THUNDERPLUMP

The Completionist Chronicles Book Eleven

DAKOTA KROUT

ACKNOWLEDGMENTS

Wow. The 11th book in a series. My wife Danielle deserves a medal for her saintly patience with my relentless typing.

My fans--my friends--you get a wild round of applause for your unwavering faith in my ability to keep you smiling, and to my Patreons Lilly Hawk, Garrett Griffin-Morales, and Mike Rylander.

Thanks for helping me to keep plumping the thunder.

PROLOGUE

<Heed my words, my Progenitor of the Ice.> The words of the Jotunn rang within the mind of the third eldest of the Frost Giants.

He had been hoping for this moment, the honor of being the first of his brethren to hunt down creatures from the summer lands. There was no other reason the Mythical World Boss himself would reach out to alter the path Brisingr had been set to roam.

Hours passed as he waited with the patience of a glacier for additional instructions to be offered to him, his anticipation shown by managing to take *two* entire steps during that time. He had traversed dozens upon dozens of miles of the frigid land where frost and ice had held dominion for millennia—ever since they had *last* driven beings from the summer lands out.

<One *settlement* is already reaching far beyond their station, and it is time to make an example of them. Return them to the ice, and ensure that all warmth within a thousand miles has been chilled.>

"I hear. I obey." Only when the attention of his sovereign turned away did the giant's features, intricate carvings beneath layers of glaciers and packed snow, begin to break into what could be interpreted as a smile. It was a terrible, cataclysmic grin showcasing the abject, insane glee he was feeling at the moment.

"*This*. This is it. Finally, after enduring with the persistence of winter's long freeze, I, Brisingr, will be able to freeze out my brothers. I shall take the position of first disciple for myself."

As his feet came together, steadying his stance, the ground around him for hundreds of miles began to quake. With a deep inhale that caused tornadoes and hurricanes to form across the continent, he prepared his words. For one moment, there was abject calm, then his deep, resounding bellow reverberated across over a thousand miles as he called upon the children of the Jörmungandr.

The surface layer of the world shook as thousands, then *millions* of monstrous creatures began to stir from their hibernation. From the most humble yet ferocious Penguin to the great permafrost Wyrms tunneling below the bedrock seeking hidden settlements, all were called to fulfill their ancestral oaths. One and all began to converge on his location, leaving behind all territories, abandoning internal battles, prepared to starve instead of finishing their hunt… all to be a part of the gathering horde.

Brisingr stepped forward once again, each footfall reshaping the geography below him as his gaze remained locked on a collection of low, snow-covered hills. Approaching the mounds, he reached out with surprising care and grasped the nearest of them. With a slow, steady pull, he revealed a mass of frozen fur that seemed to have no end. The frost giant casually looped it around his neck, completing his preparations for the long walk.

"Now, I am dressed for the job I want." He let out a deep chuckle and strode along at a steady pace once more, scarf streaming behind him in the gale-force winds created by his passing. His monocle gleamed in the dim light that passed through the ever-present cloud layer, and Brisingr began to softly hum.

The tune that reverberated out from him was a standing call to arms from all of the creatures within range. A steady pressure from his immense Charisma, which drilled against even the strongest of mental defenses that would keep the beasts from ignoring his initial call. Eventually, none would be able to resist.

As the daylight turned to darkness, the giant found himself nearing the edge of a vast chasm, an abyss so deep it seemed to plunge nearly halfway to the core of the planet itself. Brisingr had been here many times before; he had witnessed when the Jotunn *itself* had done battle against the Sagedom of Vanaheim. Even *he* felt a chill down his spine as he remembered how the Mythical World Boss had dug its fingers into the planet and bodily hurled the entire continent into space… before chanting an incantation that caused it to detonate. From there, the Jotunn had commanded the debris to shift into the fallout that, even to this day, caused an eternal winter on the planet.

Without missing a step, the giant continued toward what would be an impassable obstacle for any other being. "I now see your wisdom in choosing *me*, great Jotunn."

His chin tilted up, and his eyes raised to the swirling storm above. The ambient mana of the world collapsed toward him as if drawn in by a black hole, gathering in his right eye and being amplified a thousand-fold by his icy monocle.

A beam of energy colder than the depths of space spiraled outward in a triple helix, striking the dense clouds overhead then sweeping along in a straight path in front of the giant. Where his gaze passed, the clouds solidified into blocks of ice, plummeting from the sky and into the gaping chasm barring his path.

Even as he continued forward, the void was filled in a straight line. The brand new, icy bridge held his weight without issue, as he had known it would. Hundreds of thousands of creatures swarmed across with him, and the great migration to destroy the upstarts had officially begun.

"What weapon should I use to showcase the might of the everfrost?" Brisingr mused to himself, the wind from his lips sending thousands of creatures careening off and into the void surrounding the bridge. "A storm that separates flesh from bone, freezing both once they have been parted? No… then they would never look upon my face and understand the hopelessness of their goal. An arch of ultimate ice that descends from the heavens, ignoring all defenses and eradicating the heart of their settlement? …Perhaps. Yes, that sounds… appropriate."

"First, I will destroy their only hope. Then, I will dismantle anything they have managed to build. Last, I will encase them in ice for a thousand generations." Brisingr slowly nodded as he allowed the plan to settle into its final form.

"Novusheim… enjoy the last fleeting warmth you managed to force upon us. I thank you for your sacrifice, for you shall be the stone I step on to climb to higher heights."

CHAPTER ONE

A high-pitched whine filled the dimly lit chamber Joe was working in, signaling the beginning of a cascade of energies that would cause his ritual to detonate if left unchecked. The Ritualist's Aspect Inscriber flew back over the area he'd just completed, quickly scratching out lines of mana and aspects and replacing them with corrected, stable versions that overlaid the original and substituted them perfectly. Sweat dripped freely down his brow as he raced the clock, hoping to outpace the imminent explosion.

With a final quick, efficient motion, he set a line between the second and third circles that drained the overflow and stabilized the entire diagram. When it didn't blow up, the Ritualist let out a long sigh of relief. The charge that had been building up in the room—a mix of the chaotic energies of Jotunheim, the odd, fiery semi-liquid that was aspects, and the catalyst of mana that bound them together—released a brief hum of harmony before quieting and fading into background noise.

"Did it work? Hmm… can't tell yet." With fluid and precise movements, he altered additional symbols in the ritual circles, each adjustment subtly changing the flow of energy. Joe's deep knowledge of rituals, at no less than the *Master* rank, combined with his high skill levels in Ritual Lore, began to shine through. Little by little, he shifted the ritual's purpose by removing the original creator's intent and substituting his own. "Come on, work. This is the last one I need for the quest."

After rescuing Daniella and bringing her back to be integrated into Novusheim, things had settled into a fairly routine pace for Joe. First, he had delayed replacing the towers that kept the Town safe, forcing the large population of warriors to defend against the random Beast Waves on their own, without much magical support. Once he felt that his point had been thoroughly proven, the Ritualist had gone to the council and bargained for additional privileges, solidifying his rise into the upper echelons of the burgeoning Dwarven Oligarchy.

His casual lifestyle had only been interrupted when he went to spend time with his friends or attend the events they were participating in. Joe had made a resolution to be there and cheer them on outside of combat and serious situations. For instance, Jaxon had taken an interest in local theater and had successfully played his part as an ice sculpture in two plays back-to-back. The Chiropractor was so pleased with himself that Joe didn't have the heart to explain that he was part of the set—not the play—and even then, only because the theater staff had been too terrified to deny him access.

The Town itself felt like it was in a holding pattern, slowly building up its strength and population as the residents gathered all the courage they needed to push through the bottleneck keeping their settlement from being a system-recognized City. On the plus side, morale was steadily increasing as the walls expanded, and the quality and quantity of goods being produced gradually increased.

After the bargaining had been completed, the next thing Joe had done was hole himself up in his workshop, creating better versions of Town defense rituals. Even though he could always use new ways to deal damage—just in case they came across a creature that was resistant to what his towers used—the Ritualist felt that his time would be far better used by creating *enhanced* magics instead of just *more* of the same.

The problem was, designing a new ritual from scratch required a deep knowledge of the spell model that he was going to base it off of. One of his current frustrations was the fact that he didn't have a large foundation in standard spellcasting and had already made multiple ritual variations of the spells he was capable of completing. That meant he could either create ever-more variants, learn and practice new spells until they'd reached an acceptable level, or retrofit his darker rituals to be more generally useful.

Seeing as how the last of those options also aligned with a quest he had gained, Joe had decided to pursue that one.

"Ritual of Dark Reach." Joe toyed with the words as he pulled out sections of the original ritual and replaced them with his personal symbols. "I wonder what you're going to end up being after I'm done with you."

As he made the last stroke with his Aspect Inscriber, Joe carefully leaned back and carefully scrutinized the liquid fire that was hanging in midair. His piercing gaze hovered over each swoop and swirl, finding no errors, no matter how carefully he searched. Easing his hand forward, he tapped down, putting the pads of his fingers directly in the center of the ritual and channeling his mana into the hopefully cleansed ritual.

Power drained out of him, and the oversized circles shrank down until the largest of them surrounded his hand. Finding himself flinching back, the Ritualist forcefully calmed himself and smiled as he realized that the circles had moved *with* his hand without needing to be forced to move by his Willpower. He waved his appendage around, and the ritual moved with it easily, as though it was stuck to a glove. "Okay, that was unexpected, but it's nice… *if* it works."

Selecting the far wall as his target, Joe pointed his hand toward it, and immediately a bolt of pure darkness launched across the chamber, striking the far wall and expanding to fill its entire surface with a field of clinging, churning shadows. The fact that they moved on their own and had rounded edges brought a frown to Joe's face. "Odd. This was supposed to make a twenty-foot section of spikes, not whatever *that* is. Did the ritual fail?"

Only two and a half seconds after the shadows began moving, they faded away and left the wall as blank as it'd been originally. He made a mental note to put up some kind of art, like Daniella had suggested, then sent a flash of intent back into the ritual. Once more, the far wall was transformed, and this time he threw himself forward to test it, trusting his Exquisite Shell to keep him safe.

You have been rooted! Strength check failed. Resistance check failed. You are unable to move from this spot for 1 more second.

The darkness faded away, and Joe dropped a couple of inches to the ground, a pleased, if somewhat surprised, expression on his face. He turned to his notes and carefully detailed his experience, adding his thoughts on how to improve it further in the future. "I can see where it went wrong. I'd intended for this to turn into a field of something like caltrops, but my mind had been on holding or slowing creatures moving through the area, not slashing them up like spikes would've done. Maybe I should see if Grandmaster Snow would offer some insight on how to be specific while still being ambiguous enough to allow the ritual to grow in unique ways."

Once he was satisfied with how everything had turned out, he shifted his attention to the notifications that were waiting for him.

Quest complete: Redeeming Rituals. You have cleansed your fifth ritual of at least Journeyman rank! Reward: Ritual of Cleansing (Expert).

The Ritual of Cleansing can be set in any area to remove aspects of intent from ambient mana. There are many benefits to this process, including but not limited to a calmer, less chaotic atmosphere in the area.

Eyes glittering with excitement, Joe swept all of his notes, ritual tiles, and other various knickknacks off of his desk, prepared to let them clatter to the floor. Instead, he scooped them into his spatial storage codpiece at the last minute. While he enjoyed being dramatic, the Ritualist still knew better than to make a mess or damage his research. Without taking another moment to relax, he began etching the Expert-ranked ritual onto a tile, quickly building it up over the next fifteen minutes, then half hour, hour… time flew as his intense focus and excitement enticed him along.

Before he knew it, he was putting the final touches on the ritual. As the last circle was completed, and he pulled his Aspect Inscriber back to admire his work, the stone tile shattered, filling his workshop with a blaze of fire and a detonation of mana.

The Ritualist was *hucked* across the room, slamming into the wall and being held there as the explosion rebounded, having nowhere to escape, thanks to being confined inside the vault. Joe's Exquisite Shell was blasted with power and aspects, a quarter of the potential damage going directly through his magical protections and scoring deep lines into his flesh, thanks to the odd true damage the flames inflicted.

Exquisite Shell: 4,845/12,479

Health: 691/2,599

When the energies finally expanded themselves, Joe collapsed to the ground wheezing. Raising his charred, shaking hands, the Ritualist began to pump himself full of healing magic. He could only thank his lucky stars that his Exquisite Shell had held up, forcing his blood and inner organs to remain mostly in position.

"What… the *abyss*… just happened?"

Caution! Rank of materials too low to contain magic! Attempting to force… failed! Secondary attempt due to Master rank… failed! Third attempt due to Lore skills interacting with Occultist Profession… failed!

Caution! This is the first time all three attempts have failed. No additional attempts can be made until all three limiters have come off of cooldown.

"Okay, I don't like *that*." Joe looked at the stone tile that he used for almost all of his rituals: rather, he looked at the square-shaped pile of dust that it'd been converted into. "It's not like I'm using any random *rock*. I've been making sure to use compressed stone, perfectly shaped and glossy. It has to count as at least Rare in that case, right?"

Thinking about the words he'd just muttered, the Ritualist had to hold himself back from facepalming as he groaned. "Rare rank? How many times do I need to remember the well-established fact that material can only *consistently* hold magic up to one rank higher than it is? I've seen that with enchantments, alchemy, and now, I guess, rituals. Feces. Havoc can never find out about this."

Burble?

"Don't worry, Mate, I know exactly what to do to fix this issue." Joe consoled his coffee elemental as he threw open the door to his workshop, stepping out into a town that had been transformed over the last few days. Everyone was wearing a smile, or in the case of the Dwarves, wasn't *actively* scowling. "Time to upgrade my tiles from stone to metal. Let's go boost my Ritualistic Forging skill until I'm an Expert."

Novusheim was thriving, rapidly becoming a center of innovation for the residents, and a beacon of hope for the humans still under the thumb of the Elven Theocracy. As Joe went from one fun, interesting crafting project to another, he joined the rest of the Town in wearing a brilliant smile.

"Jotunheim is *awesome*."

CHAPTER TWO

Sparks flew off of the glowing pool of aspects as Joe brought his ingot hammer down, shaping the raw energy into yet another Ebonsteel mug. A few careful hits later, the shining material solidified into a room-temperature metal coffee mug studded with jewels. The Ritualist grunted as he tossed the finished product to the side, where it clattered into a haphazard pile of mugs exactly like it.

As he wiped his forehead, more out of reflex than anything, Joe looked around in disgruntlement. "He's late. Why's everyone *late* these days? We live in a wasteland where staying outside for any length of time means freezing into a block of ice. There's practically no luxuries at all, since Havoc won't let me make personal homes or even apartments yet. So why, oh why, does everyone still find a way to be late?"

Just as he finished grumbling, the Dwarven Expert smith Joe had managed to hire, Growmore, threw the door open, carefully walking in as if he'd fallen off a high place and landed squarely on his rear. He noticed Joe's stare and shook his head slightly. "Sorry I'm running behind, lad. It's the end of the quarter, if ya know what I mean."

Joe took a deep breath, ready to explain that, in fact, he had no idea what the Dwarf was talking about. He paused as he noticed all of the other metalworkers looking at his teacher and wincing in sympathy. Instead of his planned biting retort, the Ritualist managed a simple question: "I actually *don't* know what you mean, would you mind... telling me?"

He'd trailed off somewhat during his sentence because of all of the jaws dropping and eyes widening, as everyone in the area looked at him completely aghast. Somehow, he'd broken a cultural taboo, and he had no idea how. The smith stared at him as well, before coughing into his hand and sending a meaningful glance around the room. Then he drew close to Joe, "You understand what it means to have high Characteristics, at least somewhat. Let's draw this out so you get to feel as awkward as I do right now. What does a *very* high Constitution do for you?"

"That's... a lot of things. You can resist poisons better, you can go longer without eating, you don't get sick as often." Joe paused, hoping he'd hit the nail on the head, but now the smith was grinning and motioned for him to go on. "I don't know, lots of that stuff?"

"Yeah, pretty much. An easier way to describe it would be to say that you're able to put off a lot of your bodily functions for a long period of time." The Dwarf raised a frizzled eyebrow, waiting to see the moment of realization dawn on the Ritualist. Slowly the grin faded, and he tried a different tactic. "You can *put off* lots of bodily functions. You're resistant to poisons. That doesn't mean you can *ignore* those things. At least, not for longer than about three months, also known as a quarter."

"Are you telling me that you haven't taken a poo-"

"Three months, yeah." The smith clapped Joe on the shoulder as he walked past him to the forge. "We all appreciate the automatic destruction of that poison. Good job on your magical latrine; you're saving the environment and definitely doing the Celestials' own work."

It took a moment for Joe to comprehend what was being told to him, then his eyes narrowed. "It's *not* a toilet! Do you mean to tell me that everyone has been using the Aspect tower-?"

"Do you want an answer to that, or do you want to learn better forging techniques?"

The Dwarf had a perfectly valid point, and Joe decided that he was done asking questions about anything unrelated to the craft... after just *one* last question. "Do you know what rank of materials that would be considered? Three months, so Uncommon at least?"

That had the entire smithy laughing, and Joe and his instructor dived into the work. Over the next several hours, they worked on various hammering techniques, folding metals, and the heat of the air that had to be held when working with higher-rarity materials. The air of the forge was thick with smoke, filled with the pungent scent of molten metal and burning materials. Every once in a while, someone would break into a string of curses as the building forcefully reverted their finished product back into liquid, followed by a round of jeering from the others.

At the center of the building was Joe, his face illuminated by the intense light coming not only from the furnace, but his own particular crafting material. Beads of sweat were collecting on his shiny head, only to be swept away by his near-passive spells. Thanks to his magic keeping him comfortable as he worked, Joe was able to lend his full attention to every movement of his body.

Each strike was careful, purposeful, calculated, and often accompanied by a gruff instruction from Growmore. The deep-set eyes were staring at Joe's project, less than an inch away from where the hammer landed multiple times a second. The Dwarf had witnessed countless failures and multitudes of finished products, and every minute of his time was extremely valuable. So, each time a 'more force', or 'watch that angle', or any other seemingly offhand comment tumbled from the bearded mouth, Joe tried to redouble his focus on the area that had been found lacking.

Today's efforts were particularly challenging, as Joe was working from a template that was right on the edge of both his skill level and *barely* falling within the purview of Ritualistic Forging. An athame was one of the few blades that also had effects on rituals, and even if Joe didn't need it for his personal crafts, it was something that would be extremely useful for the coven of Ritualists that he had made a sign-up sheet for and posted in the Town Hall.

Far too many rituals required various sacrifices—either of blood, materials, or creatures—depending on how dark or potent the final effect was. Every time he ran into one of the darker ones, Joe was reminded of how happy and pleased he was with his choice of specialization. The option to avoid the messy reagents that his class typically required was a massive boon on its own. Then there was the ability to perfectly add singular aspects at a time, allowing him a level of control and finesse that others could only dream of. Hence, his current project.

Some people are Reductionists. For everyone else, there was an athame.

If Joe understood the tool correctly, the small blade would allow for careful partitioning of all sorts of finicky materials, instant coup de gras for living sacrifices—even if the Ritualist using it didn't hit a critical area—and could even be used as a weapon in a pinch. The major downside was the fact that creating the athame required a Student rank in Ritualistic Forging or Journeyman rank in a general forging skill. That made low-level Ritualists terribly dependent on outside classes, yet another barrier to entry for the extremely difficult-to-practice class.

Joe made a silent vow to give one of these to anyone who joined his coven as a present. Hopefully, he'd be able to make it a tradition that inducting someone else into the class came with a gift like this. "Huh. You know, maybe that's where basic class gear originally came from."

"If you have time to daydream, you have time to heat the

metal *there* and cool the air around it with this fan." Growmore barked at the Ritualist, who snapped his mouth shut and started pounding harder.

Ritualistic Forging was proving to be an incredibly stubborn skill to improve, seemingly resisting him at every turn. The aspects would bend in ways he hadn't expected mid-strike or simply refuse to take the shape he was attempting. Still, every failure only made him more determined to master this craft. At the very least, he needed a high-Journeyman level skill so that he could attempt to create Jotunheim Alloy. The alloy was the only Expert-ranked metal Joe had access to creating at the moment, but he was simply not skillful enough to actually create it.

"Gotta get my forging up to Journeyman, so I have a chance at making Expert metal, so I can write out a ritual on it." Joe let out an annoyed huff of air, "It's never just *one* thing I have to do, is it?"

As soon as the allotted time that Joe had paid for was up, several hours and a multitude of attempts later, Growmore snatched the most recently completed blade out of Joe's hands and critically studied it, flipping it over and inspecting it from every angle. "It's a pile of feces, but at least you don't stink as bad at forging as you did at the start of the day. A few more decades of dedication, and you might even be *good* at this. Remember, it's not just about hitting your metal until it's in the right shape. It's about understanding it, feeling it respond to you, and reciprocating those feelings."

"Intent matters." Joe nodded in understanding, speaking aloud the phrase he was trying to use at least twice a day when crafting. "I could really feel it today; how it was messing with me. I think that once I'm past this bottleneck, I'll have a much easier time of it."

"Mmm." Growmore grunted at him, tossing the knife back and offering a rare word of encouragement. "Mastering a craft is just like going for a long, long run. You start out fast, gaining quick levels and advancing rapidly. This isn't always a positive.

Usually, it's actually setting you up for failure. Ninety percent of all metalworking aspirants reach the Beginner rank and fall off, deciding to go with a different profession, for whatever reason. At the Beginner levels, all the way until you're a Journeyman, continuing to learn is like running on a slow incline. It's difficult, and you can't see much progress."

"But then you get to the top of the hill, look back and see how far you've really gone? You get motivated again?" Joe's hopeful question made the instructor let out a bark of laughter.

"Don't put words in my mouth, *Student* Ritualistic Forger." Growmore walked away without clarifying further, much to Joe's annoyance.

Congratulations! Personal instruction under an Expert of the craft has taught you well! Ritualistic Forging (Student V → Student VII).

"Welp. Thanks for helping me grow more." Joe grabbed the filthy towel the Dwarf whipped at him as retaliation, waited for his Neutrality Aura to clean it, then rubbed his face vigorously to try and scrub the tiredness from his eyes. He'd been in this *furnace* of a building for the last half of a day, at the minimum, and was ready for a change of pace. Tossing the towel back onto the rack, Joe stepped outside in preparation for going on a stroll and inspecting the defenses.

His ears twitched as the clanging of the forge was replaced by a gentle rustling sound. He turned and saw Daniella sitting at a small table just behind the entrance of the forge, her delicate features completely out of place in Joe's mind after having been surrounded by hairy, grimy, cussing Dwarves for hours. He waved to get her attention, and she perked up, grabbed a roll of papers, and rushed toward him.

"Are you finished for the day? In there, at least? I can't bring these in, they're too valuable, and I'm sure a hot coal would 'accidentally' land on one of them." She pulled one of the scrolls open, giving Joe a glimpse of a type of structure he'd never seen before. "I have no idea why they don't even *want* access to Elven buildings. They'll be able to have all the benefits of their work, even without having to deal with any of the Theocrats!"

The Ritualist could only chuckle as she puffed out her cheeks and ranted, motioning for her to join him on his walk. At first, the icy evening air was refreshing, but it only took half a minute for the first chilled debuff to appear, and Joe started directing their meandering walk in the direction of the walls. "What's on your mind, Daniella?"

"I want to petition the council for a workspace, so we can start having proper ranged weapons out there." She motioned in the direction they were walking, and Joe nodded for her to continue. "Almost everyone who has abandoned the Theocracy came here without their weapons, since they were confiscated by the Elves when they became prisoners of war. For everyone else who's trickling in just because they want a change of pace, there's nowhere to repair their weapons. This is a specialized Bowyer workshop, and using it will get us ranged weapons on par with Elven Warbows."

Joe let out a low whistle, looking closer at the blueprint she was offering. "You've someone who can make them?"

"There's a couple," she answered somewhat evasively, making Joe raise an eyebrow at her. "They would need special dispensation, since they're out in the first suburb still."

"That'll be a hard sell." The Ritualist shrugged, knowing he could probably pull enough strings to make it happen. "What's the other one?"

With a twinkle in her eye, Daniella waved the other scroll at him. "Oh, this little thing? It's just an elemental playground. If built correctly, it'll attract elementals, which all sorts of different magical classes can tame or bind."

"Ambitious." Joe's answer was short, but his brevity was due to his interest—and thinking about how he could present these options to the council. "I'm guessing there's a reason the Dwarves don't have something like this already?"

Daniella nodded, her face serious but a smile playing around her lips. "The Bowyer requires a specific type of cleric-treated wood, while the playground requires environments for each of the elementals you wish to entice. This should go without saying, but I'm betting there will be a ton of frost elementals available, and they'll be perfectly useless against the enemies here."

She pulled the scroll away with a wry smile and an arched eyebrow, and only then did Joe realize that his fingers were closing on empty air. "My goal with all of this is to start getting some hefty contracts from the council. But I clearly know what to show off to get people interested enough to see what else I have to offer."

He flushed slightly as he realized that he'd just tried to grab her scroll and start studying it without permission, then caught his breath as her final words made his heart race. "*Ahem*. Sorry about that. Yeah, let's give it a whirl. It might not work, but if it does, not only will we be able to use the Elves' specialties to make ourselves prosper, but it will be an *interesting* step forward in the variety of buildings our Town has. That can only be good, right?"

"My thoughts exactly. They'll *definitely* go for it."

CHAPTER THREE

"No."

Even though he had been expecting it, Joe had to keep his face still so that he didn't show how annoyed he was at the instant rejection. "It's always such a pleasure to get *your opinion* out of the way first, Master Frenzy. Truly, of all the members of this council, you have the most stony stare. Now, if you would switch that over to a stony *silence*, I would–"

"Joe. Enough of the jests." Grandmaster Snow waved her hand tiredly. "If I wanted to be around bickering rivals, I'd attend the front lines of our defenses, not sit at this prestigious table. I'll admit, I too am wondering how you think a structure devoted to the weapons of our enemies being built among us is the best path forward in the short-term."

"Thank you for the opportunity to make my case, Grandmaster." Joe inclined his head at the ancient Dwarf, showcasing his very real respect. "The fact of the matter is, we only have a fraction of the ranged weapons we need. My towers are filling that void, for the moment, but as more and more Beast Waves arrive, I'm certain they just won't be enough. A single point of failure is *still* a failure."

When he paused to gather his thoughts, no one interrupted. Joe took this as a sign that they recognized the issue as well but were just too proud to admit that fact. "As you all know, we're surrounded by very tall walls. I don't know a single member of the Legion who carries a bow, a crossbow, or has more than a few simple spells for a little bit of range. Imagine if we could turn the advantages of our enemies against them when they come calling. We have thousands upon thousands of humans ready to wield these weapons. Trusted individuals, yes, as well as defectors who are trying to prove their dedication to our cause. Let me make this happen."

The counselors conferred for a few moments, and Frenzy took it upon himself to speak for them. He practically spat his words at the Ritualist, working to meet his eye so he could try and intimidate the bald human into lying. "Even if we say no, aren't you just going to go and do it anyway?"

"Frankly… I'd rather just not have to find out," Joe calmly stated, not bothering to join in the staring contest the Dwarf was trying to initiate. He held up a gem-encrusted coffee mug, then pulled a few more out of his storage while handing them out. They were definitely *not* bribes. "The first time I ever made this item was the first time I found my first piece of Jotunheim's history. Back then, I didn't realize what it represented, but now I see it as the clue that it was. All of you who have the ability to see what I'm talking about, please feel free."

"Ebonsteel eternal… coffee mug?" The Grandmaster was the one who actually followed through. "Is this a joke? Oh… I see what you mean. 'The design was perfected throughout the ages, though this mug was first forged for a general on the front lines of the fifty-eighth of a hundred waves on Jotunheim as he struggled to defend that plane's first and—to this day—final City.'"

"If this is correct," Joe looked around the room with his deep-set eyes, trying to push through to everyone who would have a say in this decision. "Then every upgrade we've struggled through to this point will be *laughably* easy compared to what we *will* be struggling through. Going from a Village to a Town only required twenty-five waves, but the next rank will have four times as many. If it follows the same pattern, that means there will be twenty waves with elites. At least ten Boss Monsters. Then, likely some super creature that's leading all of them. If we aren't prepared to attack at range, we'll be inflicting paper cuts on their toes instead of critical strikes on weak areas."

Silence filled the room for a few moments, until a Dwarf Joe didn't recognize, likely a proxy for one of the council members, rubbed at his beard in deep thought and spoke quietly. "Could it be that our entire history with the Elves was intentionally fostered to ensure that there'd be no way for us to break through the bottleneck that is Jotunheim, the prison world?"

"How dare you impugn the honor of our ancestors like that!" Master Frenzy lashed out instantly, his eyes flaring with heat as he reached for a weapon at his side, only to find that his greaves had been sewn to his seat with some deft Mana Manipulation.

The Grandmaster stared at Master Frenzy until he stopped struggling to fight, then she turned her attention to the Ritualist. "It's a fact that our records do not have the true reason why our conflict has raged for so long. An outside power inciting us so that we would be forever trapped is *not* outside the bounds of possibility."

"This design is Daniella's–"

"Elven *sympathizer*!" Frenzy ground out.

"–as are the new designs for the high-ranked towers we're going to be installing over the next few days. She's been instrumental in helping us to bring our defenses to the next level so far. If she's good enough to fortify our Town, why can't she donate her skills and knowledge to enhance our overall arsenal?" Joe shrugged lightly, an annoyed expression lingering on his face. "If it's only because she made a mistake in her past, I submit that none of us should have *any* say in *any* matter that–"

"Yes, yes, there are plenty of strawman arguments on both

sides." Grandmaster Snow cut him off. Her fingers drummed on the table in front of her, leaving divots behind in the dense wood as she considered the pros and cons. "Your… *friend* has much experience, not to mention research notes and blueprints from the Elven Theocracy. If she's truly being so generous as to want to have these created, why is she withholding them from the council instead of donating them directly?"

"Why does *any* Dwarf charge for their expertise? If everything she can do is public domain, how would she earn her own living? Not to mention the very real concern that, as soon as the documents were presented," here Joe turned to stare at the wiggling, red-faced, furious Dwarf glued to his chair, "They might be 'accidentally' damaged beyond usability."

"I'll allow it… for two reasons." Snow held up her hand to prevent anyone from trying to speak out over her. "I believe that, once upon a time, she was intended as the cornerstone of the Elven foothold for this world. I've had many conversations with her, and she has been privy to research, strategies, and granted blueprints that we simply don't have. The first reason I will allow it is for our benefit in terms of defense, as you put forward. The second, which I'm certain you'll like far less, Joe, is so we can use her and her buildings as bait for any of the sympathizers who managed to escape our net. When they make a move on her, the trap will close."

"That's… not my favorite reasoning ever, but–" Joe stalled out as Snow continued.

"On one condition." Her lips were thin and pressed together as she wrestled with her words. "Bringing in Elven influence is like mixing ale with water. It dilutes our traditions and makes people angry. Based on what you've told us, even our enemies recognize that there will be issues a simple exile won't fix. If you want this to happen, before anything else is erected, you will build a prison capable of containing anyone who could be a threat to us."

"Including *yourself*!" Frenzy demanded instantly, earning a dark look from everyone else in the room, though Joe noticed that not a single person countermanded him.

The Ritualist didn't mind at all, in fact, a smirk was growing on his face. "You know, tradition is like a good cup of coffee in the morning. It's comforting, reliable, and lets you push through things that might otherwise seem too tedious. But sometimes it takes a shot of espresso added to your cup to push through the toughest days. If I'm not wrong; we've got a *lot* of tough days coming at us. I'll make you your prison. But if you think it'll keep *me* in it? I'll laugh in your face as my rituals turn your insides into your outsides the first time you try to test it."

He'd intentionally waited until the very end of the meeting to put forward his request and could now swirl around dramatically and leave the room without incurring any penalties. Grasping the handle and pulling the door open, Joe paused and spoke without looking behind him. "You all know that I'm the Apprentice of Havoc. I'd like you all to understand something. It may have taken me a while… but now *I* know what that means."

As he closed the door behind him, the smirk turned into a full-blown smile as someone cursed softly under their breath.

"Well, *feces*."

CHAPTER FOUR

Everyone involved in the creation of the new type of ritual tower let out a deep sigh of relief as the ritual reached completion and winked out of existence. The only signs that the swirling, swooping spell diagram drawing from all of them had truly existed was the tower gently swaying with the wind… and their emptied mana pools.

"Did you *need* to make it so unsteady?" Socar the Mage inquired in a gently despairing voice. "Do you know how difficult it's going to be to account for its motion in the Formation we've been layering?"

Joe shrugged and waved at the tower. "I'm just going to hook up some guy wires. It should stay *very* steady. At least, that's the plan… *if* you don't want to try pushing for new levels in your skill."

An expression of pleasant surprise washed over Socar's face as he realized that Joe had come in with a plan, and the Mage paused for a moment to make his decision. "Hmm. Go with the guy wires for now, but I'll see if I can figure out how to account for it. Good call, hard to grow quickly if we're staying only in our comfort zone, right?"

"Exactly." Joe shooed off everyone else, and the majority of them started on their way to the Town Hall to get paid for the work they'd just done.

Daniella strolled over with a bright smile on her face, eyeing the 'tower' that was no thicker than a light pole that could've been seen along the road in old Earth. "It worked! I'm not surprised, exactly, but I wasn't sure if the system would accept it as a valid structure. A foot and a half thick, a hundred and twenty feet tall. What are you going to use it for?"

"It's our first Journeyman tower, so I'll have to do something extra special." Joe shot a half-grin at her, not bothering to tell her that he wanted to use this for his new ritual that created slowing fields of darkness. He was looking forward to surprising them. "The thing I'm most shocked about is that they let us set it up in the center of Town. I thought for sure it was going to be shoved up next to a wall."

Socar snorted at the imagery. "Well, unless you have space and resources for ten *more* of these, there'd be no way to balance it if it wasn't central. Before I go, last reminder to let me check out the yin affinity before you put a ritual in place. As the center, it needs to have be an intense draw of the ambient field, or the whole thing will–"

"I've got it, buddy." The smile remained on Joe's face, though it dimmed by a few degrees. "Our skyscraper masquerading as a lamppost is complete, and as long as no one sneezes too hard near it, everything should be fine."

"As if something that common would be able to take down *my* design." Daniella flipped her hair in faux-haughtiness, then dropped the act as her eyes twinkled. "What do you think? Celebrate over dinner tonight?"

"I need to go hit some metal; how about I see you at sundown?" Joe blithely answered, not quite certain why her face fell slightly. "It's only sixty or so hours away, and I need to finish up my push into the Journeyman ranks. This project is driving me *nuts* with all of its prerequisites."

"No, I totally get it!" Daniella pushed her smile wider, then turned as they parted ways. "I should really get over to the Bowyer workshop to supervise the new hires anyway. See you at sundown… I guess?"

"You got it!" Joe waved at her as he turned his eyes toward the workshop in the distance, then practically sprinted toward the forge. "Today's the day, I can feel it!"

As he entered the forge, Joe tied on a thick leather apron and looked around at the ever more familiar space. Even though he didn't see his tutor, the anvil was practically *beckoning* him, and he felt no desire to resist its call. He decided to at least get some practice in while he waited, feeling like he was sitting on the verge of leveling up to the Journeyman rank. The Ritualist began pounding away at glowing aspects, just like the other smiths in the area, though they used molten metal and glanced at him uneasily every once in a while.

A short while after he finished his newest Ebonsteel coffee mug, Growmore bustled into the forge, full of apologies and new excuses for his tardiness. Joe waved that away and positioned himself to better see and learn from the Expert Dwarf.

"Alright, human. Today, I'm going to have you work on one of the more annoying things that we have to deal with as metalworkers. I just got an order from the council for three thousand meters of braided wires that some yokel is going to use to hold something in place. It's low-level Journeyman stuff, so you should be able to pull it off and rapidly gain some levels at the same time."

Joe wasn't entirely sure whether he should groan or laugh maniacally at the fact that *he'd* be the person fulfilling his own request and getting paid for it to boot. On the plus side, as he knew exactly what the wire was going to be used for, he knew better than to offer any that would be of subpar quality. After being handed the blueprint he was to follow and making his own adjustments to convert the material cost over to aspects, he lifted his hammer and got to work.

Each of the braided wires needed to end up seven hundred and fifty meters long, and each attempt took him a full hour to complete. Between the difficulty of the task being outside of his skill range and combining with the utterly *infuriating* curse of the building—which caused forty percent of all items made to revert to base material—it took Joe a full eleven hours to get the first of the four coils completed.

Ritualistic Forging has reached Student VIII!

As soon as the metal was properly spooled, he closed his eyes and tipped back, allowing himself to fall flat on the floor. He wasn't worried about hitting his head or taking any damage, as his Exquisite Shell shifted and gave him extra cushioning to reduce any impact.

"Uugghh. *One* skill level?"

"Ya only made *one* item, whaddaya expect?" At Joe's first visible sign of his intense frustration, every Dwarf in the room burst into laughter at the same time. Growmore had tears in his eyes by the time he grabbed Joe by the shoulder and hauled him back to his feet. "Welcome to the *real* craft, my friend! It's not all Legendary weapons and life-saving armors. It's *work*, and we all have to do it."

"One of us! One of us!" The other Dwarves began chanting as Joe was shoved back toward his anvil.

"No~o~o." The Ritualist gently protested as his hammer was pressed into his hand.

"You're in the thick of it now, boyo! The first one's the hardest, but you're geared up to succeed now!" Growmore encouragingly stated, even as alternate viewpoints were made known.

"Second one is the hardest, for sure!"

"You want four of them? Then the *fourth* is the hardest!"

"Prepare to fail the rest of the day!"

"If you have the Stamina, keep that hammer in your hand."

The last comment was once again from Growmore, but even though he still had a smile on his face, the mirth was gone from his voice. "A warrior doesn't drop his sword; a wizard casts until they're drained. A smith *smiths*! Next time you lose the hammer, you're banned from the forge for twelve hours."

Deciding against testing his tutor, Joe got back to work.

Fifteen hours later, a second spool of high-end braided metal wires was spooled, and the Ritualist's eyes were practically crossed from his intense marathon of staring at glowing magical aspects. Unable to muster up the mental energy to open his status screen, Joe gave a verbal command for the first time in… he didn't even know how long. "System… what's my Stamina at?"

Stamina: 242/1,991

Stamina Regen: 6.72 per second

"I don't think I've been this low on Stamina since I had below ten points in Constitution all the way back on Midgard." Joe chuckled gently to himself as Growmore walked over with a plate of food. Not bothering to ask any questions, he took the plate and dived into the food. In what felt like an instant, the dish was empty, and the Ritualist let out a sigh of relief. "Thanks for that. I never realized how much I use stamina while crafting. Frankly, I haven't been able to do anything to make that resource pool drop in a long time."

"Great for you, but now you owe me dinner." The Dwarf took the plate back with a grunt of exasperation. "*Pretty* sure you knew that was for me."

Joe's mind went blank for a moment, then he noticed that his instructor was chuckling and realized that he was being teased. "Abyss, does low Stamina make me think slower?"

"*All* of your stats impact each other, somehow. You want a better answer than that, find a Master Philosopher." Growmore looked at Joe searchingly. "Well? What sort of progress have you made?"

Not quite sure what else he could mean, Joe checked his skills and saw that he'd already reached Student nine in Ritualistic Forging. "*What*! But I only made one item!"

"Why should that matter?" Growmore let out a chuckle as Joe sputtered and shoved a finger at the ornery Dwarf. "What *matters* is that you're pushing through your limits, fighting against a slew of disadvantages, and still managing to produce quality items. The lower your Stamina as you work, the higher your chances of making a mistake and failing. The success of the item needs to be balanced with your resource pool extraordinarily carefully in order to consistently make items at your own skill level. Now, when you're exhausted, failing over and over, and still make me a spool of wire that I can pass on? Well. That's when you grow more."

Joe rolled his eyes as his instructor shamelessly used his own branding as an explanation. Staring at the anvil and feeling his aching muscles, he took a deep breath and picked his hammer up where he'd carefully set it down when he finished the last spool. "Does that mean, if I keep on right now, with my Stamina nearly bottoming out, success means the most rapid skill increases?"

"You're in pain, you're exhausted… sure, you might be able to get some extra skill experience, but I think you should–"

"Lay on Hands." Healing water washed out of a Ritual Orb and over the Ritualist, and he stood up straighter as the microtears and stress fractures in his arms vanished in an instant. "Extra skill experience, you say?"

A bright, glowing blob of aspects appeared on the anvil, and a moment later, his ingot hammer sent sparks flying as it slammed down. Growmore slowly closed his mouth, cutting off the arguments that would've flown out otherwise. A grudging respect grew in his eyes as he stared at the bald human who refused to stop.

"You woulda made a good Dwarf."

CHAPTER FIVE

Only seven hours passed before Joe was able to create the third spool of wire, and he held his breath with an expectant gaze as he stared at his skill sheet, hoping to see it update. After thirty seconds, he was forced to accept the fact that he wasn't pushing into the Journeyman ranks that easily.

"Abyss." Once again, he allowed some healing water to flow over his body and got back to pounding aspects.

Three hours later, Growmore walked into the smithy and tried to convince Joe to pause for the moment, but his arguments about the benefits of proper sleep and coming at this with a fresh perspective were all but ignored. Six hours later, Joe lifted a spool of wire into the air with a triumphant expression, only for it to turn into liquid metal, drop on the floor, and resolidify.

At that point, he was forced to take a small break as he worked frantically to put out the infernal flame that he 'accidentally' blasted the solidified metal with. "Seriously, isn't the entire point of these leather aprons to be fireproof?"

"Fire *resistant*, and that's with normal fire." Growmore waved down the trio of glowering Dwarves who looked like they were going to take out their anger over their projects failing due to Joe's interruption on the Ritualist's face. "If you have a career as a smith or a welder, it's just a fact that you'll eventually set yourself on fire. The mark of a professional is how quickly you put it out. As for you? Still clearly a *student*."

"For now," Joe vowed as he twirled his ingot hammer and got back to work.

One hour later, he finished spooling the metal wire and picked it up off the anvil cautiously, staring at it with the expectation that something was messing with him. Moments later, he got the notification he'd been waiting for.

Congratulations! Ritualistic Forging has reached Journeyman 0! As a bonus, all Rituals you activate which use metal you have forged will be 1+ n% more stable, where n = skill level!

"Yes! I'm officially a Journeyman! I even got a nice… wait a second." His eyes narrowed as he stared at the 'benefit' he'd just received. "I can't use metal that I *forged* in rituals. The aspects just convert over."

Before he could write off the benefit as something useless to him, the system came through with a minor clarification.

Items such as stabilization cubes are considered when your new perk is activated.

"OhThankGoodness." Joe let out the phrase in a single breath, and his faded grin returned twice as bright.

"Congratulations, Joe." Growmore clapped him on the shoulder and smiled brightly. "Unfortunately, lessons for a Journeyman are twice as expensive as they are for Students. I think we're all done here, since I'm pretty sure I just put myself out of your price range."

The Dwarf had a fairly decent idea of Joe's finances, as it came up fairly frequently while they worked with expensive materials. Between Joe's constant need for high-level cores and monster corpses so he could craft, as well as needing to pay various employees, his enormous income of aspects went out the door almost as quickly as it came in. The human sighed and fist bumped the Dwarf. "We'll see about that soon."

"What're you going to do now? Give up the anvil so someone else can work for a little bit?" someone called over hopefully.

"Ha!" Joe shook his head and placed his hands on his anvil. "No, just for fun, I'm going to see how difficult it is to make this recipe I found."

Before he did that, the Reductionist needed to craft a new ingot hammer at Journeyman quality. For a moment, as he stared at his gathered aspects, Joe was flummoxed as to how to make the tool. "I don't have any… oh right, Journeyman rank is the same as 'Special' for aspects. I guess the question is, do I just make an Expert version, or do I give my hammer some *flair*?"

"Oh?" Growmore's slightly singed eyebrows lifted, and he hesitated as if he were holding back from saying more. Joe waited patiently, and the Dwarf broke down. "Why not *both*? Tell you what I'll do. I have some very special trinkets that I've pulled off some enemies over the years. They're not doing me any good, don't even have a bedroom to hang them up on the wall as trophies anymore. Since you can do your magic mumbo jumbo and just make proper tools out of pretty much nothin', I'll make you a deal. You break these things down, add what they give you to an Expert-rank hammer, and I'll let you keep what's left over."

"I don't think you'll be able to use my aspect hammer, though. I can't just–"

"No, none of that! I get that your hammer made out of magic, sunlight, and rainbows probably isn't going to work in my hand." Growmore snorted and waved him away as Joe offered his current ingot hammer for testing. "I don't want to give these up only for you to make a tool for *Alchemy* or the like. If they're going on to better someone in my own craft, I'd be okay parting with them."

Joe shrugged at that, agreeing easily. A few minutes after he left to collect the trinkets, Growmore walked back in the room and put a small pile of wands, amulets, and what appeared to be individual metal teeth on Joe's anvil. "Every single one of these was pulled off an Elf a world and a lifetime ago. Maybe I should say, a few of these were pulled *out* of an Elf."

"I can only hope you mean the teeth." Joe chuckled but decided he didn't want to know the answer if he was wrong. While it was likely that these items had been cleaned, the Ritualist decided he didn't want to touch them with his fingers for any reason. Moments later, a Field Array was set up, and he began to reduce them into aspects.

New Special Aspect gained: Arcane.

There were plenty of Rare aspects and below, but the only thing that caught his eye was the new Special type. "Oh, I think I saw this in the pamphlet I got as a reward once. Let's see… here it is. Special aspect usage pamphlet. Arcane… boosts magical conductivity. Okay for an aspect, I guess. Just as a heads-up, I've never tried to put these in my tools before. Let's give it a whirl."

Over the next few minutes, Joe shaped his aspects into an intricate new ingot hammer, studded with various protrusions and intricate designs to get it to the point where it would allow itself to be considered an 'Expert' quality tool visually. Knowing what he did about intent, he was starting to understand that this was the tool itself having a very limited sentience. With that in mind, he slightly shifted the design to look like what he would expect an Expert to be using. Not gaudy, simply impressive quality with high functionality.

When he was finished, Joe was holding an indigo hammer that had bright veins of slowly undulating green light tracing through the entire tool.

Arcane Ingot Hammer (Expert). This Hammer, which looks like a dragon fused a sapphire and an emerald, is imbued with aspects of the arcane; allowing for a 15% increase in enchantment power for any item created by it.

Adds a 5% chance of creating an item of a higher rank (Maximum: Master.)

Requirements for use: Expert rank. You didn't think just anyone *could swing this beauty around without consequences, did you? (Bonuses halved for each rank below Expert. Example: Journeyman: 2.5% chance. Student: 1.25%.)*

"Celestials." Joe whispered as he read over the boost for getting an item of a higher rank. Even if the hammer would be able to take most of the credit, getting a higher-rank item meant a surge in skill experience, as well as… well, a higher-rank item. He remembered seeing a Grandmaster nearly cry over getting a one percent boost and so recognized how impressive this truly was.

"Mind if I take a look?" Growmore leaned in, then let out a low whistle and stared at the Hammer with a pining gaze. "Now *there's* something I'd try and buy off of ya if I could wield it. Too bad about needing to be an Expert to swing it properly; I know you're a ways off."

"Still better than what I *was* using!" Joe stated chipperly. He looked at the door of the forge, then back to the anvil, waffling between taking a break or continuing his plan of trying out his blueprints just for kicks. "Mate, I'm going in. Can I get a cuppa?"

**Burble*!* AutoMate replied energetically, doing its part to help keep the Ritualist in the zone.

Joe sipped at the fresh cup of coffee as he pulled out his modified blueprint for Jotunheim Alloy. As he studied the intricate weaves of metal he'd need to replicate, he shook his head slowly. "This is *wild*. If it's this complicated just to get the metal itself, I can't imagine what items made out of this would look like if they had a specific template. On the plus side, if I can figure out how to make this properly, I can literally come here and make my own money whenever I need it. Abyss, the council would even *thank* me at the end of the day. Pretty hard to collapse a currency that's constantly being turned into other items and taking itself out of circulation."

For the next few hours, Joe carefully followed along with the instructions, seamlessly blending aspects together with light taps of his hammer. The design itself was strange, with constantly repeating fractals, almost as though he were working to capture a harmonic frequency. In fact, one of the instructions on the document clearly stated that, if he didn't strike the metals at least every half second, it would automatically be considered a failure. Faster was better, but only if he could keep blending the material in the perfect shape.

Never before had he needed to *tap* something instead of hammer it while standing at the forge, and the impact the project was having was absolutely astounding.

"*Why*? Why are you doing that?"

"Are you making something, or were you possessed by a woodpecker?"

The comments came toward him in a near endless stream, and Joe could only laugh aloud at the strangeness of the very real project that he was working on. As he reached the final step, the aspects began to dim. From one end to the other, they shifted into metal, reaching the final point… then the room dimmed slightly as the near-finished product was reduced to base material. Even though he knew it had been a long shot, Joe felt a wash of disappointment that he had gotten so close, only for the building itself to destroy his work.

Then his hammer flashed, and the liquefying metal firmed up and set fully as a bright ingot of alloy.

Joe stared down at the huge bar, reaching out and picking it up with a grunt. "No way. Is *that* what the chance of creating an item of higher rank does? It *forces* success, even if it was about to fail?"

Congratulations! You have succeeded in creating a new item a full rank higher than your skill level for the first time. Reward: +1 skill level in Ritualistic Forging.

Ritualistic Forging: Journeyman 0 → Journeyman I.

Dozens of ideas flashed through Joe's mind over the next few moments. Part of him wanted to take the bar and squirrel it away for when he needed to pay someone for a favor. An *extra* greedy portion of his mind told him to do this a dozen more times and start a bank. But the only part of himself that mattered, the part that loved magic and couldn't wait to get even better at it, had a much better idea.

"I wonder how thin I can slice this. I bet I can get at least five ritual tiles out of it if I'm careful." Without a backward glance, Joe rushed away to his workshop, slamming the door behind him.

Everything else in his life could wait: he finally had a material that could contain the Ritual of Cleansing.

CHAPTER SIX

Joe began placing the final lines of the ritual, splitting his attention for a bare moment to ensure that his Exquisite Shell was running at full capacity.

Just in case.

He'd managed to split the bar of alloy into *six* slices, each of them slightly more than four millimeters thick. Since the deepest inscription that would be etched would only be three millimeters, the Ritualist was confident that this would work perfectly for rituals of this strength and complexity. Still, there was no reason to walk into a potential cataclysm face-first and unprotected.

The energy in the room started becoming agitated to his magical senses as the final aspect and last point of mana was invested into the creation of the dense circles of power. He had never before noticed a change in environment, though he'd always made more powerful rituals out in the open to dissipate their effects in the ambient area, or in structures designed specifically to contain them, such as the Grand Ritual Hall. Joe grabbed the front of his shirt and pulled it back and forth to get some air flow as the ritual flashed seven times, almost as though it were deciding whether it should accept its new home or violently detonate itself.

As it turned out, Jotunheim Alloy was *extremely* enchantable, and that conductivity had been boosted even further thanks to his new ingot hammer. The metal accepted all forms of energy as a superconductor, and arcane energy seemed to be no exception. As the ritual settled, Joe reached out and lifted the metal plate reverently. "Let's go activate you and see how amazing of a benefit you are for the Town."

The Ritualist could barely take his eyes off of his new diagram and was incredibly pleased with himself. This was the first time that he'd be activating a ritual that would have a hopefully permanent effect on a massive swath of land. In his mind, this was as impressive as making a ritual to change the weather or shift around the landscape. "Oh! After it's active, I should insert it into the ziggurat and finish filling all of the slots. That should boost its range even further and even give it some bonus functions. But… let's see what it does on its own, first."

Seeing as the Ritual of Cleansing was going to be a massive benefit for the Town, he had no issues appropriating dozens and dozens of paid volunteers to help him activate it. That way, the cost of their work wasn't going to come out of his pocket directly, and he was able to double the minimum number of people he thought he'd need. Joe was intimately familiar with every part of the diagram, and this wasn't going to be as simple to get running as his other single-use rituals were.

Only after he reached two hundred and twenty-seven payees did he stop his Town-funded hiring spree. Such a large crowd moving with a singular purpose drew many eyes, especially as they walked away from the buildings and out into the open areas within the wall, which were still waiting on construction crews or Joe's efforts to fill.

Almost forty-five minutes later, Joe had finally positioned the last person in the place where they needed to stand, then had to make a few adjustments from people who had been fidgeting as they waited. Finally confident, he stepped to the very center of the group and held the ritual up in the air, investing a single point of mana to begin the activation sequence.

Six illusory circles erupted out of the ritual, expanding to fill the space where everyone was standing. Clusters of people stood atop sigils, dozens of them in perfect position to form the concentric rings. The most nervous of them seemed as if they would cut and run as more mana began flowing into the ritual, and they were lifted fractions of an inch off of the ground. Joe saw one person twitch, and roared, "I already told you all, *nobody* move! If you hop off, all of your mana will be ripped out of you in one go, as well as most of your health! *Probably*!"

He tried to keep his face straight as everyone froze; if they called his bluff, there could be quite a bit of imbalance. The circles began to move faster as more mana was pulled out of him, and a whirlpool of power began draining into the ritual from all of the people actively participating. Moments later, strings of mana wrapped around each person's feet, and everyone was lifted smoothly into the air.

"Get ready for it! There's a good chance that the world itself tries to fight back against us! Tanks, get ready! Mages, start preparing barriers!" Joe had gone all out with preparations this time around, not trusting that an outside agent—such as an Elven sympathizer—wouldn't take the opportunity to attack during a massive event like this. He hadn't been lying when he said that the world itself might fight them. They were attempting to adjust the flow of energy in the area, and the chaotic energy of Jotunheim itself might resist being smoothed out.

Only a few months ago, Joe would've looked at someone with pure annoyance if they had told him that 'ambient energy' might have its own desires, but many painful lessons had taught him the truth. Almost all power had some form of intent in it, and given the concentrated energy on this planet, there had to be something with underlying control.

The Novice circle, the innermost one, began to spin and flip, acting as a gyroscope around Joe, who was still holding the ritual tile in position. Though a few people seemed surprised, it was unlikely anyone would get sick; their Constitution would be plenty powerful to get through this event. As the second circle—Beginner rank—activated, the air around them was *blasted* with an expanding sphere of power. Much of the mana that had been collected so far moved around the farthest point of the ritual, collecting like a thin eggshell before vanishing from normal vision.

As Joe took his next breath, air rushed into his lungs so powerfully that he got a head rush from the amount of oxygen he'd just sucked in. He blew it out, then took a much shallower breath and found that it was what his body had gotten used to. The Ritualist nodded, letting his lips curl but otherwise remaining entirely focused on channeling, splitting, and enhancing the mana that was rushing into his ritual tile. "Third circle will be activating momentarily! Hold on tight!"

Of course, most people were flopping around completely uncontrolled, only the mana wrapped around their feet holding them from being thrown off, like a roller coaster with the worst seat belts ever. Only Joe was completely stationary at this point, but he didn't feel too bad. After all, *they* were getting paid for this. He wasn't.

Each subsequent activation of a ritual circle caused a nova of smooth power to flow out farther and farther from the center of the ritual. Things were moving extraordinarily smoothly until the Journeyman-rank circle activated—at which point Joe was extremely happy that he'd made contingency plans for defense while he was otherwise occupied.

Your efforts to defy the will of the world by bringing order to chaos have turned the eyes of the World Boss upon you! Calculating! You are activating an Expert-ranked ritual, which authorizes the Jotunn to test you with a Unique-ranked Tribulation!

Lightning Tribulation not selected! Heart demon Tribulation not selected! Elite Combat Tribulation... selected*!*

The space outside of the twirling ritual was suddenly filled with twelve-foot-tall whirlwinds of ice crystals and fog.

Shrieking wind pummeled the area, and in the next moment, hundreds of monsters appeared with a cataclysmic **bang** as they were teleported from wherever they had been moments before. For several long moments, the unprepared monsters stared at the dug-in defenses, as surprised to be there as the defenders were to see them.

There was nothing Joe could do to help fend off the beasts, and he could barely split his focus enough to even see that there were a half dozen types of creatures he didn't recognize. It didn't take a genius to understand that a Unique-ranked Tribulation meant that the monsters around them were going to likely be that rank themselves. The enormous cyclops that had nearly destroyed their Town and their hopes was only one rank above these creatures. While they were a lower rank than *that* monstrosity, the Ritualist literally couldn't count how many creatures had appeared out of nothing.

Combat began with a massive fireball engulfing the head of a creature that looked like an oversized bear. The impacted beast screamed in fury, retaliating with a web of lightning that erupted from its flaming maw. Whatever the energy touched had enormous electrical discharges move along it, followed by pulses of ice energy that raced along the freshly created tracks.

Joe tried not to panic too much, even though he'd hired only a dozen or so defenders. The arrival of the creatures had drawn lots of attention. Even if there hadn't already been a huge crowd gathered to see what was going on, the air displacement of their teleportation had long since drawn the eyes of the guards stoically defending the walls. Already, horns were being blown, and the expanded audience of onlookers was rushing in with weapons drawn. Strikes that could shatter boulders landed on shields and fur, the two sides fiercely defending themselves and their homes, in their own way.

Not only were the monsters high-ranked, they were the elites of their groups. Every single one of them was a force to be reckoned with while alone, but together, their synergistic powers wreaked havoc on the front lines of combat. Nearly thirty seconds passed before a proper platoon of Legionnaires arrived, driving into the battle like a hot knife through a gentle breeze.

Then the Expert-ranked circle activated, and Joe had no time or attention to give to other events. One last thought lingered in his mind just before his talents were tested: he had a feeling that the people fighting on his behalf were going to have some harsh words for him. No one had expected the sudden invasion or that the walls and towers might be completely avoided like this.

A fresh wave of mana, over two hundred thousand points that had been collected since the start of the ritual, blasted outward with enough force that the monsters caught just on the outside were shoved away, albeit gently. The Dwarves took advantage of that instant of the monsters being on the off-foot perfectly, felling dozens of the beasts in mere moments. However, Joe was focused on how the eggshell of mana formed by his ritual had esoteric patterns and bright sigils, as though he'd written a dense lecture's worth of magic on the air itself.

The ritual settled, and Joe noted that it had formed into a dome, or at least that was what he could see of it. There was a good chance that it extended underground, but checking would require digging—also known as inviting burrowing monsters to assault them during future Beast Waves. Still, the dome covered half of the Town, even displaced from a central position as they were now.

A quick check on his living batteries revealed that nearly a quarter of the short-term employees had passed out. Joe winced as the ritual continued draining them, but he couldn't do anything to stop it. The spell diagram was in its final stages, only having a few minor cleanups to complete, such as settling formulas after a last-moment checkup. As the very last of the magical instructions were written on the world around them, the eggshell quality in the air vanished.

Everyone involved, conscious or not, was gently placed onto the ground.

Class quest updated: Student Reductionist II. Create at least five Unique crafts using aspects: 1/5.

Elite Combat Tribulation cleared successfully! You are now able to impact the world around you at the Expert rank without needing to undergo further tribulations!

"Well, all *that* tells me is if I try to do something higher, I have to get ready for another 'Tribulation'. Abyss, at least it worked." Joe looked around at the blood-soaked field, featuring hundreds of bodies, and prepared himself to have no mana for the next full day. Standing tall, he marched forward, bellowing instructions.

"Get those monsters out of here! Collect all the fallen; we've only got a short window to bring them back! Anyone with grievous injuries, find a healer! Anyone who's not going to make it, try and position yourself near the other dead folk before you go into the light! Make it *easy* on us to bring you back, people!"

CHAPTER SEVEN

With so much help, it was a work of mere minutes to frisbee the bodies of monsters off into the distance and reverently stack their own people in close proximity to each other. As soon as it was confirmed that no one else was about to die, Joe hurried to the side of the bodies and activated his most powerful deity-granted spell: Mass Resurrection Aura.

Immediately, he felt weakened, nearly fainting, as his access to mana was removed for the next twenty-four hours. On the positive side, Joe knew that, for the next few seconds, he was visually striking. His body was wrapped in a thick layer of shadow, with tendrils extending out from him and sinking into all bodies within range. As soon as the darkness engulfed them, the corpses began to move, breathing steadily and sitting up in confusion. Scores of portals opened as humans stepped out of their respawn rooms, each person having a look of relief on their faces that they weren't going to be losing a handful of days just because they had been in the area.

As the darkness faded from Joe, his face sagged in utter exhaustion. Tiredly ensuring he hadn't missed anyone, he began carefully walking back to the ziggurat, with the Expert-ranked ritual glowing in his hands.

The Ritualist would have to wait a full day until he could fully examine the effects with his magical senses, but he could already feel them. The intense pressure of the magic in the air had always been the same as someone rubbing his entire body with sandpaper. It was an abrasive, constant sensation, and coupled with the massive increase in gravity that a large world generated. But now? Now the air felt like… nothing. Air back on Earth, perhaps?

In other words, the previously stifling sensation was now completely unnoticeable.

With a sidelong glance, Joe eyed the plethora of notifications awaiting his attention. "Eh… might as well do this so I get all my messages at once."

The Ritualist started wading through a crowd of messengers who had gathered as he finished his ritual and resurrected the fallen, intent on reaching the ziggurat and being done with this project once and for all. None of the Messengers enjoyed being ignored, so all of them began shouting in an attempt to get his attention. The cacophony blended it together into a single, unified message: the council was demanding an explanation for his actions.

It was easy enough to ignore them for the moment, since placing the ritual and letting it unfurl over the Town would answer most of the questions—not to mention gaining him quite a bit of understanding and accolades. Stepping up to the obsidian pillar, Joe reached out and brushed a finger on the side.

Three rituals have been selected. Would you like to add another at this time? Inserted rituals can be adjusted, added, or removed once per 48 hours. Yes / No.

"Yup, that's why I'm here." Joe cheerfully waited as a slot extended from the monument, which was perfectly shaped and sized for the ritual tile in his hand. That caught his interest, as the previous tiles had been shaped *slightly* differently. "Huh. I wonder if that's a function of the monument. Did I somehow subconsciously request that size? Or did it just know that… no, it had to be a function of it."

Joe rubbed at his forehead, blinking his eyes rapidly. He tended to ramble when he was exhausted, and he only ever felt this drained when one of his resource pools was completely empty. Loss of Stamina made his body feel tired, and an empty mana pool made him want to spend the rest of the day in bed. Pushing thoughts of sleep to the side, he placed the tile and allowed it to be sucked into the monument.

There were some changes happening, he could tell, but soon the flat, glossy side of the structure was replaced with an enhanced image of the ritual: swirling fractals in perpetual motion. The pattern was soothing, almost hypnotizing.

Ritual selection 1 summary: Active daylight, night-time light adjustment.

Ritual selection 2 summary: Bodily fluid collection.

Ritual selection 3 summary: Temporary housing solution.

New! Ritual selection 4 summary: Energetic Stability boosted. Range increased by 50%. Fragments of intent are actively being stripped from the ambient energetic flows. Calculating… spells and skills down to the [Novice] rank can be used within the bounds of this effect. All bonus stability will be added as a percentage increase to the success of skills and spells.

Zone notification! The Town of Novusheim has been declared a 'Prosperous Town'! Within the bounds of their settlement, all abilities down to the Novice level have been stabilized! Whether it turns into a capital of warfare or a Sage-filled university, it is indisputable that their ability to grow will outstrip all others while this bonus is active!

As a reward for being the first settlement on the world to achieve this state, for one full day, any current or new residents of the Town may choose any skill or spell to automatically learn at the Novice level!

You have activated a new ritual at the Expert level for the first time! +800 Class experience, plus 1600 bonus Reductionist experience!

Your skills have impacted a massive number of people, as well as creating a semi-permanent effect in a large area. Skill experience doubled for all relevant skill usage.

Skill increases:

Magical Matrices (Journeyman 0 → II)

Ritual Lore (Student IX → Journeyman 0). Congratulations! By reaching the Journeyman rank in Ritual Lore, you will find that intuitive leaps for the creation or altering of rituals are easier to attain!

Smithing Lore (Student VII → Student VIII)

Calculus and Number Theory (Student V → Student VI)

Mass Resurrection Aura (Apprentice VI → Apprentice VII)

Joe had been using his Knowledge Spell as much as possible, but it was kind of like taking your vitamins. If you keep up a good schedule, excellent. But as soon as you miss one because of life getting in the way, it becomes hard to remember to do so as often. Yet, even with using that spell, he'd never seen so many Lore skills increase at the same time, certainly not naturally.

He took a few moments to study the other notifications and tried to think about how they would impact the Town in the short-term. "Okay, anyone who's been on the fence about defecting and joining us is probably going to jump ship right away. So we should prepare for a massive surge of population. Next, we need to put a full-time guard rotation on this monument. As for that reward… I don't see a list popping up. That means a free skill or spell, no limitations, huh? Still, whatever I grab isn't likely to be very useful at the Novice rank."

Joe waited for a moment, just in case the system decided to prove him wrong, but nodded in understanding when it did not. "I'm sure a full skill list would be balance-breaking, especially if there was some way to determine which of them were at a higher tier of rarity. So I'm guessing… we have to specifically ask for a skill or ask to be able to do something and let the system interpret it however it wants. Therefore, if we know the name, I bet we can get a better, more exact one. I should start asking around."

Quickly assigning a few Legionnaires to guard the area until he could get a more permanent set to take the job, Joe started walking toward the Town Hall—much to the relief of the messengers still waving for his attention. "This is one of those times when it'd be a good idea to use my connections to ask a Grandmaster. Whew, asking advice without being in a dire situation? Have I been possessed by an ancient sage?"

He would've used Query to ask Tatum directly—as having his deity give him a proper answer would be even more effective—but he didn't mind having a few opinions. Someone opened the door for him, and Joe reflexively thanked them while meeting the glare of the receptionist he had wanted fired. "You're still here?"

"I'll outlast you by *decades*." The receptionist grumbled with a deep scoff. "Enjoy your chewing out session."

"It's just a formality." Joe walked into the chamber with his head held high. An hour or so later, he stumbled out, shaking his head and blinking. "Well, *that* was a roller coaster of emotions. I'm still not sure if they were ecstatic or furious. Happy-angry? Hangry? No, that's if they're hungry and angry. Hmm. I need to make up a new word for this, but… sleepy time first."

Hurrying over to his bubble, Joe flung himself on the pile of treated furs that he was using as a bed, burrowing into them and falling asleep almost at the same moment. When he woke up, he still had no access to mana, but the countdown was *much* closer to finishing. Languidly stretching, the Ritualist unhurriedly got up, looked at his filthy clothes in disgust, and resigned himself to having some negative Charisma modifiers until his Neutrality Aura came back online.

Not sure what to do with himself—lack of mana was a *major* inhibitor—Joe decided that perhaps he should take the time to work on either physical skills or his control of Ritual Orbs. His original plan to ask for assistance in picking a Novice skill had been derailed by the intense meeting, but he had plenty of time before he had to choose.

There was an inherent knowledge that came along with system messages, and when it had stated they had one full day to choose, that meant nearly two weeks of standard time. A full *Jotunheim* day. No rush, in other words, but still a short enough time that there was a large incentive for people to defect and join their cause.

As he was walking over to an area that had been earmarked for training, Joe noticed large clusters of Dwarves and somewhat familiar people talking with each other in low voices. Not wanting to snoop, but also wondering what was going on, he walked slightly closer so that they were in earshot.

"But so many of them?"

"-gotta know that vetting them is going to be a nightmare, right?"

"*I* think it's a good thing. We need them, and they have to sign on in order to be citizens, right? Contract magic is pretty powerful."

Even without further context, Joe understood that the flood of arrivals must have started already. He grit his teeth as he imagined the morale modifier in the Town falling like a rock, but hoped that the new effect from the Ritual of Cleansing would more than offset that. Not having much else to do, and still wanting to feel somewhat magical, he called up his stat sheet to see what had changed in the last... days? Hundreds of hours, at least. "Jotunheim time is the *worst* time."

Name: Joe 'Tatum's Chosen Legend' Class: Reductionist
Profession I: Arcanologist (Max)
Profession II: Ritualistic Alchemist (5/20)
Profession III: Grandmaster's Apprentice (15/25)
Profession IV: None
Character Level: 27 Exp: 392,972 Exp to next level: 13,028
Rituarchitect Level: 12 Exp: 76,950 Exp to next level: 1,050
Reductionist Level: 8 Exp: 39,391 Exp to next level: 5,609
Hit Points: 2,648/2,648
Mana: 0/8,726
Mana regen: 0/sec
Stamina: 2,008/2,008
Stamina regen: 6.73/sec

Characteristic: Raw score

Strength (bound): 188
Dexterity: 189
Constitution (bound): 188
Light Intelligence (Bound): 202
Wisdom: 185
Dark Charisma: 151
Perception: 189
Luck: 123
Karmic Luck: 25

Upon seeing the changes, it took Joe a few minutes to understand why his Constitution had continued to increase, when almost nothing else had. Then he snapped his fingers, a goofy grin on his face. "Artisan Body! Totally forgot that it was going in the background. I *love* passives! Let's see, it's at Apprentice five right now. Nice. It must gain extra experience from increasing high-threshold Characteristics. It'd take me *how* long to train Constitution…? Almost forty hours of continuous effort for a single point? Uh, no."

Recognizing that training his Characteristics was going to be a nightmare of a time investment, and he could increase his Combat Ritual Orbs skill anywhere, the Ritualist shifted directions and started strolling toward the ladders leading to the top of the walls.

After a short climb, he walked along the extended, temporary bridges, until he finally arrived at the outermost camp within the walls. Hundreds upon hundreds of people were milling around down there, talking to each other and trying to get their bearings. Joe plopped down on the edge and watched them for a while, amazed that so many people would show up for the promise of such a seemingly low-end reward.

"Either they know something I don't, or they would've taken absolutely anything offered as soon as the system told them about this. Are their living conditions just *that* bad with the

Elves?" Pondering that thought for a few moments, the Ritualist decided that, whatever reasons they had for coming here, their past didn't matter anymore. Now they were here, and them becoming members of the Town would be a mutually beneficial situation for everyone involved.

As the sky darkened further, he let out a sigh of contentment. It had been a great day, filled with amazing—a notification he hadn't seen in a long time appeared.

Luck is two thresholds below Intelligence! 1% chance to make a terrible decision has come into effect!

"Terrible decision? What terrible de… *Abyss*! I forgot to meet Daniella at sunset!" Joe scrambled to get up but slipped on the icy surface of the wall and fell off. He let out a scream of frustration as the ground rushed up at him.

CHAPTER EIGHT

Joe had dusted himself off and retreated back to the innermost part of the Town with all the dignity he could recover. Part of him kept saying not to worry about it, that no one would have seen him fall. But… in a world of superhuman Characteristics, he knew there would be at least *some* scuttlebutt about it.

Finally returning to the core of the Town, the Ritualist walked into his workshop just as the countdown ended and the barrier blocking his mana was removed. Like a cloud spinning up to become a full-fledged thunderstorm, he felt his mana pool begin to output tremendous energy. Joe paused on the spot, closing his eyes and focusing on condensing and smoothing out the flows of power through him. "Come on, Coalescence, you can *do* it!"

The only time he had enough willpower to maintain the effort to increase the skill in the usual way was when there was only a few drops of mana within him, compared to the ocean that he normally contained. The lattice of energy rapidly grew, quickly surpassing his ability to hold on to it, but he still felt that he had managed some–

Mana Manipulation (Journeyman I → Journeyman II).

"Okay. Not what I was trying for, but I'll take it." A quick glance at his status sheet informed him that a single point in the skill had increased his maximum mana pool by sixty-one. With the energy suffusing him once more, Joe felt more energetic and focused than he had in the last twenty-four hours. He tapped on his table for a moment, trying to recall what he'd been up to, then his eyes went wide as he remembered that he was supposed to be finding and apologizing to Daniella for blowing off their meeting. "Celestial feces, that's an *insidious* debuff."

As he walked down the street, looking for the Architect—but assuming she'd be in the new Bowyer workshop—he spotted Jaxon in the distance. Just for fun, and to test out the new, peaceful feeling of the environment, Joe cast one of the only spells at the Novice rank that he still had. "Message, Jaxon. Hi there, buddy! Have you already picked out your new spell? If so, what was it and why'd you take it?"

A few moments later, a return message slithered into his brain, the mana flavored by the Chiropractor's personality. Joe winced; it was almost the exact feeling he would expect if he were getting a relaxing massage then someone started licking his ear. "I don't know who this is, but you sound like Joe smells. Has someone figured out how to send advertisements directly into my brain again?"

"Again?" Joe wondered softly, deciding that there was no point in pursuing that line of conversation further. His friend turned a corner, and the line of sight requirement of the spell was broken.

Congratulations! Message has reached Beginner 0! As you have managed to use a Novice skill perfectly on Jotunheim, your skill experience has drastically increased! Message can now reach any known entity within 3 miles! Cost in line of sight is 1 mana per word, but 5 times that outside of line of sight.

"*That's* the reason the skill we get for having this zone of ordered energy is going to be so good!" Joe mused to himself, rubbing his chin as he thought about how his skill had just jumped three levels from a simple conversation. "Being able to use skills we shouldn't, and *perfectly* at that? Interesting opportunities for growth."

Luckily, he'd kept his focus on his destination and entered the Bowyer workshop for the first time since building it. As he stepped inside, the air seemed to be thick with a rich medley of scents—nearly as intoxicating as the Alchemy Hall after so long without being anywhere near a forest. The rich, earthly aroma of freshly cut yew and ash hit his nose, mingled with the resin-heavy fragrance of pine and cedar. For a long moment, he stopped stock still, practically transported to when he was a teenager looking for sticks in the woods behind his house to use in sword fights with his friends.

He kept his eyes closed. Joe told himself that he was simply basking in the new sensation, certainly not squeezing his eyes shut because they were prickling at the sudden nostalgia that hit him. As the woody overtones faded slightly, subtler fragrances filled his nostrils. The oily tang of leather, burning or at least melting beeswax, a hint of herbs that must have been put together as an upsell for anyone who wanted to buy a care kit for their weapon.

Finally in control of himself once more, Joe took a deep breath and opened his eyes. Daniella was at the counter, waiting for him patiently. He stepped forward and started to speak, only for her to hold up a hand and shake her head.

"Joe. It's *you.* I get it. As soon as I heard about the monster swarm teleporting in, I knew you would be… occupied. I'm sure you came here as soon as you had your head on straight, right?"

"Yeah." The word came out in a blast of air, the sigh of relief being completely overblown due to the power of his lungs and their ability to fill with vast quantities of compressed air, thanks to his recent efforts. "What the-!"

"I've been seeing that happen a lot." Daniella chuckled softly and motioned for Joe to take a seat. "Did you ever see the king and queen on Midgard? They had a similar thing going on. If they moved even a little, all sorts of terrible things happened to the papers that were strewn on tables. Anyway, I'm actually glad you waited before you came here, that way you can focus entirely on our conversation and not be distracted by the enormous task list you make for yourself."

"Your patience and understanding is above Legendary, reaching Mythical." Joe tried for a joke to get past his awkwardness, but she merely responded with a wan smile.

"We are already pumping out about thirty bows a day, with an order for approximately twenty-six thousand of them from the council to outfit the defenders along the walls. It's not like I was sitting here pining for you; I'm *incredibly* busy." Daniella tapped the table, and a blueprint appeared on it, pulled from some storage device he couldn't see. "I'm sure you're wondering why I wanted some of your time. Here it is. Essentially, I've been working on this design, and I can't figure out where I'm going wrong."

Joe raised an eyebrow, leaning forward slightly to get a better view of what she was pointing at. He could practically feel his Architectural Lore skill spinning up as he swept his gaze across the document, as certain areas started highlighting in various colors. Structural integrity issues flashed red, small areas were a dead, black color indicating problems that would destroy the building. Conversely, areas that had enhancements or impressive options were in greens and golds, indicating a perfect state of production.

"Got it... well, if you look here, you can see that the doorway being placed in this spot cuts directly into the main mana matrices of-" For the next few hours, they went over the blueprint from top to bottom, with Daniella taking notes and redrawing sections on a separate document. Once they'd finished, she transferred those fixes over to the original, and soon the entire document was glowing mostly green, with gold accents at perfect sections to indicate that something was even better than strictly necessary.

It wasn't until she rolled up the document with a pleased expression on her face that Joe realized he hadn't even asked what the design was for. Of course, he had a very good idea, thanks to his study of it, but reminded himself that asking questions ahead of time was usually a good idea. Before he could say another word, Daniella plopped an ingot of Jotunheim Alloy on to the table and pushed it over to him. "As thanks for the help and the teaching. I didn't know that you were already a Student in Architectural Lore. I gained two entire skill levels."

"Student rank in my Teaching skill, too." Joe nodded his head slowly. For some reason, he'd thought this meeting was… something else. But, it made sense that Daniella, someone as focused on their career as he was, could multitask at the minimum. He hesitated before taking the payment but understood that she was likely making sure that he didn't feel taken advantage of. "You know, I'd be happy to do all of this just for the pleasure of hanging out with my friends, right?"

"Oh, *re~eally*?" Daniella leaned closer, a mischievous smile playing across her lips. "Well, if you do that much for your friends, what would–"

Congratulations residents of Novusheim! You have fulfilled all requirements to upgrade your settlement rank from Town to City! All but one, that is. Beast Waves will begin arriving once per 8 hours for the first 24 waves. The time between waves will drop by 2 hours every 25th wave! Succeed where everyone else has failed. After you win, don't forget to claim the light of the bifrost for your city, becoming the central hub for all Import and Export from other worlds.

The first wave begins… now!

Beast waves completed: 0/100.

"Daniella… I'm so sorry, I need to go." Joe stood up decisively and started walking toward the door.

"Wait! Here, I commissioned a special weapon for your friend. Heartpiercer? She's really out-leveled the weapon that she's been using." Daniella rushed over to a locked compartment, popping it open and pulling out a bow made of a dark wood decorated with various fragments of bone. "We used the sinew of the cyclops you defeated to make the string; it has a six hundred pound draw weight. That's six times harder to draw than the upper end of an English longbow, and it should last her at least a few more skill levels."

Joe, slightly confused, took the weapon and stored it in his codpiece. "Uh. Thanks. I'm sure she'll appreciate it?"

"I hope so!" Daniella stated brightly, gently shooing him toward the door so he remembered to get gone. "You guys seem to have some great chemistry, and this will help her keep you safe."

"What? That's–" The door closed behind him, cutting off the icy wind that had blown into the shop as soon as it was opened. At least, Joe hoped that was why the door had swung closed so rapidly. He wanted to go and clear up the misconception, but he could already hear his towers blasting monsters with various chemicals and spells.

The Ritualist could practically imagine the panicked defectors rushing to fill the bunker towers in time to survive the leading edge of the Beast Wave. With a growl of frustration, he started running toward the walls, mentally shuffling through his stack of rituals and wondering which ones he should prepare to save the most people possible. "I'll *absolutely* be going back and talking to her about that. *Later.*"

Luck is two thresholds below Intelligence! 1% chance to make a terrible decision has come into effect!

"*Quiet*, you!"

CHAPTER NINE

The overstressed ritual towers whined ominously as they geared up for another blast, causing Joe to flinch as an incandescent, staticky ball of flames shot forth and engulfed a group of screaming Penguins. He didn't like the fact that his eyes and thoughts were on the tower instead of the creatures below. "Don't blow up until I'm past you, don't blow up until I'm-"

"They're *everywhere*!" came a scream from below, although that particular voice was cut off very quickly.

Looking ahead, Joe could see that paper-thin sheets of ice had arced up and over the outermost walls, the hallmark of Verglas Leaping Leopards. Members of the Legion, as well as various volunteers hunting for experience, were already hard at work smashing the reflective surfaces, stemming the tide of Penguins and Salamanders swarming up and over them.

"Message! Heartpiercer Mcshootypants! Are you seeing this? Where are you right now? I have a new bow for you."

Moments later, his Archer friend's mental voice sounded in his head, prickly and sharp as though his brain was trying to hug a porcupine. "Joe? Look, I'm pretty busy. If you're talking about the battalion of oversized Penguins waddling toward us like they own the place, kinda hard to miss that. What's this about a new bow?"

"Yeah, there's been some misconceptions, and now I have a weapon for you that's apparently better for your level and skills." There was silence from the other end for a few moments, then she gave Joe a quick synopsis of where she could be found on the walls.

He felt the connection cut off and altered his path to meet up. Omnivaulting over the large gaps in the killing corridors made him nervous, not because of the height or his fear of slipping, but because the paths closest to the Town already had the frontrunners of the Beast Wave moving along them.

"Ice Leopards, Penguins, Salamanders, Hoardlings... it's like a menagerie down there." As he threw himself over another gap, Joe sent his Ritual Orb of Intelligence spiking down into an oversized lizard that looked like an elite. By the time he reached the apex of his jump, his weapon had gone through the top of the surprisingly soft creature's skull and nailed it to the ground. A bubble impacted nearby it, sending a wave of acid over the creature as the Ritualist retracted his weapon. "One down, a bazillion to go."

Even with how clustered the defenders were along the top of the wall as he got close to the entrance, it was easy to pick out Heartpiercer. She was in a league of her own, sending a constant stream of arrows at creatures and scoring critical hits with almost every single attack that landed. Unfortunately, some of the beasts were either fast enough or moving in a chaotic enough pattern that the arrows that went wide missed completely. Joe spun in a forward roll, landing on his feet next to her a moment later. "Yo. Have a bow."

He dropped the weapon from his codpiece, and she caught it in her off hand. For a moment, she seemed confused, but that wasn't Joe's problem. He pushed off again, this time aiming for a tower that wasn't sending out Dark Lightning Strikes like it should be.

"Oh, *abyss* yes!" Heartpiercer's voice echoed through the air, and the Ritualist chanced a glance back to see her drawing her bowstring and releasing it over and over again. Unfortunately, he couldn't see the arrows she was projecting at the enemies. She would let go of the string, and a creature down below either stopped moving entirely or staggered heavily.

"'Kay, *that* was a worthwhile pit stop." Joe murmured as he arrived at the base of the tower and jumped to the top. A quick glance at the ritual told him all he needed to know: it was almost completely out of power and was in energy conservation mode, set to target already-damaged beasts that would be taken down in a single hit. "It's not broken, just needs a good recharge. Easy enough."

Pulling his tablet—actually an Expert-ranked Ritual of Remote Activation—out of his codpiece, Joe pressed a few areas and the tower in front of him was swallowed by a quick-moving ritual circle. He grunted as mana flooded out of him, but in only a few seconds was ready to bring in the replacement. Tapping three different buttons after adjusting the image of the tower—so that it would align with Socar's Formation correctly—another ritual circle appeared at the top of the wall and zipped upward, leaving behind dense stone and metal that resolved into a ritual tower moments later.

Static electricity crackled over the top of the tower itself, and a blast of power leapt from its peak and began moving along the ground. Joe stared up at the tower, looked down at his tablet, and scratched the back of his hand out of sheer annoyance. "Who put the Tower of the Crawling Storm in the Dark Lightning Strike slot? Pure laziness, that's what it is."

It was nearly impossible to tell what sort of ritual was on top of what tower, which was why they'd come up with the various arrangements in the first place. He shook his head and sent a quick message to the person who was supposed to be in charge of the structure storage yard, then moved on to the next tower that needed maintenance.

As the final twenty percent of monsters were slowly whittled down, Joe was panting for breath as he switched out yet another tower. He looked down in the killing corridors with longing eyes, watching as the Legion practically screamed with laughter and glee at having a target-rich environment. "Well, at least the Dwarves are having fun."

Every once in a while, conversations from down below would float up and were mostly ignored. But Joe had to chuckle at himself as he heard, "No one can understand their language! That means there's no one to report war crimes against us!"

"Yeah! I have a canister of thermite-infused napalm I've been *dying* to try out!"

"Welp, I hope their commander is keeping an eye on them. That would go right through any wall it got splashed on." Joe stared down at the group that was yelling so boisterously, letting out a sigh as he recognized the markings on the armor of the Dwarf holding an oversized canister. "*O~o~of* course. That *is* the commander."

On the plus side, the last of the beasts were mopped up enough that the Dwarves apparently decided that trying out their experimental weapon would be wasteful. Joe breathed a sigh of relief as the notification came in.

Beast Waves cleared: 1/100! Next wave will arrive in 03:45:24.

"Not even four hours to get everything in place?" Joe took a deep breath, slowly letting it out like an air compressor being drained. "That means... when the twenty-fifth wave hits, we're going to have maybe one hour between waves, and by the fiftieth? It'll just be a constant, unending stream. Abyss, no wonder only one city has ever managed to form here."

"Joe!" The Ritualist turned as he heard a voice, but he didn't see anyone. The voice sounded again, and he realized that it was coming from the ritual of communication that he'd tethered to his Hoardling-hide belt. "Are you there? Come in, Joe. How does this blasted thing work?"

"Aren't you a Mage? You should be able to figure that out." Joe chuckled as he spoke into the device of his own making. There was a half-joking concern that his party member wasn't actually a wizard, but instead was simply adopted by a magical cat who allowed him to play pretend. "What do you need, Socar?"

A few moments later, the voice on the other end of the ritual came through much louder. "People are panicking in here, Joe. Lots of Penguins got into Town; no one was expecting such a brutal Beast Wave. Where are you? The council is convening and no one knows how to get a hold of you."

"I'm on my way. I was doing tower maintenance for the whole wave." Joe was already racing toward the center of the labyrinth, but he kept the communication device in his hand as he went. "What do they think *I* can do about this?"

The Ritualist could practically feel the shrug that he knew his party member was performing at the moment. "No idea. I think they just want to look like they're doing *something*. Keeping people calm and all that."

"Right, well, I'm *actually* doing something," the bald man grumbled, carefully not speaking into the ritual. "I'll be there in under five minutes."

As Joe approached the entrance to the Town Hall, he could hear someone shouting above the noise of the chattering crowd. "—at least a dozen more bunkers inside the walls, a high-powered bow on loan to any archer, regular maintenance crews walking the killing corridors and fixing the walls. Don't worry, people of Novusheim! The council hears your concerns, and we're working to ensure your safety. Go back to your work and hunker down as needed."

Joe felt a powerful hand wrap around his elbow, and he was pulled smoothly through the crowd and into the Town Hall. The concerning part was that he couldn't see anyone holding him, and from the way he was moved through the press of people, it had to be some kind of Mage hand spell. Grandmaster Snow nodded at him as the door opened by itself, closing as soon as Joe was inside. "We are declaring a state of emergency, and martial law is in effect. I don't suppose you intentionally kicked off our settlement advancement?"

"Of course not." Joe brushed off the space where he'd been

grabbed, not sure why it had made him so uncomfortable. "I had no idea we were approaching a hundred thousand residents already."

"I have your assignments ready." Snow stated to the room at large, flicking a half dozen folders through the air. Each of them glided smoothly along and landed in the hands of their intended recipient. "If we're going to make it through this oncoming storm, we need to put aside all of our differences and share one unified goal for the short-term. You all have two options when I tell you to do something. You can act, or you can argue."

Her gaze swept around the room, meeting each of theirs in turn. "If you agree with me, act immediately. Complete the task, or at least move on it to the best of your abilities. If you *don't* agree, argue. Tell me what needs to change and why. At the point where I agree with you, you should agree with me. That means you *act.* What will kill us faster than anything else is letting me assume that you do agree, then not doing the job. If you think I'm wrong, and you don't say anything, it's on *your head* if the task fails. Do we all understand?"

The group responded, some of them surly, some of them with perfect military bearing. However, everyone voiced some version of, "Yes, Grandmaster."

"Good, then here's what we're going to do." Speaking incredibly rapidly, Grandmaster Snow laid out her vision for the next fifty Beast Waves, and Joe could only stare on in silence as she went through detailed schematics, tactics, and strategies that they would be employing. "-and the enchanters are at work on the walls right now. As soon as the final section has been altered to fit with the rest, we'll begin phase three in that operation. Joe."

The human was so astounded that he was practically dazed, and the Grandmaster had to repeat herself before he snapped out of it. "Yes! Grandmaster!"

"Havoc tells me that you might have a solution for our mana issues. Fix them. You have until the twenty-fifth wave, if you take any longer than that, things are going to get decidedly dicey. The resources of the entire Town are available to you. Get the job *done*."

His mouth fell open as he realized he'd just been given carte blanche to pursue a goal he had been racing toward practically since he'd arrived on this world. Regaining control of himself, Joe gave a sharp nod and ran toward the door.

"The conditions are right. It's time to get the Mana Battery recharging stations operational. *Abyss*, yeah!"

CHAPTER TEN

Filled with a sense of purpose, Joe was rushing on his way to his workshop to gather resources, make plans, and ensure that the connections would be perfectly stable in conjunction with the Ritual of Cleansing. So laser-like was his focus that it was only when a hand reached out and grabbed him that the Ritualist realized that someone had been calling his name.

"Master Joe! Pardon me for laying my hands on you, but you'd requested someone to gather you once your prospective students had all arrived. The sign-up sheet was fully filled." The Dwarf that Joe turned his gaze upon was wearing robes, an oddity among almost all Dwarves, except for one, small, specific group.

"Cleric? Oh! The new coven!" Joe took a few deep breaths, trying to decide what would be a more efficient use of his time. Diving into his work or starting a coven as originally planned, so he could start handing off the low-level, less important tasks. The internal struggle resolved itself quickly, and the Ritualist nodded at his minder. "The observatory?"

"Indeed, Master Joe." The two of them hurried over to the strangely esoteric facility, Omnivaulting or flash-stepping. With the current threat to the Town, mere walking wasn't an option. Every single person in sight was moving at full speed the *entire* time they weren't exactly where they needed to be.

Flinging the doors open before him, Joe strolled into the hall and scanned the large crowd that had gathered. To his surprise, more than two-thirds of the group was comprised of Dwarves. His surprise faded somewhat as he saw Princess Dawnesha calmly sitting at the forefront of the group, flanked on either side by high-ranking members of the Legion.

Aside from the staccato beats of his footfalls on the impressive flooring, the room was entirely silent, as if every person was holding their breath hopefully. He came to a halt, composed himself for a moment, then began speaking. "All of you want to change classes to become a Ritualist like me?"

Instantly amending his statement, Joe's gaze firmed up as he stared into every eye that would meet his. "Well, perhaps not like me, but a Ritualist in your own way. Everyone here understands that this is going to be an expensive, long-term commitment before you have a vast amount of power, correct? If you want to leave, feel free to do so at any time. However, if you miss my classes, there are no do-overs. If you vanish after getting the Ritualist class, or do things that are against Novusheim's laws, I'll revoke your class, and you'll be left classless."

Seven humans started sideling toward the door, along with a few Dwarves. Joe pointed at one of them and barked, "You! It's fine if you leave, but why *were* you here?"

"Well… I've seen you work before, and I didn't want to do this just because it *is* easy, but because I *thought* it would be easy." The man chuckled and rubbed the back of his head then powered on out the door without another word.

"Okay, good point. I should mention, this is a class for people who are ready for intense study and a lot of effort. Not for… whatever the abyss *that* guy just told us. Need lots of rational thinkers here." When no one else left, Joe clapped his hands and motioned for everyone to follow him. "Excellent, you're all accepted. Come with me, we've got stuff to do. I'll lecture as we go, and we're going to start learning by doing. Oh, I know that usually there are fees and such for class training. Don't worry, I won't be making you pay... with *money*. Mu-hu-hahah."

One more person left after he chuckled darkly, but Joe was fine with that. If they didn't have a sense of humor, they wouldn't make it in this field, anyway.

"The fundamental requirement of the Ritualist class is a vast pool of mana and the ability to channel it without destroying yourself. This can happen with burnout, passing out during a ritual and having it go supernova, or even just building the ritual circles incorrectly and causing it to draw on your health pool instead of your mana." The Ritualist didn't bother to look back at the group while he was speaking. Anyone who had made it to Jotunheim had plenty of Perception, but he did pause every once in a while to see if everyone *understood* what he was saying.

He blinked a few times in surprise as he saw that roughly two score people remained, and *all* of them had a notebook out and were writing down what he had just said, with the exception of the princess. The Ritualist's eyebrow began to twitch as he saw that she had a servant writing things down so she could focus on his words and actions directly. He held his tongue for the moment, just glad to see that everyone remaining was taking this seriously.

Joe felt a surge of hope that they'd actually follow through on gaining and progressing their class. The entire time they were walking back to his workshop, he was giving a rapid-fire lecture. When they entered the facility, they filled the space to an *almost* uncomfortable level.

"That's plenty of background information for you, for now. Time to put you to work. Everyone here is going to get a different Novice ritual design, and you're *not* going to attempt to create or activate it. Now you know where the workshop is, and you know where the observatory is. Mage Socar has been put in charge of the observatory, so if you need anything in there for study material, speak with him."

The hopefuls looked at him curiously, and Joe realized he hadn't explained himself very well. "Your task for the moment is to take the ritual I'm going to give you and map the node points on it to different star clusters. It shouldn't take you too long, as the pattern should be exactly the same, and it's only a Novice diagram. Once you've completed the task successfully, we'll work to ensure that you have the Lore skills you need. After that, you'll be joining me for some ritual activations to see what they look like and how they feel. Princess, you are *not* allowed to have any servants do your tasks for you. Everyone may work together, but there is no offloading or paying. Exchanges of ritual-based favors *only*."

He didn't miss the flash of annoyance that crossed the princesses' features and was glad that he'd set this requirement. Joe quickly sketched out twenty different Novice rituals, everything from the Ritual of Glimmering to the Little Sister's Cleaning Service. There was one standout individual, a bearded Dwarf who had a near-fervent expression on his face. Before reaching for one of the ritual tiles that Joe had inscribed on, the Dwarf saluted him gratefully and tried to respectfully take the item.

The Ritualist liked that. Respect was nice. Holding up a hand, he pulled back the proffered tile and started going through his stack.

"Hold on. Do this one. If you find that it's too easy, come back, and I'll give you another one. If you complete three of these before I send a message to join me for practice pumping mana into a ritual circle, I'll let you *activate* one before we do a bigger project. Actually, that goes for everyone." Joe handed the Dwarf a Ritual of Glimmering, which would be extra easy to complete, thanks to the brightness of the star cluster.

The Dwarf let out a gasp, and his eyes unfocused. "It… it *worked*! I got a Class Change chain quest!"

"Mmm. Right, I'm a class trainer. Gotta be careful about

telling people what to do. All rewards are coming out of my pocket." *That* realization put a different spin on why there were usually fees and other such nonsense with class trainers. Still, activating a Novice ritual required practically no time or attention from Joe at the moment, so he was fine with what he'd promised.

After almost everyone had been shooed out of his space, Joe offered a salute to the princess, who was standing less than patiently in the room. "Hello, Princess Dawnesha. For what reason do I have the honor of your extended presence?"

His demeanor toward her seemed to take the princess aback, and it was a few moments before she spoke. "I can't say I'm pleased with your *attitude*. I'm sure I've done nothing to deserve anything less than friendship with you."

Joe put a polite, practiced smile on his face, as if it was his one thousand three hundred twenty-fifth day of working customer service. "Well, I don't know if you've noticed, but I've literally built almost an entire city, killed a World Boss, put down a silent coup... it's been a busy time. Frankly, the fact that I needed to find out that you were *alive*, let alone on Jotunheim, from a third party... what kind of friend lets their friend think they died?"

Taking a breath and shrugging helplessly, the Ritualist continued, "By the way, the Dwarf who told me about you let it be known in *no uncertain terms* that you were staying away from me because I was considered unsavory company. Now you've shown up only because I'm offering something you want? I'm looking for the part of our relationship that tells me we're on good terms."

"Ah. I see." She bobbed her head in understanding. "Fair enough. Thank you for the ritual; I will go and get to studying."

The door closed behind her, and Joe could only shake his head slightly in amazement. "I guess, to be fair, she didn't make any excuses or deny what I was saying."

Shaking off the odd encounter, Joe walked into the up-armored vault, enjoying the way his recently acquired vault door released a pneumatic **hiss** as it slid open in front of him. He sat at the small desk and started tapping his quill on its surface. "I need to make these recharge stations; do I have any quests I can complete at the same time?"

It had been a while since he'd opened his quests, and Joe groaned in frustration as he saw that there were several quest complete notifications that he had ignored and forgotten to open later. There were even a few quests he'd gained and completed or made progress on without realizing he even had them, which helped to mitigate his frustration a little.

Class quest complete: Student Rituarchitect I. Create 10 Rare-ranked buildings: 10/10. Reward: Ritual of Mass Repair (Student). Access to Student Rituarchitect II.

"Well, that one was kind of easy. I think I finished that in a couple of days just doing routine tower replacement." Joe chuckled fondly as he happily accepted the new ritual. He didn't have very many multi-target utility rituals, so attaining them was always a treat. "I wonder if I can pull out the portion of this that lets it have multiple endpoints, then use it with my Rituals of Communication to make magical cell phone towers. You know what? That's going on the list."

As he jotted down a note, he let the information from the other quests roll over him.

Class quest gained: Student Rituarchitect II. Create five separate buildings that function together well enough that they can be combined into a single building after they are built. Then, create walkways between them and turn them into a single facility. Buildings created: 0/5. Facility created 0/1.

Class quest updated: Apprentice Reductionist III. Reduce 10 tons' worth of Rare-ranked materials to aspects: 9.35/10 tons reduced.

Class quest gained: Expert Ritualist. You have created a successful coven that has raised a Student Ritualist. The mark of an expert is being able to raise them to Journeyman. This is your task. Journeyman Ritualist promoted: 0/1. Reward: plus 10 to skill: Teaching. +1 to all Ritualist associated skills. Access to Expert Ritualist II.

If it were at all possible, Joe's jaw would've detached from his skull and fallen all the way to the floor. The rewards on the final quest or utterly *insane* to him. It took a few minutes before he realized what had happened. "This quest… is absolutely supposed to be for someone at the early Expert ranks as a Ritualist. I'm already a Master… Celestial feces, if I get more quest rewards like this, I'm gonna get cursed again for breaking the balance."

He pondered that for a moment, cracked his knuckles, and nodded firmly.

"Worth it."

CHAPTER ELEVEN

After a half dozen hours, Joe had finally come up with his plan for completing the first Mana Battery Recharge Station. "This goes here, this here. Good. With the complexity, if I assume every portion is at this difficulty, and I put in my best effort… it'll kill me ninety-nine times out of a hundred. This is ridiculous."

Tossing the documents into storage, he groaned and remembered that he had as many resources as he needed to spend to make the project work correctly. "With an unlimited budget, I *should* be able to hire someone who can actually make it in the next few days."

Taking out a single page, he studied the Mana Collector, which was the easiest of the modular items to make. Thanks to the seemingly endless supply of ambient mana on this world, it would even be able to easily collect power constantly. On a lower-strength world, like Midgard, it would struggle greatly to get even a single point of mana a minute. Unfortunately, that was where Joe had run into his first problem. He gently slapped the paper with the back of his hand in frustration. "It collects *endlessly*, and I can't see any way to turn it off or measure how much it has inside at any given moment. This is practically *begging* to self-destruct spectacularly."

The Mana Condenser was no better, essentially being a giant coil of high-end metals and gems that forced any mana input to take up less space, concentrating the power to a terrifying degree. Once again, there were *no* safety measures added. It would last longer than the collector, but that just meant that when it went critical, the explosion would be that much more powerful.

As for the Mana Transfer Output? It was so inefficient in its design that anything that was dumped into it would practically turn the air around it into energetic soup. Simply being near it would be a hazard to his health bar. "*Why*? Why would Havoc give this to me and say it's ready to go? He has way too much pride in his craft to short sell me on this."

There were only a few reasons that he could think of, and Joe sighed as he realized that most of them started and ended with: "That means, for this rank of enchantment, this *must* be the best option. Perhaps it's intentionally inefficient so that it helps to get rid of excess mana? Maybe making it more efficient would cause a bottleneck and lead to the bad ends I was worried about?"

Grumbling about the situation, Joe reluctantly pulled the documents out of storage and continued studying the diagrams Havoc had handed over.

Half an hour later, he found himself trying to decide if it was worth attempting to build a Ritual of Enchanting around them, or if he actually *should* use the power of the purse that Grandmaster Snow had granted him to hire a half dozen-enchanters and put them to work. With one last attempt at understanding the documents, the Ritualist finally gave in.

Slapping a hand on the table, Joe pushed himself to his feet and nodded firmly. "Both. Step one is to get Havoc in here to at least supervise, if not put these together himself, then make him train me so *I* can build them. Bring in a few other enchanters because I need more than one of these. Yes. It's decided."

Throwing open the door to his workshop, Joe stepped outside, only to come face to face with a Dwarf holding three ritual tiles raising his fist to knock on the door. "Uh. Hi! I finished."

Joe was nonplussed for a moment, then he realized what was going on. He looked at the Dwarf up and down, then reached his hand out. "You did all three of them? Where's everyone else? Did they finish as well?"

"A few people did, but I stayed until I did all three." The Dwarf had bags under his eyes, as though he'd been keeping his eyes wide open the entire time that he had been gone.

"Huh. Alright. What's your name?" As his new pupil opened his mouth to respond, Joe forestalled him with an upraised hand. "Wait, no. Don't tell me. You can take up space in my head when you earn the class. What's your class currently?"

The rapid fire questions didn't faze the Dwarf, but Joe's final question caused the tip of his nose to turn bright red for some reason. "*Ahem*… currently I'm a Neophyte."

"You're a vampire? Err… I mean, maybe not a vampire, is that a werewolf?"

"What? No. I've had a class of Neophyte my entire life, and I've been unable to change it." The Dwarf grumbled at his own words, looking away in shame. "It gives what is essentially a free ride in skill levels up to the top of the Student ranks, but makes it impossible to push any of them up to Journeyman or beyond. It's supposed to allow me to train under almost any class trainer. But… for some reason, whether I have a hidden curse or a broken title fragment stuck in my status, I've never been able to find a class that will allow me to take their class change quest."

The Ritualist stared at the candidate and tried to put into words what he was thinking at the moment. "Okay, yeah, tell me your name."

"They call me… Baumann the Broken." The Dwarf had completely flushed red while saying this, and he looked like he wanted to crawl into a hole and vanish for a while.

Clapping a hand on the Dwarf's shoulder, Joe pulled him

into the workshop and sat him down. "Look here, Baumann. You don't have to worry about that nasty title for very much longer. But let me ask you something… when you change your class, do you lose your bonus to skill growth?"

"Technically yes, but I get to choose a single skill to have doubled growth for until the Master rank." At this, the Dwarf puffed up his chest, only to remember his current situation and allow a wry smile to show. "Or, at least, that's how it's supposed to work, but I've been stuck without another class for about three hundred years. Hence the… Broken."

"I don't want to scare you, but I want you to put your class change quest on hold for now." As Baumann started to protest, Joe held up a hand and pulled out a piece of paper. He began frantically writing down every skill he could think of that would be useful for the Dwarf to attain before losing his incredible skill growth. "You've the potential to become the best Ritualist in all of the worlds in no time flat. Well, maybe not surpassing me, but that's just because I'll be the one you're learning from. Anyway, here's the skills I have that I think you should pursue. You know what? Let's throw some gathering skills in there as well. Tailoring? How do you feel about art? Freestyle drawing and such? You're going to have an *incredible* foundation for this magic."

As the list rapidly grew, Baumann's eyes went wide. "You want me to learn *more* skills that aren't class related? That's… wasteful!"

A cocky grin appeared on Joe's face. "I'm an *omnicrafter*. I can make anything, out of anything else. But I need the skills to do it. I'm a Master in Ritual Magic already, but I have nothing in tailoring, leatherworking, enchantment support… trust me on this one. You know what? Better than that, I'm going to give you a Guild invite and make you my direct… disciple. Huh. I wonder if that's what Havoc did with me? Anyway, show me what you can *really* do, and I'll make sure you're the most powerful Ritualist in the world, after me."

By the time Joe had finished speaking, Baumann's eyes were

blazing with excitement. "It's a deal, Master Joe! Also, I have several of these skills on your list at the peak of Student rank, especially the ones that are aligned with the Oligarchy's most valued members. Metalwork, smelting, mining, enchanting, sculpting, golem crafting, and the like."

Joe gulped hard, trying to keep his drool from making a mess on the table. "Yeah, I think you're going to like this class a *whole* bunch. First thing, I need you to go to the Pyramid of Panacea and start learning alchemy. Jake *seems* scary, but he's *actually* terrifying. He'll like *you* a lot though, and if you can't change classes to what he does, he can't steal you away. It's perfect."

"My class change quest just updated. It's… you were serious? How can you have a disciple? You could have an apprentice, or something, but a disciple?" Baumann seemed almost listless, the intense emotional roller coaster he'd been going through seeming to burn him out for the moment.

The Ritualist nodded at him, understanding his confusion. "My guild is transforming into a sect, and I've been guaranteed the position of… well, don't worry about it. It's pretty high up there. I'm going to be turning one of the suburb areas into a guild town once we're a full City. That should let us upgrade into a full sect and collect our people, especially if we have control of the bifrost here. Plenty of room for expansion."

The Dwarf shook Joe's hand, eyes glazed as he stumbled toward the door and out into the cold. The Ritualist watched him with an extremely pleased smile on his face—bordering on smug—then startled and raced toward the door when he remembered that he was supposed to be doing things out there as well.

His search for enchanters was on, but they were doing a phenomenal job of hiding from him. Asking dozens of business owners and even some council members got him no closer to finding wherever the enchanters were staying currently. Eventually, Joe was starting to get so frustrated that he considered interrupting Grandmaster Snow. Happily, before he made a foolish decision—as his anemic Luck Characteristic was pressuring him to do—Joe remembered that she'd declared martial law and set all enchanters to start working on the walls.

Carefully considering whether his requests would be shot down, Joe still decided that he needed the help, and he *had* been ordered to requisition whatever he needed. Only an hour later, Joe had four Dwarves who were extremely pleased to have the chance to work indoors again.

Only when they started talking amongst themselves did Joe realize that he might've made a mistake.

"Will you look at that?" The Dwarf with the most elaborate beard braids chortled as he stared out of the small window of the workshop. "Snow's coming down thicker than the pile of Elf bodies made by my most recent superweapon."

"Now *this* is the life. I can't believe our peers are still out there, fussing with that ridiculous bouncing enchantment the council is making us inscribe at cost! They had the chance to get out of work without breaking martial law and instead chose to slowly freeze to death? Unbelievable." The voice was slightly muffled, as the person speaking had their nose buried in a dusty tome of advanced enchantments.

A third, who was sipping the coffee Joe had provided, nearly spat the precious liquid out as he joined in their laughter. "All hail Master Joe, breaking us out of work detail. Smarter than he looks, that one. Nothing says planning for the future like getting a group of Expert Enchanters on his side early on, know what I'm saying?"

The last of them, who'd been silent until this point, watching the various expressions crossing Joe's face during the conversation, had a slightly different take on the situation. "I don't know... something about this doesn't sit right with me. There were near a hundred of us, and almost everyone outright refused without even considering it. Are we stuck with an ongoing, continuous contract? Are we going to be forced to do low-level ward maintenance or another menial task?"

"With our expertise? Peak Enchanting Experts?" The

impressively bearded first Dwarf scoffed, beard jingling as he shook his head at the naivete of his fellow. "Master Joe Eunuch, what *will* we be doing? All this talk about experimental designs is fun, but–"

The Ritualist didn't hear the rest of whatever the question was, a deep ringing filling his ears. Taking a few deep breaths, he called himself enough to meet the eyes of the Enchanter and grind out, "What did you call me?"

"Master Joe," the Enchanter responded with an innocent grin and a mischievous wink at the Dwarf sitting next to him. "I just added in your status as a fully hairless individual."

"Is *that* why everyone flinches when they look at me?" Contrary to the expectations of the Dwarves, Joe started laughing harder than he had in weeks. "Cultural customs… are the *worst*! Not having *hair* means that I'm at the same status as the most elite warriors assigned to protect Queens and Princesses? I thought they were grossed out, but they were *nervous*?"

He thought back, working hard to remember every interaction he'd ever had with Princess Dawnesha. As far as he could remember, she had always seemed perfectly comfortable around him—never wincing, always being willing to get into his personal space—and finally, *finally* he knew why! Wiping a tear of laughter out of his eye, Joe looked at the dumbstruck Dwarves and shook his head. "Don't worry, you'll stay plenty busy here. In fact, if I'm not mistaken, I can hear our *lead* Enchanter approaching even now."

Joe's words were practically punctuated by a scream from a Dwarf who went tumbling past the window. A guttural voice followed along shortly after, "You should've accepted the *coupon*! It's barely even expired."

"Wait…" Beard-braids' eyes went wide.

"Is that–" Coffee drinker choked and started coughing, and the cautious Dwarf turned and tried to escape out the back door… but there was no back door.

A moment later, Havoc appeared in the room, having

kicked open the solid metal door that Joe had put in specifically to accommodate the chaotic Grandmaster, leaving a foot-shaped dent projecting an inch from its surface. "Joe! You said the Town is paying for all of this, right? What kind of budget can you allocate for… side projects?"

CHAPTER TWELVE

"Approximately two hundred hours since the start of the first wave until the twenty-fifth hits. That gives me about eight days in total to get these projects done before we'll be completely overwhelmed." Joe would've been far more concerned over the situation, were it not for the fact that he now had a Grand-master and four Experts working for him.

The ritual towers in the distance were constantly lighting up the night sky now, ceaselessly firing into the crowds of monsters. Watching for a moment, the Ritualist decided he may have overestimated how much time he truly had. "If the size of the waves grows each time, it's not just that we're going to have a constant stream. We're eventually going to have multiple waves fighting for the right to hit us first. Then we'll have a huge ocean of them surrounding us on all sides."

Then he had a truly terrifying thought. "What if the monsters blocking the path count as an obstacle, and the others start going through the walls? Will Snow's plan help mitigate that, or… no, I have to trust her. If *I* thought about that, the war council definitely has."

For the moment, he was lost as to what he should be doing.

The first of the Mana Battery Recharge Stations should be up and operational with only a couple dozen hours of work, and the next ones should come out even faster after all the kinks were worked out in the production process.

His individual combat skills weren't particularly versatile against so many monsters, and Joe didn't want to climb the walls just to start picking off weak beasts. "Class quests? Yes. Let's do that. I really want to go back to the den of ice wraiths I kited along to help me destroy that Elven settlement, but I think if anyone sees me leaving Town, it might start a panic."

He felt his gut clench as he thought about Havoc warning him against leaving. Joe repeated it incredulously. "'The last time you vanished through your little shrine system, you took all of the ritual towers with you'. Abyss, don't these people understand *extenuating circumstances*?"

Trying to decide between additional training, working on creating an upgraded set of rituals, or checking on the class-change aspirants, Joe stepped back to clear his head for a minute. As he thought about what to do, he started casually checking in on the situation outside of the walls. Multiple relay stations had been set up—basically little ritual bubbles that allowed official messengers to know where to have a runner bring their information in order to get it to the next link in the chain as quickly as possible.

Popping into the bubble, the Ritualist was greeted with a salute, this particular gesture a version extended from a member of the military to a civilian leader. Joe responded in kind, motioning for the Dwarf with the markings of a Scout Lieutenant of the Legion to relax.

"I have wave reports from the eastern front." She approached with a heavy scroll and unfurled it for Joe to look over as she spoke. "Between the first wave and now, we're estimating that the number has doubled. We're expecting back-to-back waves, like a fire sale on claws and frostbite."

Joe scanned the numbers and blinked a few times before rubbing his temples. "Abyss. I never expected the upgrade to be anything like this. Seriously, why was there no… I don't know, *intermediate* step?"

The Lieutenant nodded at him, stroking her mustache in thought. "You're talking about a 'Special' rank settlement. Those get shuffled to the side of the main upgrade options, and their upgrade paths are extremely limited or difficult to manage. For instance, you're part of a guild. There's only a few paths your group could take if they decided they wanted to own an entire settlement. They could turn it into what's essentially a massive factory, if they were a crafter's guild. Or, if they're all fighters and the like, it can turn into a mercenary town, pirate haven, or even a smuggler's den."

"A Sect?" Joe hopefully offered, wondering if he was about to get the information he'd been seeking on how to upgrade his guild.

She raised an eyebrow at him, but nodded. "At the Special rank, it would only be a minor Sect. I think the next step up from there is orthodox or demonic sect, depending on the majority of the alignment of your members."

"Don't know what that means, but thanks!" Joe chipperly stated, his gaze going distant as he thought about the future. "I wonder where we'll all end up? I don't know about you, but I think we should pull everything to a beach world. Set up some climate control around it and chill for a few decades. Or centuries."

The Lieutenant looked at him strangely. "I'm almost positive that Jotunheim has no beaches you'd want to lounge on."

"No, I mean, when we all *leave* here. After getting control of the bifrost?" His comment was met only with a blank expression and a shrug. Joe's words were filled with disbelief. "You don't think you're going to come along? I mean, whatever you want to do, I don't really know you. But it would be kind of hard to be here alone, don't you think?"

"Um. Master Joe, I think you may have some misconceptions. The Dwarven Oligarchy is planning on fully dominating this planet, and I don't think you're going to be convincing any of my people to leave." She tilted her head to the side slightly. "Why would we? There's plenty of meat, enormous monsters to sharpen our blades on and test our new inventions. Not to mention all of the space. We can grow to our hearts' content and choose a few thousand miles where we can dump all of our pollutants so we never have to think about them again. This world is a paradise for us."

"But... the next world...?" For some reason, Joe simply couldn't understand the words this Lieutenant was spouting at him.

She gave him a formal salute and spoke in a clipped tone. "Master Joe, I truly believe I can speak for all of us when I say that this *is* the next world for us. As far as the Oligarchy is concerned, we're staying. This is either our home forever or our final resting place."

The Ritualist felt like he'd been punched in the gut. Internally, a part of him started screaming and cursing about wasting his best materials on buildings that he wouldn't be bringing along with him. All this time, he'd been throwing everything he had into every part of the settlement, assuming that this world was a stepping stone for them, just as it was for him. If what the Lieutenant said was true, that the Dwarves were digging into this soil and had no intention of uprooting themselves...

Dazedly saluting in return, Joe turned and walked away as he tried to absorb the shock he'd been given. He looked around at everything that had been built so far, structures that had been his responsibility to create. The Ritualist had literally *given* them away, assuming that he would forever have access to them. Instead, he realized that his choices were permanent. "I don't have a blueprint for the observatory! I need to go scan that. What about the, no, I should..."

He blanched as he looked over at the Pyramid of Panacea, which was now owned by Jake the Alchemist. Joe's voice came out as a whisper. "Surely *Jake* wants to go to the next world, right?"

Rushing over to the pyramid, he used the door knocker to get Jake's attention, eventually being let in after nearly five minutes of waiting. As soon as he saw who had allowed him access, Joe understood the delay. "Ah. Baumann. Glad to see you're being as diligent as ever. Did Jake take you under his wing?"

"He did!" The Dwarf's eyes were alight, and his smile was bright enough to blind a Penguin. "The venerable Sage started with teaching me Alchemical Lore, and when I reached the Beginner rank by the end of our conversation, he started teaching me in earnest. Please, come in! He's waiting for you but didn't want to allow you access because he thought you were perhaps coming to collect me."

"But… *I* sent you here." Joe shook his head and walked into the building. His thoughts were muddled at the moment, and he didn't trust himself to have an existential conversation on this level with someone he'd only just met. The words 'the Oligarchy will never leave this world' were bouncing around inside of his skull, echoing like a mental curse had been placed on him.

The moment he laid eyes on Jake, the Alchemist looked up at him and narrowed his eyes ever so slightly. Instantly, the cauldron he was hovering next to started boiling over and the man cursed as he swept the falling liquid into glass tubes and buckets that had clearly been placed there for that purpose. "Joe, you have no idea how rare a Neophyte is. If you think I'm going to give him up before he has the most firm foundation in alchemy possible and has been *completely* convinced to advance my craft, you–"

"Jake, please. I'm not here about that." The Ritualist slumped onto a three-legged stool, heaving a deep sigh. "I just found out that the Dwarves are planning to remain on Jotunheim. I don't understand it, but I need to know… when we open the bifrost, are you going to come with me and bring the Alchemy Hall with you?"

The Alchemist's elated expression sank faster than lead

precipitate in a cooling concoction. "Is it time for this conversation already? I thought you knew. There I was, thinking to myself: why else would he give me full ownership of this building? Short version, then. There are a multitude of reasons, but *no*, I will not be leaving this world. At least not with the pyramid."

"But. Jake, I need to know those reasons." Joe's confusion was starting to shift into anger as he realized that all of his hard work was only going to benefit others, and almost none of it was going to have a lasting impact for him. "I don't want to have to start over, not again. I entered Midgard with nothing, then all of the gold I collected there was useful only as crafting material in Alfheim. The bucketloads of reputation I accrued on *that* world became worthless as soon as the Oligarchy fell, then we arrived here. I'm not going to do it again. I'm not going to another world and starting at the bottom *again.*"

"Well... then *you* should plan to stay on Jotunheim forever as well." Jake stated calmly and cautiously. "Otherwise, the next step is going to be you once again at the bottom of the well as a frog, staring up at swan flesh and wishing for a taste. Eventually, you might become an extremely powerful, influential person on this world. But... no matter what you attain here, a new world is a *new* world. Do you even know what they use as currency on Vanaheim, for instance?"

'No. How could I *possi*–"

"Cheese," Jake informed him so seriously that Joe couldn't doubt him. "It is an endlessly renewable resource, but not so much there. There's a secret cabal of penguins at the center of the world that collect tithes of cheese and use it in an attempt to rebuild the core of the planet. Now. Back to the issue at hand, the pyramid cannot survive another transfer in its current state. Too much of its material has been devoted to the magma drill. The walls are thin, and will take years—if not decades—to even out."

Joe hadn't even considered that aspect of this building, but of course the drill had to have material for its piping, and that had to come from somewhere. "But, someday? Would you continue onward?"

"The most I can say without putting a larger target on your back is that it is not an option for me. If I fly too close to the sun, I'll be *noticed*. This is as close as I can realistically shift, and even now, I am reliant on the cloud cover for, how to say… succor?"

Chewing on the information he'd just gained, the Ritualist stayed silent for a few minutes. "I'm not a Dwarf, Jake. I don't build cities to last until the end of time. I'm building so that I can have accomplishments to bring with me to higher worlds. Right now? I don't know if I want to keep investing my best resources. Not when I know it's a one-way transaction."

Jake let out a deep sigh and reached out and patted the air, as if he were trying to console the human but didn't want to get his hands dirty by touching his actual back. "There, there. I believe that is your language's comfort words. Look. You never know. Perhaps your work here may echo into other realms in ways you can't yet imagine."

CHAPTER THIRTEEN

His work was beginning to suffer. Joe knew it. He didn't know what he could do about it. Rituals that took him an hour to perform were dragging on for two, even three sometimes. The blueprint Daniella had given him for an elemental playground lay forgotten and untouched on his work table, a prime target for any Dwarf who wanted nothing to do with Elven technologies.

Conversely, he was making a great progress with his Ritualistic Forging, due to constantly taking out his frustrations by beating on aspects with hammers. Not even sure how much time had passed, Joe only snapped out of his ruminations as the athame he'd been working on completed and gave him a notification he hadn't seen before.

New item created! Congratulations! By pouring your intent into your work, you have created a brand new, unique twist on an item! As you have crafted this item without assistance or using a template, rewards are doubled. A template for the recreation of this item has been added to your storage device!

Class Experience (Ritualist and Reductionist) gained: 1,000

Ritualistic Forging (Journeyman II → Journeyman IV)

Quest updated: Student Reductionist II. Unique items created 2/5.

Athame of Rising Discontent. This ritual style dagger is perfect for the burgeoning War Ritualist intent on overthrowing a system of government. The longer they have been perceiving themselves as 'put upon' by those in a leadership position above them, the more precisely their rituals will be directed by this blade. Adds a +1% 'shred' buff to any war ritual that inflicts damage.

Shred: A debuff that makes wounds 50% more difficult to heal.

"Whoa, no, what?" Joe stared at the blade that was practically oozing malevolence and started shaking his head immediately. "Nope, not letting something like this out into the world with my name on it as its crafter. Field Array, an~nd it's gone."

Letting out a deep sigh, Joe stored his ingot hammer away and started pondering the situation with a calmer frame of mind. Growmore, who wasn't currently his tutor, but still worked in the workshop, looked him over as he sat down. "I was wondering when you were going to stop abusing that anvil. All better now?"

Almost calmly, Joe reiterated the situation for the Dwarf, who grunted in understanding as the issues were revealed. "Now I'm just not sure if I'm okay with starting over all over again. But… when I first came to this place, Eternium, I promised that I'd ascend all the worlds and win."

"Win? What're you going to win? *Life*?" The Dwarf rolled his eyes and stomped closer, then gave Joe a full-on punch to the gut. The human didn't even move, though the hairy attacker received a shadowy slap across the face for his troubles. "Look at you. You're strong; didn't even flinch. You have power incongruent with your level and status. Are you going to tell me that isn't *enough*? Are you going to stagnate now? Let me warn you… a pickaxe paused never strikes gold."

When the human remained silent, Growmore shook his head and pulled on his beard. "Well, Joe, here's a simple question for you. Are you planning on leaving and ripping away our defenses when you go? Just because you aren't *technically* the owner of each building, does that mean you can't forcibly move it?"

Blinking a few times, the human realized that he didn't know for sure. He pulled out his tablet, zooming in on the area, and finding that every building he'd created with a ritual was still marked with a bright dot. "No one's revoked my access... okay, Jake did, but no one else."

"Yeah, does anyone even have the *ability* to remove your mark from the buildings that they 'own'?" Growmore snorted and tossed a hand in the air while he turned away. "You could walk away and take everything you've done for us with you. It's your *right*, certainly. But would you want to do that? Condemn the rest of us to whatever fate we have remaining here or force us to move after we've decided to survive here if at all possible?"

"No." Joe whispered. "That's not who I am. Your lives are worth more to me than that."

"I think you have your answer. Now stop being a complete downer and get out of the workshop so we can make some super cool swords." Contrary to his gruff attitude, the Dwarf walked Joe out, even giving him a hearty pat on the back. "Get out there and impress me."

"Yeah. Yeah! It's just *stuff.* I can literally always make more stuff, whenever I want, wherever I want!" Joe gulped down a few breaths of icy air, shaking his arms to try and pull himself out of his funk. The Dwarf closed the door behind him, and Joe marched away with a determined expression, headed straight for the shrine to Tatum. "If I don't want to be forced to restart completely on whatever world opens after this, I know exactly what I need to do."

He checked his inventory, where a variety of cores glittered. "Before I leave Jotunheim, I'm going to have an Artifact-rank natural aspect jar. If I have endless access to creating items or buildings of at least that tier, I'll never be permanently poor in any world. Luxury, weapons, defenses, or bribes... I'll be able to rely on myself, no matter *what* the local currency is."

Joe snorted as he thought back to what Jake had warned

him about with Vanaheim using cheese as its trade goods, then froze in place as something Baumann had said suddenly clicked in his head. "Wait a second… did he call Jake a Sage? Was that literal? Or was it him exaggerating in order to get brownie points with… nope, not going to ask about it. Not my circus, not my monkeys."

With a fresh attitude, he slapped his hand down on the altar and searched through the list of teleport locations for his destination. "Spooky underground crevasse. There you are."

Having selected his destination, Joe blinked away in a flash of purple light. Ten thousand one hundred and seven miles away, the bald Ritualist reappeared, immediately collapsing to his knees and vomiting violently on the icy ground.

You have teleported through a contested area! The local Pantheon have extracted a toll on your travel and alerted their followers that you have arrived somewhere in their territory. Note: They cannot give any specifics. Only that you have arrived somewhere within one hundred miles of a shrine dedicated to them.

Mana remaining: 1/8,787.

After heaving for a few moments, barely remembering to take the opportunity to try and condense his mana further, Joe wiped his mouth and got back to his feet unsteadily. "That's new, and I really, *really* didn't like it."

On the plus side, the fact that he hadn't been set upon in his weakened, practically helpless state, was a good indication that none of the ice wraiths had remained in the cave. Walking into the crevasse filled with otherwise abject darkness except in a single spot, Joe's stride didn't slow, nor did he slip or stumble on anything in his way. In less than five seconds, he'd crossed the open space and was standing before the carved out entrance to an intentionally-designed area.

"Let's see what secrets you're hiding in here." He crossed the threshold of the cave and found himself absolutely unable to move. Joe couldn't blink, though he could still breathe, and after a moment of panic, he saw that his mana pool had stopped refilling. Struggling as hard as he could yielded no movement, so the Ritualist tried to remain calm as he waited for an explanation. Nearly half an hour passed before a screen appeared in front of him, but this one was clearly *not* generated by the system.

No, so far as he could tell, it was a flat screen television indistinguishable from Earth technology. A cursor appeared on the screen, and soon words began writing themselves out.

Calculating time spent. Internal clock damaged. Assessing mana storage. Calculating the passage of time based on deterioration of stasis fields. Calculations complete.

Greetings, noble adventurer! If you are reading this, several things are happening at once.

Firstly, you are caught in a stasis field, and your mana regeneration is being diverted to replenish the depleted enchantments of this vault.

Secondly, the defenses and communication array is coming online.

As soon as Joe read the final line, the ground behind him—actually an extended hatch—smoothly rose up and sealed him in the room. Then the text on the screen changed again, and Joe read as quickly as he could, the words vanishing as fast as he managed to comprehend them. For the first time since he'd walked into the area, Joe was glad he was unable to blink.

Congratulations! You are being granted a quest. Before we get to that, some background information for you. You have entered the Seed Vault of Spite, owned by the Magi Ascendant. Please note, if you are strong enough to resist the effects of the stasis field, this otherwise mandatory quest becomes a polite request.

If Joe could move, he would've snorted at that and rolled his eyes.

Based on the calculations of mana depletion, it has been approximately [10,000] years since the last time this vault has been recharged with non-chaotic mana. Thank you for your [temporary?] service of refreshing it.

Ten millennia ago, our frontier/vacation/safari/resort that was the world of Jotunheim was brutally assaulted by the children of the Great Serpent, led by the Jotunn and its progeny. At first, the primitive use of physical might against our magic was laughable, but at some point during the conflict, two of our Grandmasters were caught and swallowed by the

Jotunn, allowing it to complete its ascension and become a Mythical World Boss.

At that point, all of our inhibitors lost their efficiency against the entirety of the monsters, as they fell under the direct control of the Jotunn. Enormous clouds filled the sky, and a deadly cold began to emanate from the barbaric creature. We believe it gains additional power from being in an area that is utterly frigid and prepared this Vault deep within the bowels of the planet to one day retaliate and disrupt its goals.

Frankly, as the name suggests, this Vault was made practically out of pure spite. It is filled with seeds which will grow into a type of flora that can survive in only *the harshest of winter conditions. The plants that will erupt from their fragile beginnings grow faster in bitter cold, radiating intense heat so long as the temperature is below—calculating for current language—[negative thirty degrees Fahrenheit]. Upon being slashed, smashed, pulped, or swallowed, new sprouts will form from at least 15 separate fibers and grow faster.*

In the unlikely event that we lose the war against animals, these seeds will ensure that the world our enemy reigns over becomes inhospitable to them.

The fact that it will give you a fighting chance against them is irrelevant to us but certainly a boon to you. Do not plant them anywhere within a mile of where you intend to live.

Your task is to gain control of the seed bank and spread the seeds wherever the ground is frozen. In order to accomplish this task, you must swear a binding oath that you will plant these seeds in at least one frozen area on the planet Jotunheim.

Failure to swear this oath will result in the room becoming locked down, in which case, we appreciate your sacrifice and will use all of the mana generated by your body to empower the defenses and stasis fields until a proper candidate arrives. Control of your vocal cords and facial muscles will be returned to you as soon as the options are presented. Please choose one of the following.

1. Swear the binding oath. This will show your commitment to using this weapon, unlocking the vault, and releasing control over your Mana Regeneration.

Reward(s): access to the seed vault. A spatial seed pouch perfect for preserving seeds of extreme magical potency.

2. Refuse and attempt to disable the vault mechanism. Reward: see option three.

3. Remain in the vault and be drained until you have succumbed to starvation. Reward: our gratitude for your sacrifice and for recharging the degraded mana cells and enchantments.

Immediately after he had finished reading, Joe was able to move his head once more. He blinked furiously, spitting curses and trying to leverage his motion into releasing the rest of his body.

It appears you are attempting to select option two! Is this correct?

"No!" Joe relaxed and took a few deep breaths. "Whoever this Magi Ascendant is, they seem like a real piece of work. But, can't say I'm not impressed with all this. The Jotunn is my enemy as well, so… I choose option one? I swear to use the seeds on a frozen area of Jotunheim."

Oath acknowledged! Binding via karmic thread.

Joe saw odd lines of light for a fraction of a second, then he gasped as it felt like he was poked in a dozen places by incredibly thin needles. Immediately, he was released from the force keeping him contained, and he stumbled forward.

A small treasure chest, completely out of place in such a futuristic setting, lifted out of the ground and opened its lid. Inside was a small bag, almost too small to fit his fingers into. The Ritualist grabbed the pouch, more than a little annoyed with the rigmarole of the situation, and opened it to reveal hundreds of thousands of seeds no larger than a fleck of dust.

Glaring at the screen, Joe walked toward the wall that had closed behind him, which opened up with a cheerful noise and a slight **hiss**. Keeping his eyes on the glowing rectangle, the Ritualist pulled out a pinch of the seeds and tossed them—without looking—out of the door.

Oath fulfilled!

At the same moment a proper system notification announced his follow-through, the same text appeared on the screen. Unfortunately, the information on the screen was quite concerning.

Oath fulfilled! Self-destruct sequence initiated! 3… 2…

"*Abyss!*" Joe hurled himself across the crevasse, barely getting his hands on the altar before the Vault behind him was hidden behind a hazy, wavy field of energy. The Ritualist was yanked *viciously* backward as it collapsed into something reminiscent of a black hole. Just as his hand slid almost completely off of the shrine, he chose a destination at random and teleported away.

CHAPTER FOURTEEN

Two hops across the planet later, the Ritualist appeared on the ground next to the shrine in the center of Novusheim, panting for breath and pushing against his chest to physically tamp down the nausea of mana deprivation. Even with the maelstrom of sensations flooding him at the moment, he couldn't hold back the grin splitting his face. "Now *that's* what I call a successful expedition. Got powerful magical items, barely had to work for them, and didn't die. Power fantasy complete."

After a few moments to allow his mana to build up, he pushed himself to his feet with a groan and started walking toward the ritual tower staging yard. Joe had been gone long enough that he knew *something* must've cracked, fallen apart, or been outright destroyed. "Make some extra towers, hook up the rituals, then I'll go and figure out if I should use these seeds. Maybe I should pop over to the greenhouse and see if Herbie Thymebeard can figure out if they're a trap."

Before all else, he knew that the Town needed boosted defenses. From the moment he returned to Novusheim, the sounds of combat had been drifting through the air. Even with his recent misgivings, Joe had every intention of personally creating and deploying each tower… but that train of thought was derailed as he walked into the staging yard.

His eyes widened in disbelief as masons, enchanters, and what was clearly an engineering corps bustling around, constructing multiple towers at the same time. Some were halfway done, some were already nearing completion. As far as Joe could see, stone spires were punching through the skyline—literally through it, as the false sky was an illusion—and each was built with the exacting precision that Dwarves brought to their crafts. Bauen, the lead engineer and clearly the person in charge of this project, waved Joe over while wiping sweat off his brow.

"Ah, excellent! You're back!" The Dwarf waved at the dozens of towers that had gone up in Joe's absence. "Congratulations, we can't expand the walls out any further at the moment, so everyone working on a project out there was re-tasked with making your life easier. All we need from you is rituals up at the top of these monster blasters, and they'll be good to go."

Joe nearly started dancing with glee as he realized one of his tedious tasks had been taken off his plate. "I see you've been busy! Kind of weird, but I never even considered having someone else build the towers. I… this is going to give me back *so* much of my day."

"Yeah, and why should you have all the fun?" Bauen chortled as he wrapped an arm as thick as an oak tree around the Ritualist's shoulders and pulled him along to showcase what they were doing. "These front ones are all at the Rare rank; the higher tier are at the back, behind the bunkers. Abyss, those are a beast and a half to put together."

"Pretty resource intensive, I know. On that note, how do we have the building slots for all of these? Also, where are you getting the materials?" Joe had a pretty good idea of how many open building slots there'd been before he went on his little trip, and this… was way past what should've been possible.

The engineer smirked at Joe and raised an eyebrow. "I just

told you. They take about a beast and a half to put together. Since these towers up front are roughly eighteen feet tall, and Penguins are twelve feet tall, you can do the math yourself. Converting the bones to a framework for stone and other material to be put in place works just fine."

Chuckling to himself at some joke Joe didn't quite understand, Bauen continued, "As to the building slots…? Well, we're approaching ten thousand monsters put down in the last couple of waves. Not a single one of them got to the center of Town. I tell you what, the morale bonuses have been *stacking.* We're going to have to be careful not to use everything that's available to us, or we'll be pushing into a Metropolis as soon as we finish upgrading to a City!"

The Dwarf was so proud of himself for that line of thinking that Joe didn't want to bring the mood down by articulating how *terrifying* that would actually be. They just didn't have the resource centers that such a large settlement would require. Their mines were shallow, food was gathered by hunters—or various people delving into the greenhouse—and all in all, their foundation was simply nowhere near sturdy enough. Frankly, even if he didn't want to admit it to himself, Joe was concerned that they may not even survive the current upgrade they were fighting for.

Still, the Ritualist felt like it was Christmas morning and someone had just handed him a bag full of time. As he walked along the towers, looking for any issues, he noticed a few glaring ones immediately. "Hey, right there, these towers are supposed to have a topper, but… did you leave it that way on purpose?"

Bauen winked at him and put a finger to his lips. "Shh, you're spoiling my surprises! Yes, we're completing those sections separately so that we can have a bunch of buildings that are *almost* complete and not counting against our total building slots. That way, if you need to throw something together really fast, you can. Or, we can slap the top on and send it out right away if we need a replacement. We're trying to maintain a consistent amount of them, just in case additional buildings draw in additional monsters."

"Good call. I'm thinking that perhaps now *isn't* the time to test that." Joe's words pulled a rueful chuckle from the duo, and they split up. The Dwarf had to get back to supervising, and Joe could start working on his to-do list! The thought put a smile on his face, and he started toward the observatory with a spring in his step to check on his Coven.

Walking into the specialized facility was always an interesting experience. It was a combination of the liminal space of a library, and the bustling activity of a new tech startup. People were keeping their voices down but nearly constantly murmuring to each other as they tried to understand the projects they were working on. Joe's eyes roved over the area, watching as the hopefuls pointed out certain stars to people working on similar rituals to them or laid on their backs with their hands folded behind their heads, quietly searching for the patterns they needed to pick out.

He remained quiet for a few minutes, and just before he was going to call everyone over, the stars above faded as someone activated a Ritual of Glimmering in conjunction with the star pattern, filling the enclosed area with light twice as bright as the sun. Dozens of people shouted in frustration, but only *one* was screaming in pain.

"I know *that* sound." Moving at full speed, Joe Omnivaulted over the various groups covering their eyes, aiming directly at the person screaming. He landed directly atop the Ritual of Glimmering that had dropped from their hands, feeling his Exquisite Shell resist the minor heat damage that such a bright light generated at this proximity. Realizing that he was already standing on the ritual tile, Joe simply directed his will at it and cut off the flow of mana.

The room was instantly back to its dusky state, the scream cut off, and dozens of people looked around blinking owlishly as they tried to clear the spots from their vision. Joe stared down at princess Dawnesha, his lips pursed as he tried to decide if he was angry or impressed that she'd activated the ritual. Angry, because he'd told them all not to activate any of these without permission. Impressed that she had managed to do it at all.

Then he remembered that she was a high-level cleric, along with whatever class she had been before that, and Joe settled on anger.

"I seem to *recall* telling everyone exactly what they should be doing. Specifically, I gave you all homework and tasks to complete, while making it clear that no one was supposed to activate these rituals. As you can see," here he paused and waved a hand at the Dwarf, who had blood weeping from her nose, ears, and eyes, "There's a good reason for this. Luckily for our friend here, all of the rituals I gave you were *my* design, and I included a kill switch in case of a situation just like this."

He paused and took a breath, staring the princess down as he spoke. "But as you all may have noticed, I only just arrived. If I'd been even a few minutes later, the ritual would've completely drained her health pool, as she had invested all of her mana in it already. I'd be *shocked* if Luck wasn't one of her peak characteristics."

Feeling that he'd made his point and that she had suffered enough to learn the lesson, Joe turned away from Dawnesha and began pacing through the room. "My intent with this stargazing lesson was to get all of you Lore skills that will be heavily beneficial for your growth. Getting the Lore early allows you to grow it at a similar pace as the main skill itself, and they'll work together to let you reach higher heights, faster. *Skipping* steps will kill you. Some of you humans are able to go to respawn and get back up in a few days. Others—you know who you are—will just stay dead... or become an Elf."

At least half of the class shivered at that. "Our next lesson is going to be on controlling your mana as you invest it in the ritual, how to *cut* that flow of mana, and how *not* to blow up an incredibly rare structure if you lose control of your ritual. Lesson number one: you should *not* try to throw the ritual tile away from you after investing your entire mana pool and a good chunk of your health. That only makes it harder for me to intercede."

Out of the corner of his eye, he could see the princess wilt further. Joe decided to move on and started a lecture on the Ritualist class; attempting to get the Lore skills of everyone in the room up to an acceptable level. Over roughly half an hour, he had the aspirants show him the star patterns they'd figured out—secretly copying down their positioning while nodding along as if they were merely doing *themselves* a favor—and tried to answer any questions they brought to him.

Then, someone came to him with an inquiry he didn't have a ready answer for. A serious-faced Dwarf was pulling on her mustache, staring at the sky above them, and her voice came out with a near dreamy quality. "Master Joe, what's the difference between Novice-rank star clusters and Beginner rank or higher tier? I mean, do they correspond to higher-tier rituals, and how?"

Joe went silent for a moment as he considered her words, hoping that he appeared as a wise teacher instead of a low-level tutor frantically scrambling for an answer. His eyes lit up as he realized he had a way to figure out the answer. Covering his mouth, he subvocalized, "Knowledge. Ritual Lore-"

Ritual Lore is at Journeyman zero! The spell knowledge is still in the Student ranks and cannot be used to increase it further.

"Abyss." He could feel the mana draining out of him, so he quickly named two of his other skills so as not to waste the benefit. "Enchanting Lore. Alchemical Lore."

Enchanting Lore has reached Student IX!

Alchemical Lore has reached Student VI!

Congratulations! Skill 'Knowledge' has reached Journeyman 0! As a bonus for having this skill reach the Journeyman ranks, the same skill may be selected twice for a level increase if it is under the Journeyman rank. Note: doing so replaces selecting two separate skills during that usage.

"Gah, missed it by *that* much." Joe muttered to himself. Looking up slightly, he met the expectant eyes of his students and coughed into his hand. "Excellent question. Would anyone like to hazard a guess? I'm sure we all know that finding the answer on our own, without outside assistance, helps us grow slightly faster. Anyone?"

The stares turned into pondering, unfocused glances as everyone raced to think of the answer first. Though he wouldn't admit it, Joe was doing the exact same thing alongside them. This early in their interactions, he didn't want these people losing confidence in his abilities—he was a Master of Ritual Magic and the only class trainer who existed.

Finding himself able to wander without drawing eyes, Joe wiped his forehead, an unnecessary but calming gesture. "Whew. Barely dodged *that* bullet."

CHAPTER FIFTEEN

Joe was having so much fun with his lessons that he found himself staying far past when he'd planned to leave. In fact, the only thing that broke him out of lecture mode was the dozens of horns and alarms going off outside of the observatory. Thankfully, he didn't have to give an explanation to his students as to why he turned on his heel and sprinted away.

Most of them were hot on his heels, needing to take up their own positions among the defenders. Since the Beast Waves were a near constant at this point, the alarms sounding as they were could only mean one thing.

A Boss Monster was approaching.

As he sprinted toward the walls, the Ritualist directed his orbs up into the air above him, allowing mana to flow as they unspooled and took on a familiar shape. Chancing a glance upward, he ensured that the repaired ritual hadn't gotten kinked or damaged while opening and **tisked**. Making a new Ritual Orb had been the easy part, comparatively. Joe had simply found an Expert smith and let them use his blueprints.

No, the annoying part of the process had been unspooling all of the wire that had been in four orbs then piecing it all back together from scratch. "Seriously, if Jaxon hadn't found that pair of needle-nosed pliers for me, I have no idea when I would've seen Morsum again."

The spell bound in his orb activated, and mana flowed through the hovering ritual circles. Darkness collected around the Ritual Orb of Constitution, scattering moments later and revealing the Pseudo-Lich head. The bright flames dancing in its empty eye sockets shifted slightly, and Joe knew that he was being stared at in annoyance. "Mor~*sum*."

"Yeah, well, I didn't exactly plan for your orb to be chopped in half by a Grandmaster wielding laser swords. Don't worry, we've got plenty of creatures that need killin' today." When Joe finished speaking, the skull released a gurgling sound that could have indicated interest or just a buildup of blood in the back of its throat. Then the Ritualist was leaping, landing atop the walls and running toward the entrance of the labyrinth they'd built around the city.

The Beast Wave below was relentless and unending. But, thanks to the joint efforts of the people of Novusheim, the enormous monsters were being continuously pelted with arrows, spells, and ritual effects. Every tower had become a beacon that showed the best place to attack densely packed monsters, and dozens of the enormously hard-to-kill entities were being slain each second. As he ran past them, Joe tried to pick out which of the towers had been built via ritual and which had been constructed by hand.

He gave the game up quickly, since it was far too obvious.

Anything that'd been built by a ritual was seamless, as if it had been poured into a cast and created as a single whole. In a way, it had. The Dwarven constructions, on the other hand, were not only created from hundreds of individual pieces but were also etched and embellished in such a way as to show some of the history of the city-to-be, as well as showing who had worked on them by their artistic style. "Seriously, even on these? These towers are *disposable*. How much faster could they go if they didn't-"

Joe shook that thought off. Trying to convince a Dwarf to put unadorned structures together was like asking him *not* to laugh when one of his towers lit a Penguin on fire. It just wasn't going to happen.

Closing in on the entrance, Joe scanned the miles-long stream of monsters, looking for the telltale signs of the first boss. "Can't believe it's already the tenth wave. Abyss, that means I've burned through almost half of my allotted time to get the battery station up and running."

A deep bellow from a scout rang out. "Boss Monster spotted! It's one of those cats, three times the usual size! It's got a squad of elites on it! Thirty seconds until it approaches the–*no*!"

The sharp gasp drew all eyes to the scout, and the shocked human got a hold of himself and shoved his hand at a forty-five degree angle away from the entrance. "It's coming over the wall! Archers!"

"Aim for the legs!" The experienced battle commanders among the Dwarves took over, snapping out a half dozen instructions as a beautiful leopard soared up from the ground and landed *on top* of the wall.

"Oh, feces," Joe breathed, barely able to get the words past his lips. So far, none of the monsters had been intelligent enough to land on the walls and use them as paths, but it seemed that had changed. The Boss Monster sprinted along the wall, leaving a bridge of ice behind it wherever it went. A handful of elite leopards were right behind it, and they followed their leader, but only for a few moments. Then, one of them jumped off of the wall, but not toward the city as expected.

No, it jumped out into the seething tide of creatures, creating a bridge for them to join combat on top of the walls.

Every few seconds, one of the elites would leap off, and by the time the fifth had jumped, the first to go had circled around and jumped *up* again. For the first time, the ranged attackers on the walls were having to fight with the enormous beasts at the same altitude, and they quickly became overwhelmed. Bows were swapped out for blades, and quick-reaction forces from the

Legion scurried along the new battleground, working hard not to slip off and over the edge of the battlements.

Joe lost track of the surge happening at the edges, his eyes tracking the movements of the Boss Monster itself. It was barreling along the walls, slamming into as many defenders as possible and sending them tumbling. As he watched, it suddenly shifted, skidding about a dozen feet before crouching down just like a regular cat and *pouncing*. Claws extended, the leopard let out a savage growl as it arced above the killing corridor, landing on the next wall over and beginning its sprint anew.

"*Feces*!"

Shifting his own momentum, Joe grabbed an outstretched arm, feeling like his own was about to tear off as the Dwarf twirled in place and hurled him back the way he'd come. "Thanks!"

"Never have to thank me for chucking a human." The laughing Dwarf's voice floated to him over the din of battle.

The Ritualist wasn't exactly sure what to make of that comment, but he didn't have time or attention to spare on it. He quickly began calculating how fast he could return to the center of Town, his face paling when he realized that the leopard was going to get there first. "Message! Heartpiercer Mcshootypants! Boss Monster incoming; it's going over the walls. We need to slow it down or slap it down between the walls. Thirteen seconds until it reaches the interior of the–"

"I'm on it; stop talking." The bristling sensation of her thoughts hit Joe's mind like someone had whipped a hedgehog into it.

Wisdom +2!

Able to focus on his own race and trusting that other people were pulling their weight, Joe pushed all of his effort into Omnivaulting faster. On his third push, his foot hit a sheet of ice at a bad angle, and a small notification appeared that he had made a bad choice due to his low Luck threshold. With a grunt of effort, Joe *forced* the magic flowing to his feet to realize that ice was water; it just had its molecules slowed down a *lot*.

As he slid across the surface of the ice, toward the edge of the wall and a forty foot drop while barely maintaining his balance, Joe dumped mana into his skill and *shoved*. Fifteen feet in every direction around him, the ice coating the top of the wall shattered and blasted into the air, trailing along behind the Ritualist like the tail of a comet as it hurtled through space. As his upward momentum slowed, the ice caught up with him, and he kicked off it with yet another Omnivault; shifting his direction and blasting forward, getting ahead of the leopard.

Strength +1!

Dexterity +1!

Omnivault (Master II → Master III). Congratulations! As you have increased in Mastery level, all of your Characteristics have increased by +5!

He grunted as his muscles contracted, grew denser, more malleable and controllable. His mind sharpened; the individual hairs on the lower left lip of the leopard leapt into perfect view —he could have done without that, actually—and his plans came ever-more intuitively. Joe backflipped, landing on the second-to-last wall before entering the Town proper, leaning down and slapping his hand on the stone as his momentum was bled off. "C'mon, Heartpiercer…!"

The boss leopard flung itself from its position, eyes locked on the shimmering bald man daring to stand in its way. It let out a warbling snarl as it crossed the distance, paws and claws outstretched to rend his–

Thwack.

An arrow that had flown a massive distance slammed into the back leg of the leopard, shifting its spin violently and causing it to miss its landing. It slapped into the edge of the wall just in front of the Ritualist, bending sharply and smacking its head on the stone before twisting and dropping down into the killing corridors. As it hit the ground, the low growl of fury that floated back up caused the hairs on Joe's arms to stand on end. "Nice shot, but that thing is *ma~ad*."

Luck +2!

Checking over the edge, Joe met the gaze of the beast, which was gleaming with a ferocious intelligence that made the human's heart sink. A smattering of arrows flew through the air toward it, and the local ritual towers charged up and started sending a mélange of arcane energies in its direction. The creature practically scoffed as it began moving with unnatural agility for something its size, dodging most of the attacks and shrugging off the rest of them—weak blows that it accepted in exchange for not being hit by the most damaging of them.

"Not a fan of this thing," the Ritualist muttered to himself as the leopard spun in place and shot off down the corridor, chased by spells the entire way. "I just need to get ahead of it and figure out some way to make it stay in one place while-"

Joe went silent as a voice cut through the cold.

"Here, kitty, kitty! How adorable are *you*? Listen, I have this Anatomy skill I've been *dying* to advance. Well, killing to advance, but you get the picture!"

"Change of plans." Joe started moving faster. "I need to put that beast out of its misery before Jaxon finishes experimenting on it. War crimes are one thing; letting *him* have free rein is another."

"Ooh-*hoo*-hoo! So feisty! Come, now, let me *adjust* your attitude and finish this pet project of mine."

CHAPTER SIXTEEN

Literally bouncing off the walls, Joe flung himself through the open area in an attempt to catch up to the leopard and join his friend in taking it down. As the flicking tail of the Boss Monster came into view, the Ritualist sent out his orbs and struck from behind. To his surprise, the creature didn't move, instead flexing its body and taking four strikes while preparing a pounce.

Damage dealt: 892 mixed damage!

Jaxon came into view, standing calmly in front of the leopard, his expression a wild mixture of anticipation and bubbling enthusiasm. The great beast leapt, a menacing twenty-foot-tall, sixty-foot-long missile of pure muscle and fury. For a moment, it appeared like the Verglas Leopard was going to go over the obstacle in its path, as it seemed less interested in a duel as it was in getting to—and destroying—the Town Hall.

Fortunately, Jaxon had other plans.

The Chiropractor leaned forward so far that it appeared he was about to collapse to the ground, but just before he struck the surface of the snow, his grin widened to a full-on maniacal smile, and his legs began to pump. He bolted forward, ducking under the extended claws and snapping jaw, aiming a series of jabs at its belly as it sailed over him. There was a flash of metal then a splash of blood that coated the cheerful man from head to toe.

"Ooh, the needle *is* still useful at this rank. Interesting. I had thought I'd have trouble opening your hide, but I unzipped you like I do my pants before stepping closer to the urinal!" Jaxon's taunt went ignored as the boss scrambled to keep moving. "Are we running? Wait! A rib bone is showing! I need to *study* that."

As Joe got closer, Jaxon moved so abruptly that the bald man lost sight of him. By the time the Ritualist found his friend again, he was above the cat and allowing his hands to shift into their new Living Weapons form. As if he were doing upside down dumbbell flys, the Chiropractor clapped his hands together on either side of the leopard's neck. This allowed the adolescent hydra heads to begin pumping their paralytic toxins into the beast, forcing the cat to release a growl of pain and displeasure.

Only managing a few additional steps, the boss tipped and fell, already twitching and thrashing as its massive Constitution score forced the paralytic to weaken and dilute faster than it would on any lesser being. Joe's hopes that his friend would use the opportunity to end the beast were dashed as Jaxon pulled his hands back and shouted at them. "That will only hold it for a few seconds! Quick! Count its vertebrae!"

Then the snake-like fingers wiggled across the body of the massive beast, pressing against various bone structures, feeling gaps and protuberances, and only every once in a while sneaking a bite of tasty flesh. "Jaxon! Don't play with your food!"

"Abyss! He's getting closer! Joe doesn't stop my fun, exactly, but he *changes* it. *Faster*, fingers!" The snaky fingers redoubled their efforts, but Jaxon was thrown into the air as the cat regained its footing and pushed upward, bucking him off before starting to run—albeit at a much slower pace.

Joe Omnivaulted past Jaxon, spinning up his Ritual Orbs and launching a Dark Lightning Strike on the slightly maimed creature. Other than a deep hiss of displeasure, there was no visual reaction from the boss. Clearly, the toxins had mostly worked themselves out, because its speed increased.

"Whoa there, we're not done!" Jaxon flashed past Joe, sprinting in a serpentine pattern that allowed him to dodge past the tree-trunk-esque legs of the boss. Arriving at the side of the creature, he reached out to grab it, only to trip and fall, bouncing off the ground in a burst of snow.

"Abyss, Jaxon!" Joe bellowed in annoyance as his friend once more failed to do lasting damage. His words trailed off as Jaxon twisted in the air, grabbing onto the lengthy tail of the leopard just before it went past him. Then his friend got his feet under him and began skiing across the snow, being dragged along at a high enough speed that he kicked up a shower of powder wherever he went.

He couldn't see exactly what the Chiropractor was doing, but a moment later heard, "*Adjust*!"

Near instantly, the leopard changed its trajectory and slammed face-first into the wall. Now that it was completely stopped, arrows began striking it from above with pinpoint accuracy, and a half-dozen spells blasted against its skull. Jaxon burst out of the snow a moment later, rushing over to Joe and sliding to a stop next to him. "Joe! As it turns out, they use their tails like rudders! Change the direction of the tail, change the direction of the cat. Easy enough. Sadly, not all that different from the lesser versions. Still, I'm one step closer to being a Grandmaster, so that made this little jaunt worthwhile."

"Glad you're happy, Jaxon." A particularly impressive Dwarf jumped off of the wall, spinning end over end while holding a massive broadsword. The stocky individual let out a deep bellow, sword cleaving out and removing the leopard's head as the final hit. "Looks like we're done here; let's go clean up the rest of the monsters and see what sort of damage got done to the outer barricades."

"Nah, I've got lunch plans." Jaxon waved as he started back into Town. "Don't forget to grab something for yourself; you can't live on coffee alone! Fun fact, most animals can't eat coffee beans in the first place, caffeine is just jitter-inducing poison. Kinda like feeding chocolate to dogs—it's not a great look."

"I can and I *will* live off coffee!" Joe retorted instantly, holding up a mug and having it filled by Mate in the same second. He lifted the drink at the fallen boss, paying his respects to it, then tipped back the coffee and drank deep. "At least, *someday* my Constitution will be high enough that I can live on coffee alone."

As the hot drink warmed him from the inside, Joe hesitated. His plan of going back to the outer walls suddenly seemed... inadequate. There were plenty of people who could fix up any damage, and literally thousands of Dwarves and humans that were fighting against the monsters directly. There were better things that he could be doing to help. The Ritualist looked back longingly but walked into Town, following Jaxon's footsteps through the fresh snow.

His destination was the greenhouse, where he hoped Herby Thymebeard would be stationed. Otherwise, Joe had no idea how he was going to be able to find the Dwarf. A small flash of inspiration struck him, and he tried to use his Message spell, only for it to return with static the same moment he sent it. The Ritualist clutched at his head, forced to bear the cacophonous noise until it finally cut out. "Ooh-*kay*, I hope that's a side effect of attempting to send a Message spell through the greenhouse. Would that be the aspects of scattering coming into play? Well *there's* a nasty trick I could play on someone if I needed to distract them in combat."

Happily, it was easy to find the person he needed to speak with. Unfortunately, after initial pleasantries, the Dwarf grabbed him by the back of his neck and his belt, bodily throwing him out of the building after Joe showed him the satchel of seeds. "You outta your mind? Just *one* of those gets loose in a dungeon-waiting-to-happen like this here greenhouse, and we'll have to blast it with artillery spells until it's nothing more than melted slag!"

Joe had hit the ground and rolled, coming to his feet and not bothering to brush the snow and dirt off of himself; knowing his Neutrality Aura would take care of it. Pausing for a moment, the Ritualist tried to decide if he was getting better at navigating delicate situations, or if he was simply growing accustomed to being thrown around. "Did you at least get a good look at them? Are they safe to use?"

"No, they're absolutely nowhere *near* safe." The Dwarf was still eyeing the satchel with a hearty amount of distrust, so Joe stuffed it in his pouch to get it out of sight. "Also, they'll do exactly what they say they will. Don't plant those anywhere closer than five miles away from us. If you think dandelions spread quickly, you should see the growth factor *those* have as an underlying stat. Creatures walking over them are going to cause them to creep closer to the city either way, but… is five miles enough? Make it seven."

"Or should I just not use them?" Joe questioned the only expert of plants that he knew. "If they're that dangerous–"

"You should absolutely *use* them," Thymebeard told him with a glower. "Just not anywhere closer to us than eight and a half miles."

"I noticed that the distance keeps *increasing*…" The Ritualist stated leadingly, earning himself an eye roll and a half from the Dwarf as he threw his hands in the air and returned to his post in the greenhouse. Alone once more, Joe pulled out the satchel and looked at it carefully, making sure there were no holes, and he wasn't leaking the seeds anywhere. "Well… he *did* say I should absolutely use it. But now I want to be nowhere near it when I do that."

The seeds were so tiny that, if he didn't have his Exquisite Shell on, they could easily sit in the fur of his clothing and stay hidden forever. He contemplated the vegetative weapon in his hands and slowly formulated a plan on how to use them.

As there was no time like the present, he hurried over to his workshop and started throwing together a modified Ritual of Bubble Travel. Luckily, the satchel informed him how many seeds exactly were in storage, so he was able to make a plan for perfect distribution.

When everything was completed, he stepped outside of his workshop, only to be greeted by thirty of his Ritualist aspirants. "Ah! Perfect timing! I was just about to activate a ritual, and this would be some great hands-on experience for all of you. Where's everyone else?"

The members of the group grinned weakly, muttering and looking amongst themselves while shuffling in place. Finally, one brave soul shrugged, "Everyone else decided that they'd rather be out there fighting, working on their current classes, than trying to get this one. Lot easier to punch a Penguin in the beak than it is to figure out a star chart and then pay for the privilege of all the materials you need to activate a ritual, just so you can make your ears bleed by using it wrong."

The human speaking didn't seem to realize that he was being glared at by the Dwarven princess, and Joe decided not to call attention to that fact. "Fair enough. Welp, they miss out! Here! A present for all of you. This is an athame, and is a complex utility item that's useful immediately for the class. Without having an advanced level in smithing or Ritualistic Forging, you'd be getting one of these only when you could make it."

There were multiple mutters of appreciation as each of his aspirants took a subtly glowing dagger from the pile. "Consider this a reward for your hard work in mapping out the star clusters you were assigned. Now! Who wants partial kill credit for the rest of the monsters that attack the city?"

That earned him a few confused looks, until the Princess clarified, "You mean the rest of the wave? We got a notice that the Boss Monster had been slain, so it shouldn't be too much longer."

Joe grinned and held up the ritual tile he'd been working on. "Nope, I mean *the rest of* the monsters that attack us. Come with me. I've got something neat to show you."

CHAPTER SEVENTEEN

"Gather round, gather round!" Joe started pacing in a circle as the crew of Ritualist aspirants shambled into position. He didn't miss the fact that they appeared jittery and somewhat nervous, eyes flicking to the ritual circle etched on the tile that he was casually carrying around. The princess especially seemed to be on edge, and he was glad that the lesson had sunk in so well. "Don't worry, this isn't active. Even if it breaks, it won't hurt you… too much."

Now that he had a captive audience, Joe dove into why he placed everything in prime number positions, then used them as an example so they could *feel* the difference. Once the loose group had settled into a sequence that made his Magical Matrices skill purr in pleasure, he explained exactly what was going to happen.

He went over everything from how the ritual circles would appear under their feet, to how quickly it should pull mana from them. "That was why I asked how full your mana pools were. If you have a larger pool, you're on an outer circle, as that's where you'll do the most good. If you're in the inner circles, don't feel bad; you'll be channeling their power, which will help your own power grow. Just... do your best to control it."

A hand shot up, and Joe arched an eyebrow as he looked at the man waiting patiently to ask a question. "Is there any chance we explode from channeling their mana?"

"Very *small* chance," Joe admitted after staring at the man for a long moment to show his displeasure with this line of questioning. "Much more likely, you'll pass out or have other issues before then, so speak up if things are going sideways for you. No more questions; this is ritual magic, not rocket surgery!"

Half a dozen more hands had shot up, and he was beginning to sweat through his Neutrality Aura. Applying a light touch of mana to the ritual tile, Joe activated it and began filling the ritual diagram with power. "Remember to hold your athame! It should act as a conduit for your Mana Manipulation skill, and if you don't have that skill, it should help you get it! Probably! If not, I recommend that skill as one to spend your free skill point on, because getting it otherwise is a pain in the rear."

He looked around, seeing a ton of confused faces, as though what he had just said came out garbled. Then Joe was hit by a wave of nerves at the fact that more than two dozen people were surrounding him holding knives all of a sudden. Then the ritual began drawing mana from everyone, and there was a collective, "*Oof!*"

"Yup, that'll happen! Breathe through it. Embrace it; you might even get a channeling skill! Who knows! Not me!" Joe let out a laugh, doing his best to imitate a combination of Havoc and Jaxon. Then, very softly, he muttered to himself, "If I can get rid of another half of this group, it'll be a lot easier to do small group training."

Another scan told him that he was likely on the right path, as a quarter of the aspirants had turned green from the side effects of having their mana rapidly drained. Joe hummed lightly, his vast reservoir of mana practically untouched from a ritual of this strength. Moments later, a bubble of force came into being above his open palm, and he lifted the satchel of seeds above it. Very gently, *very* carefully, he inserted the opening of the storage device into the bubble and instructed the satchel to eject all of the seeds.

Thousands upon thousands of magical capsules poured into the contained space. Even with all of them out in the open, they took up less space than his closed fist. Joe shook his head at the thought that these were likely potent magical items, more powerful than he had the means to create on his own at the moment. "I still have so far to go. *Awesome.*"

With a flick of his fingers, the orb shot into the sky and vanished into the distance. He clapped his hands together and looked around brightly. "All done! That'll travel seven miles from the center of the city, then start depositing seeds in a wide circle around us. Congratulations on activating your first successful, non-self-lethal ritual. Look at that! Not a single one of you passed out."

Immediately following his declaration, everyone smiled or clamped their mouths closed—just in case. "Now, follow me up to the walls, so that we can get a good view of the… whatever is going to happen!"

He marched away, ensuring that everyone could keep up with him by maintaining a leisurely sprint toward the walls in the distance. Not wanting to individually grab and jump everyone to the top, Joe directed the aspirants to a ladder. They climbed up, finding an area that wasn't too busy with archers or various supply runners.

"Master Joe…" the soft voice caught Joe by surprise, and he looked over to see a hand half in the air. His eyes followed the limb down to come to rest on a lady. She stood just under five feet tall, had a pixie cut hairstyle, and was staring at him nervously. "I don't mean to… um. What was that ritual supposed to do?"

"I believe I told you?" Joe furrowed his brow and tried to think if he'd actually stated his thoughts out loud, or merely been thinking them extra loudly in his head. "No, I absolutely told you. It's out there dropping seeds in a circle around the city. Any chance–"

The Ritualist paused, realizing that *perhaps* asking someone who was clearly a human if they were part Dwarf was a bad idea.

She nodded, but didn't lose the confused expression for some reason. "But why? Won't those seeds just die in the cold? There's no soil, no water?"

"Oh! Gotcha. They're *magical* seeds." That didn't seem to be enough of an explanation for anyone, so he expounded upon that slightly. "They're a gift from the previous civilization that inhabited Jotunheim. They were a super weapon against creatures that thrived in the cold. Apparently, when planted in snow, or in super cold areas, they're supposed to grow rapidly using an exothermic reaction. Somehow. Again, magic."

That earned him a few nods, but Joe could only shrug. At this point, they officially knew as much as he did about the flora. "While we're waiting, anyone have any questions?"

"Yeah!" The pixie-cut lady spoke up with much more enthusiasm. "Back to the constellations, I think I have an answer. Well, at least, I got a skill level for it. But I was hoping to get your answer now. That way I can adjust where I went wrong and learn more at the same time."

"O-oh! Uh, yes, that's a great idea, but we wouldn't want to deprive everyone else of the chance to think on it, right?" Joe looked around at the group while nodding sagely.

"I'm good with it. I couldn't come up with anything." One guy shrugged and motioned for Joe to go on. Multiple other people glommed on to this, and soon Joe was surrounded by expectant eyes twinkling as brightly as the constellations they were hoping to hear about.

Feeling like he had his hand caught in the cookie jar, Joe began speaking slowly, trying to put his own insights into an understandable format for other people. "Why would the constellations play into rituals? Anyone?"

There were no takers. Joe cleared his throat and spoke more firmly. "Well, the fact is, it's *not* just the stars way off in the distance. It's the sun, the moon, the tides, the landscape, even the local alignment of ambient energy. That last one I've been learning from a wizard specializing in Formations. The yin energy of Jotunheim is apparently real rough on anyone trying to use fire-based attacks, yet the 'yin alignment' of the creatures we light up is also the reason the strikes are so effective."

Now that he was on a roll, the words came easier. "The more in tune with our local nature we can become, the better. However, that's much more important and effective for Formations, whereas we can think of constellations and the… celestial bodies, I suppose would be the phrase? Yes, if we think of the celestial bodies as powerful magical circuits and align our rituals up with them, we're tapping into the mega-powerful magical circuits of the universe and applying them at a much more microscopic scale. The universe likes itself, and it likes patterns. Allow it to do something it's done before, and it'll do it far more easily."

A notification appeared, but Joe waited to open it until he finished his thought. "When it comes to certain high-tier rituals, they can only be performed under specific constellations after *ensuring* that they're perfectly aligned. Think back to Earth, for those of you that have lived there, and think about the pyramids in Egypt. They would be a great place to do a grand ritual, because at specific points of the year, they perfectly align with Orion's Belt. Being a Ritualist, and understanding what we do, is like having a backstage pass to the programming language of the universe. Which is *Perl,* if you were wondering."

No one laughed at his joke, but he figured they would eventually figure it out and chuckle. During the thick silence that followed his lecture, Joe took a moment to look at the notifications that had appeared.

Skill Increase(s)

Teaching (Student I → Student II)

Calculus and number theory (Student III → Student IV)

Skill gained: Celestial-Arcane Interaction Lore (Novice VIII). Congratulations! You have taken a huge leap forward in understanding how the celestial bodies of the universe interact with the arcane energies that you are tapping into. Increasing your understanding will allow you to increase your understanding faster. +.5n% faster skill gain for Celestial-Arcane Interaction Lore, where n = skill level.

Current: 4% faster skill gain for Celestial-Arcane Interaction Lore.

"What?" Joe double-checked the skill he'd just gained, making sure he was reading it correctly. "The only thing the skill does as it gains levels… is allow itself to gain levels *faster*? Is it actually possible for skills to be narcissistic? I *really* hope that it gets some bonuses as it ranks up."

Since his teaching skill had increased in level, Joe knew that at least some of the people around him had gained *something* from what he said. What confused him was why his Calculus and Number Theory skill had increased; as far as he could tell, he hadn't said anything that should've had an impact on it. The Ritualist could only shrug and hope he would find answers to his questions in the future, and decided to simply bask in the warm breeze that was easing some of the stiffness of his chilled skin.

Joe's eyes popped open, a slight frown on his lips. "Warm breeze? What?"

"Master Joe! Look! The world is on fire!" The words just didn't come from one of his aspirants, instead it came from a scout nearby that had acknowledged the Councilman when his group came up to view the horizon. "It must be an attack from an outside force, but… I don't understand what's going on!"

Alarms started going up all around the city, and Joe realized that the seeds were exactly as effective as advertised. Two major concerns popped into the Ritualist's mind at that moment, and he very carefully kept them to himself. "Perhaps I should've informed the council of my plan. Hmm. Oh, well. Whatever happens there is fine. But… maybe I should have planned some walkways for us to get out of the ring?"

Joe could only hope that anyone looking at him only saw a

serious-faced, powerful person considering a grave threat stoically. His eyes shifted to the side, reading over his status to ensure that his Neutrality Aura was in place, which should help him to cover the physical signs of his sudden anxiety. Clapping his hands lightly, the Ritualist looked around at his group with a smile and motioned toward the ladder.

"I think that's just about enough for today; why don't we all go into my workshop, shut the door, then, and *only* then, discuss today's work… and the excellent reward you're getting for your efforts and for *waiting to discuss* those efforts until no one can hear us."

CHAPTER EIGHTEEN

The knock on his door came even faster than he was expecting, but Joe was still ready. He threw open the entrance, a wide smile on his face as he took in the visage of his old party member, Major Cleave. He lifted his hand in greeting, opening his mouth to exchange pleasantries, but she cut him off with a brusque, "Really, Joe? A ring of fire around the entire Town? Is that meant as a Town defense, or are you trying to slow cook us all?"

"Are they calling for my head already?" Joe tutted and put his hands on his hips. "It's an effective method of damaging monsters ahead of time, and as it grows, it may even wipe out the entirety of the Penguin caste of monsters."

By the way she glared at him, Joe knew he'd said something that the Dwarf in charge of the defense of the walls didn't like to hear. "As it *grows*? That fire out there is going to get *worse*?"

Joe pressed his lips together, refusing to speak until he was certain that the words he was going to say weren't going to open him up to further blame. "That's not really *fire*, per se. It's magical plants that use extreme cold to grow and propagate rapidly. In fact, because we're at the center of the ring, you should've felt the same warm breeze that I did."

"Can it be called a warm wind if it's fifty degrees below the freezing point?" Cleave snorted at him, though she did seem to be letting some of the tension in her arms and shoulders go.

The Ritualist crossed his arms, deciding against pretending to be polite about this issue any further. "Yes. It can. When the usual gusts hit negative *seventy* below freezing, that can at least be called 'warmer'. If a ring of fire—which is entirely contained by its own nature—will help protect the Town, then that's what I'm going to make."

"It's contained? How?"

Joe ignored the question for the moment, instead going deeper into his workshop and grabbing a few stacks of ritual tiles off the table before joining Major Cleave outside. The Ritualist went perfectly still. He hadn't been expecting such a large crowd of angry civilians to be surrounding his workshop, but…

"*What*? Are we doing this *again*?" He directly challenged the glaring civilians. "You have a problem with the things I'm doing to make sure that we win? Well, *too bad*! If you want protection to look a certain way, then *you* should be out there making it happen, not complaining that it *is* happening! Are you all so *bored* because you haven't had to deal with any monsters getting into your shops recently that you came out in force to parade around? Forget this. I'm putting a Ritual of Quarantine on my workshop. If anyone comes within a dozen feet of it, better be ready to projectile vomit out of your–"

Major Cleave stepped forward and lifted a device that was shining brightly, and as she spoke, her voice was magnified fifty fold. "The council, and therefore the Town, has already conferred about this new development and found councilman Joe to have done Novusheim a great service. As he's already stated, we need defenses, and we need resources. There have been very few expeditions setting out since our arrival, and over eighty percent of them have been initiated by, funded by, or directly spearheaded by Master Joe."

She went on to explain that the council would be taking the

lead in sending people out in the near future, using the Fast Travel network that Joe had set up as a starting point. The Ritualist himself simply looked on incredulously, the mounting frustration he'd been feeling stripped away as he realized that she really *had* just been checking to make sure there was no other malicious intent behind his actions.

"Hmm. Major Cleave, I guess I can't fault you for doing your due diligence, even if it's *annoying*," he muttered, loudly enough to get a sidelong glance from the Major. She continued speaking in hopes of collecting a large group of volunteers. When there was a lull in the conversation, Joe realized that he'd just been asked to lead a few more expeditions.

Shaking his head, he spoke louder so that the assembled people could hear him, the Ritualist offered an olive branch. "Nope! Currently I'm focused on Town defense and making sure that we survive to have an official City. After that, who knows? But, I'll facilitate expeditions when possible. If anyone needs funding or *specific* help, either myself or one of my new students will help you out."

Then, ignoring any further conversation—whether positive or negative—Joe Omnivaulted to the top of his workshop, kicking off the roof and arcing away in the direction of the celestial observatory. "See, this is why powerful Mages need to have enormous towers away from civilization. Everyone wants *something*, and half the people are angry when they get it. Then, even when everyone calms down and realizes it was for their own good, the meteor the mage called is already en route and can't be stopped."

As he landed near his destination, Joe walked a few more paces until he arrived at one of the messenger stands that had been set up. Pulling out a note, he wrote out a few questions and handed it to the messenger on duty, along with a small ingot of alloy. "Please deliver this to Grandmaster Havoc. I'll be waiting for a reply, but I need to know what his progress toward completing his project is."

"Grandmaster H-Havoc? On it." The messenger licked his

lips and nodded, even if it was somewhat nervously. The ingot of alloy vanished into his pocket, and he turned and ran without another word.

Leaving the cold of the day behind him, Joe stepped into the observatory and firmly closed the door behind him. Then he walked straight to the center of the room, pulled out the bean bag chair that he'd been using while bubble-traveling around the world, and sank into it while watching the ceiling above him. Letting out a deep sigh, he pulled out a blank notebook and started detailing all of the constellation homework that his students had turned in. "If I use the first section of my notes for Novice stuff, then write out progressively harder combinations, I could turn this into a legitimate lore book."

The sound of his quill scratching over parchment, combined with the low voices of people in the room, generated a soothing ambience that acted as a balm to his frayed nerves. When he had completed his writing, he closed the notebook and his eyes. "I really jumped down Major Cleave's throat there, huh? It's not like I don't have plenty of precedent to point at. I do something, other people come after me for it, then we work to resolve it… but that wasn't her fault. It was never her fault."

Feeling fairly guilty, he sent a Message spell to the Dwarf, who replied almost instantly with a stoic acceptance of his apology. The spell instantly leveled up to Beginner one, almost as if in acknowledgment of his attempts at being a better person. With that weight off of his mind, Joe was able to calm down and assess the situation in a different light. "It seems like the council is fully on my side, *finally*. I can't even count the number of sticks I've had to break on them, but maybe now we toss them a carrot. My plan is always to incentivize good behavior and make sure to immediately punish… Abyss, I *am* turning into an Oligarch."

That thought drew a rueful chuckle out of him, and he bent his thoughts toward finding an effective reward that would be useful for everyone in the city. "Only thing I can think of is how massive this world is. I think... perhaps the best thing would be to expand the network of Fast Travel shrines. But how do I do that without having to go there myself?"

Perhaps it was the fact that the stars were twinkling above him, or that the environment was just right, but as Joe's eyes landed on Jotunheim's version of the North star, something **clicked**. "I've been doing all of the work already, why don't I just combine it?"

Pulling out a large sheet of parchment, he hurriedly began sketching out his thoughts. "Endless monsters, which means I'll have as many aspects up to the Rare rank as I could ever desire. Even when the City is completed, we'll have to deal with Beast Waves forever. I can use that to work in our favor; just like that we have our building supplies."

The first building in what would become a production line was sketched on his parchment. "The A.S.P.E.C.T. tower will hold all of the aspects, and I'll need to figure out how to hook the aspect jars up to the next piece. Hopefully, I can get Grandmaster Havoc excited about this project, and he'll point out some areas to improve."

Joe tapped on the open space then started sketching. "With the excess power generated by the Mana Battery recharge stations, we could have a fairly endless source of mana to fuel the rituals and construction. Good. We have a power source; we have materials. Next is a permanent ritual that creates the shrines, and finally someone on the end of the production line that uses the Ritual of the Traveling Civilization—already in place—to put the shrines out there in a grid pattern until we have access to the entirety of the planet."

The Ritualist stared at the parchment in disbelief. Even though it was a rough plan and was missing a few key components, he was holding in his hands their best chance of gaining access to the entirety of Jotunheim. "I can even leave here, after my students are trained up to an acceptable level, and leave them in charge of running this and performing all necessary maintenance. It's... this is probably my best plan ever."

Making a few additional changes, the Ritualist scanned the document one last time and stored it away. Right now, they had much more immediate problems. Still, he made sure that he wouldn't forget this, because there was *no one else* who could possibly bring this to fruition. It was a heady feeling to realize that he was the only person who could accomplish something of this magnitude. "But before that, more work. Lots and lots of work. Let's see if I can figure out the star clusters that coincide with the Ritual of Slaughter. I'd love to revamp that to be even more powerful."

Over the next few hours, he rapidly gained skill levels in his Celestial-Arcane Interaction Lore skill, breaking through into the Beginner ranks—then all the way up to Beginner six—before he was interrupted by a messenger with a return message from Grandmaster Havoc. As Joe packed up his documents, his bean bag chair, and prepared to go and meet his mentor, he couldn't take his eyes off the cluster of green and purple constellations—plural—that he thought might meet the minimum requirements for the Ritual of Slaughter.

"I'll be back to look at *you* more closely," He promised the stars in the sky, which twinkled with a–perhaps imagined–subtle sanguine malevolence. Then the Ritualist hurried off, because Havoc's message had only consisted of two words.

It's ready.

CHAPTER NINETEEN

"Sorry it took so long to get back to you; we were so close to finishing the project that I had to force these lay-abouts to push past what they thought were their limits." Havoc cheerfully called out around a freshly lit cigar as Joe entered the workshop. "But, enough about that! Look at these beauties! The prototype is complete, with room for ten batteries up to the Unique rank."

Joe wasn't entirely certain what Havoc was apologizing for. "You didn't take very long at all to get back to me. I sent that message when I went into the observatory, and it came back almost right away."

"Right away? *Oooh.*" The Dwarf chewed on the end of his cigar for a moment, looking Joe up and down. "Huh. Well, don't suppose you were taking notes on what you were working on, were you?"

The Ritualist cocked an eyebrow, "Of course I was. You want to see them?"

Pulling out his notes on the star patterns that he'd been observing, Joe wiggled it in front of the Dwarf, who snatched it out of his hands and opened it up. He started flipping pages, and Joe's concern started mounting higher and higher as he saw that every page being flipped was filled out with meticulous, tiny handwriting. "Yep, that's what I thought. You went in there just after the end of the Boss Wave, wave ten, right?"

"*Ye~es…*" The Ritualist already knew where this was going but braced himself for it to be worse than he expected.

"We just finished up wave eighteen. There's already preparations in place for the next boss coming with wave twenty." Havoc tossed the half-filled notebook back to Joe, who caught it and stored it in his codpiece in the same motion. "You've been stuck in there for just shy of three standard days, I'd say somewhere around sixty-four to sixty-eight hours. High Constitution is one abyss of a focus aid, especially if you have some way to keep yourself clean and hydrated the entire time. As you get higher level and even more powerful, you'll run into the same issue over and over. *All* of us are running into that problem all the time. So, a note for your future. Going into seclusion is a bad idea, because you come out and realize a city has grown up around you."

Joe was cursing internally, though he had to admit he'd gained quite a bit from his time locked in study. A cursory glance at his notes revealed what he already knew—he had filled out the Novice section so completely that he could hand this over to a new Ritualist and have them gain the lower skill at the Beginner rank. "With the low lighting, and how it never changes, I must've drifted off a few times. No wonder I feel so rested."

"Enough about you. Come and take a gander at my triple-combined enchantment that hasn't exploded in our faces!" The Dwarf wrapped a meaty hand around Joe's shoulder and pulled him along. "Between my expertise and my ability to tease Experts to get the most out of them, we've put together one station at the Unique rank. The next ones will come together thirty times faster, because now that we've made one, all five of us can work on separate versions. Each station rank adds space for up to five additional batteries, starting at the Common tier, and skipping the Special tier. That means you can recharge up to twenty batteries at the same time on this table, if you have enough ambient mana to make it happen."

The Dwarf's enthusiasm for his craft was starting to get Joe excited as well, so he asked what he thought was a natural follow-up question. "How much mana per minute does this thing output?"

"Yeah, *way* too much." Havoc chuckled as he brought his hand close to the artifact and the surface of his skin began to char. There was a manic gleam in his eye as he turned his head to Joe and met his horrified gaze. "I managed to *crank* those numbers up. A well-*enchanted* Mana Battery, going off of your design, has a maximum storage of forty thousand. 'Course, the ones that you make with your little rituals are about half as efficient as if you did it by hand, so they top out at about twenty thousand. All that to say, each battery put on the pad over there can regain approximately seven hundred mana per minute, letting you refill your largest Unique batteries in a little under thirty minutes."

Joe blinked at that number, trying to decide whether he should say what he was thinking or simply congratulate the Dwarf on the success of his enchantment and move along. Unable to stop himself, he voiced his thoughts. "I don't mean to sound... *ungrateful*... but that seems a little low?"

Havoc paused and turned fully to look at the Ritualist, puffing smoke gently out of his nostrils. "I'm just going to stand here quietly while you put a little more *thought* into what's going on here."

"Um. Oh. Twenty at a time. Got it." Joe winced as he realized that he'd just insulted the Grandmaster with his casual dismissal of his hard work. "Yeah, so that means... fourteen thousand mana output per minute. All pulled from the ambient environment. Got you. Can we please get back to complimenting how awesome this is?"

"That'd be a *great* place to stay, conversationally," Havoc allowed after taking a moment to let Joe tense up. "Let's talk about what sort of protections this bad boy needs. At any given moment, it should have something like, oh, let's throw out an approximate of one hundred thousand mana condensed into the center of it. Someone gets a good attack on the station, it's not just your house that's going to be on fire. It's about half the city. On a positive note, if your ritual that is stabilizing the air in Town fails, it doesn't just cause this to explode anymore."

"Oh! That's good! I was worried, because if I'm not around to run maintenance or add mana to it, that ritual could fail pretty much anytime." Joe tore his eyes off the artifact—which looked like a poker table with a miniature nuclear reactor strapped to the bottom of it—and found that the Dwarf was staring at him with extreme exasperation. "What?"

"I said it doesn't *just* cause this to explode. It'll still do that, but at least we put in a failsafe that should give us about five minutes to evacuate. Also, we, uh, added a little feature that's become standard on our war golems." Havoc chuckled darkly as he watched the realization dawn in Joe's eyes.

The Ritualist backed away from the device that he was almost positive wasn't healthy to stand near, realizing that what he'd been calling 'table legs' in his mind were actually powerful coiled springs hooked up to a small block of ice. "Let me guess… if the machine starts to overload, it melts the ice, setting off the springs and sending the recharge station flying. I'm hoping it's set to fly *out* of the city?"

"Nah, just *up*." Havoc watched his bald protege for a moment before squinting and leaning forward slightly. "Let me make one thing very clear to you, human. This is *not* something you can intentionally overload and throw at a big, bad beastie. If this thing goes **boom**, lots and *lots* of people die. Not only that, they'll for the most part be vaporized. Your little Resurrection Aura isn't going to do much when all that's left of them is mana-irradiated ash, and my people are scattered over half the continent."

Joe thought back to when he'd first opened a vault in this world and had sent an overloading Master-rank ritual soaring toward the sky. Shaking his head, he gestured helplessly to the recharge station. "We've sent something into the sky and blown it up before, that led to a bad time. It dropped… I don't know, a couple miles of snow and ice in the area as the clouds collapsed. I think we should go the other way with it. Maybe shunt it into the shaft that the Pyramid of Panacea dug through the crust of the planet? Drop it, in other words, instead of sending it up?"

Havoc chewed on his cigar a little more, before shrugging. "You want to make extra work for yourself, you go right ahead and do so. Anyhoo, how many more of these do ya want? I'm thinking we should have at least ten before we get to the fiftieth wave, so we can have a backup battery charging for every possible tower out there."

Blanching at the thought of so many doomsday devices casually active at the same time in the small space they currently called home, Joe put off the Grandmaster for the moment, promising that he would think about it and get him an answer. "Before that, where do you think we should store this?"

"For now?" Havoc jabbed a thumb over his shoulder, "Put up a slightly larger bubble ritual thingy in the center of Town. We'll keep it safe by making it *appear* to be completely stable. No one would think that we'd leave something so dangerous practically out in the open, and that means they won't snoop."

Joe gulped at that thought but realized that there was plenty of truth in what the Grandmaster was saying. "Yeah, but they'd never think we'd do that, because it's pretty *dumb* to do that."

"Now you're getting it." Havoc chuckled while pulling out a few batteries that he'd swiped from the ritual tower staging yard. "Come here, I'll show you how to use this thing. Oh, I also recommend you spend a whole lot more time choosing who gets direct access to these. Uhh… and, probably give them a big fat raise."

"Because it could explode at any minute, and they need to keep their mouths shut?"

"Yeah… yeah, that's a good reason, too." Havoc looked to the side and coughed a few words that sounded suspiciously like 'maybe to also replace their bones after a few months', which was an oddly specific cadence to the coughing that was hard to miss.

The Ritualist decided to ignore that for the moment and just take the gift horse he'd been given. After spending a few minutes looking over the Unique-rank enchantments, which had been set into Unique-rank materials, Joe glanced around the room and asked, "Any chance I can lift this with less than ten people?"

"Ahh… 'lifting' it isn't exactly what I'd recommend. Also, no." Ignoring Joe's look of pure frustration, the Dwarf simply laughed and started setting enchanted cores on the felt-top 'poker table' portion of the design; in the spaces where cups or drinks would go. Immediately, the Mana Batteries began drinking in the condensed mana, and the wavy, crackling radiance around the table noticeably dimmed. "So, if you ever need to do maintenance on one of these while it's active, I highly recommend tossing a few batteries in to pull in the energy. Also, do the maintenance *real* fast."

"Yeah, no kidding. I have no idea how I'd go about replacing my bones."

"Shouldn't be a problem for you." Havoc brushed off his concerns. "You've got all those fancy healing abilities, after all. Let's start with the basics. Pretend for a moment that you're really boring and do want to keep all of your fingers, and you *don't* want them to have scales or the like. In that case, first you put the battery in like this…"

CHAPTER TWENTY

Walking away from the new addition to the ritual tower staging yard without looking back was a test of his willpower, but Joe tried to keep his body language calm and his breathing even. "If I don't make a big deal out of it, why would anyone else? There's only one of them right now anyway, not a sequence of Chernobyl events all lined up in serial waiting to melt down and take out the last vestiges of the Dwarven population."

He tried to stop that line of thinking but couldn't stop himself from nervously giggling and adding one last thought. "No, we won't have the meltdown sequence all set up until at *least* next week."

With that, he was finally able to break away from his doomsayer mindset and turned his attention to what should be happening in the near future. With the Dwarven engineers and craftsmen building ritual towers, training up a cadre of Ritualists to arm them, and now having a hopefully permanent energy source to provide the fuel, Joe's daily task list had dropped to 'I get to do whatever I want to do'. As he realized this, the constipated grin plastered on his face settled into a much more natural expression, and his attention began roving the area within the walls of the city.

"Should I do enchanting first? No, that's a bad idea. That'd take away time from Havoc and the others, and we need them to finish the additional recharge stations." Joe pondered his other crafts, feeling a little leery about losing days at a time going back and observing the stars. "I've been making a lot of metal recently, so maybe I should go and exercise my right to alchemical training while I still can."

As he walked toward the Pyramid of Panacea, Joe activated his Knowledge skill, double selecting Alchemical Lore to bring its level up to Student eight. "Glad I remembered to do that before I was in eye or earshot of Jake. Don't want to get caught 'skipping steps' again."

The door of the pyramid was one of the only ones in the entire city that he needed to knock on and still wait to enter. It irked him slightly, but standing in the cold gave him a few moments for self-reflection, and Joe chuckled at the realization that he was starting to feel entitled to his position in the current social hierarchy. "I guess that's just what happens when you have an entire city that has no houses or personal living spaces. Everything is a workshop or a public space. Kind of weird, when I actually think about it."

The door opened, once more revealing Baumann instead of Jake the Alchemist. "Master Joe! You're back! Excellent, I've got to tell you, Jake has really been awesome to work with. He's also.... very persuasive about my aptitude as an–"

"Jake, if you steal him from me, you lose the temporary bonus!" Joe called out succinctly. Then the air itself seemed to freeze in his lungs as an aura of bloodlust washed over him for a fraction of a moment. He looked to the side, meeting the eyes of the highly talented Neophyte, and nodded slightly. "You shouldn't have to worry about him trying to sway you over anymore."

"Oh... yeah, that's... that's what I was going for. Yes." The

Dwarf's nose was once again bright red, showing that he was beginning to blush.

Wondering if he'd just made a terrible mistake, Joe surreptitiously checked his messages, but there was no notification of his Luck threshold impacting him. "Doesn't mean that it's not, just that it isn't telling me. Yet."

"I see that you've returned and are ready to dive into the deep end of the alchemical pool," Jake commented with his usual bland, stoic monotone. "Good. I feel that you have been wasting your precious time learning from me. Instead of specializing in excellent, useful areas, you've been tinkering with lesser crafts. Does that change today?"

"In a manner of speaking," Joe returned with a sheepish grin. "I managed to offload all of my other responsibilities, besides teaching, and I'm going to take a few dozen Beast Waves' worth of time to improve my overall crafting ability. But-!"

The Ritualist quickly made an addendum to his words as annoyance crossed Jake's face, and he started to turn away, "But I came here first! Because I know it's the most useful."

"Hmm." Jake seemed to decide against pressing further and simply waved toward the cauldron in the exact center of the pyramid. "I suppose you are going to take the best spot once again and still not recognize its absolute intrinsic value. Might as well get on with it, then."

"I *recognize* it. I *built* this place!" Joe defensively argued. Those were the last words he spoke for at least a dozen hours that did not have some significance to the task at hand. Jake had a masterful plan in mind and set Joe and Baumann against each other to see who could pick up a new potion, new trick, new style, faster and more efficiently than the other.

The Neophyte and the Ritualist went head to head, with the Dwarf gaining a skill level every single time he attempted a new recipe, whether he completed it or not. Joe, on the other hand, had no interest in losing to what was supposed to be *his* star disciple. His pride demanded that he put every effort he possibly could into succeeding, so as not to be shown up. Throughout the entire process, Jake's voice was constantly speaking directly into their ears, guiding them through difficult Draughts, complex Vials, and edging into low-ranked Philters as Joe's skill ranks shot up.

As the Ritualist scooped a multicolored liquid out of his cauldron, pouring it into his container with a swirl and flourish that would allow it to showcase its most potent effects, he finally pushed into the Student ranks of Ritualistic Alchemy.

Congratulations! Training under a... calculating... Master of Alchemy has done wonders for rapid skill growth!

Ritualistic Alchemy has reached Student III!

Ritualistic Alchemist Profession experience gained: 1,680.

Congratulations! You have reached Ritualistic Alchemist level 7. As a level 7 Ritualistic Alchemist, you gain a profession bonus. Randomizing.... bonus gained.

Elemental Equilibrium: This profession bonus allows you to add alchemical reagents to rituals to mimic the effects of adding additional elements into the ritual or balancing out conflicting elements. All ritual-specific reagents you create will now have their elemental affinity listed and can be sacrificed to a ritual to add or negate a specific elemental effect without the remaining effects of the reagent impacting the ritual.

Joe turned his eyes to the dozens of stoppered flasks he had filled with various-ranked alchemical liquids, reading over each of them and their effects. Focusing on his two favorites, he found that, just as promised, they now also showed their elemental affinities—some of which were... strange.

Item created: Philter of Ethersync. Effect(s): Reduces loss of mana due to channeling in rituals by 18.4% (Maximum: Student Ranked rituals). Enhances the emotional connection between the activating Ritualist and their ritual circles, allowing the ritual activator to understand problem areas and gain better control of the sympathetic flows of power.

Elemental affinity: Dreams, Exceptions, Water.

Item created: Draught of Clarity. Effect(s): Focuses the mind of the ritual activator, allowing them to hold a more complex mental image of a ritual pattern in their mind. (Maximum: Apprentice Ranked rituals).

Elemental affinity: Time, Health, Lightning.

"What the what? Elemental Affinity of Dreams? How is 'Exceptions' considered an elemental affinity?" Joe's mumbling didn't go unnoticed, and a slight smile appeared on Jake's face.

"Sounds like somebody got a rank in their profession! Congratulations. You should really take some time to go and consolidate the foundation you have been building in this discipline." Jake shook Joe's hand and pushed him toward the door. "By that, I mean take your potion-quality swill and get out of this building before it is impacted by your wastefulness. Frankly, I'm shocked that you could get anything less than a perfect twenty percent reduction in the loss of mana in a Philter of Ethersync. I'm literally *shook* by that knowledge, as I've never seen it happen before."

Before the Ritualist had another moment to think, the door was already slamming behind him. A **tinkle** sound of glass shattering drew his attention to the fact that the sudden shift in temperature had caused one of the glass vials to shatter. With a muttered curse, he swept the remainder of them into his codpiece and started walking away.

"What was that... fourteen hours? Not bad." Joe looked into the distance, where the ever-present sound of creatures roaring in fury and pain emanated. "Sounds like the walls are holding, and no alarms are going off. If that's the case... done with alchemy, onto smithing!"

Hustling over to the forge, Joe found that all of the workstations were occupied and patiently waited out one of the smiths who was pounding molten metal into shape. Joe filled his time with testing various ritual components, trying to decide if he should keep his new potions for himself or hand them off to the soon-to-be-Ritualists and deciding which of the forging projects he should work on next. He was only at the first rank of Journeyman, and although he had managed to make items above his rank before, he wanted something he could do consistently. His eyes fell on one document and lit up. "Or, I could create something that lets me skip coming here all the time."

It was an ambitious project, but Joe tapped on the template for a 'Ritual Anvil' to show that he was going to be completing it today. "A small, portable anvil that's great for on-the-go ritual component crafting. It can only facilitate the creation of ritual-based items, and even though it's an Expert-ranked template, only Student-ranked items *at best* can be made upon it."

He looked around the bustling workshop and gave a small shrug. "Not like it's going to matter to me all that much; I always have access to this place when I need it. But, when I get tired of using this thing—or lugging it around—I can just offload it on a member of the coven, and they'll be eternally grateful. Good. I like this plan."

He was a full rank below the minimum requirement of being able to easily, or at least consistently, complete the project. Still, Joe understood that greater difficulty came with greater rewards. Full of energy and ready to use his muscles after more than half a day of fiddling with minuscule alchemical components in the form of aspects, Joe swung his ingot hammer at the thick bar of aspects waiting for him. His first strike was practically a thing of beauty, the hammer singing in the air as it vibrated in resonance with his own emotions.

As he worked on the project, humming slightly just because he felt good, everything just seemed to *flow*. The aspects were shaping up well, the patterns and divots created by his hammer were well ordered, and just as it felt like everything was coming together, the center of the anvil sizzled, sparked, and a small crack appeared that shot from top to bottom. The still-forming metal disintegrated into a shower of sparks and aspects, burning holes through whatever they touched—rapidly reducing the durability of the building as a whole.

"Sorry, *sorry*!" Joe shouted as a wave of complaints broke out, especially from those who had been lit on fire by the failure. Still, it wasn't even the first time today that most of them had gone up in flames, so no one was *too* upset. The Ritualist turned back to his anvil and his anvil project, closing his eyes and envisioning what had gone wrong. "Okay… think. It looked like it started at the top, but it moved through the entirety of the item too fast. So it must've been a flaw in the internal structure. Where'd I go wrong?"

After visualizing his process several times, Joe noticed a tiny discrepancy between his memory and what the template showed. "Ah… there it is. I should be able to fix that this time around."

His second attempt was even more promising. The anvil had fully formed, and he was using a chisel to tap symbols into its outer edges that would allow it to focus the energies of his class and profession into the items that would be created on it. Unfortunately, as he leaned over the still-glowing, almost completed object, a single drop of sweat formed on the tip of his nose, falling off and splashing onto the semi-solid energy of the anvil. It caused a chain reaction that made the metal collapse in on itself as if it had been surrounding a tiny black hole. Not even a single mote of light escaped before the anvil was gone.

"Here I was, thinking that putting my blood, sweat, and tears into a project was supposed to make it succeed." Since he had to either decide to be furious or try to make light of the situation, Joe went with humor.

Continuing to power on, the Ritualist felt like the third attempt was the one that would *absolutely* succeed. The anvil took shape, the symbols were formed—he had double-checked his Neutrality Aura this time around to mop up any loose sweat —but as he completed his final swing, a glow from the building itself around him collected on the surface of his project and reduced it to slag.

Ritualistic Forging (Journeyman I → Journeyman II)

"Right, I'm going to count that as a win. It clearly succeeded then was derailed." Feeling more than just a hint of despair, Joe stared at the pool of molten metal and let out a deep sigh before starting again. "Taken down by a malicious manifestation of Special aspects. I see how it is. Well, I'm not leaving until I succeed."

CHAPTER TWENTY-ONE

Seventeen attempts. Seventeen failures. On the eighteenth, the failure that would have taken the last bit of his hope was mitigated by the special effect of his ingot hammer activating and *forcing* a success. As the energy crackled out of his tool and the anvil took form, Joe was forced to hold back tears of relief. He'd promised himself he wouldn't leave until he succeeded, but the fact that he had gotten within a single hammer's blow of success at least a dozen times had well and truly *thrashed* his desire to continue.

Ritualistic Forging (Journeyman II → Journeyman III).

Feat of craftsmanship completed: Workhorse Montage I. You have gained skill levels in at least three different crafting-based disciplines while working for 72 hours straight. +1 to all stats!

"Yay, a whole skill level and a tiny Characteristic point bump," Joe deadpanned as he let his hammer slip into his codpiece. Quickly checking over the anvil and finding that he couldn't tell what type of metal he'd made it out of, the Ritualist stored the several-hundred-pound item into his codpiece and sent up a silent thanks that the legendary spatial storage device fully removed the weight of whatever was put inside. "That was surprisingly small for an anvil. What, two feet across? I wonder how dense that material really is, that it's so heavy and so small."

His body suddenly froze, as though he had been chomped by a full-grown hydra and pumped full of paralytic, caustic acid. Pain rippled through him, tingling his nerves and causing each part of him to shake to its own rhythm. The sound of a handful of notifications pinging in his head at the same time was a minor annoyance in comparison to the abrupt agony that was filling him. People were shouting, though they sounded as though he were underwater, but the words that he could make out comforted him greatly.

"Joe's down! Get a healer!"

"He *is* the healer, find someone else! Maybe a cleric!"

"No, he is a cleric, find someone else! An Alchemist!"

"No, the Alchemist is too freaky, get the Council!"

"Interrupt the Council of Masters? You're out of your mind! Make him deal with it on his own!"

"Yeah, that's a good idea."

"Oh. Didn't know that was an option. Great."

The sound of hammers ringing on metal started up again, only to be interrupted by Growmore rushing over and gripping the sides of Joe's head. "Hey, lad! Going by the lack of foaming at the mouth, puncture marks, or bleeding, it looks like you're going through a multi-threshold breakthrough. Hold tight to that thought, and just go ahead and let go of consciousness if it lets you."

That option never came, and the entire time his body was going through the agony of sudden upgrades across the board, he tried to piece together where all of the increases had come from. His Characteristics had been jumping for days, but always in small spurts. He vaguely recalled gaining a boatload of Perception and Wisdom while detailing the constellations. There'd been a boost in his Charisma not even worth mentioning thanks to his handling of various crowds as well as his students.

Dexterity and Perception once more had been rapidly growing under the care of Jake the Alchemist, and it went without saying that such an intense round of smithing would show benefits for his Strength and Constitution. Then, of course, his *mental* attributes fed into his physical ones—thanks to the perk he'd chosen when he first got to Alfheim—giving them a boost.

He pulled up his character sheet, looking at the adjustments so he could feel he had at least some kind of control.

Name: Joe 'Tatum's Chosen Legend' Class: Reductionist
Profession I: Arcanologist (Max)
Profession II: Ritualistic Alchemist (7/20)
Profession III: Grandmaster's Apprentice (15/25)
Profession IV: None
Character Level: 28 Exp: 423,159 Exp to next level: 11,841
Rituarchitect Level: 13 Exp: 87,450 Exp to next level: 3,550
Reductionist Level: 9 Exp: 53,000 Exp to next level: 2,000
Hit Points: 2,854/2,854
Mana: 6,561/8,988
Mana regen: 85.5/sec
Stamina: 1,350/2,140
Stamina regen: 6.8/sec

Characteristic: Raw score

Strength (bound): 188 → 200
Dexterity: 189 → 200
Constitution (bound): 188 → 200
Light Intelligence (Bound): 208
Wisdom: 185 → 200
Dark Charisma: 151 → 159
Perception: 189 → 200
Luck: 123 → 138
Karmic Luck: 25 → 26

"Karmic Luck even went up? Oh. That feat didn't say it excluded Karmic Luck. Interesting." Joe looked at all of the numbers that stayed steady in his mind's eye, even as his head bounced off the floor, and his eyes rattled around in his skull. "Seriously? wait a second... did I get my old moderator back, or is the new one messing with me? One, two... *five* different Characteristics hit two hundred at the same time? There's no way that's an accident."

The potent side effects of his sudden breakthrough started slowing, though the results remained. His nervous system became more effective and responsive, his bones and muscles shifted to being denser yet more supple, and every sense reached a point that was unrecognizable to basic humans. All of this combined meant that, even though he had been given back control of his body once more, his attempts at moving caused him to flail and damage himself and the floor he was laying on.

The difference from one hundred and ninety-nine points to two hundred was a qualitative shift. A single point shouldn't have been able to change everything about him so drastically, but... it did. Joe's mind had been at this threshold for a while already, so it was able to facilitate the shift well. His mind interfaced with his senses, coming into harmony at the fifth threshold. Once he had control of his senses, they interfaced with his Dexterity to give him balance, which let his muscles and bones align. Fractions of a second after he'd first started spasming around, Joe smoothly lifted to his feet and flexed his powerfully enhanced muscles.

"Whew. What a rush."

"You think *that's* good, wait until your Charisma gets on parity." Growmore chuckled as he gave Joe a hearty slap that didn't cause the human to move even a fraction of an inch.

Joe raised an eyebrow. "What makes you think that my Charisma isn't at the fifth threshold?"

"Just... you know... the whole..." Growmore waved a hand over the entirety of Joe's face, "...*thing* you've got going on here.

Hey, changing the subject really fast, you should try picking up something you thought was heavy a moment ago."

Only hesitating for a moment, Joe pulled out the anvil that he'd just created and lifted it into the air with only a very light grunt. "Huh. Yeah. I see what you mean. That's… something new. I wonder how this'll impact my ability to manipulate mana?"

"Depends. If you've got your Intelligence, Wisdom, and Perception in the same tier, you'll probably notice a marked difference." Seeing the slight smile on Joe's face made the Dwarf scoff in amazement. "Don't tell me you got *all* of that at the same time."

"Of course not!" Joe replied immediately, waiting until the Dwarf had settled down slightly to finish his thought. "I got Intelligence there weeks ago. It was only *five* Characteristics that pushed through the bottleneck. At the same time. Just now."

"Get outta here before I chase you out with this new ice pick I just made." Growmore hissed at Joe as he made a few threatening stabs in the Ritualist's direction.

"I'm going, I'm going!" Joe laughed as he walked toward the door. Or, at least, he *thought* he walked there. To his own perception, he simply strolled across the room and put his hand on the door knob, but he was followed by a sound that was not *quite* a sonic boom, but still caused the water in the air to condense into a liquid form as he passed through.

"Blasted newbie mages!" Growmore snarled as he waved a hand and funneled the falling water out of the air and away from the forges.

"No, I've been a Mage for a while," Joe informed him with great confusion. "But I didn't use a spell just now, that was just from moving!"

"Yeah, *I know*." Growmore made a shooing motion at the Ritualist. "Don't worry about it; I'm using an old classification that doesn't matter anymore. Get!"

Stepping outside, the bald man flexed and stretched, feeling how his clothes strained against his body. "It's kind of nice to have tactile feedback that says that wasn't a nightmare, and this isn't a dream. Annoying that I'll probably have to go and buy new clothes, though."

Congratulations! Beast Waves completed: 25/100.

All future Beast Waves during the rank up of your Town to a City will occur 6 hours apart; a 2 hour decrease in time between waves.

Bonus: as no monsters have managed to enter into the center of your protected zone during the first 25 waves, Novusheim has been granted a 25% total increase in morale!

You have proven your resilience! Beast Wave number 26 will start immediately, so you don't need to wait for more enemies to sharpen your blades against!

Horns began blowing, and at first Joe ignored them. It made sense that the people on the walls would call for reinforcements, as they hadn't had even a moment to switch out with fresh combatants. Only as the horns took on a more dire note, blowing a fourth time, did he hurry to see what was going on. "A single blast is beasts spotted in the distance, two are stealthy ones having entered the walls. What was three again? A Boss Monster? So... I don't even know what four toots of the horn *is*!"

There was only one way to find out, and Joe was perfectly happy to test out his upgraded physique on the way. Crouching down slightly, he burst forward with a push of his leather-clad foot, causing a geyser of snow to erupt into the air as he set off at a run. He could feel the strain of his movement, but it was no different than when he was running hard to beat his best time during his military days on earth. It *certainly* didn't feel like he was careening through the Town at over a hundred miles an hour.

But he was—and it was exactly as awesome as he'd always dreamed it would be.

The innermost wall of the Town was rapidly coming closer, and Joe was able to calculate at a glance the angle he needed to jump, exactly how much force he needed to put behind it, and how his Characteristics would mesh with his skills. "Omnivault!"

If before he had created a geyser of snow, now he was the start of an avalanche as he shot wildly into the air, crossing more than double his previous record for leaping a single time.

Skill updated: Omnivault. As you have broken through the 5th threshold of physical Characteristics, your skill sets will reflect the input of your Characteristics.

*Omnivault: jump upward (Strength/10 → Strength/5) feet directly upward from a standstill, or leap forward (Strength/10 → Strength/5)*3 feet.*

"I can jump forty feet straight up from a standstill? No wonder basketball doesn't exist in this world. That means I just leapt one hundred and twenty feet in less than a second… I should go pounce on a cheetah or something just to freak it out." Still extremely exuberant about his massive increase in personal power, he hurried along until he arrived at the nearest sentry. "Hey! So sorry, I missed the meeting where they assigned what the horns meant. What does four toots mean? Heh. Toots. Fun word."

"Uh. Yeah. Master Joe… we didn't have that signal until just now," the Legionnaire informed him with a weak salute, his eyes trained on the horizon. "As to what it means, see for yourself."

The Ritualist turned to look in the same direction, scanning the distant horizon and not understanding at first what he was supposed to be seeing. "Okay, pretty standard, monsters everywhere. Regular horizon, mountain in the distance, I don't see the issue?"

"Councilman Joe. Respectfully, Jotunheim doesn't *have* mountains."

"Oh. Oh, no."

CHAPTER TWENTY-TWO

"How far away do you think that thing has to be in order to be hidden behind the curvature of the planet?" The words fell out of Joe's mouth before he thought all the way through them. It seemed the Dwarf next to him was in an equal amount of shock, because the answer that came back was practically nonsensical.

"This planet is so huge that you could be forgiven for thinking it was flat." The scout began rambling. "At the mining camp fifty miles out east, you can look back and see Novusheim at the same level. Our walls are forty feet tall. That thing has its face covered by clouds every once in a while. Nine hundred feet? Maybe a thousand? More?"

Joe stayed silent for a few minutes, slowly coming back to himself and finding that he was flanked by battle-hardened Dwarves and nervous human defenders. Not a single one of them was paying attention to what was going on in the local area, instead focused on the far-distant threat. Closer to the battle, the clanking of armor and weapons still rang out, barely managing to break the hushed tension mounting atop the walls. Looking around, the Ritualist sucked in a breath to try and make a light-hearted comment, but one of the people in the surroundings beat him to speaking.

"Well, look who's fashionably early." The Dwarf slammed the butt of his ax handle on the ground, startling those near him. "I'll bet my beard that's a Legendary-ranked monster. We shouldn't have to deal with one of those until we're trying to create a *Megalopolis*. Not City, not even a Metropolis. You all know what that means, right?"

No one answered, but now all eyes were on the Dwarf, full of curiosity and desperate for any spark of hope. With a tight grip on his weapon, the Dwarf pumped the air and shouted, "They're *afraid*! We're so awesome they needed to send a boss *two full ranks* above our settlement!"

His whoop of exuberance fell flat for a moment, then Joe caught on and chipped in, "*Yeah*!"

Everyone in earshot exploded into cheers, banging their weapons on shields, hollering at the giant in the distance, and in a few cases even lowering their pants and shaking their rear at the incoming threat. It might have been Joe's imagination, but as the giant's eyes intermittently appeared and vanished behind the swirling clouds—like a deity playing peekaboo with them—it seemed that the expression on its face shifted to a scowl.

Quietly distancing himself from the group, Joe started rushing back toward the Town Hall to bring this matter to the attention of the council. "Good to keep up appearances in front of the troops, but… this is *absurd*. A Legendary-rank monster on a Town upgrading to a City? We need a plan and lots and lots of coffee."

Then he slid to a stop, pausing and rethinking why he felt the urge to go in person to make a report. "This is literally why we have scouts and messengers. I don't need to be doing this. I need to keep building up our defenses and maybe figure out a ritual that can take that monster head-on. Let's see, a Legendary-ranked monster, that would be… okay, maybe a different plan. I don't think I'm going to be able to put together a Grandmaster-ranked ritual before that thing steps over our walls like they aren't even there."

Beyond putting together a bunch of rituals to go on towers, which might or might not be effective against such a high-ranking beast, there were only a few options for increasing his personal power in the short-term. Joe decided to go with one of those options and sighed softly as he looked at his Ritual Orb of Constitution. "Sorry, Morsum. It's not that you're not strong, it's just that the monsters here are so much stronger that you seem weak."

The fact that the pseudo-lich head was not currently summoned to this plane of existence made the choice easier, so Joe returned to his workshop and opened all six of his Ritual Orbs, filling the room with a mess of tangled wire thread. "Right, probably should've done these one at a time. Ugh... I practically just finished fixing and re-tweaking the repaired version of this."

Joe rushed to his workshop and locked himself inside, pulling open his Ritual Orbs and carefully inspecting them. Luckily, the first several ritual circles remained mostly the same, mostly needing a shift so that additional sympathetic lines could be pulled between them and the additional circles that would be surrounding them soon.

Looking over his options for summoning things from other planes, Joe was able to easily tick off the first of them as impossible. "Celestial Wyrm, nope, that's at least Grandmaster rank. I need something that's *Expert* at the worst. A Valkyrie Shield Maiden? That's promising... oh wait, she would automatically attack me because I have a neutral alignment. This book is *very* helpful."

By the time he'd crossed off abyssal horrors, he was down to Expert-ranked elementals. Thinking about how the council had refused his request to build an elemental playground, which would make the summoning of a creature like this easier and more effective, he allowed a moment of annoyance to be experienced, then let it pass. "I could do an earthen colossus? That might be something useful against a titan like that. Wait, no, I think it would only reach its ankles. Oh, that thing is *slow*. Elemental of wind? That'd be pretty powerful in a place like this. Lots of wind, lots of snow. Also… even the *Penguins* probably have some resistance to wind."

He turned the page and found another diagram, dismissing it immediately and flipping to the next section. Before he could fully move on, he felt a warm heat wrapping around his left hand. "Mate? What's up?"

Burble.

The elemental shifted its body to look like a human hand and used its index-finger-like appendage to point at the diagram Joe had planned to ignore—then back at itself, bending the 'finger' in a way that would be impossible for anyone but Jaxon to replicate.

"You want me to use this on you?" Joe looked over the spell diagram, carefully considering it instead of skipping past as planned. "You don't ask for much usually; are you sure that you want to get so directly involved?"

The spell in question was a type of summoning, but a much more *literal* planar shift. Instead of pulling an entity out of a separate plane, it used an already summoned creature to pull in a copy of *its* plane of existence, creating an area where the summoned creature would be vastly more powerful than usual. It didn't negate attacks or send them away; it was a straightforward empowerment. In other words, not something that Joe would typically bother with. But… as he put more thought into it, he realized that this spell would fulfill one of his lifelong dreams, if it worked.

"For a short time, I'd literally pull over a chunk of the elemental plane of coffee. I would bathe in coffee, breathe coffee, and to top it off, *you* would be super empowered. I'm starting to like this plan. Are you thinking that, by getting a boost like this, you can help all of our defenders have a huge burst of energy? Or, do you know exactly what this will do? Help me out here, how many people could you pump caffeine into if I managed to activate this at the Expert rank? One hundred?"

The coffee elemental swirled in the air.

"That was… not a yes, you were adding on a zero. Right? So a thousand?"

Burble! Mate swirled again.

"*Ten thousand?* Surely you must be joking." Mate and Joe stared at each other for a moment, and the Ritualist slumped slightly. "Wait a moment. You don't know how to do math."

Burb! The coffee elemental cheerfully bubbled at him. It swirled in the air four times, and the Ritualist could only shrug helplessly.

"Okay, all I can think is you're trying to tell me you could give a boost to somewhere between a thousand and ten thousand people. You know what? Good enough. Let's start putting this together."

Joe briefly considered switching the orb that was the central focus of the planar shift spell. It made sense to him that, if he shifted it from the orb of Constitution to the orb of Strength, he would be able to make stronger coffee. Yet, he talked himself out of it by reminding himself that he didn't need coffee that could punch someone; he needed coffee that could impact those who had massive resistances. "I hope this works!"

Frankly, even if it didn't work the way he expected, Joe was sure he would still be happy with the final results. Pulling out his needle-nosed pliers—he had never given them back, finding them far too useful—Joe began pulling at the wires as he stared at the diagram in front of him. The changes to the first several circles were very straightforward, and the outer ones moved along quickly, thanks to his extreme comfort with rituals at that low of a level.

"I wonder if I can find a potion that has the affinity of coffee, or caffeine? Hmm. Probably not in a reasonable amount of time, and I wouldn't be able to access them if Jake made it for me. I'd need something at the Expert rank, at the minimum. Another time."

As time passed, the complex diagram slowly came into being. The odd, arcane runes on the outer edges were easily molded, and as he attuned the entire diagram to Mate—who sat at the center of the ritual for this part—a subtle ripple went through the entirety of the ritual. Joe checked on the sections he'd just finished, finding that several of the symbols had shifted slightly and now looked like latte heart art.

For a few moments, he tried to decide if that was an error or simply the results of the heart-shaped Ritual Orb of Constitution making itself known. "I mean… it kinda *works* for what we're going for here."

When the ritual diagram was fully set, Joe pulled out the Unique Mana Battery that usually sat in the Ritual Orb and left his workshop. "Just gotta put this on the recharge station, fill it up, and we should be good to go."

It was the first time using the recharge station, and he was understandably nervous as he approached it and slotted his battery. The fluctuations surrounding the table dimmed precipitously, and he hoped that he had just saved someone's bone marrow for the short-term. Three people were standing inside the bubble, two of them guards, one of them tasked with placing and pulling cores. Joe walked up to that employee and pulled out his Ritual Orb. "Mend. Lay on Hands."

Luck +1!

There was no visible difference, beyond the human looking somewhat confused as to why he was getting the treatment. Joe clapped him on the arm with a smile, "Yeah… we're gonna keep doing *that.* As a perk of the job, at least once a week, make sure to see me for some casual healing. Never know what kind of debuffs you'll pick up from… the, uh, the cold."

His employee nodded awkwardly, scooting slightly away after Joe instructed him to keep that battery safe for him and have it delivered as soon as it was full.

After that, he simply stepped out of the bubble and began practicing using his Ritual Orbs in conjunction with each other to expand out to the intricate, six-circle Expert ritual diagram.

While it wasn't exactly *easy*, he quickly got the hang of it. So quickly, in fact, that he realized his mental Characteristics must be playing a significant role in his use of the exotic weapons. This was quickly confirmed as his skill level began to rapidly rise.

Combat Ritual Orbs (Exotic) (Student 0 → Student IV)

"It's been so long since I first got to Midgard. I almost forgot that, if you show a higher level of mastery than your sheet indicates, it will rapidly catch up." He tossed all six orbs into the air, where they exploded like metal fireworks one at a time, forming into all six circles and linking up as quickly as his mind could make them move. "Better. Now let's see if I can get this down to less than three seconds."

CHAPTER TWENTY-THREE

With his new ritual diagram well-practiced, at least in terms of popping it open, Joe found himself itching for an opportunity to put it into play. Its battery was placed, and he'd tested it lightly by running a few strands of mana along it. Not enough to actually activate the ritual or begin its activation sequence, but just enough to test the integrity of its design. "*Should* work perfectly."

Still, the steep cost of keeping the ritual active precluded him from testing it casually. Besides the standard activation cost of the spell, there was a cost per second for keeping the Planar Shift active, as there wasn't an entity he was pulling over that could bargain on its own behalf. Joe had plenty of tasks remaining, dozens of things he wanted to do, but as much as he worried about losing himself, he truly wanted to figure out if the star cluster he had noticed recently was the one that would coincide with his Ritual of Slaughter.

"It was slightly different, so I *might* be wrong." He mused to himself as he strolled back to the celestial observatory at a cozy seventy miles per hour. "Either way, I need to see if it's something I can boost. That'd give us a great deal more firepower as a final trump card if it works."

Before walking into the building, he cast Message and sent his thoughts to Jaxon. "Hi buddy! Are you doing anything I should come and be a part of? I remember that your rendition of a tree frozen in time is absolutely masterful, and I want to get to another matinee if they're still going!"

The slithery, jubilant thoughts echoed in his mind as Jaxon replied near instantly. "No worries, no worries! We've put that on hiatus for the moment, as half of the cast are jockeying for position at the leading edge of the battle. I can't wait to show you what it'll look like, especially since I know at least a dozen of them have grown tremendously in flexibility under my personal care!"

Exchanging a few more pleasantries, just to make sure that his friendships were maintained, Joe swiftly ended the conversation and reached out to each of his other party members, as well as Daniella. Each of them was fully engrossed in what they were doing but pleased that he was making an effort to be present in their lives. Feeling like he had made a great stride forward, Joe paid a messenger to come and get his attention—pull him out of the building, in other words—after a few hours.

Then he walked inside, plopped himself down, and pulled out his notebook. "Right. Knowledge, Alchemical Lore twice."

Congratulations! Alchemical Lore has broken into the Journeyman rank!

Alchemical Lore (Journeyman 0). As a bonus for breaking into the Journeyman rank, you have gained a Tonic-rank recipe for Alchemical Solvent! Do you have a cauldron coated in leftover gunk that can't even be called a potion? Just add a spritz of solvent to have the cauldron sparkling like new! Remember, if you're not part of the solution, you're a precipitate!

"I guess I can sell that recipe or something?" Joe didn't even bother looking it over further. He already had a cauldron with a perfect self-cleaning function, as well as the ability to reduce any waste products to aspects, thanks to his Field Array. "Wait, no, I can use it to help boost my skill levels. Or maybe not, since it might not have any relation to Ritualistic Alchemy."

Shaking off the annoyance of getting a not-exactly-useful reward, the Ritualist turned his eyes to the false sky above him. Holding his notes, he compared the sigil placement of the Ritual of Slaughter with the stars, finding that they simply didn't match up. "Abyss, I really thought I had it that time. It just makes sense; they emanate a subtle feeling of death and bloodlust, and there are matches, but just not enough of them."

Scratching his head, or at least attempting to and having his fingertips bounce off of his Exquisite Shell, Joe tried to figure out what else this star cluster might represent. His quill flew across the page as he attempted to calculate the connection between the stars and the various rituals—or even just *components* of ritual diagrams—that he knew. As he studied the stars and worked on extrapolating data from them, his skill levels began to rapidly increase.

Celestial-Arcane Interaction Lore (Beginner VI → Beginner VII)

Celestial-Arcane Interaction Lore (Beginner VII → Beginner VIII)

Calculus and Number Theory (Student IV → Student V)

Celestial-Arcane Interaction Lore (Beginner VIII → Beginner IX)

Even though all the skill did was make itself gain skill levels faster each time it leveled up, it was still fun to see the numbers practically spin. Yet, no matter how he adjusted for what he knew about rituals, Joe couldn't figure out what else this star cluster could possibly be in alignment with. "For celestial's *sake*! This *has* to be aligned with the Ritual of Slaughter!"

Celestial-Arcane Interaction Lore (Beginner IX → Apprentice 0)

Joe's eyes, which he hadn't even realized were squeezed shut, shot open and allowed the alternating green and purple twinkling lights of the star cluster to fill them with inspiration. "That's it! I've got it! They would align perfectly, but only if the ritual was a rank higher than it is currently! This means, if I use the other stars as reference points, I'll be able to skip nearly a quarter of the work in determining where to position them on the next circle out. Celestial Feces… I've never done a direct upgrade of a ritual before. This *has* to be worth some skill levels."

His quill began twitching as he fiercely scribbled down his insights and began arranging the next layer of the ritual starting with the symbol positioning. "Now, going from Journeyman to Expert rank, what are the changes that I need to focus on? What is it that an Expert-ranked ritual has that the lower ranks don't?"

Far too slowly, he began writing out his insights, turning the page slightly to the side when it just felt *correct* to do so. As his Ritual Lore skill was still in the Journeyman ranks, Joe was pushing into unknown territory by attempting to craft something he didn't have a solid intellectual foundation on already. "Novice simply tells us what to do, then we add complexity in the form of targeting in new ways, additional effects, esoteric functionality, and all sorts of exceptions or specifics. Oh, maybe I could add that affinity of exceptions to this and see what happens? No, don't think about that right now!"

When he had completed writing out his thoughts, Joe found that he'd written them in a perfect circle. Unfortunately, a large chunk of the text remained dull and lifeless, Tatum's gift to understand written knowledge showing him that his line of reasoning was simply *not correct*. The Ritualist growled and started over, testing out a new line of thinking. The stars above shifted ever so slightly as he worked, and the enormous planet he was on rotated.

"It's not a force multiplier or conditional trigger. Those are simply components of the greater spell circle." Joe tapped his quill on his chin, not noticing as a large droplet of ink ran down the outside of his Exquisite Shell and off him, spilling onto the floor with dozens of others. "It couldn't be as simple as a mana sink that's far too low level. But… here's a thought."

Pulling out a couple of his Expert-ranked rituals as a comparison, Joe tried to get a sense for what they were actually supposed to be doing, in terms of the ritual's functionality. Pieces started fitting together in his mind, and he slowly nodded as an idea came to him in a rush. "It's not a perfect explanation, but these circles almost seem like they're created to pull data from the rituals current effects, analyze them, then channel it back into the ritual overall. An optimizer? Is this optimizing the performance of the ritual in real time?"

He knew he was getting close, even if that wasn't going to be the answer for every single iteration of rituals that existed. Likely, there were many who did not care about optimization or efficiency and would instead simply use the outer ring to create even more specific effects. But, for the moment, the system seemed to think he had put together a good working knowledge during his time studying.

Ritual Lore (Journeyman 0 → Journeyman II). Pretty good! Being able to use something with ease is much different than understanding it! Impressive deduction!

"Thanks, moderator." Joe muttered as he studied his ritual diagram, and tried to think of how he could interface his new knowledge with his spell work. "Now that I know what I'm looking for, I can start considering spell components that are specific for optimization and use the sigil placement to figure out which one would work for this specific instance."

For the second time during his work, Joe felt a hand lightly touching his shoulder and brushed it off. "Five more minutes; I'm nearly done."

Some quiet murmuring was ignored, and soon the presence trying to get his attention moved away. Joe continued attempting to brute force the circle generation, setting up dozens, perhaps hundreds of iterations before finding a set that seemed to come together into a cohesive whole. As he put the last line in place and began going over the new circle, he was pleased with what he saw. "I'm going to have to adjust the actual symbology there, shift the intent a bit so that it matches up with this particular ritual, but… I think I've got it?"

As he stared at the newly crafted Expert-rank ritual—which seemed to glow in the light of the stars he had positioned himself under—Joe realized he was holding a far more potent

War Ritual than its predecessor could ever hope to be. *If* it worked.

Congratulations! You have upgraded a ritual from Journeyman to Expert rank without outside assistance! That's right, we saw you go to Grandmaster Havoc and have him boost the reward you earned back then. The Ritual of Slaughter (Student) wasn't enough for you, huh? Well, that's fine. In my mind, you've redeemed yourself by doing the next upgrade by yourself, and this one was a whole lot harder. In the future, you should be able to intuit what you need in order to do things like this. I look forward to seeing you figure it out without just making new, failed versions, over and over!

Ritual of Slaughter (Expert). In addition to the previous effects, the expert version allows you to add additional mana to the ritual after it has been set off. Each Additional point of mana will increase the effects of the Ritual of Slaughter by .001m, where m = a single point of mana. Each point of mana added will also extend the duration of the ritual by .25 seconds! Up to six additional power plates can be used as inputs. This ritual must *be set up in conjunction with constellation clusters, or it will fail to activate properly—generating immense backlash as it flounders and lashes out in pain.*

We hope you have a lot of friends with deep mana pools!

Intelligence +5!

You know what? That shouldn't have worked the way that it did. Luck +3.

"Yeah… yes, I can think of plenty of ways to make this work for me." Joe traced one of the circles with his finger, shaking his head in wonder at the newly enhanced ritual.

There were a few other notifications that didn't make their presence known until this moment, and Joe felt his stomach sink as he read over them.

Luck is two thresholds below Strength! 1% chance to do absolutely nothing when an action should have been taken has activated! Twice!

Luck is two thresholds below Dexterity! 1% chance to fail a dexterous action has activated.

Luck is two thresholds below Perception! 1% chance to notice a truth that nobody will believe has activated! Twice! Three times!

Luck is two thresholds below Wisdom! 1% chance to make a foolish decision has activated.

Before he could take any time to do some self-reflection on what he may have missed, or what truth he'd found that would be so hard to believe, Joe found out where he had failed to do something important—a foolish decision. A Legionnaire burst into the celestial observatory, shouting for him.

Joe was on his feet at the same moment, storing away his bean bag and notes. "I'm here, I'm here! What's the issue?"

"Master Joe!" The Legionnaire sprinted toward him, shouting the entire time. "A new type of monster, a Boss Monster, arrived five waves early, along with a pack of elites of its own type. It was put down, but the damage to the walls is extensive. We need you out there repairing walls or at least providing the means to repair them."

"Abyss!" Joe was already sprinting for the door, and the Legionnaire twisted around and matched his speed. "Five waves early? We're only thirty-five waves in, and the walls have taken enough damage that I need to get involved personally? This is going to be a *long* siege."

"Uhh… *what?*" The confusion in the Dwarf's voice shifted to immense annoyance as he snapped out his next words. "The walls were struck during wave *forty-five*, and wave forty-six just started. Have you been hiding under a rock?"

CHAPTER TWENTY-FOUR

As soon as they were out of the doors, the sound of dozens of alarms being sounded around the Town reached Joe's ears. Clearly, nearly every sector was dealing with a breach, and the closest ritual towers to the Town were sending out their deadly payloads. "I'm just going to go ahead and say it. The soundproofing in that building is *crazy* good."

"Happy for you," came the curt reply from the Legionnaire still running alongside the councilman. "Southeast section is the most heavily damaged. No one was expecting the Boss Monster to attack from an angle that wasn't at least somewhat in line with the main entrance."

"Can you give me a rundown on that beast? I need to know more so that I can plan for it in the future." Joe's question was met with pursed lips for a long moment, as the soldier was either ordering his thoughts or calming himself down—giving Joe the chance to feel *twice* as bad about having ignored combat for so long.

"Yeah. It was a new boss, along with a set of elites that were the same as it, just a lot smaller. It was called a Pachycephalosaurus Palisade Puncher, which we already shortened to

Triple-P." The Dwarf paused and worked his jaw, trying to push past the minor tongue spasm he'd just experienced. "It was some kind of dinosaur pulled out of a glacier, set up like an oversized battering ram. The thing ran in a straight line, pretty much ignoring anything that hit it straight on. Couldn't make a dent in the blasted beast."

Joe's eyes scanned the inner wall, not noticing anywhere that they'd even cracked. "Well, it's obvious you guys took it down, so…?"

"Right, so, it was massively armored and completely mana resistant on its head, but once we were able to get behind it, the boss fell as easily as any Penguin would have. Only problem was, by the time we figured that out, it'd smashed through six walls and turned to hit the next ones. It cut a 'V' by going straight in, then straight out, somehow ignoring the compulsion to go after the Town Hall, I guess." The Dwarf sighed and pulled at his beard. "First line of defense got to have all the fun bringing it down. To be fair, I guess most of the big threats have gotten deeper than that, and they've missed out, so it's all working out in the end."

"Yeah, but not in the way I hoped it would." Joe lightly stated. "I'd be pretty happy if *all* of the Boss Monsters broke against the first line of defense. Abyss, here's a scary thought. Can you imagine how completely wrecked our Town would be right now if we only had a single layer of walls?"

Both of them shivered at that, then the Ritualist grabbed the Dwarf and activated Omnivault, launching them over the innermost wall and into the next set. "Blasted human! Dwarves aren't meant to fly!"

"Not flying!" Joe chuckled in reply. "Are we getting close to… oh."

"Yeah."

Two major sights had caught Joe's attention. The first was the swath of destruction that had been cut through the barricades. From the space where they were standing, they could see the swarming monsters outside of Town. The hundred-foot-long chunks of wall had thirty-foot holes that had been shattered in almost the exact center of the outermost one. They continued at an angle, thanks to the curve of the hallways, until the final one had been struck and ripped off the endcap of the wall. Then the pattern reversed itself.

The second and much stranger event was how the sections of walls that had *not* been destroyed were behaving. The enchantments Grandmaster Snow had ordered to be placed on them were active, and Joe was thrilled to see them in action for the first time.

Little by little, the hundred-foot-long sections of wall bounced into the air and approximately a single foot over at a time. Joe had been leery about its usefulness, but the Grandmaster had pointed out an extremely pertinent detail: when there were breaches in the wall, they could move sections so that they created funnels, exactly as was happening now. Also, when they started to have an area get overwhelmed, they could move the walls and cut off one route into the town, opening up another that would force the monsters to stop, turn around, and seek out the new entry.

"I love seeing what magic can do," Joe cheerfully commented as he set up the Ritual of Repair. These had been in such popular demand that he always kept a few primed and ready to go—for situations exactly like this one. Tapping the activation sequence, Joe pulled out a Mana Battery and set it on top of the ritual, allowing the glowing stone to act as the power source. As it connected to the wall, chunks of stone that had already begun burying themselves in the blowing snow began lifting up and rolling toward the wall, seamlessly melding back into place.

Taking a few moments to ensure that everything was running properly, Joe clapped the Legionnaire on the back and Omnivaulted forward, setting up another ritual at the wall in the same layer that had been damaged during the triple-P's exit of the walls. "This isn't too bad, give it… let's say half an hour? Then this layer will be fixed up."

"I'll inform the commander." The Dwarf stoically replied. Joe shrugged nonchalantly then threw himself to the top of the wall and across to the next layer.

While it certainly would have been easier to just walk over, the density of monsters pouring into the labyrinth suggested that attempting to set up another ritual at ground level would not be a wise decision. While his debuffs insidiously attempted to make him do just that, Joe pulled out another diagram and set it up. "Abyss. Never expected I'd need a giant stack of these. I'll have to go see if I can borrow some from the maintenance crews."

After he finished activating the ritual, he looked around and noticed that there were active rituals humming along around the entirety of the settlement. "Oh, right. It wasn't just the Boss Monster that smashed in. I wonder how bad the damage is from the smaller versions?"

He waved down a work crew, letting them know where he had set up the rituals and leaving it to them to finish up the repairs.

"Our enemies are adapting." It took a moment for the voice to be recognizable, but Joe paused as Grandmaster Snow's voice boomed throughout the entire area. "They're going after our walls, our confidence, attempting to subvert us and crack our protections. But we are still learning and growing faster than they can! Our victory over this most recent Boss Wave may feel like a tainted victory, that we've been pushed to our limits, and I know all of you are feeling the strain."

She paused, her voice losing its weary tinge and allowing steel to seep in. "On the plus side, we are *the Oligarchy*! We don't just stand on the edge of disaster, we stomp on it and try to figure out how far we can fall before catching our balance! I'm sure you've all seen the Legendary-rank monster bearing down on us in the distance. Well, the world does not punish without offering a gift in the other hand! When we defeat this giant, it will be smooth sailing to the *next two* settlement ranks! I have received confirmation that there will be *no* final boss allowed during our next upgrade, nor the one after that!"

Joe perked up at that, tilting his head and listening intently, as it seemed that the Grandmaster's speech was not yet complete.

"To that end, I am authorizing the use of three Grandmaster-level abilities that had been classified as too brutal for general use back in our previous home. When the time comes, don't try to take a peek at the devastation. Just bunker down and try not to get caught in the fallout."

There was a subtle shift in the air, and Joe understood that there was nothing else coming. "Yeah, right. Like I *wouldn't* try and see what Grandmaster-rank abilities look like in combat. Although… I hope that when she said 'fallout,' she didn't mean literal fallout. That'd be annoying to clean up."

Joe snorted at that thought; if they had radioactive fallout drop on them, he was more concerned with how long it would take his Neutrality Aura to clean the space around him than he was over its long-term effects. "I've said it before, I'll say it again. Magic is *neat.*"

As Joe moved among the defenders, he found the air abuzz with discussion on what Grandmaster abilities would be used. People were debating whether it would be Havoc, McPoundy, or Snow who showed their trump cards first.

"You're forgetting that Master Wrath pushed through to the Grandmaster rank!" another voice chimed in excitedly. "That's why he stepped down and allowed Master Frenzy to take his position; he wanted to spend time in seclusion, gaining control of his skills. I hear they were too strong for him to use anywhere someone else could see him."

There were a few other names bandied about, but Joe didn't recognize them. That did put a question in his mind that made his brow furrow and his eyes narrow. "How many Grandmasters are hidden away in this group? Why'd I have to run across the entirety of Alfheim to find three of them who would come along with us, if a sneaky half dozen were already standing around me? I swear, if I find out they gave me busy work to keep me away from the cool things happening..."

He let out a breath, reminding himself that he had a part of a pretty amazing adventure himself. With a coy smile, Joe muttered, "None of those hidden ones managed to melt the Elven capital, though, did they? That was all me and Havoc."

In fact, it had been almost *entirely* Grandmaster Havoc, but Joe liked his version of events better.

Wave forty-seven came to a close with the repairs more than three-quarters complete. As the last monsters in wave forty-eight were cut down, the defenses had regained full functionality. Joe made sure to be present after he realized that repairing the walls with his ritual also repaired the enchantments that had been placed on them. There was something extremely satisfying about seeing a wall have a final chip of stone replaced, shine like a strobe light for a half minute, then begin bouncing along in time with all of the others.

As he thought about how he could probably figure out a way to mimic that ability, using rituals of course, Joe turned his thoughts toward the Novice-rank skill he needed to choose. From the time it became available, until it was too late to get one, was three hundred and thirty-six hours. At this point, from the start of the Beast Waves until the twenty-fifth wave, two hundred hours had passed. Until now, the remaining waves had only consumed a hundred and thirty-eight hours, leaving him with only an hour and some change until the option was lost. Even then, he would've missed it, except for the fact that wave twenty-six had been initiated early.

"Whew, that was a close one." Joe chuckled nervously as he looked at the timer that was still counting down, having had to dig through hundreds and hundreds of notifications in order to find it. "Well, at least with the energy in the air stabilized, I can just ask my faction leader. Query: Tatum, which skill or spell should I choose?"

For a moment, the air around Joe's head went still, then his mind was blasted by static, similar to when he'd tried to send a message through the walls of the greenhouse. He clutched at his ears, screaming in pain from a sound only he could hear. The sound cut off, and he pulled his palms back, noting that they were coated in blood. He healed himself, unable to even hear the words he was saying to cast the spell.

Sound returned in a rush, and he looked at the notification that was waiting for him.

Occultatum is unable to answer this Query! His attempt to inform you of a Mythical-rank spell has earned him a three-day period of silence. As it is not your fault for making the attempt, and the Skill you used was forcefully canceled, resulting in backlash, you have been compensated in the form of Skill levels!

Query (Beginner 0 → Apprentice 0). Congratulations! By reaching the Apprentice rank in this spell, you are now able to reach out to your deity twice a day for Simple answers or once a day for a Minorly Complex answer.

"Wonderful, how great is that?" Joe spat sarcastically, waiting for his Neutrality Aura to clean off any remnant blood. "A whole rank in a spell they don't let me use. *Nifty*. Why not two ranks, three? It won't *matter*, will it?"

His annoyance went unanswered by the system, which he was equal parts thankful for and annoyed with. With a sigh, he tried to think of who else he should ask, and immediately his mind went toward Havoc or Snow. Unfortunately, Joe fully understood that the two of them would most likely be busy at the moment preparing their most powerful weaponry to throw at the giant.

"Jake the Alchemist it is." Without another word, he pushed off of the wall backward, flying across open space as if he were lucid dreaming. "*Ooh*, that's nice. High Characteristics are pretty neat, too."

CHAPTER TWENTY-FIVE

For the first time, as Joe approached the Pyramid of Panacea, the doors opened on their own, granting him access immediately. Understanding that it was the choice of the building itself to do so, he paused and put a hand on the wall, "Hey, thanks so much! That was *very* nice of you to let me in right away without making me wait in the cold."

While he didn't get any kind of feedback from the building, it was possible that the floors he was walking on were just a *teeny* bit warmer. As per usual, Jake was at the center of the workspace brewing various items, and his new regular addition of the Dwarven Neophyte was standing nearby, carefully studying every motion the Alchemist made.

"Jake, I'm in a jam, and I need your advice, if you're willing to give it." Joe spoke softly, not wanting to interrupt if there was a delicate process happening. Moments later, he went still—*ecstatic* that he had been so quiet. Jake didn't spare him even a single glance; every muscle on his body was taut, and every vein on his face was bulging as he stirred the concoction he was working on.

Tapping his Ritual Orb containing Essence Cycle, Joe

watched the magical version of what was happening, and had to stumble away at the sheer flood of power that was being carefully twisted and added to the mixture. Baumann had been standing next to Jake, but upon seeing Joe, sidled backward incrementally. "Please be very, *very* quiet. Any interruption right now could kill all of us—not just the three of us."

"Yeah, I can see that." Joe was filled with disappointment, as he truly had no idea where to turn for advice. "Abyss, I was hoping that he could help me with this."

"What's on your mind? Maybe I can…?" The Dwarf trailed off as Joe let out a sigh so deep that he sank to the floor in a limp, lotus position.

"About that." Joe shrugged lightly, his arms flopping out and back to his side with the uncoordinated motion. "It's nothing crazy, I was just hoping for advice from a really high-level person. I haven't picked out my new skill or spell yet, and since it says we can grab anything…"

"Yeah, that was tough. Want to see what I figured out, though?" Baumann smirked at the bald Ritualist, who admittedly had his curiosity piqued. "I think that the skill you should get is **smorgasbord*."

"Did… did you just tell me to get a smorgasbord?" Joe couldn't help but let out a huff of laughter. "How'd you do that? It sounded like you were underwater."

"Yeah, I think the system messed up by not putting any constraints on the skill or spell we could get. In an attempt to fix that, it jumbles anything that might give you a hint at a higher power skill or spell then you've earned. It works with writing the skill down, as well."

In a way, the words of the Neophyte were a massive relief. Knowing that he'd have to make the decision on his own meant that he hadn't screwed up too badly by waiting this long to seek advice. "Thanks, Baumann. I guess… I should just decide what would be the best thing for me to have, and if I should plan short-term or long-term."

"Well, you have about an hour to think about it." The

Dwarf clapped him on the shoulder, then sat down next to the Ritualist, surprising him. "I've been trying to gain some insight into Alchemy by observing the Venerable Alchemist, but it's about as useful as trying to replicate his ability to duplicate his Ichors. Pretty much useless, in other words. The level of control needed for things at this rank? All watching and trying to learn does is burn my brain."

They sat in silence for a few minutes as Joe pondered his choices, casually watching as Jake strained and struggled to shift his oversized spoon another millimeter. "*Feces*, that looks difficult."

"You're telling me." Baumann agreed with incredulousness filling his voice. "The only thing I could figure out was that he was moving each molecule independently of the ones next to it. The amount of focus and control over his craft is… utterly astounding. I can only hope that someday *I* can reach a Sage rank at least *half* as potent as his."

Joe shot the Dwarf a glance, quirking his lips and shaking his head. "Jake is a Master at Alchemy. If you keep saying 'Sage', people are going to look at him funny and laugh at you for not understanding the difference. I get a notification every time I train under anyone, and it told me he was a Master. That was like… I don't know, a standard day or two ago? Four? Time is a little funky for me right now. I'm keeping track of it only thanks to the Beast Waves. Now *there's* a clock you can set your watch by."

"Uh, *no*, Joe." Baumann scoffed at the Ritualist. "Jake is *the* Sage of Alchemy. *The* Sage. I don't know why he's showing as a Master to you, maybe that was just his teaching skill or something? Or he's intentionally hiding his true rank, and I just messed up pretty badly by telling you. If he's hiding it, the message you got would look strange compared to others, if you were paying attention."

Thinking back to his recent training session, Joe paled as he realized that there *had* been some inconsistencies. Brow furrowing, he thought back to what other parts of his conversation with the Neophyte he'd considered to simply be quirks of his speech. His words came out slowly, though his thoughts were flying through his brain. "You've told me a *couple* of times now that he's a Sage. Why haven't I picked up on that?"

"Um." The Dwarf swallowed as he stared at Jake, who, even though he was focused to the extreme, could most likely hear and understand what they were talking about. He just couldn't intervene. "Yeah, when he was talking about taking me on as an acolyte, he shared that with me as a way to convince me. As to why you never picked up on it? I don't know? It could be something he actively controls, such as a powder or spell that he uses to make you not think about it. But… maybe, with him in this state… I think I should stop talking."

Joe pulled out a notebook and started writing everything down, just in case he 'mysteriously forgot about it' in the future. As he wrote down the entirety of the conversation between the two of them, he blinked as he read over a line that was in his head, but he had previously dismissed. "Baumann. When you said 'it's about as useful as trying to replicate his ability to duplicate Ichor', you meant the Artifact-rank Alchemy product, right? Did you mean that he can follow a recipe and make it again or *literally* duplicate it?"

"Um. I'm really uncomfortable sharing secrets that I may not have realized were secrets."

"*Baumann*!" Joe wanted to shake the Dwarf to get the answers to rattle out of him, but he controlled himself so as to not mess up the progress of the Alchemist. His words came out in a soft hiss, "literal or figurative, that's all I need to know. Then I will leave immediately."

"I was being… literal?" the Dwarf started breathing heavily, his eyes flicking between the two powerful people in the room.

Immediately, Joe got to his feet and pulled the Neophyte up as well. "Thank you for this lovely conversation about the weather. I hope that you stay warm and have a very pleasant day."

"What? That's not what we were–"

The smile on Joe's face stretched into a rictus grin, and his eyes bulged out as he stared the Dwarf down. "I have *no idea* what you're talking about. Anyway, thanks for the tip about the warmer weather. Have a *nice day*."

Joe turned on his heel and walked out of the pyramid, leaving the stunned and confused trainee behind him. Refusing to say another word to anyone else, he hurried to his workshop, locked himself in, then entered the vault, and barred that behind him as well.

"System, I've made my decision. If it's possible, I'd like to take the skill or spell 'Ritual Duplication'."

Congratulations on choosing a new spell! You have gained the spell Ritual Duplication (Novice I).

Congratulations! You are the only living entity to attain the Sage rank in Ritual Magic! Reward 1 of—error—: Ritual Duplication (Novice I).

System error. Wait just a doggone minute… Calculating… Processing… verifying skill eligibility… nope, nope, nope*!*

System alert: security protocol 401-A initiated. Cross-referencing divine interventions database… scanning for unauthorized deity activity… Tatum, if this was you, I <u>*swear*</u> *you're going into the Archives.*

As he'd been expecting something new and interesting to happen, Joe was able to maintain his cool. He sat on the floor, in the lotus position, keeping his face serene and his eyes closed. "Don't look at the magic that is probably thundering around me right now. Sorry mod, not trying to make your life hard. Just trying to snag a cool reward, since it's available."

He began to gently hum, and as the moments ticked by, he had to continuously force his breathing pattern into a relaxed state. After ninety tense seconds, another set of notifications began appearing. These slowly scrawled across his vision, as though someone were reluctantly typing them onto the screen instead of dropping the entire message at a time as was usual.

System verification complete. No divine interventions have been detected. No laws of magic or bending of the universe were detected. Space-time continuum verified for integrity. Recent conversations scanned, point of origin for determination of skill verified. That's right, we had to pull in an admin and read your entire conversation log to make sure our ban on skill explanations wasn't defective. Are you really just this…?

Even though the messages paused at that point, Joe decided against opening his mouth. Another minute and a half passed, and again the reluctant typing continued.

Well, I guess you get it, Joe. One somewhat confused, shiny, absolutely-not-stolen-from-a-deity spell ready for you to have a blast with.

*You have gained the spell Ritual Duplication (**Mythical, Immutably Unique**).*

Ritual Duplication (Novice I): This spell allows you to effortlessly clone an existing ritual with just a touch, transferring all of the magical symbology, geometry, intention, component requirements, stabilizers, celestial alignments, alchemical, enchantment enhancements, and mana requirements to instantly create a duplicate ritual circle. Congrats, you are the magical equivalent of a photocopy machine, only much more dangerous.

Skill mechanics (We added some spacing because it's a pretty chunky skill, and you don't have the proper foundation to fully appreciate it.)

How to use: Touch an inactive ritual. Use this spell. Pretty self-explanatory.

Notes on limitations: only rituals of the same rank or lower can be duplicated. No stretching the edges of this spell, sorry. We highly recommend you try anyway.

Immutably Unique: Only one entity can have this spell. It's supposed to be whoever gets to the Sage rank in Ritual Magic first, but we guess it is going to be you instead. If you would be so kind, hit that rank first, so we don't have a conflict of interest.

Now we get to tell you about the fun part: why this is going to be so very difficult for you to use. First, there is a mana and resource cost multiplier set at (100-.5n)% where n = spell level (maximum 25% discount). Secondly, each additional duplication of the ritual or one of its duplicates doubles the mana and resource cost—this is only applicable to a specific ritual that has been duplicated. Creating multiple of them by hand will still allow you to duplicate each of them (once) without incurring the doubling cost.

That's about it. So. Great. I'm starting to see why your previous mod tried to nerf you so hard. Oh, I'm also taking all of your Karmic Luck. That should help balance you in the short term.

Karmic Luck: 26 → 0.

Joe waited a few more seconds, then a couple of minutes, just to make sure there was nothing else coming. Then, he got to his feet, dusted off his legs, stretched lightly, and took a deep breath.

Then he screamed, jumping in the air and swinging his arms around wildly.

"*Yes*!"

CHAPTER TWENTY-SIX

Before he knew it, he was standing atop the walls of the Town, doing what anyone that had just gained a spell like this would be doing.

Using it.

Joe glanced at his current aspect count for Damaged aspects, which was all he needed in order to cast Novice rank rituals. "A little over fifteen million. Well, I don't think I'm going to run out of these anytime soon."

Lifting his hand, he made a *completely* unnecessary gesture and drew a circle in the air using Somatic Ritual Casting. With just a hint of intent, he was able to shift the coloration of the Ritual of Glimmering and how it would output its light. Typically, he allowed the ritual to act as a light bulb, sending light in all directions around it. But for his current purposes, that would be detrimental. "Daylight with the output focused as a cone to create a flood light. Good!"

This was a nice and easy low-rank ritual, which had been attuned to its constellation. With that thought in mind, Joe decided to see if the attunement would also be copied over by using his new spell. Placing his left hand on the floating magical diagram, he smiled and muttered, "No time like the present to find out! Ritual Duplication!"

Instantly, the ritual was formed in the air above his *right* hand. Joe inspected it, seeing no difference whatsoever between his first version and the new one. Taking a deep breath, he bunched his muscles and broke into an intense lateral run, shuffling as quickly as he could with his massively inflated Characteristics. The ritual, which had only taken a few seconds to form with his Somatic Ritual Casting, was even *faster* with the duplication ability. His bottleneck was his ability to cast the spell, which at the Novice rank, was reliant on actually saying the words out loud.

Still, thanks to his physique, Dexterity, and mental acuity, it only took a hair over one and a half seconds of continuously casting at roughly ten times a second to be forced to stop. A quick check of his notifications made him let out a light whistle.

Ritual of Glimmering aspect cost:

509.44 Mana, 1,018.88 Damaged Aspects

1,018.88 Mana, 2,037.76 Damaged Aspects

2,037.76 Mana, 4,075.52 Damaged Aspects

"Just like that, I'm out of mana." He checked the rituals he had hanging in the air, shaking his head in frustration. "Thirteen of the most basic rituals that exist; that's all I can manage?"

With a grunt of dissatisfaction, he walked along the line he'd created and poked each of the rituals, activating them with a single point of mana. Immediately, a bright wave of light lit up the landscape, each of the frequencies exactly the same, to the point that it looked like daylight had come early to this patch of ground. Of course, Joe couldn't actually see the ground, due to the hundreds of thousands of monsters that were surrounding their walls at the moment.

"Feces on a stick, how many monsters are coming during each wave?" As far as he could see, there wasn't a single patch of snow visible under the enormous bodies of the beasts just waiting for their chance to try and test the defenses. He shook his head and looked at the horizon, where the enormous giant had grown significantly closer, but was still mostly hidden behind the horizon. "That's right, you just *stay* away, big boy."

With the knowledge that his mana was going to be the majority of his bottleneck for using this spell, Joe started working out how he could use it to its best effect. "If I give myself plenty of time to refill my mana, and remove all of my active effects, I could duplicate something so that I'd have fifteen versions of it."

Skill level increased!

Ritual Duplication (Novice I → Novice VIII).

He immediately redid his math, shaking his head when he realized that it didn't change the fact that he'd need to have a mana pool of over fifteen thousand in order to duplicate this ritual a fifteenth time to have sixteen total versions. Then he had a thought that made him chuckle softly. "That's a long way off. I bet, by the time I hit the Sage rank in Ritual Magic, I'll have enough mana to do it pretty easily."

That was only taking into consideration the lowest level ritual that he had, which took him a grand total of two mana to create. Anything else, which would take more mana to craft, would obviously have greater restrictions. "Still, a bunch of these in a second and a half. At some point, this'll have amazing functionality in combat. I'll get into a duel with a wizard, he'll send a fireball at me, and I'll set off a half dozen Rituals of Proximity, wind blade style. That'll pelt him with nearly two thousand wind blades a second. I wonder who'll win *that* fight. Heh."

Shoving aside his delusions of grandeur, Joe reluctantly stopped playing with his new toy and went off to do some real work. As he'd created an Expert-ranked version of the Ritual of Slaughter, he decided to get it in place immediately. While he hoped he wouldn't need to use it, Joe was almost positive it would come into play against the Legendary giant bearing down on them.

He had the template, his own creation—which still sent a thrill through his mind whenever he thought about it—but he still needed to inscribe it on an Expert-ranked material, namely Jotunheim Alloy, so that he could have a working version.

As he pounded on glowing aspects in the forge, he daydreamed about making a ritual that could do his crafting work for him while still providing experience to the skill. Unfortunately, working with Expert-ranked aspects and daydreaming was practically the same as begging to have the attempt fail, rather explosively. This time, he actually had to fight off the other smiths in the area, who were sick of him coating them in layers of loose aspects, which dealt true damage wherever they landed.

Apparently, in their minds, it was *not* the same as being lit on fire, as they had various skills that gave them resistance to heat and open flame. Who knew?

In order to alleviate the situation, Joe was banished from the best forge, directly in the center of the building, and exiled to the farthest corner, where he was surrounded by walls on two sides. By the time he emerged from the forge victorious, or at least having enough metal to make a double handful of ritual tiles, Beast Wave fifty-three was just finishing up.

"I think I might be getting better at this," Joe commented to himself. "It took me less than thirty hours to put these together. Nice. Also, Knowledge, Enchanting Lore, Smithing Lore."

As his mana was siphoned into his brain, Joe looked over the increases that he'd gained both from the use of his spell and his time working to create Expert-ranked metals.

Skill Increases:

Ritualistic Forging (Journeyman II → VII)

Enchanting Lore (Student IX → Journeyman 0)

Smithing Lore (Student VII →Student VIII)

Acknowledging his progress, Joe hurried to complete his

next project, the ritual itself, with the knowledge that the boss monster of the sixtieth wave could approach at any time. He wasn't the only person running around and preparing desperately; if the Monster coming at them in the near future was going to be anything like the Pachycephalosaurus Palisade Puncher, they needed to be ready to not only fend it off, but jump on repairs immediately. "Abyss… that was only the boss of the fiftieth wave. What is it going to look like at the eightieth? Or when that Legendary gets here?"

With his heart lodged in his throat, Joe took a deep breath and tried to let go of the anxiety. "Can't live in the future, I can only plan for it. We've got this. I'm not the only one who'll be deciding the outcome of this fight. All I can do is my best."

His arrival at the workshop didn't go unnoticed, and as Joe set out his tiles, the entire group of the Ritualist Aspirants showed up at his door with hope in their eyes, trying to finagle a new lesson from him. The bald councilman nearly sent them packing but paused as he stuck his tongue out and held it at the corner of his mouth in thought. "Yeah, come on in. I don't know how much you'll be able to learn, but I'm just about to create an Expert-ranked ritual. If you want to see what it looks like, just stay quiet and know that if it goes sideways, everyone in the room dies."

Only three-quarters of the group chose to enter the room after his proclamation, and after triple checking to make sure that none of the others would be joining them, Joe firmly shut the door and turned to those in the room with him. "Anyone outside of that door just lost the chance to gain the Ritualist class. You came here for lessons, but at the first sign of danger, *they* turned away. This isn't a *safe* profession. Congratulations to the twenty-three of you who stayed. I hope you live through the next little while, perhaps even learning something."

He started by creating a chalk outline of the ritual he was going to be carving into the surface of his metal ritual tiles. "First off, every item has a maximum flow of Mana it can contain before going critical. Typically, you can put enchantments–or in this case, rituals–of a single rank higher than the material you're placing it on. I've only been able to confirm this up to the Expert ranks, as I've never attempted to put a Master-rank ritual on something less than a Master-rank item."

Then he blinked and amended his statement. "Oh, we should work on getting all of you the skill Somatic Ritual Casting when we get to that stage. Because my previous statement has a caveat. You *can* put everything up to the Sage rank in mid-air *if* you have the ability to perfectly form it and maintain the imagery in your mind *and* the stability required while forming it. I guess that means you can put it on material at the correct rarity *or nothing*, but materials in between will simply not suffice. Hah! That's great."

Nearly everyone was furiously scribbling down the words tumbling out of his mouth, but Joe didn't even notice. He had already retreated to the recesses of his own mind as he started pulling on his passive skills to assist in the creation of the Expert-ranked Ritual of Slaughter. "Make sure you stand back, I don't want to accidentally include you in the targeting portion of this design. No, I'm kidding. Mostly. Now, what I do here will be a little different than how you do it. I've specialized twice in this class and have the ability to forgo standard materials by substituting a type of energy called 'aspects'."

As he pulled out his Aspect Inscriber, quickly inspecting it for flaws, the Ritualist continued his one-sided lecture. "Don't try this at home, or without me. Actually, don't worry about this for a long, long time. I know all of you are coming from other classes, and you must be fairly powerful at them. But, unlike in smithing, every single part of this must be exact, or you could end up with extremely unfortunate or unexpected outcomes. I'm not doing all of this freehand, even if it might look like I am. Even the chalk outline was assisted by my Master rank in both Ritual Circles and Ritual Magic, as well as a profession, and my Lore skills in Calculus and Number Theory, Celestial Arcane Interactions, and the basic Ritual Lore skill."

Brightly shining aspects flowed out of the tip of his inscriber, melting through the surface of the Jotunheim Alloy with ease as its minuscule true damage was applied to the surface of the metal. "Exactness to the millimeter, that's the requirement to be crafting rituals at the Expert rank. Unless I miss my guess, that requirement is going to be exactness to the micrometer by the time I'm trying my hand at Grandmaster rituals. Note the word 'trying'. Fun fact, I'll probably have to pick up some supporting skills so that my heartbeat doesn't throw off the depth I'm trying to press with my inscribing tool."

"*Abyss*, dude." One of the humans whispered, almost making Joe lose focus to grin at him. The Ritualist barely maintained his poise, managing to complete the line he was working on before chuckling aloud.

"Let's get into the meat of it. Here's where the number theory comes in. As I cut each line, curve, and symbol, you can also assign it a numerical value. Typically, each of the lines, especially the circle—which should be fairly obvious—can be determined with a straightforward calculation. In order to create rituals or upgrade them, as it turns out, the basic premise is to balance the ritual. My method involves making them perfectly symmetrical, using prime number theory."

On and on he talked, detailing the *why* behind every action he took, every pause between finishing one line and starting the next. Eventually, as the circles glowed with the multiple radiances that the aspects exuded, Joe was brightly lit up, and he took a moment to sweep his gaze around the circle of students. With one last flourish, the ritual design was complete, and the varied spectrum of lights shifted until they were a standard blue. The entire ritual converted to a spell diagram that existed solely as mana within the lines of material.

"If anyone is wondering, *this* is how you make magic out of math and stars." Joe let out a deep exhale, wiping his forehead out of habit as he lifted the tile and inspected it for any flaws. When he found it to be perfect, he looked around at the utterly amazed, bewildered students, and wiggled the chunk of metal at them. "Now, who wants to see an Expert-ranked ritual get activated?"

Perhaps it was the fact that the people who had stayed out of the workshop had been booted from his course, maybe it was because they were truly interested, but every single hand in the room shot into the air.

CHAPTER TWENTY-SEVEN

The first step in setting up the new Ritual of Slaughter was going over and getting Socar to approve the placement of it. As this ritual had a much higher etheric fingerprint, Joe had been concerned that it would throw off the balance of the delicate Formation Socar had been designing. Happily, there was no conflict, and Joe was able to begin dismantling the previously-placed ritual and replacing it with its upgraded big brother.

Once it was in position, and Joe had ensured that every station was set to be well-aligned not only with the Formation, but the constellation clusters, he paused for a long moment. Hundreds of people had surrounded his burgeoning coven, ready to jump in and assist with the activation of such a powerful weapon against the swarming monsters. Still, something made Joe hesitate. "Why don't I want to activate-?"

His eyes went wide as he remembered the terminology of his ritual duplication spell. "I can't duplicate an active ritual; I can only duplicate a created but inactive one. Wait. Silly brain, I can't duplicate it. My skill level is *way* too low."

Pushing aside his misgivings, as he had correctly identified them, the Ritualist began pumping mana into the design. He used the entirety of his Coven of twenty-three aspirants to make up the Novice ritual circle, as there was a perfect prime number in their presence. From there, he arranged the volunteers all the way out until the sixth circle, which had hundreds of people standing inside of it.

They would have the largest amount of mana drawn from them, and the Ritualist had no desire to see his brand new creation fail because he wasn't willing to use *all* of the help that had been offered. When he was ready, and a platoon of Legionnaires had been stationed around the site—orders of the council, after the last hullabaloo when activating a powerful ritual—he fully activated the diagram and exulted in the power he had to channel into it.

Thousands upon thousands of points of mana swirled in from all sides, and that was after taking into account all of his cost reduction bonuses. "No idea how many people are going to be required when my students are the ones activating this. I hope they get good bonuses as well, when they earn their class."

There was only one minor issue with the ritual's setup, and that was when an arrow came streaking from the battlements, aimed at the side of Joe's face. Luckily, a Dwarf shot into the air and smacked the arrow away with his shield, releasing a thundering sound like ringing a dinner bell. Dozens of people converged on the location the arrow had come from, apprehending the Elven-sympathizing infiltrator who had tried to take Joe down in his moment of weakness.

"Not a huge fan of being bait, but if it works, it works." As the ritual ended, Joe casually scooped up the active ritual tile, pulling on it gently and coming away with two sets of five plates. Checking over the information of the ritual once more, he confirmed that the first five were the flags for the ritual that would add an incremental counter to each of the monsters that fulfilled its conditions. The second set were power plates, which could have additional mana added to them during the moments when the ritual was spinning up after its trap was sprung.

As the crowd dispersed, Joe tried to mingle with it to lower the chances that an unfriendly entity would be able to keep an eye on his movements. He had to set the flags first, and that started with the Expert-ranked final activation flag. It would trigger only when something hit the structure it was attached to, and Joe set it against the Town Hall as per usual. He hoped it would activate in time to defeat whatever attacked it, instead of being a strike in retaliation for the destruction of the facility they'd pinned all of their hopes on.

The next flags were harder to plant, as the walls now moved. They only iterated when a monster went in front of them, but they also needed to be in an unmoving area so they would interface with the rest of the rituals correctly. Eventually, he had to settle with putting them on the bunkers in each of the four suburb areas within the walls. Those were the only structures that remained in the same position at all times.

"I should go check with Socar and see how the movement of the walls is impacting his Formation. Does it wax and wane in power as the walls approach the positions they started in? Or is it completely messing things up?" Joe had plenty of time to think as he raced through the killing corridors, dropping off his formation flags as needed. Eventually, he decided against going and bothering the Mage, figuring he would've brought it up if there was an issue.

Then came the question of the power plates. Joe knew what he *wanted* to do with them: he wanted to slap them on top of the Mana Battery recharge stations and have those dump all of their mana payload into the plates when the ritual activated. Unfortunately, that wasn't possible. The only time the plates could accept additional mana was when the trap was in the midst of being sprung. If he put them on the tabletop portion of the stations, one or both of the magical items would be damaged.

Then, **pop**.

After consulting with the employee who was stuck in the

bubble, Joe came to a compromise. "You're sure you are okay with this?"

"Yeah, why not? That kind of a bonus just to set this plate on top of the table if something manages to land a hit on the Town Hall? *Yeah.* I'm perfectly fine with that being my responsibility." The ecstatic individual accepted the power plate happily, keeping it in his offhand as he worked to swap batteries in and out of their recharge slots. As Joe turned away, debating on what he should do with the other four plates, the human spoke up once more. "Is this just going to be me, or are you going to make this a responsibility of all of the people who are recharging batteries?"

"Well, you and whoever your replacement is. I *hope* you'll hand that off when it's their turn." Joe tried not to sound condescending, but he also didn't think it had to be explained that there was a very limited time frame in which putting the ritual plate in place would be useful.

"Nah, I meant the other recharge station operators. We've got half a dozen of these set up around Town now. Havoc just has the others stuck in a hole so they aren't easily visible or hit. Actually, this station is gonna get sunk in about two hours, too." The casual way in which the man explained that they were ringed by doomsday weapons made Joe blanch; but instead of panicking, he decided to take the opportunity for what it was. Keeping his mouth shut, his lips pressed in a firm line, he set out to find other stations and hand off the plates along with the promise of a generous bonus if they were correctly used.

With that taken care of and out of the way, and everyone as happy as they could be, Joe turned his mind to the power plates themselves. "I wonder if I could extract this component from the ritual and put it in place for other things? All of my rituals have a specific mana input section, and... I guess the question is, if I just dumped tons of power into a ritual, would it work harder or go *boom*?"

Very specifically, Joe wanted to figure out if he could further empower the planar shift ritual and spell. With its current mode of operation, the ritual would take mana per second to keep the elemental plane of coffee phased into an integrated with this world. "If Mate thinks he could make coffee for up to ten thousand people with this active, as-is, what would he be able to do if I supercharged the ritual while he was the only creature that could harness the power? I kinda... yeah, I kind of want to try that out."

It would be a long-term project, as it would need to be tested far, far away from a populated area. If it worked perfectly, great! But that was almost guaranteed to be the *least* likely outcome. He could permanently phase a chunk of this world away, he could accidentally drown thousands of people in coffee—yes, the best way to go, but still bad—or a *myriad* of other consequences he simply didn't have enough information to even consider.

His cheerful planning session came to an abrupt halt as a deep rumbling filled the air. At first, it felt like the very edge of a thunderstorm, where you could just barely make out that something was coming. The sound grew, displacing the air and causing Joe's clothing to flap around him in the sudden wind. He pushed against it, running forward and Omnivaulting upward just in time to grab someone who had been thrown off of the battlements. Catching the Dwarf, Joe was able to push off the snow in the air and throw them onto the walls once more. "Careful, there! Any idea what this is?"

"N-n-no." Seeing a *Dwarf* shiver this violently made Joe realize that the air up here was even colder than it had been when they first arrived on this world, without any wall to slow down the wind. That put a frown on the face of the Ritualist; he'd been getting used to the slightly warmed breeze that had been blowing toward them ever since they'd planted the ring of exothermic plants.

"What in the abyss is going on?" Far off in the distance, the tangles of plants—which had creeped much, *much* closer than he had originally planted them—were suddenly blazing with an incredibly bright light. Recalling the details that had been provided about them, Joe realized that the incredibly intense cold was not hitting just them. "Those plants grow faster, releasing more heat, the colder it is around them. For them to be spreading like a literal wildfire across the surface of Jotunheim means…"

The thunder resolved into words at that moment, and Joe was nearly pushed to his knees by the actual force of the sound hitting him.

"One chance, and one chance only. Flee."

The words themselves were cataclysmically loud, and the millions of monster bodies undulating around Town were affected first. Those closer to the Legendary giant in the far distance were thrown into the air, some of them dozens or even hundreds of feet. Others cowered in fear, and those already close enough to attack the city threw themselves against it with renewed vigor.

After the sudden hush had passed, every defender not actively engaged in combat raised their weapons and shouted their own war cries back at the giant in the distance. The air practically turned blue from all of the foul language filtering outward, and Joe had to avert his eyes from some of the more… *flagrant* displays of disrespect being sent at the giant. True to his words, the giant didn't speak again. Still, their obvious defiance *did* elicit a response.

From what Joe could tell, this monster was wearing some kind of clothing. Every once in a while, when the winds allowed, light flashed off of its face, hinting at it wearing some kind of reflective eyewear or perhaps a mask. At this distance, it was simply impossible to tell. But the coat or maybe scarf of the giant had been a point of conversation for days now. Even Joe, who hadn't participated in the gossip—much—had seen how this monster was wearing something to warm itself up. This oddity was doubly curious on a world completely consumed with keeping everything frozen.

The giant's hand reached up, up, up, for dozens of seconds, until it grasped the dangling garment. Then it pulled and threw it forward toward the city. It fluttered oddly in the air as it slowly approached the ground, then, just before touching down, enormous legs made themselves visible from the base of the fur. As wave fifty-eight began, the system gave them a terrifying notification.

Alert! A Metropolis-ranked threat is approaching the city!

CHAPTER TWENTY-EIGHT

Razorscarf the Polar Polecat has been set loose to destroy you!

The message was succinct, but terrifying for its simplicity. As soon as the creature touched down, Joe's eyes could barely make it out. Still, it was enough to know that it was coming, and the beast kept them abreast of its location thanks to releasing an unending, ear-piercing battle cry as it charged toward them.

As it approached the back ranks of the million-strong swarm, Joe expected to see Penguins and Hoardlings go flying as it barreled through their ranks. Instead, just before it hit the waiting units, the ferret dove under the snow, looking for all the world like a giant mouth had opened up and **slurped** down a fuzzy noodle.

"Abyss, is that a burrowing monster?" As his question was taken up by those around him, eventually shouted until people ran off in all directions to try and put last moment contingencies in place, Joe noticed where the creature must be moving. His powerful Perception allowed him to pick out the plume of snow generated by the creature's passing. "Wait! I don't think it's burrowing; I think it's only tunneling through the top layer of snow!"

His thoughts were backed up by how the mound moved, forcing the monsters atop it to stumble or be thrown if they were light enough. Not enough to damage them, unfortunately, but certainly enough to be a noticeable disturbance in the usual movement patterns. As his shell-shocked mind tried to make a plan, a nearby scout began shouting out a report.

"The monster is a ferret, a type of carnivorous—sorry, omnivorous—polecat! Initial estimates put it at four hundred feet long, two hundred feet tall, but only twenty-eight feet wide. It looks much larger than that, but that's only its fur. This thing is *fluffy*. If you have it, switch over to a flame-based attack and burn that critter to a crisp!"

It moved with astonishing speed, especially as it was not moving along the surface, plowing through the monster horde as if they were a mere annoyance. As It sped closer, the Dwarves started shouting encouragement to each other, and Joe's senses heightened as adrenaline pumped through his veins.

"Get ready, bros!" a sergeant hollered as he unsheathed four swords, holding two in each hand. "It's about to be an all-you-can-kill buffet, and our diet ended yesterday!"

"It's war crime time!" This voice was near maniacal, and Joe's eyes tracked the speaker instantly, revealing a somewhat familiar Dwarf holding an incredibly reflective canister. "I've been waiting... *heehee*, waiting... it's been way too long!"

"Thirty seconds until impact!" The scout was still calling out instructions. The conversations died down as the tensions hit a new height. "Five seconds... *brace*!"

The ferocious ferret seemed to still be following the commands that had been injected into every monster's mind; the blasting snow tunnel was aimed directly at the entrance to the killing corridors. There was no more snow to hide under as it came within range, so the swift creature was ejected from the subnivean tunnel and revealed in all of its terrifying glory.

Ballista bolts, enormous spells, and in one case, a too-shiny canister, were waiting to greet the Artifact-ranked beast. At first, Joe thought that the world had gone silent, but then he realized that the blast from the combined power had simply deafened him for a moment, simultaneous with the tribulation-lightning-grade light that was released.

The first sound Joe could make out after that was a high-pitched keening wail coming from the mouth of the ferret. His eyelids fluttered rapidly, clearing the spots in his vision while trying to find even the *silhouette* of the creature. For a few fractions of a second, even with the immensity of the beast, his watering eyes made it impossible to focus on the boss monster.

As Razorscarf finally came back into view, the fur along the entire creature's head and over a third of its body was already burned away. The furless areas showed that the creature was less than a quarter as tall as its fur had originally suggested, not that Joe wanted to look too closely at the weeping sores it had instead of healthy flesh. Deep chunks of thermite and other superheated metals were embedded in the exposed skin, releasing noxious fumes and causing continuous damage, but... at least as far as the Ritualist could tell... the potent polecat wasn't permanently plastered on the pavement.

As a matter of fact, the crowd realized all at once that the boss wasn't holding still because it was shaking from pain. No. It had paused its assault only because it was quivering with unutterable rage.

Joe wasn't entirely certain how to describe the sound that it made, but it expressed the wrath of the creature perfectly. Razorscarf began its movement once again, lashing out like a tantruming toddler at every inconvenience in its way. The walls it was forced to squeeze between gained new gouges along the entire length of their structures. Monsters that impeded its progress were snapped up and swallowed whole. The Ritualist noted with concern how the gaping wounds and damage over time effects of the fire seemed to lessen every time the monster swallowed a lump of meat.

"No visible area affects! Almost all of its power must be tied up in speed and regeneration!" A section commander bellowed out. His observations were echoed along the walls, and thousands upon thousands of attacks streamed down on the monster —though they feared it still might not be enough. Over half of the fighting force left their positions behind, as even the melee fighters were able to actively attack the massive monster from their prominent positions while still safe on the wall. Frankly, the fact that the ferret was forced to follow the labyrinth was shocking to Joe, as it loomed above the walls—almost thrice the height of the stone edifices.

Unfortunately, most of the combatants were simply not fast enough to land heavily damaging strikes on the critter, as only its front half was exposed to the attacks they could inflict. Huge clouds of hair flew into the air each second, falling to the ground and impaling anyone who had the misfortune of being on the receiving end of their descent. Someone called out, "The fur is as sharp as razors! Watch that!"

Were the situation not so serious, Joe would've laughed out loud when he heard a nearby fighter mutter "Razorscarf. Yeah. The name is making a little more sense now."

Help came in a form Joe hadn't been expecting. As the ferret made a loop around the entire city—allowing the defenders that had stayed put another shot at landing a strike—thick shadows wrapped around the Boss Monster, and its speed dropped to nearly a quarter of what it had been mere moments previously.

The effect only lasted approximately one full second, but that was enough for *hundreds* of hits to land home. Then the beast was moving at full speed once more, hissing and spitting in pain as the gaping wounds started closing almost immediately. Joe noticed with concern that whenever the skin had closed fully, new hair began sprouting in the next moment. "Abyss, that's an armor and weapon all in one, and it's coming back so *fast*!"

Darkness struck the ferret once more, and it was slowed again, but not even for a full second this time.

Joe's Ritual of Communication lit up, and he pulled it to ear level without a second thought. Heartpiercer's voice rang through it, her shout barely able to be heard above the din of battle. "I see you out there! I'm the only one who can actually *hit* this thing from a distance, so I'm aiming the slowing ritual instead of letting the automated attack go off. Listen, alert everyone around you that the Grandmasters and Masters *can't* help with this threat. They're entirely focused on their preparations for throwing everything they have against the giant. Get the word out: anyone who has a trump card needs to play it *now.*"

"I'm on it," Joe snapped back, before repeating what he'd been told to a scout. Moments later, a glowing device amplified the Dwarf's voice and repeated what Joe had told him. As the announcement was rolling out, Joe shouted additional questions to the archer. "Do you have a good vantage point? *Any* kind of information you can give me would be helpful!"

"Dude. I have nothing." Her voice came back completely flat, emotionless as though she was doing her best to keep it together. "All I know is, without the Grandmasters intervening, there's no way to beat this thing head-on. We need to stack damage over time as much as possible. Burn it, coat it in acid, hit it with draining spells, pump it full of toxins, poison it! *Anything* that you can think of, you need to do right now! I'll focus on slowing it down as much as possible, but it's already looking like this ritual is losing effectiveness against it."

"Does anybody have *something* that'll slow its regeneration?" Another voice screamed, drowning out anything else the Archer was trying to say. "The fur is growing so fast!"

Joe cursed lightly as he remembered the 'Shred' debuff that had been applied to the Athame, a debuff he'd considered too brutal and therefore reduced into aspects. "Feces on a stick, why'd I have to go and get rid of the ritual that would have brought Morsum here? That would've been *perfect* for stacking damage over time."

As he lamented the fact that he had switched out the rituals contained in his orbs, Joe struck on an idea. It was a *terrible* idea, a no-good absolute wreck of an idea, confirmed by the slew of threshold debuff notifications that tried to fill his vision. Even so, it was the only thing he could think of. The Ritualist threw himself into motion. Whenever the tall-as-an-office-building body blocked his bounding, he repeatedly cast Infernal Conflagration, coating the ferret in ghastly flames—which **wailed** as they clung to its towering bulk.

Just as Joe jumped forward again, it seemed that Razorscarf had finally had enough.

It leaned back, rearing up on its legs and swiping at the walls blocking it from entering the Town directly. Three sections of the wall exploded into rubble before the strike had finished, and it pushed its body through and into the next killing corridor by simply dropping to all fours and skittering forward. As it lifted its paw to reenact the horrifying strike, the Ritual of Clinging Shadows wrapped around it once more, causing the ferret to swing as if it were moving in slow motion.

Joe got ahead of it, Omnivaulting over the final walls and positioning himself at the mouth of the labyrinth. "I really hope this works. *Please* work!"

The polecat *walloped* the wall, utterly erasing another set of the barricades from existence. The clinging shadows faded, and it lurched forward at the final set of protections blocking it from entering the Town directly. Joe began to channel his mana, beyond thankful that the ferret didn't simply hop over the small hurdle in its path. "I love game logic. I hope you still love me, mod! So sorry to make your life difficult. I'm a changed man, I'm reformed! Watch me play nice and not try to get around the rules for at least… at *least* a week!"

The claw-tipped paw swung down and hit the final wall…

…and rebounded off of it so abruptly that Joe could hear dozens of bones in its leg break even from this distance.

A smirk appeared on Joe's face, pleased with that outcome, even though it wasn't what he had been expecting. "That's right, you overgrown mouse! The outer walls are stone, but the inner ring is solid Ebonsteel. Not going to get through *that* so easily."

The ferret swung its other paw in a rage, and Joe saw the wall it had struck instantly deform. Any trace of a smile that had been on his face vanished instantly.

"I *did* say 'not as easily'. I never said you *couldn't* do it."

CHAPTER TWENTY-NINE

To the great relief of not only Joe, but the thousands of assembled Legionnaires and independent combatants preparing to hold the line, Razorscarf gave up on the idea of smashing through the Ebonsteel wall. Whether it was due to the compulsion or rules of this world that he could only guess at, the ferret turned and began flowing through the killing corridors once again, knocking aside and impaling any monsters.

Even with how his adrenaline was pounding through his veins at the moment, Joe couldn't help but appreciate the fact that they would only have to face this one monster, as it was offing all of its fellow attackers. "Thanks for scraping the path clean, I guess!"

As it came ever closer to the entrance to Novusheim, Joe found himself in the center of a shield wall, eight rows from the front. There was something about being surrounded by a wall of metal and pointy objects—aimed at someone else—that was truly calming to the spirit during combat. His third Ritual Orb snapped open, unspooling with a **twang** of metal, followed by the fourth, but the charred remnants of Razorscarf's whiskers had entered their view by the time his fifth orb was flying into the air. "Abyss, that thing's *moving*! I can get this diagram set up in under five seconds, and it's *still* staying ahead of me!"

As the sixth and final Ritual Orb shot into the air, exploding outward like a metal net and expanding to its position on the outer edge of the floating diagram, the front line of Dwarves slammed their shields together then heaved forward as one. The momentum of the Artifact-ranked boss was broken momentarily, and it flinched back as its sensitive nose took the blow. Swords, hammers, and spears found their mark along the flank of the beast, opening shallow wounds if they relied only on physical might.

Those who could combine their muscle with magic had a greater effect. One eye-catching sword slash—which left a flowing prismatic line of light wherever it passed—even managed to slice through the cheek of the monster from the corner of its mouth all the way back to its jaw bone. While it had been the most effective attack so far, it also exposed dozens more teeth. The monster retaliated by lunging and grabbing a half dozen people before chomping down, gore and viscera spraying out of its mouth that could now no longer close properly.

Starting to hyperventilate, the Ritualist maintained his focus as best as he could, connecting each of the metal ritual circles with various threads, forcing the individual contents of the orbs to mesh together into one cohesive item. Then he was done and ready for the next step. As he returned his gaze to the fight, the blood drained from his face.

Razorscarf was mere *feet* away at this point, shoving its way through the layers of high-powered Dwarves and humans as though it were merely pushing through a particularly stubborn pit of mud. Suddenly, being multiple layers of people away wasn't the comfort it had been. Joe grabbed Mate's Ebonsteel coffee mug, shoving it up into the air, where a lone piece of wire shaped like the end of a coat hanger wrapped around the handle and pulled it into the exact center of the ritual.

"*Planar Shift*!" With no time to lose, Joe dumped his mana

into the ritual, even as the Mana Battery at the center of the Ritual Orb of Constitution was drained down to almost nothing.

The air around him shimmered, and the light of the false sky above darkened. With a puff of air, a fragrant aroma suffused the battlefield, washing out and away from him as the elemental plane of coffee began to overlay the world of giants. Joe moved slightly, finding that there was a new resistance in the air, as though he were swimming instead of pushing through the constant light wind.

Then AutoMate erupted from the top of its container, like a genie exploding from a lamp. Always before, the elemental had been an adorable, bubbly little buddy. As more and more coffee erupted out of the mug, the intense pressure forced everyone around Joe to stumble back and the boss to slink backward in surprise and concern.

A pillar of dark liquid slammed into the ground next to Joe. Then another, and another. A fourth one struck down behind him, and the Ritualist looked upward to see his ritual acting as a tattoo in the center of the chest of a massive coffee bean. Dark liquid had surged out of the bean, forming arms and legs the size of silos that had crashed down around the Ritualist.

The elemental had taken the shape of a five-pointed star, though the five extremities were nowhere near symmetrical—the final point of the star, the head, was Mate, exactly as Joe knew the elemental.

Congratulations! Your summoned creature 'AutoMate' has been temporarily upgraded to one of the options for its Grand Elemental final form: Berry Stah.

"Dude." For some reason, the only thing that the Ritualist could focus on at the moment was the fact that the size and shape of Mate's head had only changed slightly, becoming a bit more conical while keeping the happy little coffee beans for eyes. "Your body is fifty feet tall, and your head is still… three and a half inches?"

"**Bur**. **Ble**." The elemental's voice had drastically shifted, becoming a deep grinding roar, like the sound of the machinery at a roastery.

"Right. Good enough!" Joe pointed at the ferret, which had immediately begun working to get around the empowered summon, only to be met with a reinvigorated fighting force of Dwarves. "Just like we talked about, hit it!"

Even as he gave the order, Joe began pumping his mana, as well all of his active regeneration, into the ritual to empower it further. He sank to his knees as the very fabric of reality around him transformed. In one moment, the Ritualist was standing on a blood-soaked, stinky battlefield. In the next, the velvety aroma enveloping his elemental expanded outward drastically. The air took on swirling patterns of light and dark roast coffee, stirring around each other in perfect balance, like a yin-yang symbol.

To his surprise, there was more than just liquid. From the enormous bean in the center of Berry Stah's temporary body, vines sprouted and shot out, allowing the elemental to grow even further as it transformed into a living coffee plant. Breathing became more difficult, the air now thick and stifling, but it was also deliciously imbued with blends of flavors. As his elemental prepared its attack, it began expending enormous amount of mana every instant. Steam, real steam and not an illusion like the elemental overlay, erupted from its fluid body.

"Getting kind of *muggy* in here, isn't it?"

The enormous entity rapidly shrank, concentrating its powers down from a standard brew to an espresso, then further and further until it had collected the entirety of its caffeine in a single, iridescent crystal spear. Joe thrust his finger forward, gasping out the words, "Go, Berry Stah! Use *Over-Caffeinate*!"

As his mana dropped down to just the last few dregs, the shimmering spear launched forward with a surge that felt like an entire coffee plantation exploding into bloom at the same moment. The crystal rammed through the gaping wound on the face of the ferret, pushing past its teeth and impacting the soft tissue at the back of its mouth.

Razorscarf shrieked in confused pain, the sound so loud

that Joe could only pat himself on the back for having the forethought to make the coffee mug out of metal. Porcelain would have shattered from the close range sonic shockwave.

Berry Stah didn't stop there. The purified caffeine was still under the control of the elemental, so it condensed the residual coffee around the spear, forcing the crystal to return to a liquid form and inject itself directly into the veins of the mighty Boss Beast.

Joe's eyes rolled up, and it took everything he had to stay awake, cutting the connection to the ritual and letting his expanded orbs fall to the ground like a net, dragging down two Dwarves who had the misfortune of being caught up in it. Mate and his coffee mug clanked to the ground, clattering out of view.

But it was the ferret that had the most noticeable reaction. Enough caffeine to potentially give a buff to ten thousand people with the Constitution of a Dwarf rushed through its veins. Its pupils constricted as the potent fluid hit its heart then rocketed up to its brain.

Its next attack was so fast that, even when replaying it in his memory, the Ritualist couldn't see the paws lash out. A section of the front lines was cut into five chunks, falling to the ground without ever knowing what had happened. Someone yanked Joe back, pulling him along as the Ritualist couldn't yet control his body. "Abyssal *fool* of a human, why would you make that thing stronger?"

"Didn't–"

"Yes, ya *did*–"

"–mean to!" Joe gasped out, finally having enough mental capacity to take control of his own body and pull himself from the iron grip. "It shouldn't be getting stronger. That should kill it! Or, at least, make it easier to do so!"

Going by the whirling blender that Razorscarf had turned into, spinning in tight circles and letting his fur shred any defenders that came into contact with its body, his plan wasn't working as the Ritualist had hoped it would. The Dwarf behind him shook his head, hefted his axe, and charged into the fray.

As dozens more died to its rapid movements, the Boss Monster twisted and twirled, its body following along behind as it looped up and over the first few lines of remaining resistance, coming down in the center of a group and using its exposed flesh to crush anything it had landed on and letting its fur take care of the rest.

Then it began to thrash around, its enormous bulk slamming back and forth. "Careful, it's doing a new kind of attack!"

"*Yes*!" Joe shouted as he punched the air in sheer exuberance. Anyone not actively engaged in combat shot him a dark glare, prompting him to quickly explain, "It's *not* attacking! Caffeine negatively affects the central nervous system and heart of ferrets back on Earth, and it looks like that holds true here! It lost control of itself. Avoid its flailing, and you shouldn't need to concern yourselves with intentional attacks!"

Seeing that Joe's words were correct, the Legionnaires redoubled their assault on the spasming critter, which suddenly slowed dramatically as another bolt of shadows hit it and forced its form to cling to the ground. With the enemy unable to regenerate, thanks to the constant damage over time—from not only the caffeine, but the thousands of various decaying effects stack onto it such as the lingering infernal damage of the Ritual of Infernal Conflagration—it was an easy target for the battle-hardened Legionnaires.

"Stroke! Stroke! *Stroke*!" A Master Sergeant called out like a rowing instructor as a dozen Dwarves with oversized great swords worked together to chop a path through its body, attempting to slice its head off of the rest of it.

"Yep, I think that's right." Joe put his hand under his chin and nodded. "Yeah… *pretty* sure it's having a stroke. Good call."

Feeling a warm, wet feeling on his leg, the Ritualist looked down and found that Mate was crawling up him, dragging his coffee mug along behind. Joe reached down and helped him up, clipping the super durable container to the carabiner on his belt. "Great job, Mate. You really brewed up a pot of kick–"

With a final downward cleave of their weapons, the Dwarves separated the spine of the ferret, and a notification spread outward to all the assembled defenders like a ripple in a pond.

You have defeated the Artifact-ranked Boss Monster: Razorscarf the Polar Polecat!

At the point where the creature's head had been forced open, a light began shining, so bright that it pierced directly through the false sky illusion and created an aurora effect on the cloud cover above. Joe's mouth went dry as he realized that there was an Artifact-ranked core... *right there*, ripe for the taking.

Immediately, he took a step backward, wanting to remove himself from what he was certain would be a mad dash to claim it. Yet, not a single person moved, and the Ritualist only realized why as the remainder of the notification appeared.

Quest alert! A Grieving Giant. The Legendary boss monster, Brisingr the Progenitor of the Ice, has witnessed the slaughter of its pet. If you return the corpse to the waiting Beast Waves outside of your walls, without further desecrating the body or looting it, all of the defenders who had a part to play in its death will gain five levels in their two highest-ranked skills.

A deep, reverberating bellow raced across the landscape, the fury of the giant palpable. Literally palpable—Joe could feel his *bones* vibrating under the strain.

"Abyss. That's one way to cause internal conflict. Anyone who attacked it is going to get stronger, but all of the craftsmen who're likely already eyeing the Artifact-ranked material are going to lose their *minds* if they don't get a chance to work with it."

CHAPTER THIRTY

From the moment that the giant's roar had shattered the air, the ritual towers closest to the center of the Town started falling silent. Over the next several minutes, the sounds of fighting died off entirely, and Joe had to assume that an order had been issued to the minds of all of the creatures that forced them to stop fighting and back away so that the giant could get to the body of its beloved scarf back.

"Legionnaires!" The order was snapped out. "Form up around the fallen enemy!"

Civilians were *pouring* out of the woodwork. Butchers were leading the charge, enormous cleavers held out and a manic gleam in their eyes. Leather workers were close behind, their stout clothing protecting them from the jostling of other, less physically-focused crafters.

"Hand over that body, right now!"

"Your job is done; now it's our turn!"

"Don't you dare even *think* about it!"

The mob of crafters were nearly as feral as the slavering beasts outside, and the hundreds of warriors surrounding the enormous body were barely enough to hold them back. Luckily, reinforcements arrived in the form of the people who were on top of the walls. They flooded down, adding a massive wave of bodies between the ferret and the civilians. After only a few minutes of confusion, the massive body was hoisted on the shoulders of over two thousand Legionaries, and they began moving it out of Novusheim, step by step.

Joe stayed out of it, shaking his head and merely enjoying the show. Frankly, he was happy with either outcome. He had delivered a massive amount of damage to the creature, and his contribution would likely have the Town grudgingly hand over even the Artifact core, if he demanded it. But he was stunned at the reward he could attain from giving up the opportunity to reduce the beast into usable parts. In fact, it was so shocking that it made him concerned.

"How could that giant *possibly* have the power necessary to give people huge jumps in skill rank like this?" The fact that it had come as a system notification meant that the reward was genuine, but that didn't stop him from thinking about it as he watched the show. "You know… I bet it's because the Council of Masters wouldn't involve themself for something like this, and they know that all of the Grandmasters are engaged in other work. They're expecting to boost Experts, at the worst. That's *gotta* be it."

The ferret's enormous bulk was easily visible, as its oddly proportioned body stuck into the air like a shark fin above the waves. The sight of non-combatants doing everything they could to hit the flesh and desecrate the corpse, therefore automatically failing the quest, was absolutely comical. All manner of odd items were raining down from above the ferret as it was hauled out of the city, looping around and through the killing corridors with barely a few feet to spare on either side. Crocheting needles were thrown like shuriken, vats of acid for use in soap making or other 'soft' crafts were pulled from inventories and flung.

But the seasoned warriors repelled all comers. Eventually, chasing after the monster became far too difficult for the non-combatants, and they simply remained atop the walls shouting their complaints and warning that they would be filing for a full audit of the Legion's expenses.

"Yeah, threatening their *paycheck* is going to stop them." Joe snorted into the warm air, which had remained humid after the massive form of the elemental had converted its power into steam. He was following along after the strange corpse parade, bemused by the odd event, when he exited the reach of the false sky above Novusheim. At that moment, a thick, heavy raindrop splattered against the top of his Exquisite Shell.

"What? *Rain*?" Joe stared upward in amazement as his initial thought was proven correct. Between the ring of not-so-friendly fire that he'd placed around the Town—which initial reports stated as having grown to be over four miles wide—and the sudden area shift that had been forced by Joe creating an overlay of an elemental plane in the area, the troposphere of the planet had been drastically impacted in the local area. Another raindrop hit him–oversized, as was appropriate for the world of giants.

"Ahh, that's the good stuff." A Dwarf near Joe clapped a hand on his shoulder, sending a wide smile up at him. "That right there is the first, heavy drops of rain that come down from an impending storm. We're going to have a right deluge here, and it always kicks off with a *thunderplump* like this."

"A what, now?" Joe had never heard that word before, but it sounded fun. He was always up for learning new things.

"*Thunderplump*. You know. The thing I just said?" The Dwarf eased his hand off of Joe's shoulder, apparently just now noticing that he was speaking to a completely hairless human and getting a little creeped out. "The first thick drops of a storm, right before a heavy downpour of rain?"

"Neat." Joe looked upward once more, but his excitement was entirely over the fact that—for the first time since he'd arrived on Jotunheim—there was a change in the weather. It wasn't snow, a blizzard, or an unpleasant wind. It was warm, wet *rain*. "This is good, I think."

The enormous corpse was fully out of the walls and set on the ground. Monsters swarmed forward, surrounding its body and snarling viciously at the warm-blooded defenders of Novusheim. Clearly they were wanting nothing more than to attack, but the will of the giant was able to barely hold them in check. An enormous number of Hoardlings, the only monsters that could lift the creature and still move, grabbed Razorscarf and started dragging its body into the distance.

Struck with a moment of sympathy, Joe slammed his fist to his chest in a show of respect for the mighty, terrible creature that had been felled by the greatest of drinks.

The salute was picked up by those around him and spread out until nearly everyone in the area was offering their respects. A moment later, a notification arrived that made them scramble back to their positions.

Quest complete! A Grieving Giant. Your reward will be distributed in 5 minutes. Beast Waves are resuming in 10… 9…

"Master Joe!" A human Joe recognized as one of the tower repair crew ran over to him with a panicked expression on his face, pausing and leaning forward to catch his breath.

"What? *What*? Start talking!" Joe grabbed the man's shoulders and shook him, hard enough that he broke the man's collarbone and had to repair it with a quick application of his Mend spell. "Bro. Sorry about that. Now talk!"

"We… we got all of the Mana Batteries properly charging and being replaced in droves. But, it's the towers themselves!" The panic in the man's voice had been replaced by notes of fear, likely due to the fact that Joe had not yet let go of his shoulders. "We ran out of slots in the Ritual of the Traveling Civilization! It's not letting us mark them so that the ritual can move them anymore."

The Ritualist let out a huge sigh of relief, letting go of the man and giving him a gentle pat on the back. "Okay. That's *not* a big deal, actually. It has a maximum capacity of a hundred total buildings. We can just pull the marker off of the Town buildings that are supposed to be stationary. The Town Hall, the… Pyramid of Panacea… the…"

He took a deep breath, trying to let go of the angst that filled him. Once more, Joe was forced to confront the fact that none of the most impressive buildings he'd made would be moving along with him to his next world. After a short pause, he nodded at the employee and dismissed him by saying, "I'll take care of it on my end, but that will only free up a few additional slots. Tell them they're just going to have to figure out a new method of replacing the batteries."

As the worker walked away, he muttered something so quietly that Joe almost missed it. "I have no idea why they don't just hook the towers up to the power source directly. Seriously, just plug it in. Why are you relying on batteries?"

Even though he agreed with the man, Joe had no idea how to make that a viable option. Something told him that the system wasn't just going to let them skip the step of collecting beast cores and enchanting them, or any of the other myriad of crafting that needed to go into the defenses so that they would work properly.

"Yeah, if it was easy, it wouldn't be this fun." While he had intended his words to be sarcastic, Joe realized that he actually meant them. He enjoyed most of what he did, and even the thrill of combat. "Hmm… I could do without the pain, though. Other than that, maybe just more time to figure out magic? We'll get there."

He had been making his way back to the Town proper and mistimed his jump. As he sailed over the final Ebonsteel walls, the reward for the quest hit.

Omnivault (Master III → VIII)

Ritual Magic (Master I → VI)

Congratulations, for increasing a Master-rank skill, you earn +5 to all stats!

The last message repeated ten times in a row, and the ambient mana of the world around him was sucked into his locked-down body as the ground rushed up to meet him.

His mind was filled with incredible insights into the two different disciplines, confusing his thoughts and making it impossible to respond before he slammed face-first into the ground. He stayed there, head stuck in the dirt and feet locked rigidly in position, like a javelin thrown by an Olympic athlete. The incredible inspiration kept him frozen as his mind worked to unravel what his abilities were now capable of.

Congratulations! Luck has broken through the fourth threshold!

Congratulations! Charisma has broken through the fifth threshold!

The fact that his body was working to adapt to the massive influx of Characteristic points made everything even slower. Now, his brain needed to balance the deluge of inflowing information with keeping his heart beating and air filling his lungs. As Joe began figuring things out, he regained control of his body bit by bit, finally yanking his head out of the ground like an ostrich that knew that danger had passed.

As he did so, the dirt went flying away from the sleek, crystal-clear skin of his bald head almost in slow motion. Even without being able to see a mirror, he knew that he was likely even more incredibly handsome and manly compared to how he had been even moments ago. At least, that's what the Charisma-inspired confidence was whispering into his ears.

"Status!"

Name: Joe 'Tatum's Chosen Legend' Class: Reductionist
Profession I: Arcanologist (Max)
Profession II: Ritualistic Alchemist (7/20)
Profession III: Grandmaster's Apprentice (15/25)
Profession IV: None
Character Level: 28 Exp: 432,687 Exp to next level: 2,313
Rituarchitect Level: 13 Exp: 87,450 Exp to next level: 3,550
Reductionist Level: 9 Exp: 54,900 Exp to next level: 100
Hit Points: 3,795/3,795
Mana: 7,910/10,836
Mana regen: 105.88/sec
Stamina: 2,750.5/2,750.5

Stamina regen: 7.13/sec

Characteristic: Raw score

Strength (bound): 201 → 256
Dexterity: 203 → 255
Constitution (bound): 203 → 255
Light Intelligence (Bound): 213 → 263
Wisdom: 200 → 250
Dark Charisma: 159 → 209
Perception: 202 → 256
Luck: 142 → 192
Karmic Luck: 0 → 3

Congratulations! You are the first non-native human to reach 10,000 Mana! You have gained a Title!

Title gained: Monarch of Mana (Upgradable). You are the Monarch of Mana, the first person to reach a mana pool so vast (10,000) that releasing it in one burst could permanently change a kingdom-sized portion of a planet. Effect: Once per 3 months (90 standard days, or 2,160 hours) you are able to instantly refill the entirety of your mana pool.

You do not currently have a title slot available. Would you like to ignore this title, or get rid of one of your current ones?

"Ignore this title? Who would do that?"

Answer accept-

"*Ahh*!" Joe screamed, interrupting the rest of the message from being written out; likely shocking the moderator into freezing up. "No, I was asking a question! Remove Title 'Dungeoneer'!"

New answer accepted.

CHAPTER THIRTY-ONE

By the time he got his head on straight and his body back under control, time had flowed around him like a river. Joe started walking, having to constantly readjust his mind and senses due to the discrepancies from only a short while ago.

He'd gained what essentially amounted to twenty-five percent of his total stats in an instant, and in the fifth threshold, the increases were magnified fairly drastically. "That's strange; now that I think about it, shouldn't I be in the sixth threshold?"

Joe received no notifications, nor did he have additional information on what the higher thresholds of power would hold for him. Still, when he looked at his current hidden debuffs, the particularly nasty effects that came from being multiple thresholds over Luck had not manifested. "That either means that thresholds are not every fifty anymore, or… maybe they're just aren't more of them?"

Even as he said the words, he shook his head. Of course there were higher thresholds of power. He hadn't already reached the peak; the proof of that could be seen by looking in any direction. There were Dwarves zipping around at speeds he couldn't match—in fact, for the first time, he was able to see as

Grandmaster Havoc zipped by him at full speed. The Dwarf shot him a glance, met his gaze, and seemed faintly shocked that the human was tracking him perfectly.

Apparently, he wasn't too pleased with what he saw, because the Dwarf blew out a puff of smoke and ramped his speed up further. The muddy ground under his feet exploded into the air, and the Grandmaster vanished in the distance, leaving a wake of falling material as the only indication of where he'd gone.

"Yeah, there's more thresholds." Joe chuckled as softly as he tried getting used to his body once more. Looking up, he crouched and pushed off the ground. "Omnivault!"

The land dropped away below him, and he went up, up, until he was ten feet over the top of the innermost wall, and his head broke through the illusion generated by his ritual. Instantly, the false daylight was replaced with darkness, and his vision was occluded by the massive deluge of rain pouring down. He let himself fall back down, easily absorbing the shock of his landing, in part thanks to the drenched landscape.

"I hope the water collection rituals aren't getting overloaded right now." Joe looked into the distance, where his water tower was likely greedily accepting all of the liquid falling from the sky. Then he thought through his jump, a pleased smile on his face. "Fifty-one feet up, from a standstill. Yeah, I'm not mad about *that*."

His internal celebration was forced to end abruptly as a horn weakly blasted. The single, sad note drew Joe's attention immediately, and he jumped to the top of the wall once more, happy with how casually he was able to do so now. The smile fell from his face as he looked out and saw absolute chaos.

The Ritualist bounded along, quickly finding a scout, clearly the one who had blown the horn. Looking him up and down, Joe realized the Dwarf wasn't injured, he was clearly just utterly exhausted. So much so that, when Joe arrived, and the scout saw the familiar face, he collapsed to his knees, barely managing to maintain consciousness. "Master… Joe. It's bad. The reward… it was a trap."

"Breathe, bro!" Joe encouraged the Dwarf, already understanding that the situation had rapidly devolved. Even from here, he could see the ice bridges that the Leaping Leopards left behind and that no one was actively smashing them to stem the tide of creatures pouring in. "Explain, if you can."

"The entire command structure fell into celestial inspiration. Our officers, anyone Captain rank or above, were completely out of commission. I don't know if they came out of it yet, or if they got hunted while they were unable to move." The Dwarf gestured weakly into the distance, only managing a few more words before passing out. "It was all... a trap."

"That's not good," Joe grumbled as he raced along the top of the walls. He'd wanted to get the Dwarf somewhere safer, but at least he was on one of the inner walls. The Ritualist noted with concern that most of the defenders who had come down from the defenses to help escort Razorscarf out had stayed on the outer areas of the labyrinth—leaving the areas closest to the Town drastically understaffed.

His movement through the rain caused a passageway to form, leaving shock waves of water collapsing in where he displaced the air. He came to a stop atop a parapet on the outermost wall and immediately started scanning the battlefield.

The entrance to the killing corridors was a charnel house, and one of Joe's original concerns had started coming to fruition. The mass of bodies wasn't being destroyed quickly enough, and bodies were accumulating high enough that the passageway was nearly completely blocked. Even though other issues were popping up all over the place, if Joe didn't do something to clear that space out, they would have monsters coming through the walls in no time flat.

Mere seconds passed as he dodged through the defenders, smashing any bridge of ice he came to with his Ritual Orb of Strength clenched in his hand. Then he was standing next to a Unique-rank tower that had a ritual of Infernal Conflagration embedded in the top of it, a perfect space to set up shop. His back was protected, and he had space to work. No one wanted to be too close to this tower, just in case it was damaged and the infernal ritual went critical—then infected them with a difficult-to-remove debuff.

Eyeing the expanding mound of bodies, Joe quickly set up a few Rituals of Glimmering to shed some light on the situation. "I hope people realize what's going on and can get over here and help."

He made ten Rituals of Glimmering with his Somatic Ritual Casting, then duplicated each one twice. It only took a few additional seconds to activate each of them individually, and soon he had a set of thirty floodlights blasting down at the monsters, blinding them as well as calling attention to the blockage.

Ritual Duplication (Novice VIII → Beginner 0)

"That's great, but not exactly what I need right now." Joe muttered as he focused his mind on his Somatic Ritual Casting. With an ease he'd never felt before, he held out both of his hands and generated a Novice, Beginner, then Student-rank circle. Aspects were spurting from his codpiece, and mana flowed through him as he activated the Ritual of Acid Spray.

The deluge of water falling from the sky mingled with a constant stream of acid that had tripled durability damage. While it was merely somewhat painful to living creatures, once they were slain, they became nothing more than crafting materials in the eyes of the system. The top layers of monsters rapidly melted away, but Joe shook his head in frustration. "It's not enough! More!"

As he went to create the same ritual, he hesitated and looked at the array of lights he'd just put together. Changing his mind on the fly, he created the Ritual of Acid Spray at the Beginner rank, which downgraded its potency, resulting in a Ritual of *weak* Acid Spray. He did it again and again, until he had five of the inactive rituals hovering in the air, pointed at the corpse mound and the bellowing monsters that were climbing over it. "Ritual Duplication!"

He created two more of each of the rituals hanging in the

air, resulting in a five-by-three grid square of an acid shower, then activated each of them in turn. "One hundred and sixty-six damage, tripled, times fifteen. That should be just shy of seventy-five hundred durability damage per second. Whooo, *boy*, we are just going to be making the crafters mad all *day*, aren't we?"

The torrent of caustic fluid rapidly lowered the mound, fast enough that Joe was certain the monsters throwing themselves heedlessly into the mix wouldn't be able to build it back up. With that problem out of the way, he let out an enormous heave of relief then turned to go and try and reestablish order amongst the Legionnaires.

"Wave seventy is approaching quickly! Keep your eyes peeled for Boss Monsters hidden among the ranks!" The Ritualist let out a sigh of relief as a commanding voice rose above the endless noise of combat. Major Cleave was back in action, and that meant the fighters would quickly shape up once more. "I need a runner to get the next refill of arrows from the bowyer! Who's in charge of sector seven-A? She's dead? Guess what, *bro*, now you're in charge! Stay alive, or I'll find your body and curb stomp your *skull*–"

Either she realized that her voice projection enchantment was on and turned it off, or it ran out of juice right as things were getting interesting. Either way, it was clear to Joe that he could move on to the next situation where his unique talents would be useful. A quick inspection of the barricades themselves showed that none of the damage that had been done by Razorscarf's passing had been fixed yet.

Joe pulled a face as he realized he needed to start doing maintenance once again, especially if Cleave had been correct, and another Boss Wave was imminent. "Wave seventy already? How long was I out? No wonder things got this bad; people have been doing their jobs with no instruction for… what's that? Almost three days? No wonder Havoc seemed like he was in such a rush back there."

"Triple-P spotted!" The hoarse voice of a scout shouted

from somewhere in the distance. Moments later, the call was echoed from the far side of the city. Realizing their error, the scouts added in the sections of wall that the Palisade Punchers had been spotted. As additional reports started pouring in, Joe realized that there was likely as many as a dozen of the elite variety of dinosaur battering rams closing in on their Town.

"None of this is a coincidence," he muttered to himself, casting a dark glare at the giant in the now-not-far enough distance. "It's too well-coordinated. I need to figure out a way to block that thing's vision."

A few ideas sprang to mind right away, but one of them was doable within the next few hours. Leaving behind the damaged walls, the beaten down and exhausted defenders, and the chain of command that was being quickly reestablished, Joe rushed to his workshop.

Once there, he retrieved a thin sheet of Jotunheim Alloy and got to work inscribing it. The first three circles appeared near-instantly, though the fourth circle was slightly slower, and the fifth taking even longer, as Joe directed them with Somatic Ritual Casting. While his inner dialogue screamed at him to go ahead and push his skill to the limit and try for the Expert-ranked circle as well, he couldn't afford the setback that would come with failing to do it correctly and blowing up his workshop.

Now working directly with his Aspect Inscriber, Joe created the final ritual circle of the diagram, running outside as soon as it stabilized. "I'm so glad it's raining like this; if we didn't have a nice big thunderplump like this, there'd be no way to activate this ritual."

Quickly gathering as many people as he could—using the skills he had learned back in his military days on Earth of volun-tolding people—Joe powered up the Ritual of the Ghostly Army. As the thousands of points of mana were absorbed by the ritual tile, Joe waited for things to go terribly wrong, for the other shoe to drop, as his mind screamed at him absolutely *would* happen.

Then the ritual was complete, simply waiting for the input of water to achieve the next stage of its activation. Joe hurriedly thanked the moaning and groaning people who had been sucked dry of mana and sprinted toward the water tower in the distance that had fluid cascading off of it in its best Niagara Falls impression. Nearly two hundred feet away, he geared up and activated Omnivault, leaping forward and up, managing to grab the top rung of the ladder just as he passed it. A simple shove upward, and he had access to the water source for the entire Town.

"In you go!" The Ritualist casually flipped the chunk of metal into the overflowing pool, and the water level began dropping immediately. It was fun to see the two types of ritual fight against each other, as one collected all of the fluid in a massive area, and the other stored it away in some kind of extra-dimensional space.

As the water level dropped and raised, Joe had a moment to reflect on his earlier thoughts. "Why was I so doom and gloom while activating this ritual? I knew that it had been done correctly and that any dissidents were likely far too distracted to try and mess with it. Hmm. Must be that pesky imposter syndrome popping up again. Well, I know how to deal with that!"

Seeing that his wait might be longer than he'd hoped, Joe sat down and reminded himself of a basic truth. "Imposter syndrome is just the brain not knowing what to do with the competitive advantage it's gained. Just gotta remind myself of the facts: I'm in an awesome place, surrounded by amazing, uplifting people who just wanna kill monsters as bad as I do. Of *course* I'm going to do crazy, wonderful things and be supported by them. Not only that, but I'm going to do it with *style*."

CHAPTER THIRTY-TWO

Standing at the highest point of his ritual tower of Infernal Conflagration, Joe tried to get a good idea of where the best point to block the vision of the giant would be. After a short round of internal contemplation, he set the activation of the ritual to be a quarter mile off of the ground. "Just using the Pythagorean theorem here. If this blocks vision for half a mile up and a mile long, putting it *there* should make it so that, if he wants to see past it, he's going to have to get close or get down on his hands and knees and peek under."

If either of those happened, Joe would consider it a win. Either the giant was in range or having to give up its dignity. The Ritualist inserted the variable and slapped the 'go' button, and the water that had been sucked into the extra-dimensional space was expelled in a cone of intermingled mana and mist. Unlike the last time Joe had activated this ritual, he didn't drop it on his own face. Plus, his class and huge advancements in ritual magic allowed him to optimize the spell further, practically without even trying at this point, so the visual impact was *much* greater.

Frightening visages, terrifying stares from eyes that didn't really exist, and sudden lunges in the mist caused the weaker-willed monsters caught in its effects to scramble away. The Penguins especially caused a massive logistics nightmare, impeding the progress of the slowly milling swarm of beasts. Small experience notifications began rolling in, and Joe realized that he was getting partial credit for larger monsters squishing smaller ones because they had fled his ritual.

"Neat."

Congratulations! Reductionist has reached Level 10!

As a reward for reaching this milestone level in a specialized class, you are now able to convert aspects from a lower tier to a single tier higher at a conversion of 1,000 to 1.

As exciting of a reward as that was, Joe did some mental math and realized that, even if he used his approximately fifteen million Damaged aspects, he would only get fifteen hundred Common aspects in return. Then only fifteen Uncommon from there. Useful, but in an extremely limited context. Still, every little bit helped, and he swore to himself once again that he'd be making an Artifact-rank Natural Aspect Jar before he left Jotunheim.

As the enormous cloud of fog settled into place, unnaturally staying in its position against the blowing of the wind, the Ritualist found that his action had an unexpected effect. The various elite monsters, as well as any boss monsters that had hidden themselves in the horizon-filling carpet of beasts, were suddenly released from the giant's control.

The elite creatures alerted him to this fact by trumpeting in exultation and charging at the Town.

Around the entirety of Novusheim, walls suddenly had enormous holes punched through them, and monsters started pouring into the killing corridors in droves. Joe watched all of this happen from his vantage point, taking a deep breath in through his nose, and letting out a gentle, "*Whoops.*"

He consoled himself with the fact that the monsters losing their tactics was better than allowing the giant to do as it pleased, which likely would've led to a far more devastating outcome. Even so, each time he heard the crashing of stone falling to the ground in the distance, he flinched and twitched his fingers, forcing himself to remain steady instead of rushing off to slap a band-aid on a wound that needed stitches. "Where am I needed? Where am I…?"

An oversized Hoardling rushed through the opening far below, clearly a Boss Monster by the sheer aura of bloodlust and intelligence it exuded. Even as the elites cut through the bouncing walls—using the brand new tunnels that led nearly all the way into the innermost sanctum of Novusheim—the Boss began causing issues by ignoring the easy route. Instead, it jumped at a bunker.

Huge hands reached out and slammed enormous claws into the shrieking metal and stone structure, ripping the ceiling off with an almost gentle-looking tug. Less than three seconds later, the inhabitants of that building had been wiped out to the last man.

"Never mind, I figured out what I'm doing next." Joe pushed off of the tower, Omnivaulting up and off the tower. As he reached the apex of his leap, the Ritualist leaned forward, diving down alongside the hammering rain. As the Boss Hoardling grew in his vision, magic sparked along his skin, and a half-dozen spells erupted outward and impacted the unsuspecting beast. "Dark Lightning Strike! Acid Spray! *Wither*! Abyss, that one only works on plants. Infernal Conflagration!"

Only the cackling ball of fire smashing against the back of its knee caught the attention of the frighteningly durable beast. A roar of annoyance was the only warning Joe got as a set of fists the size of a truck swung in an arc back and behind the creature. Feeling a terrible sense of foreboding, the Ritualist watched the strike that could level a city block approach his face. "Omnivault!"

Just before he would have been turned into the world's saddest pancake, the Ritualist spun in place—bald head beautifully reflecting the lights of the various spells and skills that were bombarding the creature mere inches away from him at this point. His feet pushed outward, catching against the falling rain and allowing him to arrest his momentum and soar up into the air.

The boss twisted, and the arm came back around. Seemingly without a care in the world, Joe zigzagged through the open air around the exaggerated blend of gorilla and reptile, sending out Ritual Orbs and spells to harry it and force its attention away from the remaining bunkers of people who would soon be full-fledged citizens of Novusheim. Each time it decided to ignore him, Joe would use an attack designed to maximize the amount of pain the boss felt.

His Ritual Orb of Intelligence would zip out and try to drill through its skull at the weak point of its temple, a fresh coating of acid would splash into its eyes, and he even managed to get his Ritual Orb of Constitution into its nostril and bang it around inside its sinuses for a few moments, until he lost his connection to the weapon.

"I might be a fly to you, but I'm gonna make you more jumpy than a cat lying near a rocking chair after grandma's had her sixth shot of espresso!" Joe was forced to land on top of the city wall, his mana nearly completely spent from multiple usages of his Omnivault in such quick succession. He ran alongside the path of the rampaging beast, which took out its fury on each bunker it came across.

Joe could do nothing but curse softly and clench his fist, carefully controlling his Ritual Orbs so as to leave larger and larger wounds on its hide. Just as his mana pool approached full, the Hoardling lunged forward, snagged a bunker, and shook it like a protein shaker before chucking it at a wall. The bouncing barricade broke as the bunker bashed into it, opening a new path for the Boss Monster to follow.

Having no choice but to follow along, the Ritualist moved like a whirlwind of agile mayhem, testing out the capabilities of his massively enhanced body as he got close enough to flashing teeth to individually count cavities on its canines. Joe kept his attacks and spells simple: quick zaps of lightning; sudden splashes of caustic, pain-inflicting acid; and a relentless swarm of Ritual Orbs pounding its muscles into tenderized steak.

It wasn't enough, and as Joe got more familiar with his own ability to move and consistently dodged the strikes of the boss, he became overconfident. What took him down was not the comparatively slow punches, but an arrow from a familiar archer. As the Ritualist pulled himself into a cannonball dive position, spinning four times in the air before kicking out and pushing himself upward, he accidentally lunged into the path of an arrow shot from Heartpiercer's high-level bow.

Exquisite Shell: 6,453/15,496 (9,043 Damage. Critical, sneak attack).

Even before he hit the wall and bounced off it, falling flat in the mud, Joe's Ritual of Communication lit up, and Heartpiercer's voice rang through it. "Feces on a stick! Joe, I'm so sorry; I've been trying so hard to account for your movements! Please don't be dead!"

He pushed himself off the ground with a groan, the sucking mud doing its utmost to keep him in place. Without time to respond, he ducked, dipped, and dived before pushing off the ground and hopping to the top of the wall with a single usage of Omnivault. "I'm good! Honestly, I'm just over here being impressed at how well my shield is holding up."

"Abyss, don't scare me like that." Her voice snapped back, all business once again. The ritual went dark, the connection having been cut from her side.

Joe rolled his eyes as he put his communication device back on his belt, softly grumbling, "Yeah, 'cause it's *my* fault you shot me in the butt."

Having taken too much time already, he rushed to catch up to the Boss Hoardling. It was currently standing over a bunker it had ripped the top off of, using the bottom half of the building to contain the cowering inhabitants, which the monster tossed into its mouth in handfuls like popcorn. As he closed in, watching the gruesome scene, Joe's fury reached a new height.

His Ritual Orbs raced back to him, and he pulled his arm back with the tips of his fingers pointed at the beast like a knife.

His Ritual Orb of Intelligence moved into place—just in front of his hand—and the other orbs **swished** and **clicked** into position. Finally, the Ritual Orb of Strength at the very back rocketed forward and slammed into the metal pressed against Joe's elbow. Combining his punch and mental effort, the Ritualist's meteoric descent onto the back of the Hoardlings head culminated with a shout.

"Alpha strike! *Newton's Deadly Cradle*!"

CHAPTER THIRTY-THREE

*Damage dealt: 12,143 ((263+2,376)*5 damage.)*

Critical! Damage doubled!

Total damage dealt: 24,286

All orbs take 30% durability damage based on the orb with the highest durability.

20% Ritual Orb Psi Barrier depleted on all orbs!

Caution! 2/6 of your Ritual Orbs have 40% durability remaining!

Caution! 3/6 of your Ritual Orbs have broken!

Combat Ritual Orbs (Student 0 → Student III)

Battle Meditation (Journeyman 0 → Journeyman II)

Artisan Body (Apprentice V → Apprentice VI)

Retaliation of Shadows (Expert II → Expert IV)

"Was my shadowy double slapping this thing every time it took a swing at me? Or did I gain two ranks in my retaliation by accidentally slapping Heartpiercer from such a huge distance?" Before he could find the answer to his questions, the Ritual Orbs all along the length of Joe's arm which had not been bound to a Characteristic—and therefore did not enjoy the twenty-five percent durability increase the others did—shattered in a spray of metal flechettes. The Ritualist cursed lightly as his arm went limp, then he went back to staring at the enormous hole his fist had created in the back of the Hoardling's skull.

Spells released from capture in Ritual Orbs: Lay on Hands. Essence Cycle.

Delayed skill experience granted!

Lay on Hands (Journeyman I → Journeyman VII). As Lay on Hands is a variant of the spell 'Mend', and therefore cannot exceed it in skill level, excess experience has been diverted into spell 'Mend'.

Mend (Journeyman IV → Journeyman VII).

Essence Cycle (Apprentice VIII → Journeyman IV). Congratulations! For reaching the Journeyman rank with this skill, it has gained a minor passive effect. While not being actively used, Essence Cycle now gives a 5% boost to all attempts at Mana Manipulation and increases your perception of mana by (Perception/4)%. (Current boost: 64.25%)

As his new passive skill came into effect, Joe could feel simply by the disturbance in the ambient energy field around him that the beast wasn't falling. Instead, it was turning to swat him like a mosquito that had stung it in a sensitive location. Barely managing to maintain his combat rhythm, he pushed away just before the hand struck.

What neither of the two combatants had been expecting was an oversized arrow to flit through the opening between them just before the hand hit down. The sharpened tip hit the already-cracked skull, and the powerful slap of the hand drove the shaft into the creature's brain, activating an instant coup de gras.

As the creature collapsed, Joe backflipped onto the Town wall, heaving for breath and cradling the few shards of orbs he'd managed to catch. "I know you can't hear me, but that was a *great* shot. Abyss, I just got that ritual how I wanted it. Maybe I should keep a better eye on my Ritual Orbs' durability. You know what? No. I should just make them out of better material."

Immediately, he thought about how he could remake these in the near future. "Jotunheim Alloy to make them incredibly durable and conductive to energies. Maybe figure out how I can get a sprinkle of arcane aspects in them, so it will be a superconducting superconductor, not just for energy, but for my mana? Yeah… thanks Boss Monster, you gave me the push I needed to innovate and fight even *harder*."

Taking a deep breath and making sure his final three ritual orbs were in his bandolier, Joe gave himself a once-over to make sure he was still in fighting form. With the enormous boost to his Characteristics, he didn't trust that he would notice issues if he wasn't looking for them.

The rain pouring down on him was washing away a thick, syrupy coating of blood the Hoardling had left on his Exquisite Shell—even faster than his Neutrality Aura could erase it. His body felt good, strong, and his Health bar was still maxed out. With a grunt, he remembered the massive amount of damage he had taken from the unexpected arrow and dismissed his barrier. "Let's start this Exquisite Shell from scratch."

His mana poured out of him, forming a thin layer around his body. Knowing how important it was, Joe directed his *intent* into the magic that was forming, convincing the hexagonal facets of his main defense to be even smaller, tighter together, more able to absorb damage and–

A sharp pain lanced through his mind for an instant, breaking his concentration just before a notification popped up in his vision.

Exquisite Shell (Journeyman 0 → Journeyman V) Caution! Applying Expert-ranked or higher insights to lower-ranked skills can cause rapid growth, but can also stress the skill to the point of permanent collapse.

The shell that had been forming wafted away with the wind, and Joe grumbled only very lightly as he waited for his mana pool to refill before getting his defense back in place. "Not a huge fan of having to take hits on my meat. Come on, come on… there we go."

It may have been his imagination, but as his shell formed again, it had a new, iridescent glow to it for a few moments before settling into its standard pattern. To his delight, the hexagonal facets were exactly as he'd been imagining them, and the boosted skill level meant he would be able to take nearly seven thousand additional damage before it broke. "That's like two free lives before I even start to take real damage. *Nice.*"

A wavering note blew from a horn, and shortly afterward, light purple flashes started reflecting off the false sky directly over the center of Novusheim. "I really need to figure out what these sounds mean. Seriously, you think they would post this in a public place or something. Wait... maybe they do. Everyone *else* seems to know what's going on. "

As he hopped over the walls, jumping high in the air and spinning to get a bird's-eye view of the situation, his elation from the victory over the Hoardling Boss began to wane. First came a realization, second came the view. "Feces! I forgot to rip the core out of that thing. Gah! No, Joe, we have bigger problems. Look at all the holes in the wall. That's... that's not good. Wavering note, purple flashes, was that an evacuation order? Are people teleporting out using the shrine right now?"

Simply by looking in that direction, his inflated perception allowed him to see that was *exactly* what was happening. By now, the purple flashes were practically a strobe light, as the non-combatant Dwarves had been given a briefing on where to gather, most likely at least hundreds of miles away.

Pulling out his Ritual of Communication, he tried to connect to Socar. "Are you there? Can you hear me now? Good. Why's everyone leaving?"

Almost immediately he had started getting an answer, and he listened intently as the Mage on the other end gave him the details of the situation.

"Joe? You're alive?"

"Yes, and please don't sound so surprised in the future. It cuts me deep."

"Yeah, okay!" The words coming through the ritual were half-shouted, so Joe was almost certain the Mage couldn't hear him very well. "They're getting all of the crafters and non-combatants out of Town. There's dozens of holes in the walls, but two of them are large enough that the entire stream of monsters diverted. Dwarves are going first, because they don't get respawn, but people are panicking."

The Ritualist rubbed at his chin as he came in for a soft landing on the muddy ground, turning his fall into a walk as he tried to come up with a solution. "Have any monsters made it to the center of the Town yet?"

"No, which is the only reason no one's *fighting* to escape yet." There was a momentary pause, which was followed by the Mage hesitatingly sharing some bad news. "Joe, everyone in the suburbs? As far as we know… there weren't any survivors. At all. No one at ground level made it."

Anything else the two of them were going to say to each other had to wait, because an important system message appeared at that moment.

The total population within the walls of Novusheim has dropped to 49% of its starting capacity! All experience and contribution points for those remaining in the Town have doubled! Stay stalwart; the end is in sight!

Joe was almost positive that any fighter who had been considering leaving with the main group had just had their minds changed for them. He read over the message twice, his smile curling up so far that he was pretty sure his lips had wrapped around themselves. "Oh *system*, I'm *so* glad you didn't specify anything about only *combat* experience doubling. That means all skills, specialization, and even profession experience is going to double, doesn't it? Is… is anyone going to notice if I go and boost my skill level enough to make my Ritual Orbs out of Jotunheim Alloy? My combat effectiveness is low… and other people are working on repairs… *yeah*. Let's still be sneaky about it, though."

Not hesitating for a moment, he threw himself toward the forge, which had only a skeleton crew still working within it. Joe barely acknowledged Growmore as he raced to his usual spot at the center of the forge, getting a few halfhearted grunts of annoyance from the others in the room. Aspects poured out of his codpiece, and Joe began pounding on them. "I need to be able to consistently make the alloy, if I want to alter the configuration of metal in my template for my ritual orbs. That means I need to hit Expert rank *yesterday*!"

"System, I would like to choose a fourth profession!" As he worked, Joe realized that he'd been missing out on a bonus for quite a while. "Ritualistic Metalworker!"

Calculating... Ritualistic Forging Skill is at Journeyman 7. General Forging skill not found. Skill level is below Expert rank, self-assigned profession unavailable. Checking for valid profession trainer. Profession trainer not found! Canceling profession selection–

Growmore stepped over as soon as he heard Joe speaking. "I'll act as his trainer to get him started."

Joe didn't stop working, and nearly five minutes passed until the system acknowledged the selection, and he was granted the profession he had requested.

Profession gained (4th slot). Ritualistic Metalworker. A metal worker forges weapons, armor, and trinkets that can stand the test of time. That's not for you, is it? A Ritualistic Metalworker instead focuses on creating a metallic symphony, focusing on crafting components that are solely focused on empowering and modifying rituals. By forgoing the ability to forge most common items, the Ritualistic Metalworker narrows their possibilities in the future while being able to rise up the ranks in this profession at incredible speed.

+25% success rate on all attempts to create ritual-specific metalwork items.

+25% speed of production for all ritual-specific metalwork items.

-50% success rate on all attempts to create non-ritual specific metalwork.

"Thanks, Growmore! I got it." Joe called over while taking a moment to double check his status. "Hey, I still have an open profession slot."

"Good on you, lad. Also, yeah, you get a slot every five base levels you achieve. If you're above level twenty-five, you should have five total professions," the Dwarf nonchalantly called out, not seeing how Joe's face clouded up at the realization that he'd been losing out on creating more impressive works faster because he'd been dithering over which profession to take. "It's usually recommended to take professions that work together synergistically to grow all of them as rapidly as possible, but someone with your talents? Totally understand taking a bunch of disparate professions."

As he continued hammering in his normal pattern, Joe thought about those words of wisdom that had been sent his way. "Synergy, huh? I guess that's not just a buzzword for recruiters anymore. I've a ton of supporting skills for my rituals, but pretty much everything else is a lone skill. I wonder what Omnivault would look like, for instance, if I took a bunch of skills that supported my ability to jump? I mean, I *had* them at one point, and it *ate* them, but still. Maybe I should find a circus in the next world and see what they can do for me."

Joe pounded away at his aspects for hours, his concern mounting as the recipe failed time and time again. Finally, just as he was about to give up out of the sheer knowledge that he could be successfully gaining skill ranks in fighting at this exact moment, he managed to make a single ingot.

Item created: Jotunheim Alloy.

Ritualistic Forging (Journeyman VII → Journeyman VIII)

Ritualistic Metalworker (0 → I). Congratulations! You are taking advantage of a double EXP event, and the very first item you created was at the Expert rank, outside of your profession!

"Celestial feces." Joe shook his head and turned to leave the forge immediately. "You've *got* to be kidding me. Why didn't I realize that? I just *asked* to have a fifty percent decrease in the chances of success when I'm not working on a project that's 'ritual-specific'. Well, there goes my plan to make my own money."

CHAPTER THIRTY-FOUR

Novusheim had seen better days—yesterday, for instance—and the rigged defenses were punctuated by the roaring of monsters that echoed far closer than anyone within the Town had experienced over the last few weeks as the settlement upgrade was taking effect.

As Joe exited the forge, he took note of the strangely grim sight. For a Town that was supposed to have a population of at least a hundred thousand and had always been absolutely bustling with people going about their life, it sure looked like a ghost town. "Yeesh. Haven't seen this place looking so empty since I broke my Intelligence and just couldn't see the people moving around. Let's…"

Pulling out his Ritual of Communication, Joe reached out to Heartpiercer for an update. "Hey, have you seen Jaxon? I wasn't able to get ahold of him. I figure it's because he's fighting, but… you know. If he's at respawn, I don't want to worry about him any longer. Also, any news about the Town as a whole?"

Her voice came back immediately, and the Archer's voice

was likely matching the exhaustion that she was feeling at the moment. As far as Joe could tell, she was approaching delirious, having been in a state of hyper-awareness during combat for the last week at the minimum. "Jaxon? I think I saw him out there hugging Penguins pretty recently. No, before you ask, *not* fighting them. I don't know why, but the Penguins seem to have accepted him as one of their own. As for the town, the evacuation has been moving along at full swing. Um. Yeah. What was I…? Oh. The stream of people trying to escape stopped recently. I think the Legion is cracking down on necessary crafters?

"Necessary crafters? Who are they deeming essential?" As far as Joe could tell, only those with high skill levels in combat capabilities were anywhere around.

"Anyone who was bringing out extra arrows or making them, that's been what's most important to me." Heartpiercer's reply was delayed, as though she'd zoned out for a moment due to be near-catatonic. "People repairing weapons, bringing food to the front lines… oh, and the groups that have been tasked with clearing out the monster corpses when they start getting piled up too high. I bet they'd really go for a bunch of those acid things you made. I've heard a lot of people saying overwhelmingly positive things about that."

"Okay, you should find some time to take a nap." Joe shook his head lightly as an annoyed sound came through the ritual, which abruptly went dark as she closed the connection from her side. "Or ignore me, whatever."

The total population within the walls of Novusheim has dropped to 35% of its starting capacity! Population critical! City integrity threatened.

Joe stared at the notification, wondering what was different about this one compared to the much louder one that had doubled everyone's experience gain. He snapped his fingers, making a realization just as additional data started appearing. "This isn't an alert for everyone. I think maybe it's only me that can see this? Or maybe–"

All members of the ruling body of Novusheim are called on to vote. At this moment, you have the option to cancel the City upgrade to immediately send away all monsters currently within—or directly adjacent to—the walls (291,084 monsters). They will not return for at least three full Jotunheim days, so long as you do not attempt to push into the City rank during that time.

If the 'yes' vote succeeds, all buildings within the Town will be reduced by one rank, but all current structures will be returned to 100% durability. You will gain a shield over the Town that will repel all attacks from monsters for one full Jotunheim day. All voting will be anonymous.

Private notification: As an added incentive, you will personally regain 50% of all aspects that you have invested in the structures that get downgraded. This includes creation cost as well as maintenance. Only if you vote 'Yes'.

Please vote now. This option will remain for only 10 minutes.

Current vote tally: 4 Yes. 0 No.

"They sure hit that 'yes' button real quick, didn't they?" Joe stared at the notification with great distaste. "I wonder what kind of incentive *they* were offered? Must be pretty good if they were willing to give up all of the hard work everyone has been putting in. Hmm... I wonder if they know Jake will come and kill us all if he finds out that we voted yes."

Not allowing himself to be tempted, Joe immediately voted 'no'. Then he let out a sigh of relief, as the temptation had truly been intense.

Current vote tally: 5 Yes. 3 No.

Would you like to change your vote?

"No! Stop it." The Ritualist growled at the system. He was reeling from the lifeline they had been offered, and his mind was spinning with numbers as he tried to assess the current permanent loss of Dwarven lives and how badly this would impact the morale of everyone going forward if they chose to stop now. "It's got to be getting close to wave ninety, or even later at this point, right? I should *really* keep better track of that."

Still, part of him was screaming that he should change his vote and suck down the aspects he was being offered. The sheer amount he'd get from the Pyramid of Panacea alone was staggering, and from the Town as a whole? Including *maintenance* costs? He had to struggle to control his breathing and was beginning to get dizzy as he waited for the final tally.

"I could make better defenses. Make *all* of the walls out of Ebonsteel." Joe looked into the distance, where thick plumes of smoke and dust from destroyed defenses were rising into the air. "Now we know what sort of threats are going to be thrown against us… we could prepare better. If we had a few weeks, like it's promising…"

He shook off the thoughts and crossed his arms, closing his eyes in an effort to ignore the floating temptation. That didn't help, as the screen was actually in his brain, and cutting off his vision only made it become the only thing he could see. "No, come on, council! We don't give up. Not now, not ever. Don't give in, *please* don't give in!"

At least he could tell why the voting was anonymous. As he stared at the five yes votes, he was already trying to figure out who had given in and how he could hunt them down and excise them from the council. "Stupid *message*, protecting stupid *people*."

Current vote tally: 5 Yes. 5 No. Time remaining to change your vote to 'yes' and gain your incentive: 3 minutes.

"What did I tell you, system?" The Ritualist growled at the last line of the message, which was twice as large as it had been moments ago and flashing bright green while being surrounded by smiley faces. He waited out the timer, somehow holding strong as the tally flipped back and forth a few times. Finally, it settled on an outcome.

Current vote tally: 5 Yes. 5 No. A tie means that nothing happens, and the fighting continues. Try not to lose everything you've worked for out there!

Joe was nearly gagging from the anxiety that had been eating away at him, and he took a deep breath to calm his nerves. "Good. *Good.* Now… what was I doing? No, *not* trying to hunt down the people who voted yes; every single one of them will deny it. Maybe I could put together a Zone of Truth? No, *stop* it, Dark Charisma, I know that's you. Monsters. Let's go kill monsters."

Just as he threw himself into the air to get back to combat, the ground below him shook hard enough that even the walls that were *not* enchanted to bounce did so. It almost made him miss his landing, but he had enough experience in the air to land properly. Still, a small fraction of those who remained in their defensive locations were knocked off the wall, adding to the total casualty count.

"Secure yourselves!" A hoarse voice from a scout rang out. "The giant is on the move! Estimated time of arrival for the Final Boss is at wave one hundred, eighteen hours out! We're almost done. The Grandmasters will be launching their attacks when it gets in range!"

Joe appreciated the heads up, doing a quick calculation in his head to see what that meant for him. "Waves should be two hours apart, so we're at number ninety-two? Or just about? Okay. What if we–"

A chill raced up his spine as he felt the ambient mana in the air shift away, like the wind racing toward a storm on the horizon or the ocean receding from land as a tidal wave closed in. No one else seemed to be reacting, or even noticing what he was, and Joe realized that his high level in Mana Manipulation, passive bonus to Essence Cycle, and familiarity with the state of energy in the air were the only things allowing him to recognize what was happening. Immediately, he shouted as loud as he could, pumping mana into his lungs and throat in the hope that it would amplify his words. "*Brace*! Incredibly powerful spell coming toward us!"

Even as his eyes darted around, he couldn't see what was causing the effect. It had to be a Boss Monster, but… where? Then the night outside of the walls deepened somehow, and the falling rain turned into icicles pelting them in an instant. A massive displacement of air echoed as thunder as Joe's gaze was yanked to the shield of fog he had put in place between Novusheim and the giant.

No longer was it a fog bank. Instead, an awe-inspiring transformation had taken place. The dense fog, filled with illusions and fear-inspiring instances, shifted from gas to solid in an instant. Cold so extreme, so absolute, had washed over it, that the floating shield of fog had instantly converted into a massive, perfectly clear, convex iceberg.

Staring through the ice showed odd ripples in the air, which was so still that the surrounding, warmer air, was trying to collapse in on it—but was instead freezing. Luckily, unbelievably, the icy barrier acted as a buffer, absorbing and diverting the remaining energy of absolute cold and sending it anywhere *except* at the city.

Joe's teeth were chattering as he stared at the giant, which had suddenly leapt into view, thanks to the magnification that the ice provided. He flinched as a fearsome face lunged at him suddenly, before realizing that the Ritual of the Ghostly Army was still affecting it, even though it wasn't in its original state.

"Okay… make a note of *that* for future upgrade options with this ritual." He watched as the hundreds of thousands of tons of ice crashed to the ground, sticking into it and remaining upright. "Well. Um. Thanks for the protection against your long-ranged attacks, I guess."

Luck +10 for everyone remaining in the city!

The quiet that had followed the blast of cold was finally broken as someone in the distance began laughing. Joe could only shake his head and chuckle ruefully, "Yeah… yeah, that makes sense."

Congratulations! Luck has reached the fifth threshold!

With the blast of ice, thousands of creatures had been turned into frosty statues, granting the defenders a short reprieve as the swarming monsters collapsed into a new attack pattern. They lifted their axes, began to ready their swords, or shifted into a lotus pose to try and recuperate their spent mana.

From then on, every few minutes, the ground would shake and toss them all lightly into the air as the final boss closed in.

"Good thing we all just got a big boost in Luck." Joe kept his thoughts to himself as he studied the snarling, craggy face of the giant through the telescoping effect of the ice. "*Pretty* sure we're going to need it."

CHAPTER THIRTY-FIVE

"Remember everyone, the more people that run for their lives, the better the rewards for us!" A Dwarf howled into the air, prompting a round of explosive cheering.

Joe was currently setting up a Ritual of Repair, trying to target the last remaining rubble of a wall chunk that had been smashed to almost nothing. He could only let the smile appear on his face and keep working, muttering to himself, "I don't know why, but I absolutely *love* the fact that everyone is staying here out of sheer greed at this point. Yeah, I'm sure there's a lot of 'protect the city at all costs' going on, but… this is great."

He activated the ritual, watching as stone and metal began flowing back into the fully destroyed section of wall. Frustratingly, the repairs weren't fast enough to keep monsters away from it, and the wall kept having large sections gouged out as they rushed past and through it. "Come on, magic, you can *win* this!"

Even with the accumulating damage, it was obvious that eventually the ritual would rebuild the wall large enough to stop the tide of monsters. Joe handed control of the spell diagram off to a sleepy Mage and started hurrying to the next area that needed to be rebuilt. His heightened Perception picked out a Dwarven face staring at him, running over and weaving through the crowds. The Ritualist had no intention of slowing down or stopping for the Dwarf, figuring that if he had something important to tell him, he would eventually catch up.

As he set up a second Ritual of Repair, once again handing it off almost immediately upon completion, the messenger finally caught up to him, panting for breath and glaring. "I *know* that ye saw me! You'd better be happy they paid a premium to get you this message right away, or I would've left."

"Oh, you're doing your *job*? Yeah, *me too*." Joe sniped at the Dwarf, immediately wincing and waving at the air. "Sorry, didn't mean to snap at you there, just… a lot going on right now."

The messenger let out a deep sigh. "Bro, I get it. Listen, your trashcan building stopped dissolving bodies, and now we're about to have a problem. Message delivered, have a nice day."

As the Dwarf ran off, Joe blinked a few times before understanding what was going on. "My A.S.P.E.C.T. tower! Abyss, when's the last time I emptied that out?"

With the two largest holes in the defenses being patched up, Joe made his way slowly toward the center of the city, casting spells and throwing out his remaining Ritual Orbs in an attempt to gain as much experience as he possibly could, while stopping the monsters—that was an important thing to focus on as well.

He chanced a glance back toward where the giant was still approaching them, having to turn away and blink rapidly at the brilliant, flickering light that greeted him. "What's happening out… oh! Ice flowers are burning even brighter after that absolute zero sneak attack the giant tried on us. Ha! I wonder how many monsters are burning to a crisp, not even able to get close to the Town? Not enough."

The rain of icicles had stopped, as the cloud layer up above was no longer being melted by the heat coming off of Novusheim. Still, as he got closer to the Town Center, he found that the atmosphere surrounding those who remained was stifling. Paying attention to his senses put a frown on the Ritualist's face. The reek of blood, burnt flesh and hair, and ozone generated by lightning spells mingled to make the city smell like the war zone that it was.

The closer he got to the entrance to the Town, the worse the stench became, until Joe was double and triple-checking that his Neutrality Aura was actually active and tamping down some of the miasma. As he leaped the final wall, he looked down and saw the remnants of monsters, yes, but also what remained of various warriors and even civilians who had been caught out or crushed by chunks of stone falling on them. His rituals collected all manner of things, such as corpses and unwanted materials, and it didn't discriminate between enemies and allies.

Peeling his eyes away from the open air graveyard, Joe continued rushing toward the entrance of his A.S.P.E.C.T. tower, which was supposed to be working tirelessly to keep morale-destroying experiences like this to the minimum. Dozens of people were swarming around it, pushing on bodies and trying to figure out what had jammed up the mechanism. "Hey! Everybody needs to get out of there, right now! It can't operate when living creatures are inside of it."

As Dwarves tumbled out of the three-quarters full building, Joe hoped that was the end of the situation. Unfortunately, the remains stayed right where they were. "Abyss. Let's go check the collection units."

The problem was, he needed to dive into the chum bucket in order to reach the place where the jars were attached. Were it not for his high threshold in Characteristics, he wouldn't be able to squirm between organs, push eyeballs to the side, and brush off the sharp things that would have otherwise torn his body open, even with their owners deceased. Finally, he was able to pull open the mechanism and inspect the jars, finding that they were, indeed, overflowing with aspects.

Trying not to breathe very heavily, Joe wiggled around and shoved the various organs and viscera out of his way until his codpiece was directly touching the glowing aspect jar. "Transfer all aspects to my storage device."

There was a notification of confirmation, and the jar went dark. Pleased that he'd figured out the issue, Joe started wiggling away, only for his lower half to light up incredibly brightly and draw his attention back to the jar. "What the…? It's full again? Already? Does that mean… uh-oh. It must hold all of the excess aspects in a buffer. Abyss, if this had taken a strike while it was full, I have no idea what would've happened. Wouldn't have been *good*, that's for sure."

Twice more, he had to **clink** his codpiece against the crystal surface of the aspect jar before it stayed not all the way full. A third time allowed it to remain dark and empty, and Joe moved on to the next one. He repeated this process until each of the aspect jars were fully empty, then began wiggling and squirming through the squelching, revolting masses. As soon as he plopped out of the entrance of the tower, the ritual swung back into instant effect, and most of what had been inside the container was immediately reduced.

The collection rituals began grabbing chunks of… stuff… and depositing them. Joe hoped the area would soon be clean of gore. He waited a few minutes, keeping his eyes trained on the items in the container that had *not* been reduced. There was only one reason that they would've remained where they were, and it was almost enough for him to dive back in.

"Pretty sure this thing can break down monsters up to the Artifact rank… but I'm definitely seeing some hair in there that looks like it came from Razorscarf." His eyes went wide, and he grit his teeth in frustration, "Ah. Right. There's no aspect jar for it to deposit the material into!"

Doubly frustrating, he could have had an Artifact-rank core in his hands for that exact purpose, if he had fought to keep the ferret's body in their control. Technically, he supposed he could use an Expert-ranked core to hold the Artifact-rank aspects, but he was holding out for the proper-sized container, just to ensure that he didn't waste the incredibly difficult-to-attain energy.

After all, even with enchantments or rituals, it put a hefty strain on materials to imbue them with magic a rank above their own.

With the durability-sapping true damage nature of the strange, flaming aspects, Joe was fairly certain the jar would eventually shatter if he tried to contain aspects at the Artifact rank or higher in substandard conditions. It was just a hunch, but as far as the Ritualist was concerned, it was a perfectly reasonable precaution to take. "Not exactly a bunch of Reductionists I can go out and ask, now is there?"

After leaning slightly to the left to avoid a limp Dwarven arm floating through the air, Joe decided he needed to get back to the front lines and start making a difference in a more direct manner. Then he had a thought that made him shiver, and he picked up the pace. "Thanks to the aspect collection, I literally have the power of thousands and thousands of people at my fingertips. If I don't use it to protect the city they sacrificed themselves for, what kind of a monster would I eventually turn into?"

A glance back at the charnel that was being reduced and *vanishing* resonated with him at that moment, in an odd way. His thoughts froze, and Joe missed a moment as inspiration filled him. Hitting the wall flat and tumbling to the ground pulled him out of it, but he hopped to his feet with a bright light in his eyes. "So much *slaughter*… is that it? Was that the piece I was missing with that star cluster? It's not… no, is it? Around those stars, and in between them, it wasn't *only* empty space."

In his mind's eye, he could perfectly recall the view from the celestial observatory. He lifted a finger and traced their outlines, his finger stopping at individual points where nothing existed. At least, nothing that he could *see*. Yet, somehow, he knew what was there. "These are dead stars… maybe black holes? It is a constant battle between the celestial bodies there, as they try to slaughter everything around them, including the points that are keeping themselves stable. If we assume that the stars *were* once there…!"

The diagram for the Expert-ranked Ritual of Slaughter

appeared in his hand, and he made a few circles. The death and reduction of hundreds of thousands of creatures was an odd place to draw inspiration, but he'd take what he could get. "That's it, I think. Eighty-three stars that were slaughtered by their neighbors. Just like that, I have the map I need to start working on the Master-rank version of this ritual."

Congratulations on your Master-ranked inspiration!

Celestial-Arcane Interaction Lore (Apprentice 0 → Student III).

Ritual Lore (Journeyman 0 → Journeyman IV)

Ever so slowly, Joe put away the diagram and reminded himself that now was not the time to vanish for a month or two. "It's nice to know I'll have something to do when all of this is over."

CHAPTER THIRTY-SIX

The Ritualist had never felt more in tune with his combat abilities. Being able to stay in the air for hundreds of feet at a time if he ran and leaped from a wall allowed him to cast his spells dozens of times. His greatly improved perception of time allowed him to use each second to skillfully control his Ritual Orbs to bash, slice, or impale monsters. Even though the seemingly endless horde wasn't being whittled down, he still felt that he was making a difference as the hours passed.

As the Beast Wave number slowly crept upward, Joe tried to tally the sheer amount of mana he'd dumped into his spells and various effects over the last half day or so. From the time he had finished his inspiration on the Ritual of Slaughter, the Ritualist had been keeping his mana pool at half full or below. As far as he could remember, not once had it crept up over that line.

"If I assume I've been doing this for about ten hours, which feels about right, that means… I'm closing in on four million in mana regeneration alone." A dark laugh bubbled up out of him, freaking out some of the defenders on the wall as he shot past them like a demented flying squirrel, only to be swatted out of the air by a passing leopard. He regained his balance midfall, managing to push off the wall just before he hit it. "Ha! Joke's on *you*, sucker! All you're doing is helping me boost my Retaliation of Shadows and Exquisite Shell! Woo! Double Experience event!"

With every attack, every spell, and as every moment passed, Joe was *actively* gaining experience. As his towers ceaselessly continued their arcane barrage, he slowly *passively* gained experience. Joe checked the combat logs, finding that wave ninety-nine was coming to an end, or at least the timer was almost done. "Yeah, the wave isn't over; it just can't get to us all at once. What a *ridiculous* world."

As he pushed to reach a new area, Joe decided to take a quick glance at his resource pools and let the system inform him of the skill and spell levels he'd been gaining. "Modified status, class information, and changes!"

Name: Joe 'Monarch of Mana' Class: Reductionist
Profession I: Arcanologist (Max)
Profession II: Ritualistic Alchemist (7/20)
Profession III: Grandmaster's Apprentice (15/25)
Profession IV: Ritualistic Metalworker (1/20)
Profession V: None
Character Level: 29 Exp: 462,807 Exp to next level: 2,193
Rituarchitect Level: 13 Exp: 87,450 Exp to next level: 3,550
Reductionist Level: 10 Exp: 55,700 Exp to next level: 10,300
Hit Points: 3,795/3,795
Mana: 2,531/10,836
Mana regen: 105.88/sec
Stamina: 2,750.5/2,750.5
Stamina regen: 7.13/sec

Skill increase(s).
Acid Spray (Student III → Student IX)
Dark Lightning Strike (Journeyman 0 → Journeyman VIII)
Exquisite Shell (Journeyman V → Journeyman IX)
Mend (Journeyman VII → Journeyman VIII)

Retaliation of Shadows (Expert IV → Expert IX)
Infernal Conflagration (Beginner 0 → Beginner IX)
Artisan Body (Apprentice V → Apprentice VI)
Combat Ritual Orbs (Student III → Student VIII)
Battle Meditation (Journeyman II → Journeyman V)
Essence Cycle (Journeyman IV → Journeyman V)
Ritual Duplication (Beginner 0 → Beginner VIII)

"Yep, not sad about that." Joe swept his thoughts over the increases, staring at one in particular that was bothering him. "Okay, let's break this out of the Beginner rank. Infernal Conflagration!"

Channeling the spell for a few seconds, he released it into the face of a heavily wounded fluttering Penguin, blasting its head off in a single strike. Then the decapitated bird ran around in circles for a few seconds before falling to the ground and quickly being consumed by the giggling flame.

"What?"

Infernal Conflagration (Beginner IX → Apprentice 0). Caution! Your spell has been developing a personality. Please consider imbuing your intent more carefully!

A quick check of the skill made Joe's jaw drop. At Apprentice zero, the spell was currently his most highly damaging combat ability, clocking in at six hundred infernal damage from the initial blast—and *not* counting the lingering burn that inflicted damage over time. "Abyss, my *next* most powerful attack after that is Dark Lightning Strike, and that one is only doing about five and a half hundred. Havoc, what rank of spell did you force-feed me?"

Then he was back on the attack, and the more monsters that came, the harder Joe met them with head-on ferocity. Long, long past, when he would've completely collapsed only a few weeks ago—from exhaustion, stamina loss, or mana imbalances—the Ritualist simply kept attacking. Finally, suddenly, the chaos that had become a part of his life was replaced with an unnatural stillness that stole all of Joe's focus.

The air itself began to crackle as a piercing chill swept through the air. He turned his head and looked for the giant, but his eyes only saw a mountain. He looked up, up, even farther, finding that they had long since been draped in the shadow of the Legendary frost giant.

It began to speak, and the sudden burst of air pressure swatted Joe out of the fly like an insect that had been hit by a rolled-up newspaper.

"Novusheim! I am Brisingr, the Progenitor of the Ice. Hear my name, and realize the futility of your resistance." The words flowing out of the Legendary monster's mouth flowed across the land, forcing all combat to a halt as lesser creatures were pushed against the ground. Due to the otherwise unnatural stillness from the cold that permeated the air, Joe was certain that the vibrations of its speech traveled nearly across the entire continent.

"You have been here for such a short time, yet your actions have brought death and despair to millions of the Children of Jörmungandr. You were granted warnings, extended offerings of peace over and over, and *this* is the path you chose?" The disbelieving scoff caused Mate's Ebonsteel mug to vibrate like a tuning fork. The ground began to crystallize, the very air turning to glittering frost wherever some vestige of moisture had managed to collect. "You even slew my most comfortable scarf, and for that, I *refuse* to make the final offer I have been told to bring you."

An enormous hand raced upward, its passing causing a hurricane-grade wind to sweep across the world. Its mountainous index finger touched the odd iceberg monocle on its face, and the ambient mana of the world was sucked toward the giant's face so powerfully that not only Joe, but *every* Mage with any form of sensitivity at all stumbled and went pale. "Now hear my proclamation and accept your death."

The air shimmered as the collected mana focused into the iceberg raced outward, unleashing a beam of such abject cold that it looked black; light itself was unable to move within its confines. It wasn't aimed at the Town. Instead, the giant stared up and into the distance, sweeping the beam around and drawing a circle in the clouds a hundred miles around, with Novusheim at its center.

The dark clouds that ceaselessly roiled above the world started to shift, falling out of the sky wherever the darkness had touched them.

An enormous circle of ice dropped toward the ground, creating an icy arena surrounding the Town in all directions, the frozen barricade reaching hundreds of feet off of the ground. Suddenly, the air *compressed*, and Joe let out an involuntary gasp as he felt a restriction, a confinement reaching down to his very soul.

"In retaliation for your invasion, I have diverted the boss of the ninetieth wave, as well as one hundred thousand of the Children of Jörmungandr to lead a slaughter against those you sent away, foolishly assuming they would be safe. The safe haven for your 'innocents', *pah*, your non-combatants who supplied you with the weapons you slaughter us with, will instead become their grave."

A collective gasp rose from the defenders of the Town. Many of them had accepted that this was going to be their final stand, but they had hoped that they would be survived by others who would sing songs of their bravery and remember them well.

"My frozen arena has sealed this Town, has frozen the very fabric of space, rendering any form of teleportation utterly useless." The wind stopped, having been completely blocked and finally realizing that fact. For the first time since they had arrived on Jotunheim, the abrasive, constant companion was simply… gone. After having grown used to it, the silence and lack of movement felt almost unbearable—making the fact that the flowers in the distance were letting loose flames that raged nearly as high as the walls of ice incredibly obvious.

Before anyone could attack, retaliate, or even make some

noise to try and rally their companions, one final notification appeared.

While the freezing air caused their bodies to shiver, the ominous words of the message chilled their very hearts.

Warning! Warning!

Beast Wave 100 is approaching! This wave will only be considered cleared after all monsters currently on the field have been eradicated.

Space has been frozen for the next __error__ hours! All forms of teleportation or other means of fast travel have been deactivated.

Legendary Monster [Brisingr, the Progenitor of the Ice] has sealed itself in with you! It will only be able to leave the frozen arena it has created by slaying all of the defenders of Novusheim.

Retreat is not an option. Surrender is not an option. You cannot make peace with this Boss Monster. One side must be eradicated for the spatial lock to be removed.

Warning! Warning!

CHAPTER THIRTY-SEVEN

"Infusion of Ice... Gift of Vel... Star-sword of Damocles!" With each word that fell from the lips of the giant, the hidden world of ambient mana quaked, shivered, and hollowed out as it was yanked into a new form.

His first cast caused what appeared to be icy, blue-black blood to erupt from its fingertips, pouring out and collecting into an orb in front of its face. The second spell was a combination of shaping the blood and mana along with a burst of ultra-cold air from its monocle, to create a spear over a thousand feet long.

Joe could feel the strain in the giant's voice as the third and final incantation was wrought. The spear tip transformed into a shard of ice glowing as brightly as the sun back on Midgard, and the giant fell silent as the weapon pointed toward Novusheim almost in slow motion. The Ritualist took a deep breath, coughing from the combination of frigid air hitting his lungs and the strangeness of breathing air that seemed to have not even a single unit of mana in it.

The world around him felt hollow, fake. As though he were

moving in a dream instead of sprinting at full speed toward the edge of the wall to do… something. He slowed down as he realized that there was nothing that he *could* do at this moment. Nothing except redouble his efforts on slaying the smaller monsters that were still pouring into the walls. "I really hope the Grandmasters are up to something. Otherwise… I think we're about to lose."

Jumping in the air, the Ritualist grabbed his Ritual Orb of Strength and whipped it in an underhand throw, shifting its position mid-air and catching a Leaping Leopard on the back of the neck, forcing it out of the air and throwing it to the ground far below. "Getting real sick of these *cats*!"

With a moment of horrified realization, the Ritualist realized that he hadn't thought about Queen Cleocatra of the Nyanderthals almost the entire time he'd been on this world. Immediately, he broke out into a sweat that ten straight hours of combat couldn't force on him and frantically began thinking of gifts he should start putting together. "Yeah… I'm sure she wouldn't come to this world. Cats aren't big fans of the cold. But, as soon as I leave, she's going to show up on the next world, as though it's my fault for just being slow."

Realizing that he was in the middle of a dangerous situation, Joe forced the dreadful scenario out of his head and got back to work. As he continuously cast his spells, throwing his orbs out in multiple directions to hit as many monsters as possible, his mind frantically worked to find a way to damage or impair the giant. "Can't imagine that my spells are going to be very effective against it. That thing is Legendary rank, and the only spell I have that might do anything at all is… Infernal Conflagration?"

Pondering that for a moment, Joe looked at the giant, which was still several miles away and able to attack with impunity. With a sigh, he determined that he had nothing that would be able to reach from his current location, even if he set up rituals to blast at the giant for him. "Maybe I should figure out how to cast artillery magic? That way, I could bombard it from a distance, at the very least. Pretty sure I can't get close to it, even if I ran over."

There was a subtle blue aura washing off of the giant at all angles, which could easily be mistaken for snow falling off and fluttering out. But when Joe looked at it through the telescope that his fog bank had become, his senses screamed at him that there was extreme danger. "That has to be an aura of cold. For it to set off my internal danger sense from this far away, it's probably a Legendary-ranked passive."

A sudden sucking wind pulled at Joe as he jumped, sending him tumbling through open air before managing to regain control of himself and force a soft landing by sending his Ritual Orb of Intelligence through the jaw of a Penguin, pinning it to the wall for him to slam into. As he rebounded off in an explosion of feathers, inevitably he found his eyes locked on the spear that had suddenly been drawn away from the city, taking the wind with it.

Brisingr was leaning back, and Joe realized with sudden horror that it wasn't a spear in his hand: it was a javelin.

Suddenly, a new form appeared in the air between the city and the giant; a brute of a Dwarf that Joe had barely seen since they had come to Jotunheim.

Grandmaster McPoundy walked along the open air, a hammer held loosely in each of his hands as he looked at the giant in the distance with exhaustion already evident in his slumped form. "You really had to lock us in together? Sorry to say, that was a *bad* move on your part."

For a fraction of a second, Joe was annoyed at the fact that the Dwarf was monologuing at the giant. There was no possible way that his casual tone would reach the ears of the massive entity. A frown appeared on his face as he realized that he was having no trouble understanding the words, and… magic was a thing. So, perhaps the words actually were being projected into the distance.

It didn't seem to matter to Brisingr that someone was acting so casually, and Joe felt a shift in the air itself even before he saw that the javelin was moving forward. As the projectile weapon began gaining speed, the wind switched directions and picked up further. In mere seconds, the actual spear itself was hidden behind a trail of water vapor as it condensed the atmosphere in front of it, breaking through the sound barrier even before leaving the giant's hand.

Joe listened in quiet contemplation as the floating Grandmaster Smith and Enchanter took a deep breath and raised his hammers.

"*One Hundred Thousand Refinement Echoing Hammers.*" The words were spoken like a soft sigh, as though being released only reluctantly. The Dwarf's hammers moved forward and gently tapped the air in front of him as though he were a conductor standing in front of an orchestra.

"It's really happening." The voice startled Joe, not because he hadn't realized he was surrounded by people on the walls, but because he had never seen Growmore outside of the smithy. "I hope my fellow craftsmen are watching closely… this is *unbelievable.*"

The hammers continued to tap the empty air, almost as though the Dwarf floating in the sky were starting to move into a salsa dance. Joe couldn't see any effect on the giant or the spear that was continuing to move forward at literally unbelievable speeds and could only hope the Grandmaster would speed things up a little. "Growmore… what's he doing?"

"Quiet, ya *daft* fool—oh, it's Joe." Growmore refused to take his eyes off the Grandmaster in the distance, drinking in every motion. In fact, as Joe looked at him, he noticed ice forming at the corners of the Dwarf's eye, which normally would have been cleared away if he was blinking normally. "Lad, you're looking at a Grandmaster-ranked skill. Also known as a *Legendary* skill. If we're going to have any chance of taking down that *behemoth* on our terms, it's going to be up to those that can fight at its power level."

Only the fact that they were moving at fifth threshold speeds in Perception, bodily control, and mental processing allowed them to have a conversation in the span of the incredibly swift motions of both the giant and the Dwarf directly opposing him.

Though Joe stayed silent, Growmore must have realized that he had questions, and explained quietly, so as to not break his own train of thought. "Watch him, *learn* from him. This is one of the few Grandmaster-ranked skills meant for crafting that can be directly used in combat. Did you ever wonder why they —Grandmasters, that is—are so reluctant to take the field? To a smith watching him, this is going to be as good as personal instruction gets. If someone's close behind him in ranking, this might be the push they need to put them at his level. I know that's what *I'm* after."

"There can be only *one* Sage of a discipline." Joe realized where this line of thinking was going and stared even more intently at the Dwarf. "By showcasing his skill… you think he's worried that he will lose his chance at becoming the Sage?"

"That's exactly what's going on in his mind. But he has no choice, not if he wants us to live. Well, it doesn't hurt that he's locked in here with us, and his neck is on the line as well. I bet he's pretty unhappy he has to go *first,* though." That put a greedy smile on the Dwarf's face. "I'm *so* going to be a Master by the end of the day."

Joe started seeing puffs of debris appearing in the air around the giant, and as he stared intently at the strange combat that was happening, either directly at the Grandmaster or through the telescoping ice at the giant, Joe started seeing patterns. When the Dwarf struck the air with his hammer, a plume of debris flew off of the giant in the next one thousandth of a second. "Celestials…"

"Yup." Growmore leaned forward, trying to capture everything so that he could replay it in his mind later. "I know what this skill is supposed to do. At least, I've heard rumors about it. It's a Mastery skill achieved only by those who've transcended the normal bounds of smithing. McPoundy is currently channeling this skill, and at its peak, it'll be delivering a whopping one hundred thousand precision strikes *per second.* When it gets to that point, every strike resonates with the previous, *refining* the target—whether it's metal, items, or even living beings."

"I don't know what that means," Joe admitted, earning himself a small grin from the Dwarf, though the stocky smith didn't turn to look at him directly.

"If he were using this to create an item, it would be seamlessly melded. The integrity and strength of the final product would not only be maintained but enhanced to the utmost. To even have a *chance* of creating a Sage-rank item, he'll need to use this skill to put the materials in the *most perfected* state possible."

Growmore went silent for a fraction of a fraction of a second, plenty of time to show that he was collecting his thoughts. "Sage-rank… the greatest bottleneck. Look! It's starting! If the rumors are true, once it ramps up to a hundred thousand blows per second, the strikes will become echoes of themselves, becoming self-propagating until he runs out of stamina, mana, or whatever resource it is that a Grandmaster at his level is using to fuel this skill."

While Joe was interested in seeing this happen, his eyes started getting drawn to the spear that was still closing in. As far as he could tell, nothing was being done to stall or alleviate the impending destruction of their Town. "Growmore, I think we're-"

"Stop." The Dwarf's voice was suddenly as hot as the iron that he worked when it was pulled straight from the furnace. "Either we're going to live through this, and I'm going to come away with skill advancement, or we die, and I'd never know anyway. If you get in the way of my skill advancement when I have double experience gain, I will straight up come back as a ghost to haunt you if that spear lands on my face. No, worse, I'll come back as an *Elf* and hunt you. Won't even know why. I'll just be huntin' you and won't ask questions."

Joe sucked in a sharp breath as the javelin was released.

At the same time, McPoundy went limp… falling out of the air toward the howling monsters leaping up at him.

CHAPTER THIRTY-EIGHT

Joe was perfectly positioned, already leaning forward and on the edge of the wall, to immediately push into a full powered Omnivault and launch himself at the falling Dwarf. He wasn't the only person who jumped from the walls to save the Grandmaster, but he *was* the fastest.

Bounding off the heads of monsters, Joe raced forward, arms stretched wide. The Ritualist slammed into the Dwarf on his third Omnivault, arresting their tumble through the air and getting his feet under him. He was just in time to smash into the face of a Hoardling and push up and off, expelling their momentum with his Superhero Landing title and blowing the skull of the monster into fragments. "Please be considered a leap!"

While he wasn't getting the full one hundred and fifty feet of distance that his skill could allow when he was moving on his own, Joe was completely fine with absolutely *melting* his mana pool in order to drag the Grandmaster back to safety. After Omnivaulting nine times in quick succession, the Ritualist had burned through over nineteen hundred mana and two hundred fifty stamina, but had traveled nearly a tenth of a mile before the Grandmaster had hit terminal velocity. Then he had turned around and returned both of them to the safety of Novusheim, all before the look of panic had left Growmore's face.

"Yer a *wild* man!" the Dwarf bellowed as he lifted his arms to help pull the flying duo to stable ground. "Glad you're back; now get out of the way so I can watch those echoing refinements."

"The *javelin*!" Joe yelped in fear, completely unaware of where it had gone, but knowing that it should be striking the city at this very moment. Flinching and whirling around, his eyes searched the sky until he found what he was looking for.

"Looks like Snow made her move." McPoundy wheezed out as he focused on channeling his energies. "She always likes to wait until the last moment, doesn't she? She's a savvy one… always knew she'd lead the council one day."

The weapon was less than a hundred feet above the inner section of the Town, angled up and away perfectly, but partially hidden from their view, thanks to the false sky that Joe had put over the Town. The Ritualist felt his jaw drop as he saw the strands of mana creating a barrier in the sky where the spear had struck—completely stopping it without allowing even a small noise to escape and alert the people below as to how close they had been to death.

"Are you saying that she waited on purpose? Did she time stopping that weapon so that the people in the Town proper would think it had just vanished? Is this some kind of move to make the non-combatants feel more comfortable?" Joe spit to the side as he narrowed his eyes. "We're fighting for our lives, and she's playing politics?"

"Nah." McPoundy's voice had taken on a dreamy quality. "She put it there so that no one could see her Grandmaster-ranked skills in action. Can't believe *I* didn't think of that."

"Yeah, you can." Growmore chuckled, still watching the hammer blows beating the giant in the distance.

"Heh. Suppose I can." The Grandmaster grumbled self-deprecatingly. "Like I said, *she's* savvy. I just hit things with a hammer. Oh? I managed to deal damage."

In the distance, ice, snow, and accumulated soil suddenly cascaded off of the giant in a massive avalanche. Tens of thousands of pounds of material dropped off of the creature, revealing its pristine frozen body for the first time. Just as McPoundy muttered his words, a crater appeared on Brisingr's chest, and bluish black blood erupted like a frozen volcano. The air shook as the boss bellowed in pain, and Joe felt a strain of magical backlash racing toward the Dwarf.

"Hah. Got 'im. Nearly one percent damage, *and* I took out his armor." He clearly felt the wrongness in the air coming at him, because the Dwarf curled up slightly and grimaced. "It busted through my skill, huh? Looks like it's someone else's job from here on out."

Joe began proactively casting healing spells at the Dwarf. As the build-up of power in the air lashed out and struck the Grandmaster, he stiffened and spasmed, blood erupting from his own body as a backlash from the giant managing to break his skill. "Mend! Lay on Hands! Somebody figure out how to buff him!"

Even with as quickly as the Ritualist was healing him, the Dwarf had bones breaking, skin rupturing, and blood splattering. The wall where he was laid out began cracking under him as the magical pressure built, and tiny echoes of hammer blows became noticeable across the surface of his body.

"Verglas Leopard, on our left! Elite variety!"

"Triple-P spotted!"

"We've got ice wraiths over here!"

Joe's calls for assistance were lost in the sudden ramping up of attacks by the monsters, which the Ritualist could only assume had happened because they thought the Town and walls would be destroyed, and some primal part of them refused to charge into an assured death. Not knowing what else to do, he simply kept pumping heals into the Grandmaster, as the others around them either looked on helplessly or turned their attention to combat.

A sudden shift announced the end of the backlash, but even as Joe got the Dwarf back to full health, he didn't awaken from whatever coma he had dropped into. "Abyss… I need an Evac for-"

"Move, Joe." Growmore hoisted the Grandmaster onto his shoulders, and Joe couldn't help but realize that the Dwarf was glowing slightly, energy crackling around his eyes. "I need to go find a place to absorb my inspiration and insights anyway. I'm going to take him to the forge; it would be good for him to wake up in a familiar environment."

Then they were gone, and Joe was left wondering what he should be doing. His hands were tingling, and he wiped them on his fur clothes, only for the tingle to spread from there. Glancing down, he saw the same glowing energy on himself that he'd noticed on the Dwarf but didn't get a chance to consider what it might be before notifications began rolling through his vision.

Congratulations are in order for a variety of impressive feats!

By watching a high-ranking Grandmaster at work, you have gained valuable insights into your craft!

By absorbing and dissipating a portion of the backlash energy of a Grandmaster-ranked skill, your hammering pattern has been upgraded and replaced!

New hammering pattern learned: Harmonics of Metal (Expert). This is a pattern of strikes that you will automatically use when using your Ritualistic Forging skill. It provides a 10% increased chance of successfully creating items. (Example: if you have a 1% chance of creating an item, the harmonics ringing through it will boost that chance to 1.1%)

By rescuing a Grandmaster Smith, you have gained the approval of dozens of metalworkers in an instant! Your profession [Ritualistic Metalworker] has gained a large amount of experience (2,000)!

Profession: Ritualistic Metalworker (level I → III).

Ritualistic Forging (Journeyman VII → Expert 0).

Smithing Lore (Student VIII → Journeyman V). For reaching the Journeyman rank in Smithing Lore, you have gained a recipe book for crafts related to your smithing-specific profession and skill, Ritualistic Forging. Calculating… the profession reward is a duplicate of the smithing skill reward. Condensing into an upgraded version.

Item Gained: Ritualistic Forging Manual (Expert). This tome contains the combined wisdom of expert Ritualists and Blacksmiths. It provides specific instructions for creating metalwork designed to amplify, modify, and enhance ritual circles.

As the last message rolled through his vision, Joe lifted his eyes and gasped like a fish out of water, pushing himself to his feet and out of the lotus position that he had sunk into without realizing. "I'm an Expert… just like that? Wow… Growmore wasn't kidding when he said that using Grandmaster-ranked skills out in the open could give people an advantage over you. I just thought that maybe they would be able to copy the skill or something. Not that I could grow my profession, my ability to work metal, and my knowledge of the lore itself just by being in the vicinity. That's… dangerous."

Many of the habits of the Council of Masters, and especially the secrecy of Grandmasters and above, started to make more sense at that moment. Joe tried to envision how furious he would be if he lost out on attaining a Sage rank because he gave an opponent an edge while he was fighting someone else. "Yeah… it's a good thing these Dwarves are extremely caring about their people, or I'd be worried about a Grandmaster making sure there were no witnesses. When I'm getting to that rank, maybe I should add a snippet to my rituals that causes temporary memory loss to anyone who sees them?"

His mind was whirling with ideas and schemes, but ever so slowly, he realized that he was still being influenced by the strange energy that had collected on him. As the last spark of it vanished, the Ritualist finally felt like he was back in control of himself fully. "Right, that was weird, and I'm not sure whether I liked it or not."

A glance around showed that the battle had been continuing, even while he'd been locked in his own mind, yet again. As he took stock of the situation and began throwing his Ritual Orbs around, the voice of Brisingr rumbled over the world yet again.

"Star-sword of Damocles… *shatter*!"

Joe's gaze jerked up to the spear that was still being held in place by the threads of mana that Grandmaster Snow had woven. The tip of the javelin, which was still glowing as bright as the sun, exploded into brilliant sparks, the smallest of them being dozens of feet wide.

They swept up and away from the now-toppling shaft of the spear, circling the city like a field of stars and transforming into swords made of glowing ice. As the threads of mana bulged and pushed the remainder of the massive weapon away so that it would land on the swarming monsters, the Star-swords began falling.

Joe sucked in a deep breath as he watched the swords descend one by one, with no clear pattern. The first was practically directly over his head, and he felt that, no matter how he moved or tried to avoid it, the sword of icy death would *absolutely* be landing directly on him. "Welp. Mate, shot of espresso, please. Might as well enjoy these last few moments together."

**Burble*.* The solemn reply came, followed by a burst of steam erupting from Joe's mug. The Ritualist tossed back the hot drink; reveling in the feeling of warmth even as his body shivered from the cold, as well as the feeling of dread that slashed into him from above.

"See you on the other side."

Twang

Joe and all of the others around him were knocked to their knees as a thread of mana snapped like a guitar string, the recoil *slapping* the sword and sending it out into the horde of monsters. When the falling weapon struck the ground, it vanished silently, leaving behind an area completely obliterated, surrounded by monsters that had been flash-frozen into beast-sicles.

The Ritualist looked down at the trembling coffee mug in his hand, his eyes meeting the coffee bean version of Mate's. "That wasn't fun. Not at all. Let's not do it again."

**Burble*,* Mate vehemently agreed.

CHAPTER THIRTY-NINE

The Star-swords weren't all deflected by Grandmaster Snow, and as they circled the Town, more and more of them eventually got through the barrier. If Joe had to guess, he would have to assume that most of the Grandmaster's strength had been used up in blocking the initial strike of the javelin, and she was probably running on the last gasp of mana she could pull out.

"I think the real question, for me at least, is: does that count as one of the three Grandmaster abilities? Because I think she's using Mana Manipulation directly, not actually using a skill." Joe could only hope he was correct, because if McPoundy had been correct in his numbers, so far, only one percent of the giant's total health had been dealt as damage to it. The Ritualist muttered a dark thought. "If it has any kind of regeneration at all, that might already have healed up."

"Monsters have broken through to Novusheim proper!" The shouting voice coincided almost perfectly with a blast from one of the few scouts remaining that had a warning horn. "Fall back from the outer walls; collapse into the city!"

Notice! Morale bonus lost!

Joe pulled out his rectangular tablet containing the Expert-ranked Ritual of Remote Activation, quickly zooming in on their current location. "Come on, someone better be replacing those towers if they get crushed...!"

There were over a dozen people with large mana pools who had the task of operating the Ritual of the Traveling Civilization, but even so, they weren't able to keep up with the damage inflicted by the falling Star-swords. If it weren't for the fact that most of the swords hung in the air ominously instead of dropping down, it was likely that the entirety of their defenses would be dismantled already. Grunting from the effort, Joe pulled out tower after tower on his own, replacing the destroyed edifices with fresh towers that bombarded the beasts swarming through the dozens of new holes in the walls.

Each time a sword struck among the walls, at least two sections were blasted apart on either side of the killing corridors. Either Snow's manipulations were working better than expected, or the giant had much less control over the falling stars than Joe assumed he would. But it seemed that, once an area had been hit, the swords would avoid it, even if it was filled with a much juicier target afterward.

As he replaced the last tower he could until his mana regenerated, Joe felt a subtle shift, thanks to the passive effect of Essence Cycle. The area around him felt like it had been pulled into some kind of harmony, and the arcane blasts coming from the top of the towers suddenly began hitting with much greater ferocity. The Ritualist perfectly understood what had happened. "Looks like I got the Formation up and running again. Abyss, Socar, what would we have done without you?"

Burbled. The coffee elemental bubbled darkly.

"Mate! I don't want to hear such filth coming out of your mouth," he chastised his darkly brew-ding friend. A slight cutting sound filled the air above him, not a whistling, but a sharp sound, as though the air itself was being sliced by a razor blade. Without taking a moment to check, Joe Omnivaulted forward, tucking and rolling; even so, barely making it to the edge of the blast. A wave of intense cold washed over him from the fallen Star-sword, pushed back by his Exquisite Shell's resistance to elemental effects.

Exquisite Shell: 575/15,496. (14,921 Elemental damage taken)

Chancing a glance back—finding it difficult to move his neck from how stiff it had become in the freezing air—Joe quickly had to turn away. Behind him was a pocket of unmoving statues, wearing expressions of determination and caught in between motions. "Don't... take a hit from one of those directly. Got it."

A huge part of him wanted to run back and revive everyone he could with his Mass Resurrection Aura, but focusing on the small picture right now would only result in a small result. They needed to secure the Town while the Grandmasters fought against the giants and unlock space as quickly as they could, so they could go to the rescue of the non-combatants. Removing all of his options to save only a few Dwarves would be a terrible idea, even if *they* would most likely think it was a great one.

"Keep the towers attacking. That's what I should be doing. We've got to whittle down the monsters." Joe sucked in a deep lungful of air as he suddenly realized that they actually stood a chance of eliminating all of the monsters in the area. The world was locked down. The walls of ice in the distance demarcated an area where no one could pass, from either side. Much closer to the city, there was a massive field of fire, likely dozens of miles wide at this point, where Joe hadn't seen any but the strongest of monsters emerge for hours. "There can only be a few tens of thousands left. We can *do* this."

Suddenly Joe's Ritual of Communication flared to life, and a voice he hadn't heard in far too long came out of the other end. "Hello? Is this thing working? Squawk? Squawk, quack?"

Various squawking and clacking of bills came through the line, and Joe realized his friend was likely asking a waddle of Penguins to check the connection for him. Trying to get ahead of any odd mayhem, Joe grabbed the ritual tile and began speaking into his end. "Jaxon? What are you doing? Where are you? Do you need me to come and get you?"

"Oh, no! I'm having a delightful time zipping around out here."

"Out… here? Are you *outside* of the walls?" Joe's voice was flat and unsurprised, as frankly, this wasn't even the strangest thing he'd seen his friend do.

For a few seconds, there were odd noises, followed by sharp crackling and the clear sound of a fist meeting flesh. "*Adjust*! There, that should do it. Yes! I'm outside the walls!"

Joe waited a couple more seconds before giving in and asking for more details. "Well, stay safe, but is there a reason you called?"

"Ah! Right!" Jaxon's voice gained clarity, as though he were holding the tile closer to his face to hide what he was saying from those around him. "As soon as your fog bank blocked that first icy air blast, and I could see the giant, I've been *pulled* to him! He's humanoid, but there is no way that a human frame could support that size. His bones, Joe! I have to figure out what that bone structure is like! It could be a view into the future growth of our own people."

The Ritualist was not shocked in the least. He merely nodded and planned to close the connection between them, but Jaxon continued speaking. "Anyway, I left the walls and subverted a small colony of my new feathery friends, *adjusting* their imprint to be on me instead of on him! Now I'm leaving a revolution; we are flying the coup! Now, I was wondering if you could figure out how to send me a lance, so that I can ride my Penguin into battle and poke a hole in its skin large enough to burrow in. Any thoughts?"

"I have *many* thoughts on this, Jaxon." As he spoke, Joe wheeled around and threw himself back the way he had come, toward the outer walls of the city. "I don't think I can do anything to help you, but… some things that you should know. While I was looking through the ice, I could see an aura of frost coming off of the giant. It has to be a Legendary effect, which means it's not survivable. If you get too close, I think you'll get sent to respawn before you have a chance to do much else."

"Hmm." The line went quiet for a few moments, and Joe quickly found himself alone atop the walls, looking out through the frozen magnifying glass. Pushing his Perception to its limits, he started scanning every inch of the ground where the Chiropractor might be.

It felt like it took a long time, but as soon as Joe realized that there was a delta formation of Penguins skidding along the ground *against* the stream of other monsters, it was only a matter of a few seconds until Jaxon came into view. "I see you! Did you… wait, you just asked me for a lance. Did you bring any weapons? Explosive canisters? Do you have a Grandmaster strapped to you that I just can't see? What do you think is going to happen, Jaxon? I don't want you to get sent somewhere on the other side of the world if we fail here."

"Oh, don't worry about me! I've got my handy-dandy hands, and my slithery snakes are *hungry*!"

"Snakes are cold-blooded, Jaxon! It's going to be twice as hard for them up–"

His words died in his throat as he felt a shift in the air, which had always been followed by the giant using an ability of some kind. The Progenitor of the Ice had noticed Jaxon, as evidenced by the words that rolled across the world.

"Finally! A challenger, even if it is a joke of one. An interesting choice of ways to die, to be certain. For your valor, I will obliterate you with my full might." Before the words had even finished reaching Joe's ears, the freezing energy collected in the giant's monocle swept outward, washing over Jaxon and the entire group of Penguins he was leading. Once again, the absolute-zero temperature of the attack stopped all light from moving within its bounds.

In an instant, it was over. A small iceberg had formed, encasing the entire creature unit. As the giant's angry stare returned to the city, and it began walking forward once more, Joe let out a deep sigh and turned away. "Well… back to the defense of the town I guess. Gahh, *Jaxon*."

"Joe! Can I get your opinion on something?" Jaxon's voice

came through the ritual, though it was muffled in an extremely strange manner. "If you were trapped at the center of an ice cube, how would you go about getting out of it? Hypothetically, of course."

"You're alive!" The Ritualist practically shouted into the communication tile. "First off, how? Second… buddy, I have no idea. Start wiggling?"

"Oh! I can do that!" Joe let the Chiropractor have a moment to himself, then repeated his question asking *how* the man was still alive. "Ah, yes, I was not supposed to tell anyone. I don't suppose you remember quite a while ago, your Alchemist friend, the scary man with a hunch that refuses to allow treatment? Strange man, that one. Anyway, he put a Legendary injection up for sale, and someone purchased it?"

"Are you telling me-" Joe started, only to be cut off.

"Correct! That *wasn't* me. He had made a better version, but it was experimental. I got it for a great deal, as I had quite a bit of excess funds. I don't know if you will quite understand this, but in my industry, tips are a large part of how we succeed. So, I've been generously accepting all tips from my customers, even when they make noises about 'change' and 'breaking' the ingots."

"Unrepentant theft is all I'm hearing." Joe chuckled softly as several events over the last few weeks clicked into place in his mind, such as Jaxon laying out in the snow next to the Elven Town Hall, pretending to be frozen solid, but then being able to move without issue. "Are you immune to ice damage now?"

"Ehh… not exactly. It's just that no ice damage under the *Mythical* rank will put me down. So long as it's only ice damage, I will always be able to survive with at least a tenth of my Health. But, I *am* immune to freezing! The pranks I've played on my Penguin friends…" Jaxon chuckled heartily for a few seconds. "The first one I converted to my side? It screamed so loudly when I popped out of the snow, that I thought I had accidentally stabbed it in the eyeball! I guess it's their turn now;

all of them are pretending to be frozen solid. I'm *on* to you, Flipper, you rascal!"

"Look, buddy, I'm glad you're okay for now? Um. Yeah. I'm not sure how else I can help you, but if you think of anything, give me a call back. I need to go… help." The Ritualist lamely ended their conversation, not sure how else to do so.

"Sounds good. Look for me at the top of the giant's head in a few hours. I'll be the one seeing if it has four quadrants of a skull, or if there are additional plates. Spoiler alert: *I'm* betting there are going to be additional plates."

"…Yeah." Joe closed the connection and pulled a face. "I'm not gonna be the one to tell him his penguin friends aren't pretending."

CHAPTER FORTY

A sharp clanging of swords, staccato thudding of arrows, and the guttural cries of wounded beasts filled the frigid air. Novusheim's once-bouncing walls now groaned and creaked under the weight of the relentless assault from above and within. As the Star-swords of Damocles fell and impacted section after section, monsters clamored through the holes, thrashing against them and widening the breach for the next monsters that followed.

Even with Joe's collection rituals going strong—pulling in fluids or discarding lopped off limbs to be reduced—the cracked stones of the wall were stained with soot, blood, and had sparking fractal patterns that zapped anyone who got too close to the failing enchantments. Every second that passed filled the Ritualist with dread, as he expected the entirety of their defenses to fail in only a few minutes.

Major Cleave, still alive and in charge of the defense, was bellowing above the tumult. "Fall back to the black walls! Watch out for that warped and bent section; it could go at any time. I want a double rank standing behind it ready to catch whatever busts through. If you can't stand on the walls, form ranks! The bravest of you dudes and dudettes out front—*shields up*!"

Archers, almost every single one of them a human, were releasing a continuous stream of arrows over the walls, completely blind as to where they were landing. But, from the sounds of the pained screams, it didn't matter so much if they aimed or not. Still, for every monster felled, there were *thirty* fighting to take their place.

Strangely enough, there was another Dwarf Joe didn't recognize trying to take command of the Legion within the Town proper. "Focus on me! I want this battle line shifted to a diamond formation here, full phalanx up front! If you're listening to the wall commander, you are *wrong*! Listen to the Town defense coordinator, me!"

"We're all literally about to die, and someone's still trying to grab scraps of power?" Joe shook his head and seamlessly moved into *ignoring* the Town defense coordinator. From the look of the unmoving ranks of Legionnaires, he wasn't the only one. Perhaps the fact that Major Cleave had been out on the front lines with them this entire time had increased their loyalty, or perhaps they were simply too tired to move, after getting into position. Frankly, it was a coin toss as to which was most accurate.

The Ritualist gently shoved a Dwarf off of the Ebonsteel wall, freeing up a spot for himself to target the monsters that were at the last layers of their defenses. He was *pretty* sure the Dwarf would land without getting hurt, but just to soothe his conscience, he threw a Mend spell after the descending, flailing form. Then his attention was completely devoted to sending his Ritual Orbs into thoracic cavities, craniums, and whatever it was that wraiths had. Skulls, kinda, but wispy… Joe shook his head as he realized that his mind was wandering; the sleep deprivation was wearing on him, due to the intense few days of being awake.

As he threw out spells and spheres, Joe glanced intermittently at his Ritual of Remote Activation. He let out a curse as he saw how quickly the towers at the farthest areas of the walls were crumbling, though he nodded slightly in appreciation as one of the towers of Infernal Conflagration fell and exploded into a massive fireball; taking hundreds of monsters with it in a cataclysmic burst. "Hey, not bad. Also, yeah, I *knew* that was going to happen."

He was trying to celebrate the small victories as they came, but as more and more sections of walls collapsed, and dust rose into the air, it became apparent that they were still outnumbered more than sixty to one. The creatures, sensing weakness and finally being able to do something about it, increased the pressure, ramming into structures, screaming their hunger and rage at the defenders that simply wouldn't give up.

Taking a quick glance backward, Joe saw where all of the non-combatants were gathered at the center of the ring of Legionnaires. Almost all workshops had been abandoned at this point, as everyone waited to see the final conclusion of the upgrade to a City. If they failed, everyone fully understood that they wouldn't have a second try.

At least, the Dwarves wouldn't.

Trying to ignore that intrusive thought, Joe began casting his spells faster. "If I have time to imagine terrible scenarios, I have time to *attack*. Infernal Conflagration!"

As the spell struck home, a gratifying screech of pain returned to him. Joe celebrated by casting a Dark Lightning Strike, finding that the dopamine hits of inflicting damage to the creatures destroying his new home satisfied his Dark Charisma in a *sublime* fashion.

Another wall crumbled, and a tangled mass of beasts fell through it, tumbling into the normal entrance to Novusheim. Major Cleave pointed down at the incursion, shouting at the top of her lungs over the echoing boom of falling debris. "Brace yourselves!"

The rabid monsters hit the first line of defenders and broke against them. If Joe hadn't been so numb to the sounds of combat at this point, the wet, sucking sound of metal meeting flesh and bones snapping as hammers swung out would have been sickening. Instead, it sounded like *winning*.

The front line managed to stand firm, but as more monsters flowed through, the pressure continued to mount. After the first half minute of combat, the shield bearers began to buckle and let out low, hoarse shouts as they pushed back against the hefty beasts. The second line stepped forward, putting their bodies against their brethren and pushing with all of their might. With the additional strength, the Dwarves steadied, even as the third line stepped forward and stabbed with sword and spear over the shields barely holding the monsters back.

Joe threw himself over the combat, sailing through the air and landing on the ground near the wall, needing to toss himself up and over half a dozen Hoardlings to get into position at the breach. Pulling out his tablet, he adjusted one of the ritual towers that was still active, setting it to hit just a tiny bit below and to the side of his location.

Moments later, a bolt of darkness shot through and created a zone of Clinging Shadows, slowing the surge of beasts to a crawl. Setting the tower to continuously attack as soon as it was off cooldown, Joe began drawing ritual circles in the air. "I'll try to close this bottleneck! Somebody help me watch for leopards!"

A triple-circle diagram rapidly formed in front of him as Joe put together a Ritual of Infernal Conflagration without any of the safety features he normally put in place for the tower version. "If this explodes, that means either a monster hit it, or I made it poorly. I'm not about to make it poorly, so if it does go boom, that means it takes a monster down. Works for me."

One ritual circle floated in the air, followed by another, then two more. Taking a deep breath, Joe activated his Mythical-rank spell as rapidly as he could. "Ritual Duplication!"

The four floating rituals turned into an oversized ring of twelve as he propagated them in front of his face. Then, hoping he hadn't made an error in its design, he rapidly activated each of them in turn. The resulting circle of circles reminded him of a gatling gun: flames appeared in the center of a ritual and launched, followed fractions of a second by the next one in line. Since the ritual required three seconds to generate and launch the orb of fire, it made for an almost perfectly continuous stream of cackling, screaming, tittering fireballs flying into the faces of his foes.

Joe fell back as the heat of the rituals quickly mounted, doing the math in his head and coming up with an acceptable seven thousand, two hundred infernal damage that would be dealt each second by this ritual. "That's almost enough to take down a Hoardling every second. Good enough for now, I hope."

"Legionnaires! Step back! Step *back*!" Major Cleave's orders were followed cleanly, the centuries of experience each of the members of the Legion had shining through in that brief moment. With each step they took, they formed a tighter wall, supporting each other and protecting not only their comrades, but creating a perfect block against the Penguins that were attempting to bounce over their heads. "Good! Resume!"

While the Legionnaires had gathered more densely, which was good for their safety, the tradeoff was that it allowed more beasts into the open area between the defenders and the walls. Those atop the Ebonsteel sections were immediately cut off from support, unless they had some way of crossing the distance without touching the ground. Joe scanned the area, recognizing that the situation had become extremely tenuous.

The weight of the situation was bearing down on him, though he recognized that it wasn't nearly as bad for him as it was for those fighting in melee combat. The seemingly ceaseless arrows that had been streaming down began to peter out, stopping altogether as the supply lines were cut off, and the Archers ran out of ammunition. Watching the ranged attackers, Joe could see the moment that they decided that, if they were going down… they were going down fighting. Archers all along the walls pulled out various close-range weaponry and picked out a target to jump on.

He winced as they geared up for their last hurrah—and only

partially because of how terrible his Omnivault skill informed him that their jumping form was. As Star-swords continued to crash down, breaking clear lines through the outer walls, Joe decided he would join the Archers. At least, he'd join them in jumping. Unlike them, he would jump *over* the monsters and continue fighting from the inner ring of Dwarves.

As the defenders on the walls prepared to make their final, valiant stand to give the Town a moment of reprieve, an unnatural silence rippled outward. In that brief lull, where the furious hearts of the monsters were frozen for a moment, and the limbs of the Dwarves shaking with exhaustion stilled, only one sound could be heard.

Tap.

Tap.

Tap.

Joe's eyes were drawn to the sound, along with everyone else's that were in range. There, casually stomping down the street as if he owned the place, was someone that lit a fire in the hearts of everyone who remained.

Grandmaster Havoc walked right up to the malformed Ebonsteel wall, just as it collapsed under the weight of the monsters' assault. The triumphant call of the monsters cut off as he approached them, their bodies refusing to move forward toward this specter of death.

The Dwarf took a deep breath and shouted in a rising crescendo of song.

"Are ya *ready*, Dwarves?"

The silence lasted only a fraction of a second longer before the remaining walls of Novusheim shook with their response.

"*Aye, Aye, Major General!*"

You have entered a raid area! All experience gain has been paused and will only be calculated at the end of the raid or when leaving the raid area.

The Lord of Slaughter stands with you! -30% sensation of pain. 25% damage dealt with melee weapons. 10% reduced damage taken from all sources.

CHAPTER FORTY-ONE

"I *sa~aid*," Havoc howled out as he slapped a brave but foolish Leopard out of the air, turning it into a fine bloody mist that settled back over its compatriots. "*Are ya ready, Dwarves*?"

"Aye, Aye, Major General!"

The Grandmaster looked back at the thousands upon thousands of defenders, a smile on his face as he saw that every single one of them was staring right back. He clapped his hands, and a Hoardling lunging at him was suddenly missing its torso. Its arms, neck, and head fell as one piece, and the legs as another. "I can't *hear* you!"

"*Aye, Aye, Major General*!"

"Ohhhh… These monsters are frozen, popping up from the frost!"

"Ice, cold, war, crimes!"

"What should we do, bring the fight to the Boss?"

"Ice, cold, *war, crimes*!"

"Is losing and dying something you wish?" There was a momentary pause after this phrase, but the Dwarves got into the swing of it.

"*No*! War crimes!

"I hear you all, let me grant you your wish!"

"War crimes, war crimes!"

"Ready? War crimes, war crimes..." The Dwarf held up a large metal box with an oversized button on the top of it.

"War crimes, war crimes!"

"*War cri~imes...*! Here we go~o!" Havoc screeched as he *slapped* the button. The box shattered with a scream of tortured metal, exploding into dust as the vibrations of its noise spread out for miles around the Town.

Joe reached up and found that his nose was bleeding, even though he hadn't taken any health damage from the sonic wave that had just raced out. Looking around hopefully, the Ritualist looked to see if all of the monsters had just died, but they were still throwing themselves against the defenders, now even more ferociously than before. "Not sure what he just did, but at least we're taking less damage and dishing out more."

The battle raged on, now with Havoc standing in the hole of the walls and practically daring monsters to try and get past him. All by himself, the Dwarf held off the incursion from that area, allowing the tight ring of fighters to catch their breath and regroup. Joe checked on his rituals hanging near the entrance, seeing that they were still continuously dropping infernal fireballs on the beasts without showing any signs of instability.

As the fighting intensified, Joe waited patiently for some visible effect from the Grandmaster's actions. Every few seconds, he would chance a glance at the Dwarf splattering low-level monsters through the air, wondering when—the Ritualist had a thought that made his eyes narrow, and he watched Havoc's face. "Did he hit his button too hard? Was the box supposed to–"

He caught a glimpse of the Grandmaster as the Dwarf turned to look back at the people inside, and Joe's eyes went wide. "He looks *sheepish*! Don't tell me he spent hundreds of hours preparing, only to get over-excited and break his weapon!"

Penguins started zipping around the corners, Hoardlings

started running faster, and leopards threw themselves over the lines of defenders and into the back ranks. Major Cleave apparently felt that something had gone wrong as well, and her orders echoed out: "We have a surge! Mages, target the openings and prepare to launch area-of-effects in five seconds! Archers, target Penguins and cats! Ready... *fire for effect*!"

A huge stream of various magics impacted the entrance of Novusheim, the arcane energies rebounding off each other and causing the air in that space to warp. There was a momentary reprieve, but then the monsters continued racing in, faster than ever. Joe checked on his tablet, letting out a soft curse as he saw that every ritual tower outside of the inner wall had fallen, and there was no way to replace them.

The outer walls were gone.

As he fiddled with his ritual, planning to drop the remainder of the inactive ritual towers along the Ebonsteel walls, Joe heard a cheer. Fingers freezing, he looked up at the entrance and saw that it was empty. "What's happening?"

Confusion was rampant, but as Havoc trudged away from his position, he threw a hand in the air and waved to gather their attention. "Sorry about that last little push. I had to make sure that none of the, ah... *stuff*... got inside our Town. That meant I had to aim it out a bit, but, ahh... War Crime complete! Watch out for the falling stars and the final boss, but otherwise, it's safe to go outside!"

Joe was happy to avoid the mad scramble that occurred as the packed lines of fighters separated immediately. The Starswords of Damocles were closing in, with dozens of them still in the air and now nearly over the positions of the outermost fighters. He shifted his attention to what was going on outside of the walls, though he had to wait a few moments as the debris from the last of the collapsing walls settled enough to see through it.

For the first time since he'd arrived on Jotunheim, he was actually *wishing* for the otherwise-constant wind. As his ability to perceive the enemy was returned, Joe took an involuntary step back, making the sign of the cross on himself as he saw what was waiting out there. "Celestials... that... yeah, that's a war crime if I've ever seen one."

There were still tens of thousands of monsters, but none of them were moving under their own power. Stone and metal had grown through them, grotesquely in many cases. Elite monsters had what appeared to be metal arachnid limbs that had burst out of their abdomen and lifted them off the ground as they struggled to get back into the fight. Many of the creatures were obviously still alive, thrashing against the automaton limbs that were using their bodies as building material.

Even as he watched, the odd amalgam of flesh and crafting materials began moving again. The hundreds of thousands of beasts were slowly turning around, and those in the very back lines began charging toward the Progenitor of the Ice that was closing in. Havoc's voice called out, "How do you think he'll like a taste of his own medicine? Look, everyone! I stole his army and made sure they'd do *anything* to die! They're going to fight hard for us, so be prepared to jump in after the last of them go down."

Major Cleave reinforced his words with an order, her voice suspiciously mellow. "Priority one! Avoid the falling ice! Priority two, get what little rest you can while the giant is distracted. I highly recommend *not* going out there and taking a look. Go ahead and trust that the Grandmaster has the situation under control for the moment."

Hundreds of people dropped to the ground and fell asleep on the spot, knowing that they might only have a few minutes to recover. Joe envied them. Even with as exhausted as he was at the moment, there was no way he would be able to fight through the fear of missing out on what was coming next. Still, he tried to take the time to relax as best as he could, collapsing on top of the wall and watching as the entire landscape shifted, due to the massive swarm of abominations that were closing in on Brisingr.

"Ah, my Apprentice! Hanging out to watch the show?" Havoc plopped down next to Joe, his face a mask of maniacal glee only offset by the deep bags under his eyes denoting absolute exhaustion.

The Ritualist could only nod at the inquiry. He was fascinated by the leopards with skeletons reinforced by high-grade metal, who were creating ice bridges onto the feet of the giant. "I've got to ask, Havoc. If you could've done something like this before, why didn't you? This fight, all the lives lost? When you could just subvert the whole army?"

"Nah, that's not how my abilities work." At first, Joe was almost positive that the Dwarf wasn't going to expand on that statement further and was frankly shocked when he did. "First off, breaking the seal the Oligarchy put on me was the biggest time constraint. Snow was finally able to pop it around wave seventy-five or so. For obvious reasons, she was… *hesitant.* It's not like I'm going to let her put it back on, after all. Heh."

Hearing those words put a chill in the Ritualist that had nothing to do with the environment around him. Speaking with a raspy voice, and wondering where all the moisture in his mouth had gone, Joe pressed for more information, since his mentor seemed to be in a chatty mood. "You said that wasn't how your abilities worked? Can I ask…?"

"Well, I'm the Lord of Slaughter for a reason." Havoc pulled his cigar out of his mouth and blew a stream of smoke into the air in front of him. Looking at the vapor critically, the Dwarf lifted a finger and drew strange patterns into it. As he pulled his hand back to his side, Joe noticed that the attack patterns of the monsters in the distance had suddenly changed. "'Oligarch of Slaughter' is more accurate but doesn't roll off the tongue as easily. Anyway, if I want to be able to do something like this, I need *samples.* Lots and lots of samples. Then I need to run tests and experiment until I can take over the bodies of the creatures. Needed about, oh…"

He seemed to be doing some quick math in his head, and the answer nearly made Joe gag. "One-eighty to two hundred thousand of each type. Couldn't get to the wraiths, just weren't enough of them, or the Pachycephalosaurus Palisade Punchers.

So, you know, if you see any of those, start blasting. It's unlikely; they should have been cleaned up by the control group already."

Havoc's grin was a terror to behold as he continued to reminisce, "Anywhoo, at that point, I have the knowledge on the creatures themselves, but I need to blend up a few—say ten thousand of 'em—if I want to be able to make another control canister. Not exactly something I can just toss out whenever I want. Plus, if I'd done this earlier, the fresh monsters coming in wouldn't have been impacted, and… what a *waste*, am I right?"

"Yeah, haha… wasteful." Joe tried to swallow, his very dry throat fighting him the entire time. Some of Havoc's actions, especially from back on Alfheim, were shining in a new light. It was nice to know why the strange gray mist that had turned the Elves to automaton statues didn't seem to affect him, even though he was almost certain it had gotten on him at some point. The Dwarf simply hadn't had enough time to collect 'samples' of humans. Or, at least, he hadn't been able to collect enough corpses to make it happen.

"Ooh! It's starting! Let's see how the big nasty reacts to having to put down the beasts that are supposed to be under its control." A few moments passed in silence as Havoc watched the battle in the distance, then he broke out in a deep chuckle. "Already at two percent health ripped off of him! Take that, brother. I'm one hundred percent ahead of you and only just started."

Joe took a moment to parse that quiet statement, remembering belatedly that Grandmaster McPoundy was Havoc's actual brother. Finding some common ground, the Ritualist turned to describe the odd inspiration he'd gained, when he was caught by a sudden blast of wind and sent tumbling through the open air.

"*You* dare *make me slay the children of the Jörmungandr*?" Brisingr howled across the distance, shifting his stance and moving into a full sprint instead of the leisurely walk he had been maintaining.

"The Geas prevents this form of treachery! Enough of these games! *Die*!"

Lying on his back and staring up at the false sky above him, Joe could only hear one sound.

Havoc laughing.

"I guess war crimes are a thing here, too. It's good to know where the line is drawn so I can cross it more effectively."

CHAPTER FORTY-TWO

The shaking of the ground grew louder and more violent with every passing second, only the sheer size of the giant keeping it from having already crossed the distance between them. Havoc was still sitting on the wall, pointing and laughing at the Boss Monster closing in on them. "Ha! Look at that: his foot is on fire from those flowers you planted. Wait a second… even better, they're *growing* on him!"

Joe pulled himself back onto the wall, following the finger that Havoc was pointing. Just as the Dwarf had stated, it appeared that the plants had found a fertile location to sprout, using the Legendary aura of cold that was pouring off of the giant. The Dwarf shook his head and turned to stare at his Protege with admiration. "I've heard about people wanting to set the world on fire just to watch it burn. It's an honor to meet one in person."

"*Not* why I did that." The human stated heavily, taking a few moments to wonder if the ring of flame he planted would actually eventually cover the entire world. He shrugged gently, "You know, I guess if it does cover the entire world, at least this place will warm up for a while. According to the plants' system information, they'll stop growing when the temperature is above a certain point. Also, they only produce the fire when they're growing rapidly, so I think that it'll be fine."

"Well, I suppose," Havoc stood up and slapped his knees. "That boss ain't going to stop himself."

Off in the distance, a tiny speck appeared just in front of where the giant was charging along, launching into the air and landing a blow on the giant's face that caused it to tumble backwards, falling to the ground and bouncing along for about half a mile or so before coming to a halt. Words echoed back to them, belated due to the distance. "*Flaming Fist Furious Flurry of Endless Uppercuts*!"

"You've got to be kidding me." Havoc let out a groan as he looked into the distance. "They sent *Wrath*? He's barely got his attacks under control as it is, and they let him–"

"No." The air vibrated next to Havoc's head, instantly matching Grandmaster Snow's pitch and tone. Joe was entranced by the literally masterful control of Mana Manipulation that must take to complete, so much so that he nearly missed the venomous words she was saying. "He was *not* one that I authorized and is going to fail. Havoc, unless you can do something, Wrath just made us lose this war. Only three Grandmaster's abilities were allowed. If we unleash the last of them, we're going to have to–"

"Don't say it." Havoc growled at her, only to be blatantly ignored.

"-surrender. Fully and unequivocally." Snow's voice drifted off in the breeze, and no further messages were delivered.

The atmosphere was suddenly tense between them, as Joe and the Grandmaster stared into the distance, where a single Dwarf wreathed in flame was sending strike after strike into the giant. Unfortunately, without the element of surprise on his side, the physical blows were doing worse than nothing: the new combatant was slowly being overpowered by the aura of frost, and his flames were rapidly dwindling.

"Half a percent. Maybe a quarter. You..." Havoc's skin

began to writhe and wriggle as wires or some other worm-like item shifted within him. "I don't often cheer on the monster, but in this case, I'd be okay with making an example out of that–"

"We just need a new plan, Havoc." Joe winced in sympathy as the giant lashed out with a lightning fast backhand, swatting the Dwarf in mid-air and sending him flying. Unable to gain control of himself, the Dwarf continued on in a straight line—only for a beam of absolute cold to follow in his path, enveloping him entirely and turning his flying form into an icy comet that trailed across the sky.

Brisingr paused for a full thirty seconds, until a resounding **boom** traveled faintly through the air. Then a bright smile appeared on his face, and the giant spoke once more. "All the way to the edge of my frozen arena. Deeply satisfying. I will say, I appreciate having some sense slapped into me. What was I thinking, coming at you without thought? Let's take a moment and remove that last spark of hope I feel warming your hearts, invaders."

Hands raised toward the clouds, the Progenitor of the Ice began chanting as blood poured out of his hands and into the spell circle that began forming from jagged blue lines. "I call upon the entropic final temperatures of the farthest reaches of the cosmos! Imbue my strike with your ethereal hues. Ensure absolute destruction of my target, allowing no shield to deny my strike… I offer blood, power, and an agreement of no collateral damage whatsoever in return!"

The hanging lines of light were surrounded by a small, localized blizzard. The eyes of the giant shifted slightly, looking upward. Joe tried to follow its line of sight but found that his own false sky was impairing his view. Refusing to let that stop him, he threw himself straight up with a powerful Omnivault, bursting out of the illusion and going still with horror at what he saw.

As far as he could see, the clouds above them were glowing with incandescent mana. Directly above the heart of their Town, an enormous spell circle suddenly expanded outward—

comparable to a Grandmaster ritual circle preparing to accept mana. "Essence Cycle!"

The colors of the world immediately shifted, and Joe could only stare on in numb acceptance as he watched the very essence of the frost giant mingle with the spell, empowering it further, due to its sacrifice of its own health. There was no time to warn the Town, to figure out a solution. The churning clouds were captured, then *twisted* by the stream of mana. For a brief moment, they spun so quickly that they formed the eye of a hurricane, allowing Joe to look out and see the true night sky, filled with stars, for the first time since his arrival on this world.

Then a column of ice appeared—appeared, not *dropped*. From the edge of the atmosphere of Jotunheim, down into the very heart of the city, ice in a very specific shape had appeared.

Joe forced himself out of the state that the Essence Cycle skill imparted on him as he dropped through the false sky once more. His eyes had trailed along the column the entire way, and as he re-entered Novusheim, he found that his worst fears had come to pass.

The Town Hall was completely encased at the base of the pillar, the frost not spreading an inch farther on any side.

As the Ritualist landed on the ground, he found that it was shaking, rumbling, and he began bouncing along with it as he wondered what sort of effect this spell was about to have next. "Did it freeze all the way down to the mantle, and we are going to have a situation like the Elven capital on our hands? An earthquake? Is it just going to fall over? Maybe if we can melt it fast enough–"

The rumbling stopped, and Joe looked around nervously. Motion just above him caught his eye, and his jaw dropped almost in slow motion as he saw the massive form of Brisingr flying above the Town in a full body tackle.

"*Hup*!" The giant bowed his head slightly and hit the pillar straight on with his shoulder. Then his momentum took him out of the Town, and he vanished for a brief moment before landing on the other side of the walls, already nearly half a mile away.

Fully expecting that the remaining ice of the enormous pillar was going to be falling on them, Joe threw himself against the edge of the wall and bunkered down, keeping his eyes trained on the sky above. Instead, all of the remnants of ice vanished almost instantly, leaving behind a bare space in the sky...

...and a hole in the ground where the Town Hall had once stood.

Event status: Novusheim's upgrade event to go from a Town to a City... failed!

We regret to inform the citizens of Novusheim that the conditions for achieving an upgrade for your settlement have been failed. As a result, 'Novusheim' the 'Town' will automatically be reverted to a 'Hamlet' once the Town Hall has been rebuilt.

Please note, the Town Hall must be rebuilt for further progress as well as settlement management purposes. Once it has been rebuilt, all facilities, structures, and benefits will be downgraded to reflect this new status. Any resources or assets invested during this event are non-refundable.

We recognize the hard work and dedication shown and encourage you to rally together, rebuild, and regain your esteemed status!

Caution! Any ongoing Beast Waves will still sweep over this area.

"We... lost?" The choked cry came from one of the nearby humans that had stayed and fought through the entire upgrade process. Joe looked around numbly, finding that there wasn't a single person, Dwarf or human, that was not in a total daze at the moment. Warriors that had been utterly unyielding against the onrushing swarms of enemies now hung their heads in despair. Across the entire Town, weapons slipped from fingers and clattered onto the frost-coated ground.

"Look at that. The way the mud froze really changed the way the Town looks from above." Joe blinked at the nonsensical words, looking around to see who had voiced such an unimportant detail before realizing that the syllables were dropping out of his own mouth. "I think I might be in shock."

It didn't seem real. They'd fought so hard, brought everything from the weakest fighter to the greatest superweapon to bear, but all of their blood, sweat, and tears, had been for nothing.

As the remaining defenders began to languish in their defeat, the ground began trembling once more. A single glance showed that the frost giant was pacing toward them, almost *creeping* toward them. At this distance, now less than a tenth of a mile between them, the breath that carried its words left everyone colder than the harshest winter debuff ever could.

Brisingr taunted them, triumphant and clearly calculating how to eradicate the rest of them most efficiently, "Behold. The consequences of your defiance. The result of your refusal to follow the demands of the *Jotunn*! Bear witness to the protectors of Jotunheim, and take honor in your defeat to the Progenitor of the Ice!"

The discarded shaft of the javelin that Brisingr had thrown at the start of his entrance into combat was now in his hand. He lifted the enormous block of ice up above his head, rearing backward to bring it down with the full might of its body.

Not a single soul moved to stop him.

Sucking in a sharp breath, the muscles of the giant contracted, and it began to swing forward.

A sharp sound, like ice shattering, rang through the area. The giant *flinched*, its head snapping to the side as it stumbled and tried—and failed—to regain its balance. "*What?* What's happening?"

To the absolute shock of everyone watching, Brisingr bent in half, then he heaved and vomited all over the ground, the wave of icy bile splashing up and breaking against the Ebonsteel walls of the city.

CHAPTER FORTY-THREE

"What happened?" Joe's head snapped to the side to stare at Havoc, who had just let out an explosive sigh of relief. "Is that something you did, Apprentice?"

"Are you *kidding* me? What could I have done to make that thing sick? I've nowhere near that kind of firepower in my rituals." Not seeing an easily available answer, the Ritualist merely decided to take the time they'd been given and put it to good use. "We need to evacuate as quickly as we can. Those ice walls that came up and made an arena! I'm pretty sure that, if we can get to them and climb to the top, we can escape. It only said that teleportation had been locked down inside the arena, it didn't say that we were *stuck* in here."

"Nah, don't bother." The Dwarf tapped his cigar, letting a cloud of ash fall to the ground. It didn't escape Joe's notice that, where the dust landed, the ground evaporated and vanished. "Until this big boy is put down for good, they'll prolly radiate the same kind of cold he does. You won't be able to climb over them. No one will."

Before Joe could start arguing with the Dwarf that they needed to do *something*, he felt a strange shift in the air. Before now, that had been an indicator that the giant was about to unleash a devastating ability. But this? It felt... strange. Instead of the air being sucked dry, it was being *suffused*. The ambient mana rapidly rose to an extreme height, to the point that Joe felt his skin prickling as his hair stood on end.

Vwamp.

A ritual circle appeared in mid-air, above the giant hole showing where the Town Hall had one stood. Around the Town, in five separate locations, ritual circles appeared in the air and began to spin. Joe watched in amazement as the five circles around the area shifted in coloration away from purple or green to a stark, neon blue. They began spinning faster and faster, until their very movement was causing static electricity to form.

Just as it appeared that the circles would become unstable and detonate, the collection of energy shot to the center of their individual rings. Then, each of the five circles sent a beam of pure mana at the two circles that had appeared above where the Town Hall had stood. Three of the beams struck the outer, Expert-rank bright purple circle. The other two bypassed it and went into the innermost, green circle.

Everything started to click for Joe as he noted the locations of the floating ritual circles that were supplying mana. "They were still at their positions? Even without ritual towers to resupply? Come on... the bonus I promised isn't anywhere near *that* good."

However it had worked out that the workers in charge of filling Mana Batteries were standing by at the Mana Battery Recharge Stations, Joe could only be absolutely grateful that they had remembered to slap the power plates down when the Town Hall got hit. He considered the two ritual circles that were currently spinning against each other, with various energies being created and sparking along their trajectories. "It's not going to be enough... the Formation is broken; all of the work that Socar did to set us up for success was destroyed."

As tiny, shimmering tokens of energy zipped from all

around the Town and into the center of the floating ritual, Joe felt a hint of despair fill him. "Oh no. It's... there *is* no creature that has set off all of the conditions. There's no *target* for the ritual! It's just going to detonate and take all of us out with it."

Just before he could completely give up and attempt to dismantle the ritual, a shimmering orb containing five of the silvery tokens flashed over the wall and into the very center of the ritual diagram. The bright green inner ring was spinning on a horizontal axis, and even though the silvery moats of light were tiny, it was barely able to contain all of them. The outer ring was spinning on a vertical axis, and as the seconds passed, it began to dim slightly. "What? How is it targeting him? He didn't..."

A Star-sword of Damocles crashed down, freezing another area and vanishing. The Ritualist stared at the other lights hovering around. "Wait... Brisingr put his blood into those. Does that count? Putting the essence of yourself into the attack counts as you being there?"

"Nifty bauble you made there. Kind of looks like the inside of a pomegranate that's about to blow up." Havoc threw an arm over Joe's shoulder and pulled him tight. At first, the Ritualist thought it was a gesture of affection, but as the arm squeezed down, and he began to struggle to breathe, the Dwarf leaned close and whispered in his ear. "If we survived all of *that*, just for you to vaporize the Town, I'm going to press this button and crack the planet in half."

The sound of Brisingr emptying his stomach once more completely drowned out all other noise, and the giant pushed itself up off the ground and into a standing position. "What did you do-"

Unfortunately for the enormous entity, the floating ritual now had a clear line of sight.

**Bwamp*!*

Energy discharged as a lance of fire, striking the giant in the center of its face, just above the nose and directly between its eyes. As its glabella shifted from subarctic temperatures to hotter than a fresh espresso, Brisingr shouted in rage and jerked away, only for his eyes to cross and make the Boss clutch at its head. The Progenitor of the Ice fell back to the ground dry heaving, and the energy escaping the ritual cut off.

Scrambling for an answer, Joe scanned the entire Town, looking for anything that could explain the strange phenomena. "Why's it sending that out as a single beam instead of as a cascade of sparks like it did the last time the Ritual of Slaughter was activated? Is it… there! All that's left of the towers around the city are the original placements for the Formation Socar put in place. It's not the expanded version, but it *is* the single-target lance of flame, exactly as he said it would be. Maybe because there are no other targets, it's unable to bend around obstacles?"

"Or you just have too much pressure buildup." Havoc slowly released his grip, swiftly stowing away the button he was threatening the Ritualist with. "Hard for magic to get fancy when it has tens of thousands of points of mana pouring into it every second."

His mind flashing to his Mana Manipulation and Coalescence skills, which had stagnated *hard* since arriving on Jotunheim, Joe nodded in understanding. "We need to figure out a way to get that giant back on its feet."

"Terrible idea," Havoc growled at him. "I just need to make that wall stop existing. Then the fire can attack directly."

The Dwarf pointed at the metal barricade and snapped his fingers. Joe looked over in the direction that he was gesturing, going still and blinking in surprise as he saw that nothing had happened. Havoc lightly slapped Joe, sending him tumbling. "Do you really think it's *that* easy? I don't have an answer for everything!"

All scheming came to an end as Brisingr pushed himself up once more, glaring at the Town. Immediately, the Ritual of Slaughter lanced into him, but this time the giant was prepared. He started moving side to side, but the ritual tracked him perfectly, its gyroscopic nature allowing for any angle to be followed. Finally, a giant hand was lifted into the air and blocked the flame. A smell like a backyard barbecue washed over the area, and Joe's stomach growled in spite of him knowing where the smell was coming from.

"-llo, *hello*! Can anyone hear me?"

Without looking, Joe reached down and snatched up his Ritual of Communication, which was glowing brightly and marked with a small 'J'. "You're okay! Did you get out of the ice?"

"Joe! You're alive! Did it work? I thought it did, but then everything went dark, and the floor became the floor again instead of the wall." Jaxon's voice was coming through woozily, as though he had taken a blow to the head.

"Jaxon, what are you *talking* about?" Joe bellowed into the ritual, blinking in shock as the giant in the distance winced along with his shouting. "No. Don't tell me-"

"I've been in here working on its eardrum for the last... I'm not actually sure how long, time is... it is very strange right now." The Chiropractor's voice faded slightly, but as he started speaking again, there were small, wet, meaty sounds coming through along with his words. "I felt the giant trying to attack, so I *adjusted* its eardrum. I don't remember what happened right after that, but I thought it worked. Everyone still alive? Wait, let me try that again. Everyone still alive, who *was* alive before the giant tried to attack?"

"I really want to know how you got there, but right now we are–"

"It's a pretty easy story. I caught a ride on a mecha Penguin that was zipping along and crawled up the side of the giant when I landed on its leg. I'm looking forward to seeing you again soon. Not to put too fine a point on it, but I have some *serious* burns over a good chunk of my body from where I had to push through your fire flowers that had sprouted on his leg." Jaxon let out an uncharacteristic groan. "That's not even the worst of it. Joe, do you have *any* idea how many spiders were in this giant's ear canal? Why is that a thing, Joe? Joe? *Joe*!"

"Jaxon, I'm going to ask you a very serious question, and I need an answer right away." The bald human had one of his hands clenched on the top of his head, the other on the ritual, and would have been yanking out his hair if he had any. "Is there *any* chance that you got some of the seeds of those plants stuck in your clothes?"

"I did, but don't worry. I plucked them out as they started to sprout and put them in my storage glove. Again, the whole 'burns on my body' thing is really keeping a lot of my attention at the moment."

Trying not to get too excited, not wanting to count this as a win before it was over, Joe spoke as calmly as possible. "Jaxon, adjusting its eardrum was a stroke of genius. You're amazing, and I also need you to get out of there. Before you go, can you pull out those seeds and scatter them around in there? Wait, just to be sure, it's really cold in there, right?"

"If anything, it's colder inside than it was outside." The sounds of the small, meaty thumps stopped, then Joe heard the Chiropractor snap his fingers. "Adjust. Plants are out. This is one cold-hearted giant, but his mind is about to be *burning* with ideas!"

Brisingr let out a moan, clapped a hand over his mouth, and turned to the side in time with Jaxon saying 'adjust'.

The Ritualist took a deep breath and steepled his fingers over the ritual tile. "Please just drop the plants and run, Jaxon."

CHAPTER FORTY-FOUR

"Why'd you tell him to leave? It seemed like he was making an impact." Havoc rumbled at Joe, watching as the giant finally found his feet and sprang up, his craggy face a rictus of abject fury. "Look, now it's *just* angry instead of suffering extreme vertigo *and* being angry."

The Ritualist was already shaking his head, though he kept his eyes locked on the ear the giant had been pawing at. Until he saw Jaxon escape intact, he was going to be worried for his friend. "No, this is better. That big hit that took the Progenitor of the Ice down? That was likely thousands of stacks of Adjust in the making. At the end, I'm sure you saw Brisingr recovering faster and being less impeded by the strikes. There's just no way for our friend to build up enough stacks again before we get wiped out. But a flame-emitting plant infection? Damage over time is the only thing that's going to work against something like this."

"Yeah, because I'm *hobbled*." Havoc grunted with great annoyance. "If I didn't have to worry about the constraints of the Oligarchy, or the rules of engagement for settlement upgrades, *we* wouldn't have to worry about this ice giant. I'd blend it up and use it to chill my drinks. That hobbles you, too, by the way. If you were able to toss around Grandmaster-rank rituals, you would've gotten the notification as well. Abyss, if you could throw around *Master*-rank damaging spells or skills, you'd still be *warned* at the minimum."

"But Masters *can* still be in play?" As Joe saw what appeared to be a speck of debris fall out of Brisingr's ear, he turned to Havoc with serious eyes. "How much can we bring to bear?"

"Thinking like an Oligarch, are we? Not going to be 'who'll give me permission', but 'how much can we get away with before they stop us'? I like it." The Dwarf flashed a smile at the Ritualist but still shook his head. "There's a strange effect with the rules of engagement. Essentially, we can use any Expert-ranked skills or effects we have, as many times as we want. That's because we're trying to prove that we have what it takes to be a City. Well… we were, at least. I liked that Town Hall. It had style."

Joe followed the glance over at the enormous hole and rolled his eyes. "Can I get a couple of geomancers to fill that hole? It's making the Grandmaster *sad*!"

His sarcastic comment was followed to the letter, and the Ritualist was slightly taken aback as a half-dozen Mages began rolling and massaging the ground in an effort to be the one to balance Havoc's mood for him. The Grandmaster himself nodded slightly. "You know what? I *appreciate* that. I'm going to take it at face value, even though I know you were being a brat. Anyway, we could use one Master-rank spell or skill through the entirety of the upgrade… usually."

"But because they sent a Legendary monster at us…" Joe stated leadingly.

"Pretty much. Hit the nail on the head." Havoc took a puff on his cigar. "You know, all of this was posted clearly in the Town Hall, and you could've had all of this information weeks ago."

"Prove it," Joe quipped as he gestured at the rapidly refilling crater.

"All right, point taken." Havoc gathered himself and gestured at the giant that was sending blasts of ice at the Town. "Shouldn't we be doing something about that, though? No? Okay. We get three Grandmaster abilities, and up to twenty-one Master rank—which are mostly used up. We've burned through most of that before we even got three-quarters of the way done with the Beast Waves, and Snow has been riding the edge of what is allowable by continuously using her manipulation skill instead of a proper combat one. Frankly, we should've lost by now, and if there was something one of the other Masters could do, she would've put that card in play."

As Joe absorbed the information, the duo separated, flinging themselves away from an incoming flurry of icicles the size of his ritual ziggurat. Trying to figure out where the attacks were coming from, the Ritualist looked up, only to see that Brisingr had tried to slap the Town directly. "I didn't even see him move!"

A net of woven mana, thousands upon thousands of lines, had intercepted the open palm. Still, the sheer proximity of the appendage allowed the Legendary Boss's aura to generate and drop ice onto the area. That, combined with his previous momentum, was causing the deadly pelting that was being *mostly* repelled by the dedicated defenders. Only when a solitary person was hit dead-on did they go down from the debris field. Otherwise, where there were clusters of people working in tandem; they were able to divert the ice and avoid the worst outcome.

Joe studied the attacker, trying to find some point of weakness that he could exploit. It was on fire from within, its strikes were being blocked—for now—so the greatest concern was the collateral damage it could cause merely by existing. "There's got to be *some* Master-ranked people who can deal some permanent damage against this thing. Where are they hiding? Why aren't they getting involved?"

A terrible realization hit him, and he winced as he looked over at the now-nearly-filled crater. "Now that I think about it…

I've almost never seen the Council of Masters *not* sitting in the Town Hall. Havoc! Where's Snow? Does she have the rest of the Council of Masters with her?"

"Yeah, I'm not going to give you any indication of where she's set up. That's a good way to let your enemy know where to strike." The Dwarf pulled a face and shook his head. "Also, I'm pretty sure I know what you were guessing, and you were correct in your thinking. Let's just say there were a *lot* of people in that building, and how about we don't cause a panic for anyone."

"Abyss... who else might be able to distract this giant so we can put together a better weapon? Anyone who could put some damage over time on it?" Joe sent the questions at the Grandmaster rapid-fire, and as the Dwarf opened his mouth to bark at him, he instead paused in thought. "What? I don't care what it is, just give me an option!"

"Well, there was *one* Master who was secured for his and our safety at the start of Beast Wave ninety-five." Havoc began to chuckle, "You're going to hate this, but Master Stu wasn't evacuated. In fact, I'm pretty sure they have him hanging out in the observatory watching the stars because it has such great soundproofing."

"I don't care what it is, just give me an option!" Joe repeated, firmly ignoring the words that had just come out of the Grandmaster's mouth.

"Joe!" Jaxon's distant voice carried over to his ears, and the Ritualist turned his head... only to get an eye full of something he never wanted to see. "Do you have any spare clothes? Mine were on fire, I had to strip off everything and leave it behind. My gloves are okay, but... oh, speaking of butts, could you please heal these third-degree burns? The chill of the air is helping a little, though I'm sure I would be more comfortable if I were healed up."

"*Buddy*." Instantly over his embarrassment on his friend's behalf, Joe turned his eyes to his friend and inspected the terrible wounds covering his body. "*Mend*!"

"Ohh! *Cold*!" The Chiropractor yelped as the healing water splashed onto him. "Oh wait, no, actually, that's a little warmer than the air. Warmth! Yay!"

As his friend's skin returned to something resembling normal, Joe arched an eyebrow and tossed the man a spare fur cloak. "When did you strip everything off?"

"As soon as you told me to drop everything and run, I did!" Jaxon proudly announced, slithering into the cloak without undoing the buttons.

Joe looked down at his belt, noticing that one of his ritual tiles was still glowing. "Ugh. Havoc… Stu is going to be absolutely *insufferable*."

Without waiting around to see what the Boss Monster would do next, Joe took off sprinting for the celestial observatory. He had to evade a few icicles and kept his eyes on the last handful of Star-sword fragments that were floating around, but that was completely doable. The farther he went, the fewer obstacles were in his way, if he was not counting the much denser population of defenders.

Arriving at his target, he threw the doors open mercilessly, letting them rebound off the walls as he launched himself inside, already scanning the area for Stu. As soon as he saw the Dwarf, Joe's eyes narrowed, and he launched himself over. "Why would they put you in my bean bag chair?"

"*Your*… ew!" Stu was pulled from whatever meditation he'd been doing and tried to hop forward and out from his position. Instead, the bindings on him went tight, and he was pulled down onto the Hoardling fur cushion. "What have you done on this thing? When is the last time it was washed?"

Unwilling to get into a verbal spat with the Master of Sarcasm, Joe reached down and gripped his shoulder, prompting the Dwarf to lock eyes with him. "Stu. We are *losing*. But I have a way for you to help. You'll have the largest audience we have left, and you'll get to ply your trade as a way to finish your community service. I *personally* guarantee that I'll have your sentence completely eliminated for your help."

"Ooh... a quest." Stu's eyes twinkled with mischievous light. "It's been a long time since *I've* been granted a quest. Give me more details before I agree."

The Ritualist held up his ritual tile. "This is a communication device, and the other one is right next to the eardrum of the giant attacking us. All I want you to do is get out there, get its attention, and whisper poisonous words until it's a quivering, sad sack. Can you do that?"

Stu stared at the ritual tile with an amused expression on his face. "I accept your quest, on the condition that I get to ask a minor favor of you when I'm done."

"If it isn't unreasonable, then yes. Before you ask, Grandmaster Snow will be the party who decides if it's reasonable or not." As soon as he finished speaking, Joe felt a strange **click** in his mind that signified a quest he had offered being accepted. He grabbed the bindings and found that they were title-locked. "I, Joe, Councilman of Novusheim, authorize these bindings to be released immediately."

The strings of mana that had been woven through the leather straps and chain links faded, and Master Stu smoothly stood up from his spot on the bean bag chair. "Let's go make an angry giant so filled with rage that it can't possibly use its best abilities against *my* people."

As they walked out of the observatory, Joe realized that perhaps he should fill the Dwarf in on the situation. "Oh... I don't know how long you've been stuck in there, or if they've been telling you what's going on."

"Far too long, Joe," Stu stated breezily, though his smug countenance fell flat as soon as they stepped out into the open air.

"Right, so, all but the last layer of walls were completely destroyed. All of the monsters are dead except the Legendary Boss Monster. The Town Hall was cratered, and as far as I know, the entire Council of Masters—besides Grandmaster Snow—was frozen solid, then shattered, from a single spell. Any questions?"

CHAPTER FORTY-FIVE

The Master of Sarcasm didn't wait even a moment to get to work, slowly ramping up the phrases he was saying into the ritual tile. Much of it was utter nonsense to Joe, but from the pleased expression on Stu's face, he was getting the reaction he desired. "Oh, yes, this'll do nicely. How many times have I ever been able to slowly turn the mind of a Grandmaster against itself? The skill gain alone… what's this notification? Doubled experience? Oh-ho-*ho*! I see those chains were more for keeping me out of the loop than for keeping me out of the fight."

"All right, I need to go and see if I can get some better information on–" Joe looked up as the giant swatted at the woven dome of mana, flinching back as it followed up by punching the weave with a powerful haymaker. The air rumbled, and Brisingr snarled in fury as it was blocked yet again.

"I see that the Ritual of Slaughter is still trying to melt your face off, ya brute. Good." Joe shook his head and started walking, turning to have a longer conversation with the Dwarven Master. "Anyway, Stu… Stu? Abyss."

The Dwarf was nowhere to be seen, having likely used some kind of stealth or movement technique to escape Joe's company as soon as he was distracted. The Ritualist ground his teeth, hoping that the released prisoner would still follow through on the quest. Full of frustration, he could only rush back to the fight and hope that he hadn't just unleashed an angry, spurned ex-councilman on his own people. "Wait… I should be worried more about *my* people, not his people. I know for a fact he likes *them*."

At that moment, Brisingr chose to unleash another flurry of blows, howling in fury. When each of them was deflected seemingly effortlessly, the giant took a few steps back and opened its arms wide. This time, instead of trying to use his body to break through, hundreds of beams of concentrated frost began collecting on its hands, arms, and eyes. Even with the danger level rapidly rising, Joe couldn't help but feel a deep sense of pride as the beam of fire continuously attempted to drill into the giant's face.

"Heh. I bet it's hard to stay focused on casting a spell while knowing that twisting to the side even a *little* means your eyeballs will melt."

The giant began chanting lightly, or at least that's what Joe thought at first. Then he realized that it was actually *mumbling*. The concentrated magic lashed out, freezing anything that was unfortunate enough to get in its way—except for the beams that were launched at the Ritual of Slaughter. Those were either deflected by various Legionnaires holding enchanted shields that could work as barn doors or struck the lance of fire itself and were dissipated, due to the incredibly dense concentration of power.

Joe found himself dancing around at least a dozen bolts of frost that seemed to veer toward him, and each time they struck a surface, the area around the point of impact was transformed into a frozen spike trap. "Yep, I have no interest in seeing the kind of damage that would do if it hit me in the chest. Move, *move*!"

He had to hand it to the defenders, the Ritualist was absolutely in awe of their sheer *tenacity*. In the span of time he'd been gone to release the Master Dwarf, dozens of Mages had gotten together and were pooling their resources. Even as Joe raced back to the front line, the Mages worked with practiced synchronization, directing mana and spell components into a rapidly growing spell circle. He got close enough to listen to some of the incantations being spouted off—at a pace that would make an auctioneer sit back and applaud—just as the spell completed.

The floating diagram vanished, winking out as though it had never existed. Moments later, it appeared once more, this time atop the giant's head, spinning in place and appearing for all the world as though Brisingr had just gained a magical crown. As Joe waited to see what effect the spell would have, the Mages working in tandem had already started on the next one. "Huh. Must have a delayed effect. I was kinda hoping–"

Another spell from nearby activated, sending out a spiraling shell of mana that punched into the chest of the giant and detonated. Splashes of blood hit the ground, and chunks of icy flesh fell hard enough that it sounded like a short-term hailstorm had come through the area.

"A tenth of a percent! Keep it up!" the Mages called out encouragingly, though their voices were raspy and ragged. "A few more like that, and when this thing drops, our contribution is going to be massive."

"Do it for the Legendary resources!" one of them quipped, obviously a joke that had been made multiple times already, going by the subdued reaction.

As if sensing determination, or at least their unwillingness to give up even though they had already lost, the giant brought his hands closer together and allowed the next spell to build in his hands. It launched off with far more force than the group of Mages had managed, hitting the net of woven mana and detonating on impact. The spell acted like a shaped charge, and after its initial payload was delivered, there was still the remainder of the destructive energy that had to go somewhere.

Joe glanced back, seeing the Mages who had landed a blow

standing perfectly still, their faces a mask of determination. "No, *abyss*. Their faces are frozen in that expression."

Realizing that his spells were succeeding where he was otherwise failing, Brisingr redoubled his efforts. Ice walls formed in the air and were sent at the fallen Town like fly swatters dropping from above. Columns of energy lanced out, creating fields of crystalline spikes that impaled dozens. Finally, the giant once more hefted the haft of his spear and closed his eyes in concentration. "Unparalleled is my mastery of ice! Whirlwinds of snow, blinding reflections, imbue on this staff an iceberg without imperfections!"

A massive ice storm coalesced around the tip of the staff, growing out until it covered nearly half of the giant's body. As quickly as it had come, the mana faded, leaving behind a changed weapon in Brisingr's hands. The Progenitor of the Ice gave his new warhammer a few practice swings, generating whirlwinds and tornadoes that swept dozens off of their feet and sent them tumbling. Then his gaze turned back to the city, and he swung the hammer with a grunt.

Bo~oong.

The warhammer struck the Mana Manipulation threads, releasing a sound as though ten thousand pianos had all of their keys smashed at the same time. Joe didn't like the smile that swept across the giant's face at that moment and frantically searched for something that he could do to…

He paused, his frenzied sprint slowing to a run, a walk, and then a complete stop. Warmth was circling around him. Not his body directly, but everywhere within the walls demarcating the area still protected by Grandmaster Snow. The hot wind was blowing against his back, and he was almost terrified to turn around and see what could possibly be generating so much heat that the buffeting chill from Brisingr was pushed away.

At the center of the Town, an enormous fire was burning, and the ground below it began to melt and twist. It grew hotter, enough so that the Mages around it who had been caught by surprise threw up barriers to block the intense heat that was boiling off of it. Thanks to his Perception, as well as focusing on the area, Joe could hear snippets of the conversation that was happening.

"-Did you *do*?"

"I didn't do anything, you–"

"Please tell me we didn't just make a volcano–"

"--no way, all we did was fill in the ground here. You don't think that the shift of bedrock is acting as a cork, and now it's going to pop?"

The flames flashed brightly, once, three times, and by the seventh, they were so bright Joe had to turn away. With a final wave of heat, the radiant feeling on his skin began to fade, and the Ritualist turned back to see what fresh threat had appeared. When he saw what was waiting at the center of Town, he realized that perhaps he was starting to get numb to important, life-altering events. Otherwise, he would probably be shouting in surprise like the people around him, or even screaming in delight as some of them were.

The Town Hall was back, sitting there as though it had never been struck with an unblockable, non-survivable, Legendary spell specifically aimed at it.

Event status: Novusheim's upgrade event to go from a Town to a City... Um! Wait.

Calculating... Escalating issue... Joe protocol activated... **Cal***culating...*

Issue successfully elevated.

What? Okay, let me see... building destroyed, event failed, why is this even on my desk? Oh. What. It came back? It can't come back. *No, it doesn't matter; it's right there in the messages. 'Novusheim' the 'Town' will automatically be reverted to a 'Hamlet' once the Town Hall has been rebuilt. See? What do you mean there's more?*

It... the Town Hall wasn't rebuilt, it was revived? You're kidding. No, you're right, that's... technically different. What? Voice to text is on?

The world around them went gray for a moment, and Joe felt an incredible pressure that seemed to freeze time itself. Due to that strange phenomenon, he had no idea how much time passed. But when color came back to the world, the odd message had been replaced with the standard, game-style notification he was used to.

We are pleased to inform the citizens of Novusheim that the conditions for achieving an upgrade for your settlement have been reinstated! Successful clearing of wave 100 will result in the settlement upgrading to a City, so long as the Town Hall remains intact.

A review of the situation shows that your refusal to accept death has been mirrored in the very aspects that make up your Town Hall. Keep it up, we believe in you!

All of that was well and good, but Joe only had eyes for the skill that had increased, even though all experience gain had been halted due to Havoc using his raid buff.

Mental Manipulation Resistance (Apprentice IV → Student 0.)

Joe shivered as he examined his memory, wondering what had been stripped from the people around him and if he could trust what he thought he'd seen. After only a few moments, he was broken from that downward spiral of questioning by Brisingr absolutely *losing* his mind, swinging his warhammer in strike after strike—Joe noted with great concern that the weave of mana had begun to fray.

"I destroyed it! I cast it into the ice!"

"No," a syllabant voice called out calmly. "You *didn't.* You failed. Just as you will fail here. This is why you have never been able to be the favorite of the Jotunn… why you will always be remembered as a lesser giant, instead of a Titan of Ice!"

The Ritualist turned and saw Master Stu shouting into the ritual tile. He could practically see the threads of doubt worming their way into Brisingr's brain. A glance back at the giant showed literal smoke pouring out of its ear, and Joe could only shake his head in sympathy as the huge Boss stumbled a few steps back.

"Abyss, I want to *beat* him, not break his heart!"

CHAPTER FORTY-SIX

As realization of what was actually happening in their reconstituted Town washed over the surviving members of the Dwarven Oligarchy and remaining humans, the tone of the battle began to rapidly shift. Where before, people were starting to give up, perhaps eyeing bolts of frost and wondering if it would be better to catch one on the face instead of having to go through all of the turmoil of re-upgrading the Town, now it was as if a jolt of energy had been poured directly into their bloodstream by a friendly coffee elemental.

Joe put a hand on his lower neck, feeling his pulse racing as he saw the shift in action. Hours, days, *weeks* of relentless combat suddenly felt like it *hadn't* been a waste. The Town Hall was there, standing unassumingly and in perfect condition against a backdrop of destruction: rubble, smoke, corpses frozen to the ground that the Ritualist's collection services couldn't pull out. The calm normality of the structure was like a beacon of hope. The cherry on top had been the intense heat washing out and over everyone, removing stacks of debuffs from the constant chill.

Brisingr seemed to be collecting himself and was recovering

from his shock. The colossus had been practically savoring the rare opportunity to join combat, but now its face was rapidly twisting into confusion and *frustration*. Between the reborn Town Hall, the swarms of monsters that were catching up to it and slashing into its mostly unprotected flesh, and the Master of Sarcasm pouring words into its flaming ear, the giant was fighting a battle on two fronts.

Its body *and* its mind.

Massive, bewildered eyes darted across the scene, one of them grotesquely magnified thanks to its monocle. It spoke, and Joe was forced to lean into the wind to maintain his footing. "This cannot be. I destroyed your hope with a spell that could end a moon. This is a betrayal of the system; there *is* no other explanation. You *can't…* take this *away from me*!"

The momentary lapse ended, and Brisingr lurched forward and began pounding on the weave of mana with a guttural roar. Every strike sent tremors through the Town, the shockwave of the blow mingling with the discordant sounds of the taut lines of vibrating mana. The defenders flinched away each time the hammer came down, as they could see the protection distorting, shimmering, and failing in places.

Major Cleave took charge of the situation, guiding the Legion into a frenzy as she shouted, "*Watching* the rampaging giant isn't going to help us, dudes and dudettes! Form a line. Looks like *we're* going to have to show the Grandmaster how to properly stop a warhammer! Mages! Look for weak points to aim your spells; I'm going to recommend the giant hole in its chest that Grandmaster McPoundy conveniently opened up for you!"

Dozens of other orders poured from her mouth, the mark of either an experienced commander or a master logistician. With a clear limit on how much time they had left, the Mages worked in tandem, faces contorting in concentration, sweat forming on their faces and dripping down into their eyes, despite the chill in the air pushing back against the last bit of lingering warmth.

Something about what the major had stated made Joe realize that perhaps there *was* something he could be doing at this moment. "Weak spots… how can I use my strengths against this fiend?"

"Looks like that boss has stayed still for too long! The main swarm of Havoc's monstrosities are *on* it!" a Legionnaire gleefully called out, drawing Joe's attention over to the grotesque blend of machine, beast, and what—in any other situation—could only be called *dark* magic. Now more metal than flesh, the remnant Beast Waves were clamoring up Brisingr's legs, biting, tearing, in some cases drilling into areas that Joe assumed were chosen by Havoc to attempt damage to necessary tendons and support structures.

"I'm not a huge fan of being on the side of abominations. Really kind of makes me think like *I'm* the bad guy here." Joe muttered as he skidded to a halt under his Ritual of Slaughter and began tinkering with it. "Gotta adjust this. I wonder if it'll be able to accept my input while it's still being fed mana. Oh, snap… I just realized… this has been going way longer than it should. How in the abyss am I going to deactivate it when this is all over? Or will it just reach a critical mass of instability and—no, stop that! One problem at a time."

The Ritualist fiddled *eminently* carefully with the controls of his ritual, working to sink into a light meditation to filter out all of the noises around him. This close to the active magical diagram, most of what he had to ignore was the crackling roar of pure mana being relayed in, then the thundering, warbling sound of that energy being converted to fire and beamed away. Making his last tiny change, Joe pushed his will and power into the new targeting coordinates and swapped them with what was currently in place.

Gasping in expectation of pain, he flinched and rolled back. Luckily, he didn't need to figure out how to respawn himself—the Expert-ranked ritual took the instructions from his Master rank in Ritual Magic smoothly, integrating and infusing them without causing noticeable instability. The beam shifted slightly, drawing a slow line across Brisingr's face as it came closer and closer to the massive iceberg monocle.

Upon reaching the very edge of the glassy surface, the entire superstructure of the ice crystal lit up like a light shining through a fiber optic line. The giant pushed backward, shaking his head to regain vision through the suddenly super-bright eye patch. Joe watched carefully, trying to determine how much damage his concentrated beam of fire had been doing. After inspecting the destruction so far, he decided he had made the right call. "There's almost no noticeable injury on its face. Maybe he got a bad sunburn from it? I think?"

While the Ritualist was uncertain if actual defacement was being done to the Legendary Boss Monster, the fact that one eye was blocked with a light as bright as a close-range star meant the unrelenting blast was finally having a noticeable effect. Joe wasn't certain how he felt about deploying his current pinnacle in war rituals, only for it to—at best—act as a debuff to Brisingr's vision. Still, he *was* glad that he was at least doing something useful.

Steam was rising from the point where the beam met the ice, but as soon as it was away from the fire itself, it immediately re-froze. A quick calculation informed the Ritualist that there was a chance the ice would become so cloudy that it would impair the creature's vision, even without the light being added; and Joe was able to release a sigh of relief.

"Not sure how else I'm going to be able to help, so unless another idea strikes, I'm going to instead focus on finding a way to dissipate this ritual when it's no longer needed. It would suck pretty bad to win, only to immediately lose. I'm *done* being called 'General Pyrrhic' or 'teamkiller bro'."

Feeling like a tiny island of calm in the center of an ocean of chaos, Joe sat on the ground and worked on scratching ideas onto his papers. Almost all of them were crossed off nearly immediately, but a few of them made the short list for powering down his best attempt at a doomsday device. "You know, I think the real problem is going to be getting the power plates off of the Mana Battery recharging stations. By now, they're probably welded to its surface… hmm. I *do* love a good conundrum."

As bolts of frost begin striking once more, the Ritualist was forced to refocus on the giant threat. All of the long range weapons had been carted over to one side of the Town, and stacks of ballistae continuously launched massive bolts of metal tipped with enchanted, sharpened barbs.

Someone had even recently recharged the ritual towers on that side of the wall, but the enormous bubbles of acid were doing absolutely *nothing* in terms of damage—nothing except coating the enormous body in layers of ice that acted as armor against future attacks. Joe pulled out his tablet and replaced those structures with others that were still available for transport.

He had to cycle three of them out, as they had taken damage from one of the Star-swords of Damocles and began teetering as soon as they appeared. But soon, Joe had towers of Dark Lightning Strikes up and running. Joe chose those instead of a more damaging variant, such as a ritual tower of Infernal Conflagration, because they had a similar 'influence on aether', according to Socar.

The way it had been explained to Joe was that the acid bubbles and lightning strikes were interchangeable, and they wouldn't monkey with the Formation. "Yeah… now that I think of it, changing the output of the Ritual of Slaughter at this moment would be… *not good.*"

"*For Novusheim*!" Hundreds of voices shouting in tandem yanked Joe's attention over to where a downward swing of Brisingr's hammer had broken through the net of Mana Manipulation. The Dwarves surged forward, carrying a veritable wall of enchanted metal in the form of hundreds of shields, and parried the blow.

**Tiii~iang*!*

As the weapon twisted in Brisingr's hands, the giant nearly dropped it. Its one visible eye narrowed as it stared at the Dwarves who had managed to completely mitigate the effect of its strike. "I hadn't expected to get through your little strings so easily. I'm glad to know that–"

The Progenitor of the Ice stopped speaking, his mouth forming into a scowl as he attempted to raise his weapon… only to find that it was tied to the ground *inside* the Town by the Mana Manipulation that had previously been keeping it *outside*. "Now you are holding my hammer down instead of confronting me directly? I grow *tired* of these games!"

Even without a tool in his hands, the colossus was not an opponent that could be underestimated. Allowing his weapon to remain where it was, Brisingr leaned back slightly as he drew his right elbow down to his hip and lifted his knee up almost to the point that they touched. Then the giant dropped his fist and lashed out with his foot, delivering a powerful front kick that landed on two separate sections of the final wall of Novusheim.

The massive Ebonsteel walls shattered into countless fragments of Journeyman-rank metal. Following the momentum of the kick, as well as the wind that surged along with it, each of the shards broke the sound barrier before they had traveled three inches. An instant later, the debris **clanged** off the black walls at the other side of the city.

Dozens of workshops and warehouses began to collapse. The water tower started spraying fresh water all around as scores of holes riddled its containment. Lastly, hundreds of warriors and mages slumped to the ground, instantly defeated from the shredding strike.

Joe watched with shaking eyes as Brisingr took its first proper step *into* the Town. For a moment there, it had seemed as if Novusheim was gaining the upper hand, that the bombardment was affecting the frost giant, that they had a *chance*.

But the tables had turned once more.

The Ritualist blinked in confusion as the Boss Monster suddenly ceased moving. Brisingr took a deep inhale through his nose, his towering frame straightening, his eye flashing a deeper, brighter shade of blue as he stared down at the Town that had defied him for so much longer than he'd ever expected.

"The system intervened to save you once... all I am doing now is correcting that *error*. Enough of this." Then, in a voice that sounded like glaciers cracking from the relentless shift of tectonic plates, Brisingr began to *chant*. Unlike its earlier spell usage, these words were ancient and not translated into a language Joe could recognize. Still, the meaning was clear: yet another high-ranking spell was being cast, and this time, there were no final barriers between them.

"Hey!" Havoc's voice rang out, even as panic began to settle in on the last thousands of defenders. "That's Grandmaster rank! You're stepping outside the rules of engagement!"

The Progenitor of the Ice didn't pause his grand working, merely sending a *smirk* at the Dwarf. Dozens of spells were sent at the giant, but the attempts to interrupt or counter the spell failed instantly upon reaching the edges of the frost aura that had expanded around the giant's hands as soon as he began casting.

The air began to shimmer as the temperature fell drastically. Even as far away as Joe was, frost began forming over his clothing, and he struggled to move under the cloying effect that was rolling over him.

As Brisingr's chant began to reach its climax, the air around him froze to the point that light itself began to slow. The world seemed to tilt, and a spell *beyond* the Legendary rank rippled outward.

CHAPTER FORTY-SEVEN

The Progenitor of the Ice slowly opened the one eye it could see out of, looking down to survey the effects of its power. A grunt escaped his lips as a sharp pain lanced over his left shoulder, and he looked to the side in horror as his entire arm… fell off. "Wh-"

"Are you kidding me right now?" The voice that echoed out, the words themselves seemingly calm and gentle, yet filled with an underlying, absolute *fury*… was not the one Joe had been expecting to hear. "Do you have any idea… any idea at all, the kind of resources that just went up in a cloud of miasma from your attack on my Alchemy Hall?"

Jake the Alchemist was stalking forward, his hands out to the side—alternating between clenching and flexing—as he approached the giant as though it were a nuisance to be eradicated. "Of course you don't! Look at those hands! Hand, I suppose. You are not a crafter, someone who works with delicate reagents in carefully controlled environments. You are a brute with no *patience*. The only thing that has ever been made by your *galumphing* self is ice, and that is as a *byproduct* of your leaky mana!"

Brisingr finally managed to take a breath and howled in pain as his only arm reached over so he could clasp the wound where black blood was waterfalling out. As soon as the area had been touched, it was sealed with a plug of frozen platelets and plasma, forming a terrible, jagged scab. "You cut off my arm? I-"

"Yes. I *missed*." Jake's words were becoming more guttural. His body began twitching and writhing, the flesh bubbling like one of his many reagents that had just been added to a cauldron. As he moved, he stretched slightly, his limbs beginning to move in a rubbery, flail-like manner. As he got closer to the giant, Jake shoved a hand into a spatial storage device and began pulling.

A metal bar was all Joe could see at first as the elongated limb continued extracting the item, but finally a massive syringe proportional to Brisingr himself was revealed. "You are a sickness, a blight upon my work, but don't worry. I have the cure right here."

"Stay away from me!" As the words escaped the giant's mouth, he seemed to realize that he was backing away from a single, oddly shaped human. "What... what is this feeling?"

"*Fear.*"

Jake lunged forward, breaking into a sprint that shattered the ground below him all the way down to the bedrock. Joe was still reeling from the knowledge that the giant—who had been lit on fire, blasted with magic, punched in the face by a flaming Grandmaster, and impaled by a massive ballista—was afraid of *needles*.

The Ritualist was barely able to keep track of Jake's movements and found that what he was actually seeing was his mind replaying where the Alchemist *had* been. Brisingr wasn't about to stop his rampage over the threat of an individual coming at him, and with a surge of mana expanded his aura of cold. Hundreds of the defenders nearest the giant froze instantly, and the remainder scrambled to get away from the high-level combat that had just begun.

"Look, the frost giant used a *cold* attack." Jake's usual monotone rang out, as though he were already bored with the fight. "What a shock. Oh no. Whatever shall I do."

Meeting the boundary of extreme cold didn't even slow Jake down, merely allowing a thin layer of frost to begin collecting on his shirt where the vapor from his breath landed on his clothing and instantly froze. Brisingr lifted a foot and slammed the heel down, attempting to splatter this new combatant before he could become a threat.

As far as Joe could tell, the attack succeeded. The foot hit the ground, sending up a massive plume of debris and causing the ground to vibrate hard enough that the ice covering Joe, which had been binding him to the stone under the Ritual of Slaughter, was shattered. As he pushed himself up, the dust was cleared in an instant, and the Ritualist watched in awe as Jake stood *on top of* the firmly planted limb.

"Interesting flora. Frankly, the *most* interesting thing about you, next to the core I am going to pluck from the base of your brain stem." Jake pulled out a handful of powder, which he scattered in front of him. Unnaturally, the powder zipped over to the flaming plants and collected around them. They began growing *much* faster, winding up the massive leg and flaring with ever more intense heat. The giant growled in anger more than pain, trying once more to hit the Alchemist by quickly slapping at his foot.

"*Die*, insect!" The shockwave of the impact sent the remaining dust and snow floating in the air away in three hundred and sixty degrees, creating a zone without anything to impair the vision of the onlookers.

"No. But I am on your hand now." Jake lifted his syringe into the air, stabbing it down at the hand below him. Just before the tip of the needle, glistening with fluid, could touch the giant's skin, a torrent of ice erupted from the giant's mouth—an attack he had not yet demonstrated in this battle.

The strike was purely physical, with chunks of ice in all

manner of sizes pelting the man and blasting him through the air surrounded by so much detritus that it was practically a solid column. It bowed downward, hitting the ground in the distance hard enough to generate minor tremors all the way back in Novusheim.

Although his view was blocked by the walls in the distance, Joe had a good feeling that Jake was already on the move and running toward them. This was backed up by the way that Brisingr was frantically muttering, attempting to cast some new spell that might have an effect on his opponent.

"Unfortunately for that giant, after losing his left hand, he can only count on one thing: his *right* hand." Jaxon had come to stand near Joe and began giggling as soon as his words had escaped.

"Abyssal... *backlash*!" The giant's focus narrowed, and frosty mana began gathering in his open palm. "I understand that you needed a sneak attack at my weakest moment in order to land a blow upon me at all. All this does is further my conviction that the summer races must be expunged from this world! Though my Mana Channels may need time to recover, and my body may be broken beyond repair, I shall not fail in my mission!"

A gargantuan block of ice formed in the open palm, beginning to spin and narrow down until it was a sharpened icicle spinning at tens of thousands of rotations per second. The air began to whine as Brisingr took aim at the Town Hall, and he brought his arm up and over to smash the center of the Town directly.

**Slap*!*

Jake had arrived on the scene and grabbed the fallen arm of the giant. As Brisingr made his attack, so did the Alchemist, beating the giant across the face with his own separated hand. "It seems I needed to *arm* myself so I could get your attention. You see, we are *not* done discussing this. Don't worry... I'm not going to *let* you die until you formally apologize to my Alchemy Hall."

"Then I shall *never* die, and I will grind you down with an endless ice flow of attacks, if I must." Brisingr had been knocked back several steps, but he hadn't lost control of his spell. Where he pointed the spinning icicle, tornadoes formed and created sucking funnels that pulled those who had failed to secure themselves up and in. They hit the ice, already frozen and therefore shattering upon its rotating surface.

"We'll get around to it. For now, it seems that *I* have the upper hand. *Perfectly Prepared Material*." The arm that Jake was still holding suddenly had what looked like a shock run through it, then the entire limb fell to the ground and scattered as perfect, one-inch cubes of flesh and ice. The Alchemist took a moment to glare around at everyone in the area. "These cubes are mine. If you would like some cubes for yourself, you are free to go and collect your own from the sources. They are *not* free materials for you to snatch when my back is turned."

No words came as a reply, only *very* slow nodding of heads. No one wanted to draw the attention of this terrifying figure. As Jake rushed toward the giant once again, Joe noted with surprise that his body had finished whatever changes it had been going through. The facial features he could see were sharper, which his brain told him indicated a powerful correlation to nobility. The usually lean form had bulked out, as though the Alchemist had been supplying steroids to a thousand gyms over the years and had dipped into his own supply on the regular.

His hair was longer, and his claws extended out, closer to those of a bear than any kind of cat or bird talon. Joe whispered to himself, "At least he's not a vampire. I'd be pretty uncomfortable if *both* of us sparkled in the sunlight."

The battle raged back and forth, with both of the combatants seeming to gain the upper hand on more than one occasion. Powders and liquids flew through the air, unerringly landing wherever the Alchemist had targeted. Flesh melted, necrosis spread, and one area became brightly inflamed as tiny boils formed over the entire area.

"Itch it, I *dare* you."

Jake's laugh was cut off as Brisingr retaliated with a sweep of his hand, slapping not only the Alchemist, but tons of dirt and snow into the air and tossing them hundreds of feet upward. The giant followed up on this attack by grabbing the warhammer from the ground and *ripping* it upward. He spun around and swung with all of his might at the scattering cloud of debris. Anything that was struck was either reduced to dust or sent flying for potentially hundreds or even thousands of miles; including the stretched man that had been in the center of it.

"So close! If that was actually me, instead of the hallucination brought on by the Mycelium of a Thousand Nightmares, I could have actually taken an injury." Jake's words reached Joe's ears, and he slowly turned to see that the Alchemist was standing nearby, completely unharmed and simply recovering his Stamina.

The Ritualist began to panic. "I saw you in there, too. Is the fungus in *my* brain, as well?"

"What? No. Quiet. That isn't how it works." Jake snapped at him, before returning to staring at the giant in an expectant manner. "*There* we go."

Joe looked back at Brisingr to see what Jake was talking about, only to catch the last moments of the enormous spell circle that had been spinning on the giant's head like a crown. It collapsed in on itself and vanished, only for a meteor to drop out of the sky and slam into Brisingr's forehead, sending the giant to the ground and causing him to tumble for half a dozen bounces before coming to a halt.

"Good… I got the positioning correct. Otherwise, he would have fallen right *through* the Town instead of out of it." Jake took a deep breath and started stomping toward the giant once more, even as Brisingr grunted and half rolled, pushing himself up off the ground. "Time for you to make that apology."

"Over my cold, dead body," Brisingr snarled back, the

words coming out in a wheeze that no longer even caused the air around him to howl.

"Well, would you look at that?" Jake smirked gently as he watched the aura of cold reform around the giant. "We're already halfway there."

CHAPTER FORTY-EIGHT

The frozen, desolate wastes of Jotunheim were blanketed by a long silence as Brisingr and Jake stared each other down. At the moment, Joe wanted to be anywhere except where he was standing—directly under his ritual that could go boom at any moment—but uncertain as to where he would be any safer. "Seriously… next time, I don't care if it will introduce burrowing monsters, we're making a shelter half a mile underground, with a drop elevator that has absolutely minimal safety features."

Joe flinched as the wind suddenly picked up, knowing that the only thing that was causing the air to blow at the moment was the movement of the massive Progenitor of the Ice. Brisingr had swung his hand around, attempting to use the iceberg whirling in his hand to bisect the unmoving Alchemist. At the last moment, Jake danced backward, pulling out and tossing a handful of sparkling dust that was sucked in by the funnel of air and evenly distributed across the entire glacier.

Seeing that his attack had missed, the giant swung his hand back around, only to end up throwing a small lake's worth of water into the air. "*What*? How could you possibly *melt* my ice?

Destroy it, understandable. Make me lose control, less possible. *Melt* it? Before this moment, I would have called this *impossible*."

"Concentrated salt from the sweat of a Drythral." Jake's words seemed to be all the explanation Brisingr needed, though Joe was left wondering what type of beast had sweat salt that could melt Legendary ice. His questions would need to wait, as the two monstrous entities began attacking each other in earnest.

It was unclear what Jake *was*. He could have been nearly any age at all. If he was a shapeshifter, or at least had the ability to change his form thanks to his alchemical antics, he could be thousands of years old, on par or even older than his current rival. No matter what the truth was, it was clear that he'd spent years carefully collecting an arsenal of powders and poisons, and he used the tools he had brought along to great effect. Never once did the vials of effervescent fluids miss their mark. The powders always swept through the air and landed entirely on the giant, in the spot that had clearly been chosen for maximum effect.

Brisingr didn't hold anything back, unleashing a hail storm of icy projectiles, the smallest of them already larger than a standard wagon back on Midgard. Concerningly, as soon as the mana had flared out, it seemed that the spell became completely autonomous, and the giant was able to ignore it while enjoying its effects. His body twisted back and forth, hand and feet flying in an attempt to slap, kick, or otherwise beat on his tiny target. "If I can't end you with a direct strike, I shall fill the world with ice until you are caged enough to be crushed!"

As the giant made his proclamation, Jake hurled a brilliant yellow powder into the air. As a slap came toward him, the Alchemist held still and took the blow directly. He went flying over the surface of the world, hitting the ground and skipping off of it dozens of times as though he were a flat rock thrown at a pond. Joe scrambled away, preparing to run toward the Town Hall and hope for the best. "Feces! Jake is gone, form up on the Town Hall!"

Brisingr wasted no time between the realization of a successful blow and turning to attack, exactly as the Ritualist had feared. Yet, as the colossus turned, a chunk of frigid meat fell and bounced along the ground, coming to a rest in an open space. Joe looked at it blankly. The giant, seeing what had fallen to the ground, bellowed, "You cut off my *finger*?"

Indeed, the digit had been cleanly sliced off from the second knuckle of his middle finger. Brisingr fell silent as he saw that the streak of yellow powder was still hanging in the air, slowly drifting toward him. "No. I shall not fall for this trap."

If he had given in to his first inclinations and charged at the Town Hall, it was likely that the giant's leg would have been the next item to fall to the surface of Jotunheim with a meaty smack. Brisingr sneered at the few defensive formations that had managed to muster between himself and the reborn building, his eye filling with a cold rage.

While Joe didn't enjoy having enemies that wanted his head, he much preferred them to be unthinking, charging, frenzied brutes instead of cold, calculative killers. Instead of charging, the giant swung his hand and began directing his bolts of frost together, conjuring icicles that put the size of the building he was targeting to shame. They launched forward, only for a tight weave of mana to catch them and shatter the projectiles into shards.

"Grandmaster Snow is still *active*?" Joe tried not to be too surprised about this information, as he was certain she would hold it against him in the future if he was loud about it now. "After he grabbed that hammer and snapped her threads, I was *certain* the backlash would've thrown her for a loop."

**B-burble*!* Mate bravely agreed as it peeked up and over the edge of the Ebonsteel mug.

"Mate! What are you *doing*?" Joe grabbed the handle of the coffee mug and gently shook the container. "You should absolutely be unsummoned right now; I do *not* want you getting hurt."

After a few moments of indecision, Mate vanished, leaving

the mug empty. For extra security, Joe tossed the container into his codpiece, just to make sure that it was *absolutely* safe. Already feeling better about the situation, the Ritualist turned his attention back to the fight, blinking rapidly as he realized that the battle had shifted.

Jake was back, his body glowing in multiple areas, with various bottles laying around his feet. Joe tried to piece together what had happened, deciding that the Alchemist had likely sprinted over while tossing back healing pills of a high rank. Currently, he was dodging a storm of ice that was falling from the sky around the giant, each icicle aimed to impale Jake and pin him to the ground. Intermittently, in an attempt to throw the Alchemist off balance, Brisingr froze a section of the ground into a sheet of perfectly smooth ice.

Still, the Alchemist was always *slightly* faster than the giant. When he *wasn't,* clouds of smoke would erupt from one of his pouches, either masking his movements entirely or stacking on some kind of buff that made him move so rapidly that he could get out of a bad situation. The speedy crafter was dodging from cloud to shadow, always a fraction of a step ahead of the next attack, follow-up spell, or sweeping motion the giant threw at him.

But dodging wasn't enough. If Jake was relying on his compounds to boost his combat ability to this level, the Ritualist knew for a fact that there had to be *severe* limitations. "Come on, Jake… counter-attack! Hit him with something that does more than hurt. Make him *bleed*!"

Almost as though he were listening to Joe's advice, though he clearly didn't need it, Jake pulled an amethyst vial from his belt. He spun around and whipped it at the giant's chest, an enormous target that was impossible to miss. "*Bloodweaver's Sting*!"

The glass of the container shattered in mid-air, and the liquid inside flowed through the air in an entirely unnatural manner. It settled over the wound Grandmaster McPoundy had made, seeping through the giant's skin without leaving behind any trace of its passage. Brisingr gasped a harsh breath, took a stumbling step, and barely managed to recover before he would have fallen.

"What did you just do-" even before the Progenitor of the Ice could finish his inquiry, every wound over his body that had not completely closed had blood *slosh* out of it. The most obvious example was his separated shoulder, where the icy plug no longer stemmed the tide of fluids, but instead began high-pressure spurting the bluish-black liquid.

"I am more than happy to explain," Jake stated in his monotone, as though he were launching into a lecture at a university filled with students who had no interest in the course. "This was a combination of an Injection skill of mine that allows me to put medication into a body where it is needed. In this case, as I fear for the enormous number of blood clots you have formed, I was able to give you a potent anticoagulant. As for the reason why I am so happy to explain…"

Brisingr stared at the Alchemist, who let the silence linger for a long second before finishing his statement. "Well… obviously, the longer you wait, the more blood you lose."

"I'm not sure I've ever despised a human as much as I loathe you at this moment." The giant hissed at Jake, who merely nodded along with the statement.

"That makes sense, more than you probably know with your limited understanding of my situation." As Jake responded, the giant attempted a swift strike—clearly assuming the Alchemist was distracted. Tiny slivers of ice, at least tiny compared to what the colossus had used to this point, filled the air like a school of flashing fish. Thousands and thousands of needles of ice pierced through whatever they touched.

The ground for hundreds of feet in a line was perfectly aerated, and as the spell tracked Jake, Brisingr let out a triumphant laugh.

Moments later, that laugh turned into a deep, hacking cough as Jake sprinted through open air and tossed a pouch directly into the space between the giant's upper lip and its nose.

Upon impact, the pouch exploded into a cloud of powders, clearly some kind of poison or toxin. Brisingr coughed, waving his hand in front of his face to clear the air, not even seeing that his opponent had not escaped unscathed.

Jake fell to the ground, landing heavily and taking deep, calming breaths as he pulled out various pills and tossed them into his mouth. As he got back on his feet, Joe realized that he could see *through* the man. As the pill took effect, new flesh wriggled out of the damaged areas and wove his body back together.

The Ritualist shook his head. "I think I'm gonna to be sick."

"Don't you heal people all the time?" Major Cleave had come to stand by him at some point, and her words startled him. He looked around, seeing a half-dozen people close enough to touch and realizing that he hadn't been maintaining anything *approaching* good situational awareness. "Why is this different?"

"Uh, hello. My healing spell pretty much just washes away the injury; it doesn't force me to watch as strands of flesh grow out, grab each other with a firm handshake, then *yank* the wound closed." Joe rolled his shoulders and wiggled a little to get the image out of his head. "That looks like it hurts almost as much as taking the strike did. Maybe *more*, because you are having to grow those nerves at the same time."

Joe was not the only one disturbed by the healing. Brisingr had seen his opponent rejuvenate and slapped at the ground in annoyance, trying to splatter the man under his palm. "Just *die* already! I have things to do, goals to accomplish, and you are *all* that bars me from my proper place at the northern pole! Why is someone like you allowed to take the field in the first place? System! I *demand* an accounting!"

The world went gray for a fraction of a moment, and as color returned, the clouds above parted and allowed a brilliant bolt of lightning tinged with an iridescent gold coloration to strike the giant directly in the small of his back, sending the giant tumbling to the ground, smoke pouring off of his charred and blackened body.

System accounting complete. Brisingr, the Progenitor of the Ice, has broken the rules of engagement twice. First incident: attempted activation of a fourth, peak Grandmaster rank spell when only three were allowed. Second incident: accusing the system of favoring one side over another unjustly. There will not be a third incident, or there will not be a Brisingr, the Progenitor of the Ice.

Punishment: 10% maximum health damage per incident delivered as True Damage Tribulation Lightning.

Lastly. Just because. A bolt that inflicts only pain, but no damage. Not as a punishment, but as a show of annoyance.

Lightning struck down, a very thin bolt compared to what had hit the giant, and struck Havoc directly on the left pinky toe. "Gah—*hey*! What was that for?"

The world went white, and Joe felt agony course through him for a fraction of a second. As he twitched, he sensed that a portion of the lightning was absorbed into his foot. Without thinking, filled with rage at the injustice of an attack out of nowhere, Joe had his mana reflexively clamp down on the intruding energy.

The lightning rampaged through his foot and up his leg, but the Ritualist swarmed the area with his power, breaking the remaining energy cascade into tiny motes of energy that he dispersed through his body. Once they were contained, it took no concentration whatsoever for his body to continue keeping them under control. He glared up at the sky, and, unconsciously mimicking his mentor, lifted a fist and shook it at the sky. "Do it again, I *dare* you!"

This time, he was fully prepared for the consequences. His mana was rippling in time with his beating heart, and Joe was prepared to catch and contain a full strike. Seeming to understand that they had crossed the line, no one watching from up above took him up on his offer.

New energy detected! Options: 1) attempt to absorb into body. 2) attempt to absorb into mind. 3) attempt to absorb into mana. 4) attempt to absorb into Characteristics.

"I need more information than that," Joe growled, though his mouth snapped shut as the options expanded slightly.

1) Absorbing into body will allow you to choose a Physical Characteristic to align with [new energy].

2) Absorbing into mind will allow you to choose a Mental Characteristic to align with [new energy].

3) Absorbing into mana will allow you to infuse a spell or skill with [new energy].

4) Absorbing into Characteristics will result in a massive increase in [Karmic Luck].

"Option four is out; it seems like the world is always sapping my Karmic Luck and trying to force me to zero." Joe was still breathing heavily, but was calming down substantially. "At least that option gives me an idea of what just hit me. Some kind of Karmic retribution lightning, most likely. I need more time to think about this."

Calculating time until New Energy begins to degrade: [24 hours].

Nodding his understanding, Joe went to dismiss the notifications, when he noticed that they had arrived in a style he hadn't seen before. "What are these brackets? Notifications don't normally have that."

The answer that he received was as intriguing as it was concerning.

Joe protocol has been activated.

CHAPTER FORTY-NINE

Before he could make sense of the messages, Joe's dazed stare was pulled to the fact that Jake was standing on the back of the downed Brisingr's neck.

The Alchemist was holding his enormous syringe, poised to thrust downward. Even from this distance, as they were completed on such a macro scale, Joe could hear the sounds of Jake finishing his attack clearly.

"*Hup*!" The enormous needle raced downward, striking the skin of the giant directly above a throbbing artery.

Splutch.

Squirrt.

Jake held the needle in, forcing the massive plunger all the way down, until not an ounce of the fluid remained inside. Then, letting out a satisfied sigh, the Alchemist pulled out the needle, stored it away, and spoke to Brisingr conversationally. "Hey. How are you feeling?"

"Not… so great." Brisingr moaned as his veins rapidly darkened, and capillaries began to burst all throughout his body. While the lightning strike had knocked him flat, it was clear that whatever had been forced into his blood was the thing that was going to bring the giant down.

"I see." Jake pulled out a notebook and a quill and began writing, to everyone's shock except Joe's. The Ritualist just stared on and shook his head in bemusement. "Would you mind explaining the symptoms and feelings you're experiencing, for future use cases?"

"The Jotunn… will avenge me." Brisingr weakly swore, ignoring the Alchemist for the moment. "You will all freeze for ten thousand–"

Slap. Jake ripped off the giant's remaining arm and swung it around, slapping Brisingr in the face and sending him rolling across the ground. "Don't worry, you aren't dying yet. You haven't *apologized* to my Alchemy Hall."

"*Abyss*, dude." Joe flinched as he realized that the words had slipped out of his mouth.

Luckily, either Jake didn't hear him, or, more likely, he simply didn't care what Joe thought. The Alchemist walked over to stand directly next to the moaning giant. "I can guarantee you… the Jotunn will *not* be seeking revenge. You will describe your symptoms, and your head will be carried to the Alchemy Hall, where you will apologize or spend the next short eternity as a pseudo-lich skull. A large one, to be certain. Perhaps you can act as an antechamber for uninvited guests?"

"How dare you speak for the Jotunn! I am Brisingr… the… Progenitor of the Ice." It was clear that the giant was unable to draw in a full breath, and as he became weaker, Jake moved closer to his enormous ear and waved a powder into the air. Joe could see that the Alchemist wás speaking, but the effects of the ability Jake had used made it impossible for the words to travel back to him. However, the results were immediately apparent.

"N-no. How can *you* be *here*? This is *Jotunheim*!" Brisingr sounded like he would be sobbing, were it possible at the moment.

Jake cast a glance over his shoulder, locking eyes with Joe for a brief moment, a smug grin firmly placed on his lips as he caressed the lobe of Brisingr's ear. "I was a *quest reward*."

"I... I have extremely ragged, labored breathing. My heart rate is incredibly rapid. My pulse feels weak, with likely low blood pressure as I am seeing swirling stars. My vision is disturbed; I have nausea but an inability to vomit." The giant went quiet for a moment, his eye rolling in its socket. "Please, allow me to offer my deepest regret for the damage done to your Alchemy Hall, oh venerable–"

"Shh, *shh*..." Jake reached out and scattered yet another handful of powder into the air. Then he gripped the ear he was standing next to and began walking into the city.

The head bounced along behind him.

The body stayed where it was.

"I didn't tell you to apologize to *me*. You need to apologize to my *Alchemy Hall*." Jake hissed the words softly, and moments later, Joe's view of the situation was obstructed by the Alchemist and the head vanishing behind a crumpled warehouse.

Then, he was beset upon by an absolute *book's* worth of notifications. Before even looking at them, Joe waved away the flashing notifications and turned his attention to the Ritual of Slaughter. As the giant, its target, was out of its line of sight, the energy within it began building rapidly. "No! Gotta fix that! It's going to go critical!"

Omnivaulting to the ritual, Joe flipped open his notebook and picked the only option he had been able to think of that had made it through three rounds of 'I think this will work'. It was circled and had two little stars drawn on either side of it to catch his attention. "Venting the power it is."

There was only one good option for where to send the massive beam of fire that would be erupting outward. They needed to repair their walls, so he couldn't send it out across the horizon. Down wasn't a possibility, "So, *up* it is!"

More confident in adjusting the ritual while it was active now that he had some practice, Joe forcefully broke the targeting equation of the ritual, replacing it with a mathematical version of 'directly above'.

During the moment that the ritual did not have a target, it began to forcefully whine and shake as the power ramped up further. Still, it followed instructions and launched the beam upward, higher and higher, though as it approached cloud level the compacted energy dispersed somewhat and turned into what looked like a massive flamethrower. "Huh. Pretty sure I just made a Bunsen burner Brisingr could've used to practice alchemy. Heh. Too soon? Nah, that dude sucked."

With the imminent danger alleviated, Joe had no choice but to accept the start of the swarm of messages. He managed to set a single command, and the notifications adjusted themselves just before beginning to flash across his vision. "Set priority: settlement event, bonuses, rewards, skill upgrades, characteristic upgrades!"

Congratulations, valiant defenders of the City of Novusheim!

Somehow, against all odds, you have relentlessly driven yourself forward and emerged victorious. For the first time in millennia, a Town has successfully defeated all 100 Beast Waves, earning the right to become the first and currently only City of Jotunheim.

Due to your Herculean efforts, Novusheim is now in the process of upgrading, and will evolve from a Town to a City!

City bonuses have been earned.

1) Peaceful City. Rare reward earned due to: Settlement Title 'Prosperous Town'. Effect: It is significantly more difficult to break the laws of the city. All negative-alignment actions have a 50% increased chance of failing.

2) City of Growth. Expert reward earned due to: Achieving City status in under 1 year when starting from settlement rank 'Camp'. Effect: At the cost of a 20% increase in materials, all buildings within the territory of Novusheim can be erected 50% faster, no matter what method is used to create them.

3) City of Industry. Master reward earned due to: Achieving City status while never creating a permanent residence. Effect: All crafting attempts which require 24 standard hours or more benefit from a 20% reduction in overall cost.

4) First City. Master reward earned due to: being the first City built on Jotunheim in so long that it may as well be the actual *first City. Effect: All forms of 'firsts' when it comes to crafting a never-before-designed project, including but not limited to templates, recipes, blueprints, and prototypes, give 200% bonus experience when they are created for the first time.*

5) Only City. Temporary Artifact reward earned due to: Being the only City-ranked settlement on Jotunheim. Effect: Once per standard day, the city will automatically generate a shield that will reflect any attack, strike, skill, or spell that would otherwise destroy the City Hall.

6) Unstoppable City. Legendary reward earned due to: Defeating a Legendary Final Boss Monster (2 ranks above settlement minimum.) Effect: The City Hall will gain a Mana Cannon that can launch a bolt of purified mana twice the distance of the widest dimension of the City. The Purified Mana bolt is guaranteed to deal 100,000 damage or 10% of the target's health, whichever is greater. Each bolt requires 1,000,000 mana to generate, with a minimum cooldown of 72 standard hours.

7) Unified City of Dwarves… and Guests. Unique reward earned due to: A single, entirely sentient race claiming the First City as their permanent Capital. Effect: While on Jotunheim, the members of the Council of Novusheim may resurrect any Dwarves who have been slain on Jotunheim. All Elves slain on Jotunheim may be resurrected as Dwarves, until the Elven Theocracy establishes a City that can compete for the loose souls. Guest races (Aligned Members of Unified Races) have 10% less experience loss upon dying.

Joe forced his mind away from the notifications, finding that he was gasping for air, and his eyes were glistening. Around him, nearly the entirety of the survivors were members of the Legion, and even they were, in many cases, openly weeping. "We can bring them back? *All* of them? Wait…no… *more* than we lost?"

Several minutes passed before he was in a mental place to be able to continue, the sheer exhaustion and gratitude he felt at the moment being a heady mixture that made him want to do nothing more than lie down and fall asleep for a while. He decided that a long, healing sleep was certainly in order but could be put off for at least a few more minutes. Joe dove back into the messages, having finally moved past everything that the settlement had earned with the blood, sweat, and tears of the residents.

Final Combined City Settlement title: Novusheim the Pioneering Bastion of Lawful Prosperity and Dwarven Ingenuity.

"Long name, amazing results." Joe muttered as he got to the next section, which he was equally excited about: his personal rewards.

Raid area generated by the Lord of Slaughter has been deactivated! Releasing rewards and experience gains!

Class quest complete: Apprentice Reductionist III. Reduce 10 tons' worth of Rare-ranked materials to aspects. 10/10. Reward: A Spatial Ring that can hold up to five tons of any item ranked Rare or lower; enchanted with the ability to reduce the weight of its contents by 50%.

Class quest complete: Apprentice Reductionist IV. Reduce 15 tons' worth of Rare-ranked materials to aspects. 15/15. Reward: Rare-ranked weapon augment for your usual weapon.

Item gained: Ritual Orb Augment (Set of six.) Weapon augments allow you to hit harder and complete more actions with your weapons. As you use exotic weapons, these have exotic effects. For each of the augments, you can choose between two different uses.

1) 10% damage boost. Very self-explanatory—the augment, when attached to an orb, will increase the damage that the orbit does by 10%.

2) Ritualistic Alchemy containment unit. By loading this augment with a Ritualistic Alchemy product, any subsequent ritual activated via its associated orb will seamlessly incorporate the effects of that product.

Class quest gained: Apprentice Reductionist V. As you strive to become a Student Reductionist, you should be preparing for your future by testing multiple paths forward. Create and activate a ritual of the following effects: War Ritual of any rank: 1/1. Rituarchitect Ritual of Student rank or higher: 1/1. Utility Ritual of Student rank or higher: 1/1. Choose one of the following: Eldritch Ritual 0/1, Mind Altering Ritual 0/1, Area Healing Ritual 0/1, Area Defensive Ritual 0/1. Reward: A 5-ritual pamphlet of the optional ritual type you choose to create.

Class quest updated: Student Reductionist II. Unique crafts created: 3/5.

Experience gained during double experience event: 2,193.

"Uh... I know for a fact *that* is incorrect." Joe took a few deep breaths as he saw the tiny number that popped up. "I killed or damaged almost every single monster that came through. I know I should've gotten at least some kind of bonus for the flame moat of the flowers I planted, even if I don't get to count the ones that grew beyond what I put out there directly. What's going on?"

JP: You have reached the current level cap for your three classes / specializations. The excess experience you have gained will be held indefinitely until you gather an additional specialization. An additional specialization will increase your level cap to 50. Please note, dying will still reduce your total experience, and you will need to re-achieve level 30.

"Oh, come on! No one *ever* told me about a level cap." Joe complained to the fragment of the system that seemed to be monitoring him at all times now. "You can't just drop a level cap on me out of nowhere."

JP: Accessing all conversation logs. Accessing all notification logs. Calculating... capped level has been mentioned one time previously: 'Upon returning to Midgard, your stats will be capped at the Mortal Limit'. Level cap is a well-established fact on all worlds. See your class trainer for details... hmm. Oh. I see. Querying main system. Potential fix found.

Bonus rewards for skill gain have been calculated, and combined with various rewards from your contribution to the upgrade event. Rewards have been combined with feats of prowess. Rewards have been combined with double experience skill gain.

A new option has appeared! As a one-time offer to mitigate potential conflicts in registry, all current overage in class experience can be combined with skill gain experience. Instead of each individual skill moving up by its usage and effect, you may choose to take one of these two paths:

1) Increase the rank of all Master Skills by +1, Expert skills by +2, Journeyman skills by +5, Student skills and lower by +10. Maxed skills will gain a skill evolution or combination option. Any skills that would have gained more skill experience than this increase affords will still increase by the amount it is due. (Special option.)

2) Hold all experience until a new specialization is earned, automatically refilling Experience pool upon death to return to level 30 as needed. (Standard option.)

Joe stared at the options critically, wavering between having a permanent excess of experience or becoming arguably much more powerful in the short-term. "Gah… I guess I can always earn more experience. Plus, I'll earn it faster if I can do more impressive things… and I really want to see what a skill evolution looks like. I choose option one."

JP: As these changes will take time to take effect, you may run out of time to select what to do with the [new energy] trapped in your mana. Would you like to choose what to do with it now or risk missing out on it as it degrades?

Pleasantly surprised at the heads up—for once—the Ritualist decided to go with his gut and agreed to start the process. "I would like to bind the energy to a Characteristic, specifically… Perception. If it is what I think it is, that would be the best choice in my mind."

JP: Ok. Well, hold on tight. Here comes your current, full skill sheet as well as an updated character sheet. Please note, as soon as these take effect, you will likely pass out as your brain assimilates the information and your body updates. Feel free not to read over this, as you may not remember it upon waking up and may need to reread it at a later date.

<u>*Combat Skills/Spells*</u>

Acid Spray (Student IX → Journeyman IX) Congratulations! This spell has updated to 'Strong Acid Spray' (Journeyman IX). Spell damage increased by 25%.

Cone of Cold (Apprentice VII). Unbind from Ritual Orb to update!

Corify (Apprentice VII). Unbind from Ritual Orb to update!

Dark Lightning Strike (Journeyman VII → Expert III)

Exquisite Shell (Journeyman V → Expert 0) Talk to Occultatum to update this skill!

Lay on Hands (Journeyman VII → Expert II)

Mend (Journeyman VIII → Expert III)

Neutrality Aura (Journeyman V → Expert 0). Range of aura has doubled! No more unpleasant scents, not unless you put your nose to the stink and suck it in!

Planar Shift (Student IV). Unbind from Ritual Orb to update!

Query (Pray) (Apprentice 0 → Student 0). Talk to Occultatum to update this skill!

Mass Resurrection Aura (Apprentice VII → Student VII). Talk to Occultatum to update this skill!

Retaliation of Shadows (Expert IX → Master I). Congratulations! You have increased a Master-rank skill. All characteristics plus 5, except Karmic Luck!

This skill is evolving! Retaliation of Shadows → Haunting Shadows (Master I). New skill description fully replaces the old one. Until now, the shadows that have been retaliating on your behalf have been reactive. Now, they are proactive. Activating this spell turns it passive, binding a shadowy sentinel to the caster which is poised to retaliate against aggressors. Upon any attack or attempted attack on the caster, a shadowy doppelganger appears next to the offender, dealing a retaliatory slap worth 1+n% of the damage of their attack, where n = skill level. Current (62% damage return, no maximum.)

Should the attacker flee or succeed in defeating the caster of this spell, the shadow will intermittently materialize next to them over the next 12 hours, dealing at maximum 1% of the aggressor's total health as dark damage before vanishing unless dispersed for that visit. Note: apologies have power. Should the aggressor express remorse, the caster of this spell may cancel the intermittent effect.

Wither Plant (Student 0 → Journeyman 0). You still have this spell?

Infernal Conflagration (Apprentices 0 → Student 0)

Body/Mind Skills

Artisan Body (Apprentice VI → Student VI)

Combat Ritual Orbs (Exotic) (Student VIII → Journeyman VIII)

Battle Meditation (Journeyman V → Expert 0). You are an expert of battle meditation and have realized that life is the greatest battle of all. This skill is now a permanent, passive effect. Great for training!

Coalescence (Journeyman II → Journeyman VII)

Essence Cycle (Journeyman IV → Journeyman IX)

Hidden Sense (Student VI → Journeyman VI). Effective range of this sense has been tripled!

Magical Synesthesia (Apprentice II → Student II). You now hear magic in specific notes, which you will understand more intuitively.

Mana Manipulation (Journeyman II → Journeyman VII)

Mental Manipulation Resistance (Student 0 → Journeyman 0). You should probably seek expert help with this. You are approaching a dangerous point. The next time you get sent to respawn, you'll understand.

Omnivault (Master VIII → Master IX). Congratulations! You have increased a Master-rank skill. All Characteristics plus five, except Karmic Luck! This skill has reached the peak of the Master ranks! Only a deep insight or inspiration into the skill can increase it further. No rewards or items may be used to bypass this bottleneck. Start practicing, and study hard!

Polearm Mastery (Student 0 → Journeyman 0). But why, Joe?

Teaching (Student II → Journeyman II).

Crafting/gathering Skills

Words of Power (Written) (Student 0 → Journeyman 0)

Alchemical Rituals (Beginner 0 → Apprentice 0)

Enchanted Ritual Circles (Apprentice II → Student II)

Enchanting (General) (Apprentice 0 → Student 0)

Field Array. (Max) → Ascendant Matrix (Max). Your ability to control the finer portions of the reduction of mass to aspects has grown past the original peak. You are now able to create an Ascendant Matrix. This retains all the previous properties of a Field Array. When an aspect jar is attached, there will be no loss of aspects when reducing an item. When the Ascendant Matrix is set up in an area, there will be no loss of aspects when creating Reductionist-specific items.

Magical Matrices (Journeyman 0 → Journeyman V)

Message (Beginner I → Apprentice I)

Natural Magical Material Creation (Student 0 → Journeyman 0)

Ritual Circles (Master I → Master II) Congratulations! You have increased a Master-rank skill. All characteristics plus five, except karmic Luck!

Ritual Magic (Master VI → Master VII) Congratulations! You have increased a Master-rank skill. All characteristics plus five, except karmic Luck!

Ritualistic Alchemy (Student III → Journeyman III)

Ritualistic Forging (Expert 0 → Expert II)

Spellbinding (Student 0 → Journeyman 0)

Somatic Ritual Casting (Journeyman II → Journeyman VII)

Ritual Duplication (Beginner 0 → Apprentice 0). Watching this jump a full rank makes all of us hurt. This skill is intentionally difficult to increase. Why do you hurt us like this, Joe?

Lore Skills

Alchemical Lore (Journeyman 0 → Journeyman V)

Architectural Lore (Student VII → Journeyman VII)

Enchanting Lore (Journeyman 0 → Journeyman V)

Knowledge (Journeyman 0 → Journeyman V)

Ritual Lore (Journeyman IV → Journeyman IX)

Smithing Lore (Journeyman V → Expert 0)

Calculus and Number Theory (Student IV → Journeyman IV)

Celestial-Arcane Interaction Lore (Student III → Journeyman III)

Name: Joe 'Monarch of Mana' Class: Reductionist
Profession I: Arcanologist (Max)
Profession II: Ritualistic Alchemist (7/20)
Profession III: Grandmaster's Apprentice (15/25)
Profession IV: Ritualistic Metalworker (3/20)
Profession V: None
Character Level: ***30*** *Exp: 465,000 Exp to next level: 31,000 (Locked.)*
Rituarchitect Level: 13 Exp: 87,450 Exp to next level: 3,550

Reductionist Level: 10 Exp: 59,900 Exp to next level: 6,100. Talk to Occultatum for a Specialization reward!
Hit Points: 4,171/4,171
Mana: 3,839/11,933
Mana regen: 120.09/sec (Caution! Mana Circuits require time to heal. Go to bed. Mana regen reduced by 75%)
Stamina: 478/2,992.5
Stamina regen: 7.27/sec (Caution! Exhausted. Go to bed. Stamina regen reduced by 75%)

Characteristic: Raw score

Strength (bound): 256 → 278
Dexterity: 255 → 277
Constitution (bound): 255 → 277
Light Intelligence (Bound): 263 → 283
Wisdom: 250 → 270
Dark Charisma: 209 → 229
Karmic Perception: 257 → 279
Luck: 202 → 222
Karmic Luck: Calculating.

CHAPTER FIFTY

Joe's eyes slowly peeled open, feeling crusty and full of ick. He wasn't sure if he had come around naturally, simply due to having gotten through the worst of his exhaustion, or if it was the torrential downpour that was lapping up over his face intermittently and causing him to choke. "Ugh… what's going on?"

The deluge was falling with an intensity Joe had only ever seen in waterfalls. Every thick, plump drop was hitting the ground like a hammer against an anvil—or at least that's what his aching head informed him. Water ran through the scars, pockmarks, and crevasses that the intense war had scarred into the landscape. As his brain rebooted, Joe started looking around for signs that his water collection rituals were still active.

Looking up at the water tower, he simply sighed and nodded as he watched a massive funnel of water drain into the container… only to sieve out of it from all of the holes that had been drilled through its sides by the shrapnel Brisingr had turned his precious wall into. "I would put that on a list of things that need to be fixed, but I'm pretty sure the list of things that *don't* need to be fixed will be shorter."

Leveraging himself off the ground, Joe adjusted his

Exquisite Shell on the fly to create an invisible umbrella over his head. Taking a moment to realize what he'd just done, a smile began to pull at the corner of his lips. It seemed that reaching the Expert ranks with the spell had benefits even before he managed to enumerate them with Tatum. He started walking aimlessly, assuming that most people had taken shelter where possible.

As always, he was extremely happy with the magical protection he had gained early on. The Ritualist was almost certain he would have frozen to death or already drowned, if it weren't for the thin barrier keeping the elements off of him. The rain, while not ice, was by no means *warm*. "Gotta… find what to do next. Anxiety sprouts from aimlessness, and having a clear goal will make me feel better."

As though waiting for him to express a sentiment of that type, a standard system notification appeared in his vision.

Congratulations on nearly clearing the cloud layer above Novusheim! Time remaining until breakthrough and bifrost stabilization: approximately 30 minutes, depending on shifting weather conditions.

Warning! Once the bifrost has stabilized, all of the wandering souls Dwarven and Elven currently attempting to catch it will evacuate this world. In order to avoid this outcome, please pay the cost for their resurrection at the Ledger of Souls in the City Hall. Currently, only two people are viable candidates for activation of the ledger. Grandmaster Snow (currently incapacitated). Joe 'Monarch of Mana' (Available). All other council members are in need of resurrection!

"No! I recognize this for what it really is." Joe growled at the air around him. "This is an unrepentant money grab, an attempt to strip me of all the aspects I've gathered since arriving on Jotunheim. You can't do this to me! I'm on to you–"

Novusheim current population: 3,722 Dwarves (Stable). 8,125 Humans (Rising.)

The Ritualist stared at the tiny number of Dwarves, his staunch allies for the last two worlds. They'd lost tens of thousands of their people and were teetering on the edge of direct extinction. Practically *hopping* with angst, Joe dithered back and forth on the merits of hoping that Grandmaster Snow would suddenly swing in and open up a vault that would allow her to pay for… he paused and shut his eyes.

When he opened them again, Joe looked through the rain at the absolute devastation that was all that remained of Novusheim. Not a single warehouse was standing, and most of the workshops were finishing the process of crumbling from the weight of the torrential downpour. "Even if she gets her ancient rear over here, what's she going to do? Spend resources the Town doesn't even have? Excuse me… the *City* doesn't have?"

Joe loved exploring his magic more than almost anything that he had encountered in his entire life. A quick glance at his aspects showed that they were approaching the *millions* in almost everything Expert rank and below. "With this many aspects, I could do almost anything. Create almost anything, and… and I've already decided to give them up before making even one of them. Why do I always have to be so reasonable? *Ugh.*"

As the countdown to the bifrost opening ticked away, the Ritualist trudged through the sucking mud. It couldn't hold him back—he was pretty certain he could swim through tar pits without slowing down with his current Characteristic count—but it was somewhat satisfying to feel his mood reflected in his current situation.

The upgraded City Hall came into view, and he had to admit that its new form was… *impressive.* Atop the grand defensive structure decorated with pillars, embellishments, and inscriptions sat a massive spiraling cannon that looked no different from an artist's rendition of a railgun. Huge pillars ending in talons like the Phoenix World Boss branched off of the cannon and secured it to the enormous structure, which was easily ten times as large as its Town Hall version had been.

As he got closer, the architectural design that would confound most engineers was hidden by the nearness of the walls themselves. Enormous double doors barred his entry into the structure, but Joe didn't mind. Instead, he scanned over their design. The barriers were artfully designed to resemble the closed wings of a phoenix, and he was nearly certain that, when they were opened, they would extend as if it were a bird in flight.

It was satisfying to be proven correct as he approached, and the building recognized him. The doors swung wide, squeaking slightly on their hinges. His first thought was to grab a can of WD-forty, but the chirping sound grew louder as the doors approached their full extension, growing into the triumphant scream of the World Boss before abruptly cutting off.

Shriiawww!

"Wow! That's really cool the *first* time I hear it! I bet it's going to get super annoying to whoever has to sit right inside. Huh... maybe I somehow imbued my annoyance with the receptionist into the construction of the building? I like it *twice* as much as I did even one minute ago."

As he stepped under the shelter the building provided, he found that the cacophony of rainfall was muted. As the doors closed behind him, the building had an almost library-like silence to it. It was strange to walk through an empty building like this, when normally it was absolutely bustling with activity, *especially* over the last few weeks, as the fighting had intensified to its peak. The antechamber he was standing in, essentially an oversized office that would provide a barrier between direct access to the council and the general public, came to an abrupt halt at a set of doors that was much smaller and cozier than the grand entryway.

As he pushed through them, laying his hand on the building for the first time, a notification popped up.

Novusheim's Eternal City Hall. Current durability: 10,000,001/10,000,001.

Aspects of the Phoenix kindled: 0/10.

Mana required to rekindle one aspect: 1,000,001.

Aspects required to resurrect building if it is destroyed: 10.

"Huh... So that's how it works." Joe stared at the notification for a long moment as the door finished opening. "An interesting thought, there. Pretty sure the city could hire anyone who doesn't want to get a different job to sit in a room and devote all of their mana to either the Phoenix aspects or the Mana Cannon. An endless source of employment, at least during wartime. Also, well, this is Jotunheim. There's going to be Beast Waves all the time, and that's not a terrible career choice for the criminally boring."

Finally, his eyes refocused, and he found himself standing at the top of a sunken chamber, where the center was probably thirty feet below his current location, a platform clearly intended as a stage for people petitioning the council. It was surrounded by tiered seating, which would allow everyone on the council to have a clear line of sight at the stage below. "Hmm. Going by the size of this place, I don't think having only ten people on the council is going to cut it anymore. Or maybe we can just divvy the room up?"

Then his eyes were drawn to a pedestal at the exact center of the stage. Just above its surface floated a book he had seen before: The Ledger of Souls. It appeared to be an ancient tome, as it was bound in mystic hide and pulsing with a spiritual energy that filled him with both excitement and trepidation, but Joe knew it had been created sometime in the last day or so. It was practically beckoning him, and the Ritualist realized that it was probably the system gently pushing him forward.

"Yeah, *yeah*. I'm going! You don't have to guilt trip me anymore." Now that he had demonstrated awareness of the gentle push, it vanished immediately.

Mental Manipulation Resistance has retaliated against a foreign intrusion into your mind, carving off a small portion of energy from its source. +1 Perception.

"Abyss! Don't smack the system; that's how I get cursed!" Joe sputtered as he looked around frantically. Luckily, it didn't seem that he was going to get punished for his newly upgraded skill automatically fighting off the pull. "Is this going to mess with my ability to figure out where to go for quests and such?"

With those thoughts easing his other concerns, Joe walked onto the stage and extended a hand to open the book. The leather cover felt warm to the touch, and the pages squirmed beneath his fingers as if they were alive. "Let's see… any name in this book should indicate a slain person that can be resurrected as a Dwarf. This… *what.*"

He'd started by flipping the pages slowly, but each one of them had absolutely no white space at all. Instead, every page was completely *cluttered* with names, all the way until he got to the end of the book. Each name represented a Dwarven soul available on Jotunheim, and each soul had a number next to it representing the cost to revive them.

At the very front of the book were the most powerful of the Dwarves, but along with the names of the council members he recognized, dozens of others were mingled. "There can't be this many people more important than Grandmaster McPoundy. I don't care what this book says, it has to be *wrong*. Can this organize by how powerful people are, but only after how recently they died, and if they were most recently a Dwarf?"

The book slammed closed, reopening moments later and being filled at the start with names he expected to see. "Okay, that must mean that the others are Elves that were killed off? We'll have to do them last."

Tens of thousands of names were waiting, and Joe's heart sank as he watched the astronomical resource cost translate itself into an aspect cost. When he flipped to the back, to the start of the section that appeared to be Elves, he saw that their tally was even larger. A helpful pop-up message informed him that they were more expensive because their souls needed to be converted, and reshaping an Elven soul into its Dwarvish counterpart was *not* free.

"What's all of this going to cost me?" Joe murmured to himself, only for the book to suck the ink off a page and return it as a singular number. The total cost in resources was absolutely astronomical. Mountains of metal, flesh, and incredibly rare resources that could be found scattered across the entirety of Jotunheim. As if to make him feel better, the list of hundreds of required materials for bartering condensed down into only a handful of lines: what bringing them back would cost him in aspects.

"You know, I don't often guess wrong. Wow. This *isn't* going to cost all of the aspects I've accumulated." A smile was on Joe's face as he shook his head lightly, chuckling over the final aspect cost. Then he snarled and slammed the book closed.

"Abyssal system, I don't have anywhere *near* that amount!"

CHAPTER FIFTY-ONE

Time remaining until the bifrost opens and stabilizes: approximately 15 minutes!

Refusing to give up, Joe turned and walked away from the Ledger decisively. He may not have the aspects that he needed at the moment, but… he knew where he could get them.

**Shriiawww*!*

The double doors of the building screamed loudly as he opened them, and that helped to put a smile back on his face. "You know what? I'm going to make sure the receptionist I wanted fired has to stay here *forever*, instead."

Walking over the area he had been trapped in for the last few months felt different with no one else around. Sure, in the distance, he could point out a few people going about their business, but there wasn't even a single sign of industry happening in the City. With a sharp inhale, he realized that they had never managed to get a fighting force out to save the crafters who had been evacuated. "That explains a few of those names I didn't recognize, at least. Absolute non-combatants, but expensive because they're so high-ranked in their craft."

His target appeared in his vision, and Joe walked faster.

Finally he was face-to-face with a few Dwarves that jumped in his way, but Joe simply explained what he was doing, and they stepped aside. The Ritualist stood next to the enormous, armless, headless body of the Legendary Progenitor of Ice, and tried not to think of what he was about to do as a waste or loss of high-ranking aspects.

"*Ascendant Matrix.*" As he activated the newly evolved skill for the first time, Joe felt an intense connection with the burning matrix of lines that appeared in front of him. For an instant, he felt a flash of concern as he saw that the space the skill took up was less than half a meter total, but as his mind worried at it, the cage of energy expanded outward rapidly.

He fiddled with the power for a moment, finding that he could adjust the shape however he wanted, but with a maximum space of twenty-two meters on all sides as a square. To test it out, he created a cylinder that was smaller on one side, tapering down slightly, that fit directly over Brisingr's foot. Then, he pulled a small line that jutted out and connected directly to his codpiece. "Reduce."

Mana flooded out of him, and Joe grunted at the mental strain of Legendary resources being reduced into aspects. The process dragged on, and on, far longer than he was used to. Were it not for the knowledge that he was working with such powerful materials, he would've thought that the overall usefulness of his skill had dropped.

"Come on, I *wish* I could spend a whole bunch of time testing this, but…" A glance upward showed that daylight was beginning to break through the cloud cover. Not the much filtered light that was normally allowed through the watery barrier, but actual beams of sunlight. "Looks like I'm about to lose a whole lot of friends."

Finally, the entire foot had been reduced, and Joe moved up to the leg. Again, the process took longer than he wanted, but there was no help for it. Then he cast around, looking for something that might be easier to reduce. Joe thought that perhaps part of the reason he was struggling with this was that he wasn't reducing the entire object at a time, only a part of it. His eyes landed on the second arm that Jake had ripped off—not the cubed one—and he rushed over and began pouring energy into it. Exactly as he'd hoped, this process went much faster, and he was finished in half the time he had expected.

"This *has* to be enough."

Without looking at the clock, he rushed back to the City Hall, Omnivaulting as much as he could to cut down on his travel time. As the doors of the City Hall creaked open, Joe started to twitch.

Shriiawww!

As soon as there was enough space to squeeze through, he did, then burst through the next set of doors, Omnivaulting across the open space and landing on the dais next to the pedestal of the Ledger of Souls.

"Buyout!" the Ritualist demanded, impatiently slapping the 'yes' button on the notification that appeared without reading the message.

His pelvis began to heat up as aspects flooded out of his codpiece, so many and so powerfully that his pants lit on fire. He shucked them off and jumped on top of them, trusting that his Exquisite Shell would suffice to keep him from injury. As the transaction completed, the Ritualist pulled his—thankfully only slightly damaged—pants back on and looked around. "Where *is* everyone?"

The City Hall was still completely silent, but flipping open the Ledger of Souls showed that it was empty… then a single name appeared, and Joe revived them, too. "Ugh. I *really* hope that was an Elf on the other side of the world that just got beaked by a Penguin."

Shriiawww!

It was only when he pushed open the front doors, accompanied by the scream of a phoenix, that Joe was greeted with a hubbub of noise as nearly a hundred thousand Dwarves danced in the rain, celebrating the rebirth of their race.

The screeching doors had caught the attention of those

nearest him, and they began to hush. Silence rippled outward until the massive crowd was all looking at Joe, their Characteristics likely allowing them to see him clearly, no matter how far away they were at the moment. The only sound breaking the absolute silence was the torrential downpour, until one Dwarf nearby began to shout.

"Joe!"

"Joe… Joe… *Joe*!" The shout quickly turned into a chant, and a hundred thousand Dwarves tried to swarm toward him at the same time.

Frankly, it was terrifying.

The Ritualist tried to swing the doors shut, but the laughing crowd yanked them open and pulled him out, throwing him into the air and forcing him to crowd surf along as they exuberantly celebrated him.

You have achieved a permanent reputation rank of 'Extended Family' with all Dwarves, regardless of faction. This reputation modifier cannot be lost under any circumstances, so long as you do not personally kill more than 10,000 Dwarves.

"What, so nine thousand, nine hundred and ninety-nine is okay? Can I start now?" Joe's eyes widened as his newly enhanced Perception informed him that a bright line of gold had suddenly extended from every Dwarf in sight, lancing into his chest painlessly before vanishing. Now confused *and* uncomfortable as he was flipped through the air, Joe wondered what had just happened.

Luckily for him, a celestial event occurred that pulled the crowd's attention away. The flame from his still-active Ritual of Slaughter finally melted the last layer of clouds in a cone above the City, and a scintillating beam of light shot down from space. The intense energetic field wrapped around the ritual, and it was yanked up into the air. Its sudden, unexpected, rapid ascent caused the energy extending from the power plates to shift and go taut. The Mana Battery Recharging Stations streaming pure mana to the main ritual circle were yanked out of their positions around the City as the mana became tangible, and the devices were pulled into the bifrost as well.

Miles and miles above them, the ritual and mana stations went critical from their jumbled state, detonating as a supernova of flame that converted the clouds—for nearly a hundred miles in all directions—directly to steam.

"Somebody get a barrier over the City, *now*!" The shout came from Major Cleave, amplified by whatever artifact she'd been using to direct the defense of the City during the Beast Waves. Thousands of Dwarven Mages leaped into action, and a patchwork of energy appeared over the city. "That's not going to be enough! Rough estimation of—say it again—two hundred million tons of water dropping on us. Someone get a few of those up around in the gaps of the wall, otherwise we're going to be flooded out of here!"

Moments after she had spoken, the thousands of smaller barriers had threads of mana wrap through them, taking control and stitching the entire defense together as one cohesive, if patchwork, quilt of a shield. The dense steam that was surrounded on all sides by frozen clouds rapidly cooled and collected, and exactly as Major Cleave had predicted, a small ocean's worth of water dropped down and hit the shield.

The barrier strained in dozens of places, some small areas failing and allowing what were essentially high pressure beams of water to smash into the ground, but overall, it held strong through the sudden downpour.

This water was *hot*, as evidenced by the expanding lake around the City melting through the surface layers of snow for miles in all directions. Fog began rising up as it cooled, creating an eerie, hypnotic vision for the reconstituted race to enjoy.

"Woo! Natural hot spring! Enjoy it while it lasts!" A Legionnaire stored his armor and clothing directly in some storage device, going from fully protected to just shy of nude in an instant before diving head first into the water. Everyone stared, wondering if he had just been melted into a skeleton, but then his head popped up and he spit out a spray that caught the light and formed a rainbow around his head. "Well? What're you waiting for? Come on in, the water is fine!"

Joe was nearly trampled in the mad dash to enter the lake, but after most of the area had cleared out, Grandmaster Snow walked over to him and offered a hand. "Joe."

"Snow."

"We owe you... *Everything*."

"Great book; I'll take it."

"Huh? Enough... no more strange jokes." Snow took a deep breath and met his gaze. "From here on out, Novusheim will cover all of your training needs, as well as the cost. You want to get better at smithing? Grandmaster McPoundy will be available to you, night or day. You want space for yourself, for your guild? You can build up as much as you want, until the Guild Town is a quarter the final the City. That's not a restriction from me, but of the City itself. From here on out, on Jotunheim, you will have endless opportunity, training, and prestige."

The more she spoke, the wider the smile on Joe's face became. "Thank you, Snow. I just want you to know that–"

"Oh, and, I know it does not compare to what you must have paid to bring so many of my people back, but I was out of town until just before your ritual went *boom*. I was retrieving this, and I think it would be fitting for you to have it... *Oligarch* Joe." The corpse of Razorscarf the Polar Polecat suddenly appeared on the ground next to them as Snow waved, pulling it out of some hidden storage device. "It is perfectly preserved and should be stuffed to the whiskers with Artifact-rank materials."

"That's..." Joe swallowed hard, unable to voice his thoughts. Instead, he reached out a hand to the Grandmaster, and they shook in mutual gratitude. "I needed that, thank you. I swore to myself I would finish an Artifact-ranked item, and this... this should do it."

As he reduced the entire Boss Monster to aspects, Snow watched the process with interest shining in her eyes. "Tell me, everything that you do costs this strange energy, correct?"

"Aspects, and yes." Joe murmured, his attention still mostly on ensuring he didn't waste any of the precious material.

"That means you paid for all of those resurrections with aspects, then. I've never seen so many people brought back at the same time… if I might ask, how much did that cost?"

"Well, it wasn't cheap." Joe stated as he finished up, collecting the Artifact-rank core that fell out of the dissolving body before turning to her with a solemn expression. "In fact… it cost an arm and a leg."

EPILOGUE

Many things happened over the course of the day, after Joe parted ways with Grandmaster Snow. First, he organized an expedition to search for the remains of Brisingr that had been washed away by the melted clouds, and that took priority over almost everything else that was going on. When a dozen hours had passed, and there was no sign of the Legendary-ranked materials, Joe could only shake his head in disgruntlement, assuming that there had been some system malarkey, or a huge crowd of co-conspirator crafters had descended on the body and stripped it clean.

Eventually, they officially gave up the search for Brisingr's corpse and turned to other important, but less fun, things that needed to happen. First was the fact that the flood had washed away tens of thousands of monsters' bodies, and in order for Joe to begin the process of repairing or rebuilding structures, they needed to be carted back en masse to be reduced at the A.S.P.E.C.T. tower. While he was waiting for enough aspects to get the ball rolling, Joe finally worked on his self-set goal.

"Set up the Ascendant Matrix… complete." Joe let a small stream of energy wrap around his waist and into his Legendary spatial codpiece. "Connect the storage device, done. Now I need to devote ten percent of the total worth of the core's experience value in order to convert it."

The Ritualist let out a nervous chuckle as he compared the Artifact-rank core worth twelve thousand five hundred experience, with his thirteen hundred Artifact aspects. "I really hope the efficiency is as good as the skill purports, otherwise I'm about to be *very* sad."

Clicking the core into place on the matrix, Joe double checked to ensure that the doors to his vault were shut and locked. No one had to tell him there were plenty of people who would kill for a core of this strength, so he had taken every preventative measure he could think of. With no further excuses allowing him to procrastinate, the ritualist began suffusing the core with aspects.

Immediately, the light frequency began to shift. A core by itself was beautiful, scintillating, but radiated what appeared to be pure daylight. As the aspects flooded in, the daylight shifted to have a hint of orange, which rapidly grew in intensity until an intense, dark orange like burnished gold was the only light shining off of the core.

Then, it was a core no longer.

Item created: Natural Artifact Aspect Jar (Artifact). Maximum capacity: 12,500 Artifact-rank aspects. As this is a naturally occurring Aspect jar, it creates 8 Artifact-rank aspects per hour!

"*Abyss,* yeah!" Joe pumped his fist in the air, his eyes shining with excitement and his cheeks rosy from smiling so hard. "Only one thousand five hundred sixty-two and a half hours until it's full!"

He checked his remaining aspects and went pale, the smile slipping for a moment. "W-what? How do I only have *twenty* Artifact aspects left? The skill said… feces… it said there wouldn't be any wastage if I used *aspect jars* connected to it, why did I assume that meant my storage devices would work perfectly? Whew… I danced right on the edge for this one."

As he caught his breath, Joe heard a pounding coming from

the main area of his workshop and got up to go and see what was going on. With the core converted to a jar, he no longer had any fear that someone would be coming after it. If they were, he would politely explain that they were too late. With that thought in mind, Joe threw the door open with a smile that froze on his face, even as his eyes went cold and flinty. "*Master* Stu. To what do I owe this… pleasure? Wait, no. To what do I owe this *visit*?"

"Good, we can both be straightforward." The Dwarf had a carefully neutral expression on his face. "Here's the thing, Joe. You have the best reputation with my people that you possibly can. First, I want to warn you that even among a sweeping, people-wide benefit like that, there will still be plenty of people who don't *like* you. Keep in mind, that goes both ways. For instance, there would be plenty of Elves who think you're a delight, even though you have a hard-locked blood feud with them."

"Huh. Well. Thanks for the information?"

"I'm not finished. I'm here to collect my reward." Stu paused as he saw confusion flash across Joe's face. "I am due a minor favor from you."

"Oh." The Ritualist steeled himself and nodded at the Dwarf. "Go on. Please remember that I can have Grandmaster Snow evaluate–"

"Just hear me out," Stu interrupted with a sharp hand motion. "Look around, Joe. Look at what we've been able to do here. In no small part, this is because of you. I find myself… grateful. Because of that, I'm going to use my favor to benefit *you*. So. Here goes. Without making any demands, bribes, or threats, I ask as my minor favor that you consider leaving Jotunheim behind you."

The Ritualist stared at the Dwarf, watching as a thin strand of golden light appeared between the two of them. The light was pulsing from his own chest, clearly flowing into the Dwarf. As soon as the request was made, the line of light snapped and shattered into golden motes of energy before vanishing. Even without reading the notification that popped up, Joe understood that the debt he owed Stu because the quest he had issued had been paid in full. Arching an eyebrow, Joe slowly began to swing the door closed.

"Listen!" Stu sounded desperate, and Joe moved a *little* bit slower. "Buildings are cheaper here. Innovations are easier. Resources are plentiful. You can have all of the training and whatever you want for free, *forever*, or at least until people get sick of your demands. Sounds like everything you've always wanted, right? *Right?* Just like all your friends who stayed behind on lower worlds. They found what they wanted. They stopped. Is it your turn to do the same?"

As the Dwarf continued ranting at him, Joe froze in place, his eyes going wide.

"I know people, I understand them. You aren't someone who moves forward because you want to. You are someone who innovates on the fly and goes for interesting new experiences. As soon as you get comfortable, complacent, you're going to sit and work on one project to the exclusion of all else… forever. You'll twist it, tweak it, but it will never be enough. Your progress will slow to a *crawl.* The standing ovation that you earned from thousands upon thousands of mouths will be the *last* time someone cheers for you."

Stu stared through the crack of the door that was still open, meeting Joe's eye. "So my favor… is your consideration. I do hope you will at least *think* about it."

"Dude." Joe sighed at the Dwarf's back as he spun in place and began to march away. "Could I have, like, *one* day when I can just enjoy the win?"

Congratulations! The bifrost cascading onto Novusheim has stabilized! Time dilation aligning. All time zones have been standardized. Inter-world mail has come online.

The area has been assessed as a safe transportation point from Midgard. Current destinations available from the current bifrost location: Midgard (Unified Race, Humans). Alfheim (Unified Race, Elven Theocracy). Muspelheim (Unified Race, unknown). Vanaheim (Unified Race, unknown).

Please note, it is not recommended to travel to Muspelheim without extreme fire resistance.

Title removed: Despised by Humanity. More than double the required time has passed!

Spell gained: Beam to Bifrost. (Max). You have been instrumental in opening the bifrost on three worlds. No longer can you be forced to stay in a world you are sick of. Using this spell automatically sends you into the bifrost. From there, you can choose your destination. Please note, this spell will not work if you are imprisoned, silenced, or in combat. It requires a channeling time of 10 seconds but has no mana cost or cooldown. Feel free to travel the cosmos, knowing you can always come back.

"It's almost like the system is agreeing with Stu." The Ritualist sighed sadly. As messages flooded in from his mother, his guild, and other acquaintances he hadn't thought would be sending him mail, Joe started perusing them while walking toward the bifrost. To his surprise, humans were already flooding out of the energy bridge connecting the worlds together.

"Cool! Look at this place! I can't wait to see something other than a Wolfman for once. I've been waiting to get access to the Dwarven expansion for *forever*."

"Oh, *no*." Joe's eyes went dead as he looked at the largest group of people who had appeared. Most of them were talking to magical devices in their hands, instead of to the people around them. "*Influencers*."

As the Legion scrambled into the area, trying to figure out how to set up a protected area at the base of the bifrost, the already scattered people moved faster. Some of them were shouting about streaming secrets to their friends, some were just trying to get the Dwarves out of their area so they would be the only person seen by whoever was watching. However, due to the placement of the bifrost, they were near the edge of the current City's boundary.

As they stepped outside of the walls, they also exited the area the Ritual of Cleansing had been stabilizing. One after another, anyone who ran out into the wilds around town was crushed into the size of a marble and immediately sent for respawn.

Joe waved down a Legionnaire. "Hey, do you want me to deactivate that ritual? That should stop people coming through for a while. Or, at least… surviving when they come through."

"Nah. We just need to get a wall up. They're not doing anything wrong; they're just… strange examples of your race?"

"Agreed."

With a lot on his mind, and plenty of things that needed to get done, Joe began working closely with the rest of the council to rebuild the demolished city.

As the monster corpses flooded in, the first thing to be fixed was the expansive, whirlpool design of the walls. From there, the ritual towers went up, and the citizens breathed a collective sigh of relief that they were once more mostly defended against random monster waves.

Over the course of a week, the City was built back to its starting point, then further—dozens of apartment buildings went up practically overnight. Then came the moment Joe had been worrying about ever since his conversation with Master Stu.

He ran out of busywork.

Sure, he had plenty he could do, projects that he could jump into, a Guild Town to build on the fringes of the City, a coven to train up. But the minor favor that had been asked of him ate away at Joe's thoughts, until finally he found himself standing in front of the council, resigning.

"But… *why*?" Grandmaster Snow wasn't the only person sitting there with a completely flabbergasted expression. But she *was* the only one who seemed to be personally hurt by his choice.

"Someone reminded me that, even though I want it, I'm not really looking for 'stable and secure'. I came into Eternium with a single goal in mind, winning. Frankly… merely surviving isn't enough. I want to go and see what all of the worlds have to offer. So, even though it pains me, I'm going to. Now, I'll still be available! I'll try to come back regularly, and if you need something, I can always make a special trip."

Joe swallowed and looked away as he finished his thought. "It's just, the thing is, the last two worlds I was on, I was *forced* to leave. Now, for the first time, I want it to be my choice. Before something comes along that either destroys what I've worked for or puts me in such a bad place that I just want to go. While I'm happy, while I'm *ready* for it... I need to leave."

"This has Master Stu's Manipulation all over it. " Snow grimly stated, waving at a Legionnaire in the distance. "Hunt him down and arrest him immediately. Toss Joe into a holding tank until we figure out how to break the influence on his mind–"

"Stop it." Joe demanded in a deep tone. "Trust me when I say that he did *not* force this on me, not even a little. Now... I'm going to go to the bifrost and see what Vanaheim has to offer. I'll see you soon."

The Ritualist walked out of the council room, his heart light. Walking through the antechamber, he nodded at the glowering receptionist and pushed open the doors of the City Hall.

Shriiawww!

A smile appeared on his face as the Dwarf sitting at a desk behind him let out a low groan.

He had packed before he came to resign, so the Ritualist walked directly over to the glowing rainbow of light that would lead him to another world. A handful of people were waiting nearby, and he waved as he got close. "All right, who's coming with?"

"Count me in!" Jaxon clapped his hands and started dancing around a little. "Maybe this next world will have tiny people, and I will get to research an entirely new set of skeletons! Did you know that practically every monster on this world is almost exactly the same, in terms of its internal structure? It is like they are cloned and spit out, unless they're an elite or boss type! It got repetitive after the first five thousand."

Daniella shook her head and failed to meet Joe's eyes. "I

hope you have a great time, but… I finally got a contract from the city council. I have a *dozen* buildings to design and a pretty tight deadline to complete the quest. Um. Thank you for waiting until after they issued the quest to announce your departure from the council. I'm pretty sure I got the offer because they thought it would earn them some favors from you."

"Oh." The Ritualist tried to rein in his disappointment but nodded a few times as he wrapped his head around the information. "I don't think that's true. I saw your preliminary designs, and everyone was very excited about them. You got the contract on your own merit, and don't ever let anyone tell you differently."

Socar stepped forward, petting the cat that was wrapped around his neck. "Mind if we come?"

Joe stared at the Nyanderthal and felt his chest clench up. "Yeah… it… would be great to have you *both*."

"Meow *right,* it would be," the cat muttered, causing most of the group to look around curiously to see who was talking. For some reason, no one realized that it was the cat, or at least they did a great job of *pretending* not to realize.

"You need someone with some range," Heartpiercer grumbled while looking away. "It would annoy me to no end if you all went to the next World and died because you don't know how to take care of yourselves."

Joe saw Daniella give the Archer a significant look and simply shook his head. While he wanted to clear up the situation, this was not the time or place for it. "Okay. Off we go to the next world. We'll just take a peek, then I'll make or find a shrine and talk to Tatum about what upgrades I should be looking at to tackle that next world more efficiently."

"Good planning!" Jaxon gave him a hearty swat on the back. "I'm going to find new ways to adjust my view on reality, and become the first human Grandmaster Chiropractor."

"I like the way you think, buddy." Joe smiled as he stepped into the bifrost, allowing the crackling energy to flow around him. His teammates, his *friends*, joined him as dozens of people began waving at them and shouting their goodbyes. "Everyone ready? Let's go!"

At the same time, each of the four, and the cat, stated their destination.

"Vanaheim!"

"Vanaheim!"

"Vanaheim!"

"Meownaheim!"

"Muspelheim!"

"*Jaxon*!" Joe shouted at his friend, who looked around in confusion before shrugging and vanishing. "Abyssal…!"

Then he was shooting through the air at literally inconceivable speeds, leaving the world of giants behind him. As he traveled through space, watching the stars zip by in the distance, he looked at the planet that they were rapidly approaching.

He shouted a question to the two people and a cat who were around him, "What is that? That can't be a planet, right?"

"Who said it needed to be a whole planet?" Socar called back, studying the strange, spiky place the bifrost was sending them.

The tiny world rapidly approached them, and the Ritualist got a close-up view of the spikes they were passing. His Rituarchitect specialization sang in excitement as he realized that they were *not* spikes; they were flying past buildings so massive that they hung off of the planet and into space.

"It's an Ecumenopolis!" Joe excitedly informed his companions. "The entire planet is covered in a single city! Now it makes sense; it would be much easier to create a city at the Mythical stage on such a tiny world. I can't wait to see how they did it!"

The ground, or at least the area where they would be landing, rapidly came up to meet them. Joe estimated the skyscraper they'd been passing to arrive here was over a hundred miles in total height, and as his feet hit the ground, he wanted to *sprint* over and scan it into his personal blueprints.

"Would you look at that? Fresh meat!" Instead, Joe was met

by a strange, casual man who languidly pulled himself off a bench and stepped directly in his path. Despite the odd choice of greeting, the words didn't sound threatening, merely intrigued. "Welcome to Vanaheim, the world of the Sage's Ladders. If you don't have gouda-nuff skills, you should probably leave before you lose everything."

Startled by the odd interaction, Joe spoke without thinking, stammering out, "I'm *skilled*!"

"Oh? That so?" The man snorted out a chuckle, showing a mouth full of sharpened teeth. "Well, then I hope you're *rich*, too, or it won't matter. I'm a little low on cheddar, so I'll trade ya. You want information? I want to be paid."

The group looked at each other, shrugging slightly before motioning for Joe to continue speaking to the vagrant-looking man. The Ritualist waved around. "I'd be happy to pay you, but I don't know what you would accept. Before that? How about you tell us where we are."

"See, that's why you need to hire me as your guide. You'll never be able to find your path without a local to show you around." Bowing with a grand flourish, the man waved at the area. "You have the distinct pleasure of having arrived in Area seven, District three, subsection two-oh-one. Welcome to Th' Under Plump."

ABOUT DAKOTA KROUT

Associated Press best-selling author, Dakota has been a top 5 bestseller on Amazon, a top 6 bestseller on Audible, and his first book, Dungeon Born, was chosen as one of Audible's top 5 fantasy picks in 2017.

He draws on his experience in the military to create vast terrains and intricate systems, and his history in programming and information technology helps him bring a logical aspect to both his writing and his company while giving him a unique perspective for future challenges.

"Publishing my stories has been an incredible blessing thus far, and I hope to keep you entertained for years to come!" -Dakota

Connect with Dakota:
MountaindalePress.com
Patreon.com/DakotaKrout
Facebook.com/DakotaKrout
Twitter.com/DakotaKrout
Discord.gg/mdp

ABOUT MOUNTAINDALE PRESS

Dakota and Danielle Krout, a husband and wife team, strive to create as well as publish excellent fantasy and science fiction novels. Self-publishing *The Divine Dungeon: Dungeon Born* in 2016 transformed their careers from Dakota's military and programming background and Danielle's Ph.D. in pharmacology to President and CEO, respectively, of a small press. Their goal is to share their success with other authors and provide captivating fiction to readers with the purpose of solidifying Mountaindale Press as the place 'Where Fantasy Transforms Reality.'

Connect with Mountaindale Press:
MountaindalePress.com
Facebook.com/MountaindalePress
Twitter.com/_Mountaindale
Instagram.com/MountaindalePress

MOUNTAINDALE PRESS TITLES

GameLit and LitRPG

The Completionist Chronicles,
The Divine Dungeon,
Full Murderhobo, and
Year of the Sword by Dakota Krout

A Touch of Power by Jay Boyce

Red Mage and
Farming Livia by Xander Boyce

Ether Collapse and
Ether Flows by Ryan DeBruyn

Unbound by Nicoli Gonnella

Threads of Fate by Michael Head

Lion's Lineage by Rohan Hublikar and Dakota Krout

Wolfman Warlock by James Hunter and Dakota Krout

Axe Druid,
Mephisto's Magic Online, and
High Table Hijinks by Christopher Johns

Dragon Core Chronicles by Lars Machmüller

Pixel Dust and
Necrotic Apocalypse by David Petrie

Viceroy's Pride and
Tower of Somnus by Cale Plamann

Henchman by Carl Stubblefield

Artorian's Archives by Dennis Vanderkerken and Dakota Krout

Made in United States
North Haven, CT
04 May 2024